THE JUSTIFIABLE CAUSE BOX SET

BOOKS 1-3

ADRIENNE GIORDANO

ALSO BY ADRIENNE GIORDANO

Romantic Suspense

PRIVATE PROTECTOR SERIES

Risking Trust

Man Law

Negotiating Point

A Just Deception

Relentless Pursuit

HARLEQUIN INTRIGUES

The Prosecutor

The Defender

The Marshal

The Detective

The Rebel

JUSTIFIABLE CAUSE SERIES

The Chase

The Evasion

The Capture

CASINO FORTUNA SERIES

Deadly Odds

JUSTICE SERIES w/MISTY EVANS

Stealing Justice

Cheating Justice

Holiday Justice

Exposing Justice

Undercover Justice

Protecting Justice

Missing Justice

Defending Justice

STEELE RIDGE SERIES w/KELSEY BROWNING & TRACEY DEVLYN

Steele Ridge: The Beginning

Going Hard (Kelsey Browning)

Living Fast (Adrienne Giordano)

Loving Deep (Tracey Devlyn)

Breaking Free (Adrienne Giordano)

Roaming Wild (Tracey Devlyn)

Stripping Bare (Kelsey Browning)

STEELE RIDGE SERIES: The Kingstons w/KELSEY BROWNING & TRACEY DEVLYN

Craving HEAT (Adrienne Giordano)

Tasting FIRE (Kelsey Browning)

Searing NEED (Tracey Devlyn)

Striking EDGE (Kelsey Browning)

Burning ACHE (Adrienne Giordano)

Mystery

THE LUCIE RIZZO MYSTERY SERIES

Dog Collar Crime

Knocked Off

Limbo (novella)

Boosted

Whacked

Cooked

Incognito

SCHOCK SISTERS MYSTERY SERIES w/Misty Evans

1st Shock

2nd Strike

3rd Tango

THE CHASE

THE JUSTIFIABLE CAUSE SERIES

Hard-driving attorney Jo Pomeroy is as determined as she is sexy—in other words, a major pain in NYPD Sergeant Gabe Townsend's butt. Working together on a high-profile task force charged with busting sales of counterfeit goods has been rocky from the start. And Jo's penchant for trouble is as difficult to ignore as her spectacular legs.

The world of knock-offs isn't as frivolous as it appears. The purses are fake, but the danger is all too real—and Jo seems hell-bent on putting herself in the middle of it. Her investigations have uncovered valuable leads for Gabe's team, but they've also drawn the wrong kind of attention. Now, she's on the radar of a mysterious smuggler not afraid to use violence to evade the law. At the risk of their lives—and their hearts—Gabe and Jo must find him before he finds them.

ONE

Joanna wandered Chinatown, trying to blend into the chaotic crush of shoppers milling at each storefront and street vendor's stall. Sherry, a young investigator who'd worked for Jo's law firm for the past six months and her partner on this excursion, angled around the late morning crowd. An unusually warm November wind blew, and Jo dragged a few stray strands of her wig from her face and tucked them behind her ear.

Across the street, a gaggle of middle-aged females and what appeared to be their teenaged daughters, made their way through the throng of shoppers. Tourists maybe. Their leader, a young Asian woman, glanced over both shoulders, then scanned the area around her. When her gaze swept in Jo's direction, Jo turned her head, pretending to gawk at a near-miss pedestrian smackdown.

After a moment, she checked the group leader's progress and found the troop moving along at a good clip. Jo latched onto Sherry's elbow and tugged. "Let's go."

Against the red light, the two women darted into traffic and nearly got flattened by an irate taxi driver. Sherry flipped the cabbie off. With much enthusiasm, he returned the gesture and offered a stream of inaudible words.

Life in New York.

"What is it?" Sherry asked when they reached the relative safety of the sidewalk. Jo jerked her chin. After a moment of analyzing the crowd, Sherry nodded. "Gotcha."

The line of women marched into a clothing store on the corner and just before the last person entered the shop, Jo and Sherry quietly took up the rear. Inside, the smell of dank stifled air indicated the only breeze in the place came from the door opening and closing. They needed to open some windows.

Jo held her breath for a second while the group wound through circular racks stuffed with cheap T-shirts of every color imaginable. They reached the back of the store and everyone dutifully followed the leader to a second doorway. The young girls in front of Jo giggled.

Oh, please. For what seemed like the ten-thousandth time, Jo wondered if the older women—the mothers presumably—had hesitated, for only the briefest moment, to ponder the potentially dangerous situation they could be exposing these girls to. Even she, a ballsy attorney who took undeniable risks, never came to Tower Street without an escort.

At the bottom of the staircase, the group leader opened an unmarked door and everyone piled in. A sudden round of *oohs* and *ahs* filtered to the back of the line as each person entered. Soon enough, Jo and Sherry squeezed into a narrow room where floor to ceiling shelves on three walls were stuffed with high-end purses, shoes, sunglasses—you name it. A veritable bounty of accessories.

The leader shut the door behind them as customers pointed and perused the merchandise.

The back of Jo's neck warmed as she scanned the names on the items. Gucci, Fendi, Coach—and yes—Barelli. *Winner.*

A teenager ogled a so-called Gucci. "Is this stuff the real thing?"

"Yes," the Asian woman answered, her English clear, but obviously not her native language.

A real knock-off. What were these women thinking? If this stuff was authentic, it would be worth hundreds of thousands of dollars and wouldn't be in a stuffy, smelly storage room in the basement of a clothing store. Nope, the *proprietors* would have security devices stashed on the handles and in the pockets.

And Jo wouldn't be here trying to scrape together information about the smuggler bringing these fake goods— particularly those with her client's name on them—into the city. Once again, she surveyed the room and catalogued the different brands. For now, she focused on the Barelli handbags.

Time to go to work.

She pointed to a black tote. "The Barelli. How much?"

The tiny woman took in Jo's long coat and silk scarf —*yes, I can afford it*—and bee-lined to the tote. She snatched the bag from the shelf and held it for inspection. "Sixty-five."

Jo did her typical hemming and hawing and, for extra effect, tugged on her bottom lip. "Forty."

The woman nudged the bag closer. "Fifty? Feel. Good leather."

Feigning indecision, Jo shifted to Sherry, who shrugged. Like method actors, they'd gotten good at this. Jo handed the purse back. "Forty-five and I'll take it."

Beside her, one of the other shoppers asked about a Fendi handbag and the Asian woman glanced her way.

Time to get serious. Jo retrieved her wallet and smacked bills on the grimy glass counter. "Forty-five. There you go."

"How about that Prada?" one of the other tourists hollered.

The woman eyed the bills, looked at the shelf then came back to Jo.

Come on. Take the deal.

All at once, the woman snatched the bills and handed Jo the purse before moving on to her next customer. A flurry of activity ensued. Bags and shoes and cash exchanged hands faster than the action on the floor of the Stock Exchange. This group obviously had money to spend and by the end of the frenzy, the Asian woman had probably taken in more than two thousand dollars for items that were worth, if the shoppers were lucky, less than a tenth of that.

Jo glanced at Sherry, who nodded toward the door. Yes, they should go. For the moment, this mission was complete.

—:—

Gabe stood in the doorway of Bev Richards's office thinking the fifty-eight year old grandmother and sexy pain-in-the-ass Jo Pomeroy were surreptitiously sexually harassing him. He couldn't prove it, but every time he showed up for a meeting with them they exchanged some sort of meaningful eye contact.

And that eye contact screamed sexual harassment. Years of working to get into the NYPD's elite Emergency Services Unit hadn't prepared him for the tag team of Bev and Jo. Handling these two took finesse that he'd spent almost ten months honing.

When it came to the pushy intellectual property attorney, Gabe was all in. This was a woman who'd managed to talk the mayor into Operation Clean Sweep, a task force designed to bust traffickers shipping fake luxury items into the city. From the second he'd met her, she had, in equal parts, infuriated and enthralled him.

That first day, he'd nearly pissed himself. She'd marched into the mayor's office wearing her fancy spiked heels and a suit just tight enough to let a man's imagination run more than a little wild, and immediately Gabe started conjuring sexual positions he'd like to test with her.

Then she'd opened her mouth.

And hadn't shut up since.

He'd say this for Jo Pomeroy: the woman knew how to get shit done. Her long legs, nice rack and shoulder-length blond hair were a bonus.

Bev, the mayor's point person on Operation Clean Sweep, waved him into the office and he smacked his notepad against his thigh. Going into meetings with these two scared the hell out of him. *Suck it up, pal.*

"Good morning, ladies. Tom got called away. You're stuck with me." Tom was Gabe's boss, who usually attended these meetings with him.

Bev pointed to the vacant guest chair. "Then it's our lucky day. Have a seat."

Jo turned her baby blues on him and grinned. "Hello, Sergeant."

Apparently, she wanted to play. He nodded. "Ms. Pomeroy, you haven't called me sergeant in nine months. Why the formality?"

She flipped a page on her notepad. "Thought I'd give you a thrill."

She puckered her lips and the movement accentuated

the curve of her cheek. Once again, Gabe corralled his baser needs and grinned. "You know I always appreciate that."

Oh, shit. He shouldn't have said *that* in front of Bev. Blame it on Jo. In the months they'd worked together, they'd curbed the amount of fake goods coming into the city and figured out one guy—who they still couldn't find—was responsible for seventy percent of the items. With Jo's team helping with investigations and Gabe's team making the busts, they had fallen into the habit of one-upping each other in the verbal combat department. To his count they were about even, but he might have a few on her. Not that he'd tell her that.

As reasonable, professional people, they tended to keep the snarkfest out of his superiors' offices. Given her opening parry, she must be stoked about something, and that meant she would dive headfirst into telling him how to do his job.

Bev sat forward and held a hand to Jo. "Let's see what you've got."

From beside her chair, she swung a kitchen garbage bag to the desk and stood to dump its contents. Out of it came a large black purse, a couple of watches and a pair of boots.

All high-end.

All new.

All, no doubt, knockoffs.

She held up the purse. She'd call it a tote bag, but whatever. "I bought this one yesterday morning. My investigators picked up the rest of this stuff last night."

Bev scrutinized the watch. "All at the same place?"

"Yes."

"And you're sure they're fakes?"

"Absolutely." She held the bag closer to Bev. "See this stitching around the handle? It's wrong. Barelli trains us to know what their stitching looks like. This isn't it. I'm telling you, that place was loaded with counterfeits."

Gabe jotted notes as the women talked. "Got an address?"

She handed him a few sheets of clipped paper. "Here's everything I could find. I included a map of the inside for you."

He shuffled the papers until he got to the map. Detailed. Extremely. The woman was a pain in the ass, but she was a pro. She stepped closer to him and her perfume, check that, probably soap—Jo wasn't the perfume type—had his hot-woman radar beeping.

She leaned down and pointed to the map. "I saw a back door right here. I'm not sure where it leads and I didn't want to get caught snooping. I can send one of my investigators, though."

"I'll take care of it," Gabe said, dragging his eyes from the long blond strands sliding over her shoulder.

Egotistically speaking, he didn't like having other people do his job, but the overburdened city budget didn't allow for law enforcement to chase every counterfeiter in the city. The problem was too huge and other cases, like people dying, were given priority.

Until Jo came along with her proposal for an anticounterfeiting task force. Her law firm agreed to hire private investigators, funded by luxury brand clients, to do the grunt work. The investigators, Jo included, went out and found the hidden places people sold the goods and identified those goods as counterfeit. Jo got the proof and ESU busted the merchants. In the first month the task force was in action, they'd seized more than a half-million dollars in fake goods. Since then, it had been bust after bust of high-end knockoffs.

A political win for the mayor and a professional coup for Jo, who made no bones about wanting to form a nationwide initiative to reduce the counterfeit trade in the U.S. For Gabe and his boss, it meant being in favor with a tough, politically savvy mayor. Never a bad thing with Gabe wanting to make lieutenant.

Yep, if he did his job well, this task force would be his ticket to a better rank and higher pay grade. He liked to think of himself as an honest cop who played by the rules, but he also wasn't afraid to bend those rules if it meant cleaning up a city ripe with criminals.

By confiscating knock-off purses.

Go figure.

But the more merchandise they seized, the further underground the vendors went, making it harder to find them. The days of vendors openly peddling fake goods were long gone, but the counterfeit trade was a snake whose head kept growing back. Christ sakes, they had tourists being given directions to pick up their knockoff items in warehouses or cargo vans in neighborhoods where Gabe wouldn't send his worst enemy. These naïve tourists would mindlessly walk into war zones and risk their own safety.

For a piece of shit purse.

Bev flipped to another sheet in the stack Jo had given her. "What about the owner of the building?"

"Irving Flanagan," Jo said. "He's eighty-five years old and needs an oxygen tank 24/7. He's not our smuggler."

Gabe stuck the map under his notepad. "Yeah, but he owns the building. He knows what's going on. I'll bend over backward and kiss my own ass if he doesn't. Let's bust him under Nuisance Abatement. Then we'll get Health and Sanitation inspectors in there and let them hand out fines."

"He's right," Bev said.

"Of course he's right. That's not the issue. We need to get to the guy bringing in the merchandise. Busting the property owner won't help. The smuggler will just pay the fines for him and offer up a little extra for the owner's pain and suffering."

Bev dropped the pages on her desk and sat back. "True."

Jo drew a stack of photos from her briefcase and spread them out in rapid fire motion. *Fft, fft, fft.* "The building is big. Three stories with three store fronts. My guess is the smuggler is renting the entire building. He has the stores plus the two top floors to use as storage. I'm betting that building is loaded with counterfeits. *Loaded.*"

She reached across the desk, her body angled forward, and Gabe forced his gaze to the photos and not her exceptional ass.

Hot-woman radar in meltdown. When Jo got on a roll, it was like watching Zena the Warrior Princess fight for the greater good.

Naked.

Gabe breathed in then scanned the photos. "We'll hit it and shut him down."

She pointed at him. "Exactly. If we keep busting these businesses, they have to stop selling this crap. The gentrification alone in that area will drive the illegitimate businesses out."

He shrugged. "Then they'll move to Queens or Brooklyn and we start all over."

The Warrior Princess didn't want to hear that. She gave him a hard stare before turning to Bev. "He's in a mood today. Let's get Tom out of his meeting. I don't like Gabe anymore."

She was probably only half joking, but he laughed anyway. "Look, Jo, I'm not being argumentative."

"Uh, yeah, you are."

Maybe. "We're not going to cure the problem of counterfeiting."

She leaned over the desk and propped both hands on it. Her white blouse flopped open enough at the neckline that he could eyeball cleavage if he didn't stay focused on her face. The woman was stacked, but not in an obnoxious way. Nope, those breasts were just big enough for a man to enjoy. Right now though, he'd keep his eyes above her shoulders where her temper had turned her cheeks a nice shade of red.

"Listen up, Sergeant. My clients are being ripped off because these crooks put fake labels on bags that cost a few bucks to make. My *clients* are paying for the advertising to build their brand and these smugglers are taking money out of their pockets. And let's not even get into how this could support terrorist activities."

Oh, hell. Gabe sighed.

"Hang on," Bev said. "We're on the same team here."

"Sure we are," Gabe said.

Jo flapped her arms.

Bev shook her head. "You two are like a couple of siblings."

"Sorry, ma'am."

No point in pissing off the mayor's right-hand woman.

Bev waggled her hand at Jo. "Forget it. Give me everything you've got and I'll talk with the A.D.A. about a warrant. Speaking of Brooklyn, where are we on probable cause for that warehouse you've been watching?"

For two months, one of Jo's investigators had been sitting on a Brooklyn warehouse they suspected was filled with counterfeit goods. "Not enough evidence yet. We're getting close."

"Have we looked through the garbage?"

"Yes, ma'am," Gabe said. "Every week we go through it. Nothing there. They're careful, but eventually something will pop."

"Keep at it." Bev swung her gaze to Jo. "Anything else?"

Jo gathered the photos and handed them to her. "No. Thank you. You'll keep me posted?"

"I always do."

Gabe gathered his notes and stood. "Is there anything else, ma'am?"

"Not right now. I'll call either you or Tom after I speak with the A.D.A."

He turned to Jo. "I'll give you a lift back to your office." She opened her mouth and he held up his hand. "Don't argue. I'm heading that way."

"I wasn't going to argue."

"Yeah, you were."

"Leave!" Bev hollered.

—:—

"I'm pissed at you," Jo said when Gabe opened the car door for her. She glanced at the front seat of the unmarked cruiser, found it in a clean and fairly suitable condition and got in. He made a move to shut the door and she stuck her hand up. "I'm pissed at you and I don't know why."

"Perfect."

He shut the door.

What was *wrong* with her? She'd been edgy for two days now and taking it out on everyone in her path. And aggravating the guy who could make sure she was on hand when they took down illegal businesses wouldn't do her a bit of good.

If she had any intention of convincing major manufacturers and federal and state governments to fund a nationwide task force to battle a $250-billion problem, she had to get her attitude in check. Every day was an opportunity to prove how big of an issue counterfeiting was and if it meant her getting out there and investigating to speed the process, she did it.

The big ape known as Sergeant Gabriel Townsend slid into the driver's seat, shoved the key in the ignition, started the engine and stopped. Just halted right there.

He looked straight ahead at the side of the brick building. "I worry about you."

What? "Articulate. In other words, what the hell does that mean?"

He turned back to her. "You put yourself in danger constantly. You think you're being careful by not going alone or by wearing wigs, but it's not enough. These vendors are figuring out who you are. You're gonna get hurt. We're talking billions of dollars here and, if you're right about the guy running this thing, he won't pack his toys and go home when you're the one causing him to lose money."

He was *worried* about her? The more important part of his little admission would be the warning about her getting hurt, but there was something quite fascinating about Gabe caring enough about the pain-in-ass lawyer, as he referred to her, to admit it.

The pain-in-the-ass lawyer got a sudden hot flash. For months she and Bev had shared endless private jokes about the hot ESU sergeant, but out of respect for the man's work ethic, his ability to complete tasks in an orderly and thorough process, and simply make things happen, they'd always kept their comments on the down low.

Somewhere in the span of the last few minutes, the

banter she and Gabe typically exchanged had turned personal. Never before had he mentioned worrying about her. Instinctively, she knew something was about to change between them. And she'd probably be the one to change it.

Because she wanted to see him without a shirt.

Okay, sister, back off. She hit the window button and stuck her face out.

"You okay?"

She bobbed her head. "Hot flash. Early onset menopause."

He burst out laughing and jammed the car into reverse. "You are an effing trip, lady."

Finally, her traitorous mind controlled itself and she put the window up. Not all the way. Just in case the flash sparked again. "I appreciate you being worried about me. I am careful, but I'll keep what you said in mind. I know I can't stop the counterfeiting, but I can put a dent in it."

And we'll both be superstars.

He pulled into traffic and immediately honked at someone. "Beat it," he yelled at the driver in front of them screaming at a cabbie. "Crazy-assed people." He drove around the scene and maneuvered by a delivery truck. "We can dent it, but you need to start thinking about staying in your office and off Tower Street."

"Blah, blah. I hear you, Sergeant. I've been advised. I'll be careful. Can you go back to yelling at me? That, I know how to deal with."

"I don't yell. I speak loudly. Big difference."

Right. "It's okay. I yell too. It's how I communicate. Doesn't necessarily mean I'm mad."

"Exactly!"

He hit Broadway and floored the gas pedal. Jo grabbed the door handle and prayed she'd survive.

"Relax, Counselor. You'll live."

"Let's talk about the warrant and get my mind off my impending death."

He caught a red light, swore under his breath and stopped. "I hate driving in this city. You get nowhere fast."

"That's why I use public transportation. Much easier. My warrant?"

"You'll get your warrant. Every time we shut one of these illegal vendors down, the mayor gets to taunt his adversaries with the success of his task force."

An idea she'd worked tirelessly for. "It's a win-win. My clients are happy, I'm happy and the mayor's happy. If we can figure out who the smuggler is that's driving the volume, we'll blow this thing wide open."

And I'll get my national task force.

"We'll get him. Nobody is talking yet. The vendors are too scared, but eventually someone will give us a name. Just takes time."

The light changed and he shot through the intersection. Thankfully, her office was only three blocks up. He knew that, as he'd visited her there a couple times for various reasons. None of which required him to be without a shirt.

Jeepers. With plenty of effort, she pressed the window button.

"Hot flash?" Gabe cracked.

"Big one."

That response only led her to thinking about other big things and—*wow*—bad, bad, Jo. "I have to get out of this car."

He braked at the curb in front of her building. "Are you sure you're okay?"

Jerking on the handle, she kicked open the door. "Aside from the carnal thoughts? I'm terrific."

Gabe's head dropped forward. "Pardon?"

"Gotta go, big boy. Call me about my warrant."

"Jo!"

Before he could question her, she sped through the revolving doors and ran into the stairwell. The elevator in this ancient building was a snail and she didn't want to get stuck waiting in case the hot sergeant pursued her carnal thoughts.

What had even possessed her to say that? Seriously, she needed medication. All this time she'd kept quiet. Maybe she'd noticed *him* noticing *her* every once in a while, but he was a man and men were pigs. It didn't necessarily mean he wanted to get up close and personal.

She darted up the stairs, her briefcase and laptop making her ascent a chore. Her punishment. Had to be. She may have been psychic because it appeared her premonition about being the one to change the vibe between her and Gabe had come true.

Once again, she'd opened her big mouth and now she'd have to deal with it.

TWO

At ten-fifteen the next morning, Jo stood on the sidewalk on Tower Street listening to the yelling and general insanity that came with an ESU bust. Customers and employees inside the clothing shop where she'd bought the knock-off tote hollered, some fearful, some angry, as Gabe's team moved through the shop, their actions swift and precise.

Gabe was somewhere out here. Today he was the U-boss, the sergeant leading the warrant and as he sometimes did, had stayed outside when his men had gone in.

She craned her neck, hoping to see a signal from one of the men that it was safe for her to enter the building and start sorting through merchandise.

Nothing.

She needed to get in there, but the men would have to complete their search for occupants before they called in the precinct guys to seize contraband. With the size of this building, she'd be here all damned day.

Go in. "They're not ready," she muttered. "He'll kill me."

The rubbernecking woman next to her scurried away. As

if it wasn't normal for someone to talk to herself on the streets of New York? Please.

Still nothing from Gabe. And the precinct guys were still waiting.

Behind her, traffic crawled around the NYPD vehicles, drivers honking, some yelling profanities. All not unusual, but Jo found herself restless. Itchy. ESU had to be done with the first floor by now. She nibbled the edge of her cup. Good thing the coffee had gone cold. More caffeine in her already hyper system would not be good. A slew of people were ushered out by members of Gabe's unit. *Okay, getting somewhere now.* Clearly, ESU had taken control of the store. Which meant the room she needed was probably safe.

Screw it.

She scooted behind one of the officers leading the group out and entered the store.

"Jo," he barked.

Still moving, she waved. "I'm good."

Perfect nonanswer. Just enough to give the impression that Gabe, wherever he might be, had given her the all clear. Except the precinct team was still outside waiting to be given the go-ahead to begin their search.

No way around that one. *He'll kill me.*

She knew she was pushing the boundaries of her agreement with the P.D. when it came to being on-site at these raids. But anticipation was evil and she wanted to get in there and see what volume of fake Barellis she'd find.

At her core, she was a lawyer trying to please her client. The sooner she got inside, the sooner she'd make a call to Barelli Corporate.

At least the officer she'd run by wouldn't get in trouble. No. All of Gabe's anger would be directed squarely at her.

For a moment, her stomach pitched and she swallowed the bile forming in her throat.

She'd worry about Gabe's wrath later, because just in front of her, at the end of the narrow hallway, was the door to the room with the merchandise. Inside, two officers were dealing with what looked like a couple of customers and one of the employees, a slight man with thick dark hair. He glanced at her, looked away and then slowly looked back.

Ignoring him, Jo stepped behind the glass counter, spied the assortment of watches she'd seen yesterday, slid the door open and reached for the black display box.

There they were. The little buggers she'd been hired to find. She reached for them, ready to stash them in the plastic garbage bag she'd brought. Her own shopping trip.

Just as she pulled the box from the counter, her thoughts reeling over the successful raid, a flash of silver entered her peripheral vision. The back of her neck tingled and she swung her head toward the flash. A man stood next to her clasping a thick metal pipe in his raised hand. Jo's head whooshed. *Move.* She flinched a mere second before the pipe slammed across her right hand.

She stared at her hand as her knuckles disintegrated. For a few seconds, there was no pain, only the numbing shock and the bizarre image of this maniac attacking her with ESU guys in the room.

That changed when crushing agony barreled into her hand, a fierce blast of icy pain that brought every nerve ending in her body to screaming. The whooshing in her head evaporated. Tears—surely a reaction to the pain—filled her eyes.

Movement to her right. She turned toward it. Her attacker, someone she could probably bring down even without the use of one of her hands, loaded up for another attack. She snapped her hand back and yelped at the fresh round of pain from simply moving it.

"Drop it." Gabe's voice. From by the door. *Uh-oh.* "On the ground. Now!"

A rapid and constant click, click, clicking sounded. The man dropped the pipe as his face stretched long and his lips rolled open. His body seemed to lock up and the clicking sound droned on. Finally, after releasing a high-pitched howl, he collapsed to the floor and the clicking stopped.

She glanced to the doorway. There stood Gabe, his massive body just inside the room's entrance and that cannon of a .45 he carried aimed at his target.

An explosion of activity surrounded her. Gabe shouting demands, the third officer hustling screaming people out and the second officer standing over her attacker, stun-gun in hand. All of it came at her in a fierce, agonizing assault and she squeezed her eyes shut, forcing herself to concentrate.

Gabe moved closer, his weapon still aimed while the attacker was dealt with by Carlson.

And—*wow*—in the name of everything holy, her hand was killing her. She dared to look at it and found already purple knuckles. "Damn you," she hollered at the man. "Look what you did to my hand."

"Carlson," Gabe shouted in a voice so rough it somehow, despite all the times she'd heard him yell, stunned her. Poor Carlson. He'd been an exemplary cop for over five years, but he'd just been accepted into the elite ESU and that made him a rookie all over again.

And if the tone in Gabe's voice were any indication, Carlson was in big trouble. He must have been the one to screw up by not cuffing pipe man when they'd first entered the room. Bum luck that the combination of Jo's impatience and Carlson's mistake led to her now broken hand. This would surely earn her a lecture.

With Carlson standing over their prisoner, Gabe holstered his weapon and stepped the two feet toward her. "Let me see your hand."

Suddenly, he was in her space—all six-foot-three of him—and she stepped back. His face had hardened to carved granite.

In short, this was one pissed-off sergeant.

"I'm not going to yell," he said. "Let me see it."

Oh, he'd yell. She knew him well enough to understand that. And worse, he'd just warned her to stick to the safety of her office because the vendors were beginning to recognize her.

She held her hand out and waited. Nothing. Only breathing. Heavy, nerve shredding, mad sounding breathing.

Maybe she could minimize this situation. "It's a bruise."

He scoffed. "Right. Carlson! Get a bus."

Jo shook her head. "No. I need to bag and tag some of these items to send back to Barelli. They need to see it."

He turned those coal black eyes on her. "We'll get them bagged. Your hand needs to be looked at. Carlson. Bus!"

Another officer entered, did a swift scan of the room and headed for their prisoner.

Jo was grateful for the momentary distraction and took a breath. "Gabe, seriously. It's not that bad. Look." She tried to bend her fingers and a stabbing sensation shot up her arm. *My God, the pain.* She should earn an Academy Award for keeping her features intact and not wincing. "I can handle it. Just let me bag a few things and I'll go to the ER."

He folded his arms. "Why are you so friggin' stubborn? Carlson! Forget the bus. Get over here and help Ms.

Pomeroy bag this crap while Hutchins deals with that mope."

Yikes. Carlson would be in the doghouse for a week. And Gabe's doghouse couldn't be fun.

—:—

Gabe stepped into Jo's ER bay just as the doc slapped her X-rays on the screen. He'd known that hand was broken the second he'd seen it. Not broken, that sucker was demolished.

Thanks to him, the idiot who allowed her to talk him into her accompanying them on hits. Sure, he always made her hang back, but she didn't belong there and he knew it. Plus, she sucked at following directions. How many times had he told her not to step foot into a store until ESU cleared it and he gave her the go sign.

How many?

He always did have a weakness for leggy blondes.

Jo watched him walk into the room and her blue eyes got that hard, ready-for-battle look. Lawyers. Always brewing for a fight. "Don't start yelling."

He ignored her and turned to the doc. Phillips. "Should I wait outside?"

The doc nodded at Jo. "That's up to the patient."

"He can stay." She paused, but didn't look away. "Thank you for coming. You didn't need to."

Yeah, I did. "Someone needs to take you home."

"Okay," Phillips said. "Here's what we've got. Looks like the second, third and fourth *metacarpophalangeal* joints are fractured." He pointed to the injured knuckles on her hand. "I'll need to refer you to an orthopedist, but we can get it wrapped for you."

"So, my knuckles are broken." She looked up at Gabe and their eyes met. "The little weasel broke my hand."

Gabe nodded. "Yep."

Don't yell. Still in his tactical uniform, he shoved his hands into the front pockets of his cargo pants and curled his fingers. Before this was over, he'd be yelling. No two ways about it. He was pissed enough to make sure she never came within half a mile of any building ESU was in. But damn, he was trying not to lose his shit on her.

Or maybe he should be losing his shit on himself for letting her be there in the first place.

"We'll stabilize it," Phillips said. "But you'll need to see an orthopedic specialist. I'll get you a list." He checked his watch. "Call them today. You still have time this afternoon."

"I've got a good ortho guy," Gabe said. "She'll call." He'd make sure of that.

"I will," she assured the doctor. "I'm an obedient patient."

Her? Obedient? Not in this lifetime. "*That's* funny."

The doc laughed. "Okay, guys. I'll get someone in here to wrap that hand."

Joe waved her good hand at him. "Thank you, Dr. Phillips."

Once the doc was gone, she lowered her hands to the bed and drew one knee up. Damn, she had long legs. He hated those legs, theoretically speaking. They had taken up way too much space in his brain. The rack too. What kind of shit luck got him working with a leggy, large-breasted, smart-mouthed lawyer that he actually enjoyed?

It was the mayor's fault. Blame him.

"Did everything get bagged?" she asked. "That was a big haul. We're getting closer to catching this guy. I know he owns that building."

Gabe gave up on curling his fingers. Probably looked like he was playing with himself. Great. He snatched his hands from his pockets and folded his arms. "Yeah. We're getting close."

She flopped her good hand on the bed. "Oh, for crying out loud, just yell already. You know you want to. I appreciate that you're not, but really, I like it better when you're yelling. At least then I know where I stand."

Ten months he'd been working with this woman. For five of those months, her aggressiveness had made him insane. She annoyed him, pestered him, sometimes told him how to do his job and basically nagged him until he let her accompany ESU on hits.

Miracle of all miracles, he hadn't killed her. Yet. The thing that had saved her was the *last* five months. In that time, he learned one simple fact: Joanna Pomeroy loved her job. Much like him, she thrived on righting wrongs and throwing herself into the middle of the dogfight.

Big-time companies expected her to earn her money, and she took any risk necessary to find and confiscate the counterfeit goods that represented trademark infringement to the tune of $250 billion a year.

Gabe pressed his fingers into his biceps and took one huge breath. *Don't yell.* "You're done. From now on, you stay in your office. That's it."

"What happened today wasn't my fault. I waited."

Stay calm. He pulled air through his nose, let it out his mouth. For maximum self-control, he counted to five. "No," he finally said, "you didn't."

"I did."

Don't yell, don't yell, don't yell. But holy hell, his blood pressure had reached epic heights. If he didn't do something fast, his goddamn head would fly off. "Then how the fuck did you wind up with a broken hand?"

Okay. So he yelled.

A passing nurse—Jackie—stuck her head in. "Whoa, tiger."

He raised his hands. "Sorry."

Jackie knew him, uh, well. Considering they'd spent six months tearing up the sheets. At some point, she'd realized the only sparks between them happened in the sack and moved on. Gabe? He could have been happy with burning sheets. What single, thirty-three-year-old male wouldn't?

At least until Jo came along. Now he wasn't sure what he wanted. Aside from her naked in his bed.

Jackie pointed at Jo. "You okay?"

"I'm fine. He's harmless."

"Oh, honey," Jackie said. "I wouldn't say he's harmless."

Crap on a cracker. "Really, Jackie?"

She laughed at him and continued down the corridor. He turned back to Jo, who was analyzing him with the intensity of a sex therapist at Hedonism.

"What was that?" Jo asked.

"Nothing. She's a smartass."

"You know her, then?"

He shrugged. "I'm in and out of here. Somebody on my team is always getting hurt."

"And here I thought I was special."

"You're special, all right. You're my special pain in the ass."

Jo SWUNG her legs over the side of the bed. Gabe was brewing for a fight. He might be six inches taller than her, but she wasn't afraid of him. Not a chance. Maybe she pushed his buttons, but the thing he hadn't figured out was that, together, they were an unbeatable team. "How fitting. That's makes us both pains in the asses. Let's finish this later. I'm too tired to fight with you."

His gaze locked onto her black stiletto boot. A gift from the president of Barelli for her dedication to getting the city to tighten counterfeiting laws. One thing about working with high-end companies, they knew how to keep the fashion princess in her happy. Gabe slid his gaze up her legs. At the intensity of those eyes, her core turned to a flaming ball of lust.

The man had no idea how hot he was. Or maybe he did. His rock-hard body, coal-dark eyes and hair, and a face filled with sharp angles didn't exactly have women running from him. Unable to use her injured hand, she eased off the bed and he grabbed her elbow so she didn't fall. What with all his male hotness sending her into convulsions and all. "So, you're a leg man."

He waited for her to stand and gave her one of those shark grins he was so good at. "Breast man too."

Idiot. At least he didn't look at her boobs. Still, for the first time all afternoon, she laughed. "Lucky me. I have a set of both."

"Eh-hem."

This came from a young female doctor who stood in the doorway and had obviously heard the exchange.

"Warn your girlfriends," Jo said to her. "Sergeant Townsend is not only a leg man, he's a boob guy too. The man is dangerous, I tell you."

The owl-eyed doctor simply stared. *Sister can't hang with the big dogs.* Jo glanced at Gabe. Was that a bit of a red flush on those perfect olive cheeks? Just maybe, she'd embarrassed him. Which only increased the inferno swarming inside her.

The doctor took one giant step into the room, but stayed clear—way clear—of them. Too funny. "I need to wrap your hand. Then we'll get you out of here."

"I'll wait in the hall," Gabe said.

The doctor waggled her fingers and Jo held her injured hand out. "He's a good guy. What you heard? We were teasing. He's not a pig."

"Jo," Gabe said from the hall. "I can hear you."

"Hush! I'm telling her you're a nice guy. But forget it. I changed my mind. You're a jerk. Happy?"

The doc shook her head while she scrutinized the job ahead of her. "Wow. You two should just have sex and get it over with. Major tension."

"Nice," Gabe said from the hall.

Jo rolled her eyes. "We work together. We're not—you know."

"Well," the doctor said. "Maybe you should be."

THREE

Gabe unlocked Jo's apartment door and pushed it open. The converted building used to be Hoboken's old Lipton Tea factory and, although he preferred living in a house, the place was pretty damned cool.

Still, he'd better get extra points for driving her to Jersey rather than putting her on the ferry.

He could see why she lived here though. Between the view of Manhattan and the ferry being steps away, she didn't have a long commute to work. Using her uninjured hand, she waved him into the apartment.

"It's four-thirty," he said. "You need to call that ortho. See if you can get in there tomorrow."

She dumped her briefcase on the sparkling glass table just past the breakfast bar. "Yes, Daddy."

Smartass. "Call him now so I know you did it."

"Gabe, I'll call him. Can I take my shoes off please?"

The apartment had a combo dining room-living room layout. Surrounding a door leading to the balcony were floor-to-ceiling windows overlooking a sliver of the Hudson

River and the Manhattan skyline just beyond. To his left was a short hallway with a couple of doors. Bedroom and bath probably.

Maybe he'd ask for a tour.

Of the bedroom.

If the modern chrome furnishings in the main area gave a clue, he expected the bedroom to be just as adventurous. The only blast of color in the otherwise gray, black and white space was a bright red rug under the table. Somehow it fit her personality. All business except for the simmering spark underneath.

Yeah. He wanted to see the bedroom.

"Crap," she said from the sofa where she had her slacks pulled to her knees. "I'm sorry, but would you help me with these boots? I need two hands to pull them off."

He kneeled in front of her, grabbed a hold of the boot and glanced up. "Ready?" Her lips slid into a snarky grin. *This should be good.* "Go ahead, say it."

She must have reconsidered, because she shook her head. "No. I'll control myself. Except..."

He sat back on his haunches. "Yes?"

"Except..." She stomped her free foot. "I can't stand it. I have to say it."

Trying not to laugh became an effort. As nuts as she made him, she was entertaining. He gave into the urge and laughed. Why not? Considering he had urges happening on several levels. The professional in him ignored the brain in his crotch and focused on her lush lips that were quirked into a wicked grin. His hands were on her, his fingers moving over the suede of her boot before he gave it a good yank. "So say it already."

She leaned forward and her blues eyes sparkled. "Oh,

Sergeant," she said, in her best sex kitten voice. "I've waited so long to bring you to your knees."

Shit. The brain in his crotch snapped to, but the big brain's focus was on her bringing him to his knees and every comeback got gobbled up by that vision.

Yep, he was gone. Totally wasted.

She rolled backward, her arms held high, the victor in their battle of who could out-sass the other.

That did it. No way he'd let her win. "Sweetheart," he said, "all you had to do was ask."

"Dang it." She punched her fist in the air. "Thought I had you."

She had him all right. Good thing his cargo pants were loose, because he had one hell of a boner.

Putting aside thoughts of him on his knees in her bedroom, he grabbed hold of the other boot, pulled it off and set it next to its mate on the floor. "Call the doc. Running out of day here. Then we need to talk about you and these hits."

"Blah, blah." She rose from the sofa and pointed to the spot she'd vacated. "Have a seat while I call. I figure since you drove me to Jersey, I should treat for dinner. You up for it, sailor?"

He boosted himself to the L-shaped sofa and nearly died because he could stretch his big body into it.

He'd marry her just for the sofa. Smart mouth and all.

As soon as she made that appointment, he'd convince her that for her own safety, she should not participate in the hits. After that pipe to her knuckles, it shouldn't be hard. He'd simply lay it out for her and make her see reason. His team could bag and tag any items she needed while she stayed safely in her office.

The upshot would be that if he could create enough

distance between them, he wouldn't have to see her all the time. Maybe then they could explore the more personal aspects of their relationship.

He wouldn't mind spending the impending winter keeping Jo warm.

Gabe pulled his own boots off and stretched back. Outside, the lights of Manhattan came alive against darkening skies. He loved that city. Even with the brutality and ugliness he saw day in and day out, down deep he craved its frenetic energy. Each night, he went home to Queens where he lived in the third-floor apartment of his parents' three-family home. His folks were on the first floor, where they'd been for the last forty-two years of marriage. Maybe he was a mama's boy, but he didn't see a whole lot of reasons to move out. If they needed him, he was right upstairs. He just had to make sure his mother and her bionic hearing didn't hit on the nights he didn't come home. Not that there were a lot because, truth be told, he was growing bored with the whole one-night-stand thing.

It was, in fact, fairly disgusting at times. Sucked to get old.

"Okay," Jo said. "I have an appointment at nine-fifteen tomorrow. I'm all set. You can quit worrying."

"I always worry."

She tapped him on the top of his head. "You look comfortable. Great sofa, isn't it?"

"I want this sofa."

She dropped into the chair across from him. The one with no arms. That was a little weird. A chair without arms. Nothing to lean on.

"Sorry, big boy. It's all mine. Is this doctor you're sending me to any good?"

"Yeah. He's my buddy from high school. He still lives

down the street from me. You'll like him. Go easy though. He can't handle your wicked tongue."

"Ooh, a fresh victim? How thrilling."

He rolled to a sitting position. "I'm not kidding. Don't harass him." He flashed a grin. "He doesn't have my stamina."

"You know, when you say things like that, you're begging me to mouth off."

"I do know that. It's fun. You're not afraid to engage. Keeps me sharp." He slapped his fingers against the edge of the glass coffee table. "Let's talk about these warrants and I'll give you a couple dozen reasons why you shouldn't be on scene when we execute them."

She scrunched her nose. Such an un-Jo thing to do. "Let's not."

"The first reason," Gabe said, "is your broken hand—the ultimate proof that you could get hurt. From there, your arguments will all go downhill. My advice to you is to let New York's finest handle the bagging and tagging while you stay out of harm's way."

"Right."

He smacked his hands against his thighs. "Glad you agree. You made it easy on me."

"Nice try, Sergeant. I absolutely *don't* agree. Today was an isolated instance. Your rookie screwed up, Gabe. That's why I wound up with a broken hand. Frankly, I should sue the city."

Sue the...

"Incompetence," she said. "Who's training these officers?"

"Uh, that would be me. At least this time. And you're not suing the city. You're trying to shrink my balls. It won't work. I got balls of steel, honey."

"I know you do. That's why I will continue to go on these raids—sorry, *hits.* You and your balls of steel will take care of making sure the men do their jobs, and we'll successfully shut down the major traffickers." She waved a fist at him. "If we can get this guy we're chasing, all the other crooks stealing from my clients will be running scared. We need to shut him down."

If they were going to knock heads, Gabe wanted to be first to knock. "We will get him. My problem is these merchants are starting to recognize you. When you're roaming around looking for potential storefronts to hit, if you're spotted on one end of Tower Street, it takes less than a minute for the merchants on the other end to know. Then everyone takes their counterfeit merchandise and hides. What good does that do us? It slows down the process. Let your investigators do it. They don't have your, shall we say, *assets,* and will be less noticeable. Plus, they can rotate."

She leaned back and squinted. "Did you just refer to my tits as assets?"

"I did indeed."

"I'll beef up my disguises."

Crazy stubborn, this woman. "That's not the point. Come on, Jo. You got hurt today."

She stood and propped her good hand on her hip. "I know I got hurt, but it won't happen again. I'll admit I should have made sure you'd secured the shop, but I got excited. I jumped the gun. The rookie and I both screwed up. Put me in the Gabe penalty box and let me have it. Do your worst. Then we move on. Okay? Please?"

Please. Did he hear that right? And she admitted she'd been wrong. He shook his head, stuck a finger in his ear as if cleaning it.

Jo rolled her eyes. "Have your fun. Go ahead."

She stood waiting while he glanced out the window at the Manhattan skyline now fully ablaze. Continuing to let her tag along on these hits wouldn't do either one of them any good. And not just for carnal reasons. Images of her sprawled on a sidewalk with blood leaking from her body filled his head.

With indecision tugging him, he came back to her. Found her staring at him with those big blue eyes while she bit down on her bottom lip. Oh, man. She was totally playing him.

"Please?" Her voice was low, husky and strained. Pure emotion, not the sex kitten voice, and it was killer. "I need this, Gabe."

As much as he wanted to claim victory—he'd broken the mighty Jo Pomeroy—there was not one ounce of goddamned fun in it. He didn't want her pleading with him...at least not work-related pleading. He wanted her clashing with him. Fighting back. Making him work for it. He equally loved and despised that in her.

Maddening woman.

But he wanted her. In a bad way.

WASN'T this Jo's worst nightmare? She would rather rip out her own ovaries than beg a man for anything. Having it be Gabe only made things worse. This man matched her intelligence on every level and, unlike many men she'd run across, he wasn't afraid to challenge her.

And possibly lose.

This maniac actually *liked* losing to a strong woman. As long as he fought the good fight, he didn't care if he lost. He might yell and beat on his chest, but he'd admit when he was wrong.

Painful as it might be.

This time though, he had her. When it came to the raids, he was in charge. Whether she liked it or not, Gabe called the shots. And he had the power to isolate her. To freeze her out.

He sat back and stacked his hands on his stomach. "We're setting clearer ground rules. You stay outside until I —only I—tell you it's safe to go in. I don't care if the mayor himself tells you it's safe. Unless you hear it from me, you stay put."

She bobbed her head. "I understand."

"I know you understand. That's not the issue. You understand, but you don't *listen*. Today wasn't even a fucking nibble at what could happen to you. If that guy had a shotgun, you'd be in the morgue right now."

That set her back some. Even the most strong-willed women didn't want to imagine their bodies riddled with bullet holes. Gabe let out a long breath and his big shoulders slid down, the weight of her antics obviously pressing in on them.

"Gabe, I'm not trying to give you a hard time."

"Yeah, you are."

She scrambled to the sofa and sat next to him, touched his hand and—mistake. This man had some nice hands. Hands that could do some fairly spectacular things to a thirty-three-year-old lawyer who hadn't been under a man's spell in a long time. She took a mental bulldozer to that thought.

"I'm really not. Honestly. Being there when the warrants are executed is important to me. I do so much behind-the-scenes work that getting into the thick of it is exciting. It's the culmination of all that effort and I get to put my hands directly in it. I get to bag up the evidence. It's a rush for me and I don't get that every day."

Maybe that was TMI. Talk about sounding like a brat. She jumped off the sofa. "Wow. I'm sure you've just about solidified listening to me whine. I'll order us a pizza and crack a bottle—or five—of my favorite merlot. How's that?"

In the kitchen, she grabbed the bottle of wine from the under-cabinet wine rack and pulled the opener from the drawer.

From the corner of her eye, she spotted Gabe walking toward her. "You can't."

"Can't what?"

He pointed to the bottle. "Open that with one hand."

She stared at the bottle. *Hell.* Then she grinned up at him. "I bet I could gnaw through the glass."

"I have no doubt, but let's save that for a better occasion. I'll open the wine. And the other four. If this keeps up, I'll need it more than you."

He paddled his hands and the gesture, so fun and child-like for a man who embodied such fierce presence, gave her a blood rush.

Charming in a sort of perverse way. That's what he was.

She handed him the bottle, then the opener. *Let's see if the big, bad ESU Sergeant can handle a waiter's corkscrew.* He snapped the blade side open, dealt with the foil on the bottle and went to work on the cork. In seconds, he'd completed his task.

Incredibly irritating. "That just pisses me off," she muttered.

"What?"

"Is there anything you're not good at?"

He grinned. The shark grin. *Dangerous.*

"Nope."

"And so humble too."

"Why would I admit my shortcomings to you? Do you like pansies?"

Over the expanse of the counter, he handed her the bottle and their fingers brushed. A light touch and certainly not the first time they'd ever had contact, but this time, something sparked. Jo went rigid. No movement. Except to bring her gaze to his, which only intensified her current state.

His dark gaze zoomed in on her. "Jo?"

And oh, that voice. Warm chocolate. "Yes?" she croaked.

"Are you gonna take this bottle or what?"

"Oh. I'm sorry."

He leaned forward. Shark Gabe. "More early onset menopause?"

If her free hand weren't shattered, she'd have walloped him. "Listen, Sergeant, cut the crap."

"What crap?"

She poured two glasses of wine. "You know what crap. I dare say you're flirting with me."

"Impossible."

But the jerk was smiling at her, those perfect full lips tilting up in a way that made her think about all the places she'd like them to be. She set the bottle aside and stepped back. At this point, the counter between them wasn't nearly enough space.

Something's changed.

Being a tall, somewhat attractive blonde, she'd had her share of good looking men chase her. She'd even dated some. At least until her aggressiveness scared the bejesus out of them and they ran like hunted animals. As an alpha woman, she'd yet to find someone comfortable enough with himself to handle her.

Most of the men she'd frightened off thought she wanted to wear the pants in the relationship. To be the one in charge. Maybe she did. She wasn't sure. What she knew, without hesitation, was that she didn't want to wear the pants one-hundred-percent of the time. What she needed was a man to stand beside her, to not be intimidated by her strength. A man who would give her some leeway when she got pushy, but wasn't afraid to call her out when she went too far.

Like Gabe had today.

She supposed, when it came down to it, every once in a while she wanted to be a woman taken care of by her man.

The feminists would stone her.

Her phone beeped. An email coming in. With her eyes still on the sexy sergeant, she scooped it up and stole a glance at the screen. Her assistant. Nothing important. She dropped the phone.

Gabe rapped his knuckles on the counter. "Maybe I'm flirting a little."

"And maybe I'm not in early onset menopause."

"Good to know."

Still, he kept his focus on her and she inched backward. Somehow the space closed in and the damned heat inciner-ating her from inside wouldn't quit. All the jokes she and Bev had shared about Gabe being Mr. August—the hottest month on a man-candy calendar—zipped through her mind. Were they objectifying him? Probably. They both knew he was so much more than man candy though. Not that it made it right, but women had their fantasies too.

The stainless steel cabinet handle bumped her ass. Nowhere to go. She had to be smart here. She wanted the task force to lead to her dream of a nationwide initiative. The mayor of New York, arguably one of the most powerful men in the nation, saw her as a professional, someone determined to shut down vendors selling illegal products.

Somehow, becoming the world's biggest cliché by having a one night rodeo with a hot ESU sergeant didn't seem like a good career move.

Oh, to try it.

"It would be a huge mistake," Gabe said.

A burst of air exploded from her mouth. "I'm so glad you said that."

He nodded. "I actually hate that I said it. Right now, I could give you a pretty good go and we'd both walk away smiling."

"Shut up." Since her broken hand was out of commission, Jo threw her forearms over her ears. "I'm ready to leap over this counter and attack you, and you say that? I mean, what the hell is wrong with you?"

Then something beyond crazy happened. He smiled. Not the shark smile. The honest-to-God, Gabe-being-Gabe smile that she'd rarely seen and—*pow!*

I'm in big trouble.

She tore around the breakfast bar and he swiveled on the stool to face her. One of them should stop this.

One of them.

Not her.

Too late. His feet were hooked into the side legs of the stool, leaving plenty of room for her to fit between his thighs. He extended his arm and she nearly dove into him, slamming herself against him and kissing him. The kiss—as they say—left nothing on the table. Except maybe her flaming desire to *be* on the table. Lips clashed, tongues explored and—*yowzer*—this was beyond better than she'd imagined. Suddenly, every inch of her body expanded. That damned simmering heat spread and her skin felt too tight, too hot, too confining. Like a zipper needing to burst.

Such a mistake.

Bev would have a heart attack.

Jo jumped back and her chest hitched. "Hang on, sailor."

Gabe threw his arms up. "Not my fault."

She took three more steps back. One, two, three. She exhaled, a humongous, deep release, and then smacked her good hand over her chest. "*That,* Sergeant, was completely insane."

He smiled the Gabe smile. "You're right. Let's do it again."

Shaking her fist at him, she drooped against the wall. "You're *killing* me."

She slid down the wall until her butt hit the floor. Flipping nightmare. She finally understood the Beyoncé song about beautiful nightmares.

The heat clicked on, literally. The furnace rumbled—just what she needed—and she fanned herself. Had to be early onset menopause. Had to be. Only explanation for these hot flashes. She brought her gaze back to Gabe, who remained on the stool, dressed in his tactical uniform, looking like the hero he was. The disgusting, paralyzing, *maddening* truth hit her.

"I'm not a one-night rodeo girl."

CRAP ON A CRACKER. Gabe wrapped his fingers around his forehead and squeezed. Was he out of his fucking mind? For months this woman had driven him to the brink of insanity. On several levels. No matter what it was, she pushed and pushed and pushed. Sometimes she got her way. Sometimes not. She lived with it. Chalked it up to another day and moved on.

That moving on might be the only thing that had kept him from killing her. She knew when to cut her losses. Above all, she was a sharp, demanding woman who believed in righting the wrongs of the world.

And he wanted her. What that want entailed had eluded him, but at some point in the past few months, he'd decided he wanted to get a whole lot closer to Jo Pomeroy. In many ways.

He brought his hand down, reached for a glass of the untouched wine and slammed half. From the spot on the floor, Jo laughed and, in an otherwise quiet apartment, the sound brought relief to his confused mind.

He set the glass down. "Two things," he said. "One, I know you're not a one-night rodeo girl. I never thought that. Two, we've gotta be smart about this. We could screw each other stupid tonight and not say a word to anyone. Our secret, right? But that's crap. When people hook up, things change and others notice. Pretty soon, the guys in my unit are breaking my balls and hounding me. The more I keep quiet, the more they suspect I'm banging the leggy blonde attorney and—trust me on this—that makes me a hero. There's not a guy in my unit that hasn't thought about it. They'll have a goddamned field day."

Her eyes went big and round and she shook her head. Violently. At least she was hearing the message.

"Then," he continued, "the mayor gets word that two key people on his pet project are doing the nasty. You may have figured out by now that our mayor is good at his job, but he's a monster asshole. He'd have no problem launching us both if we embarrass him."

She sighed. "I know. I'd go from respected attorney to a

woman who can't keep her legs closed for a guy in uniform. I see the way some of the guys look at me. They're pigs."

"Exactly."

"So what do we do? Business as usual?"

He shrugged. "It'll be painful, but yeah. Business as usual." Then he grinned. Shark Gabe. "At least until we figure something else out."

FOUR

Jo sat patiently on a metal frame chair while Gabe's friend Rich—Dr. Bowles—assembled his masterpiece of a red cast. The "casting room" as Rich had called it, was the size of a small conference room with whitewashed walls and an examining table dead center. She had opted for the chair rather than the table. Along the one wall was a roughed-up counter with cabinets. On top were shiny metal instruments and a couple of electric saws with circular blades.

In the far corner stood Gabe, wearing low-slung jeans, a plain black sweater and the confidence of someone who knew how to control a room. Here was a man who, on his day off, insisted on taking her to the doctor.

When it came to men, women, and the sudden exploration of their sexual attraction, mornings after were always tough. This one was tough for all the wrong reasons. Gabe rarely got a full day off and he'd offered to drive her to the doctor when he could have been sleeping or doing whatever it was he did on his downtime.

For that reason alone she should have boffed his brains out. Therefore, she could only surmise that her morning after discomfort had nothing to do with a one-night stand. *Her* regret came from a non-one-night stand.

Tragic. Jo focused on the doctor layering strips of wet cloth on her wrist. Dark blue scrubs hung on his rail-thin body. When she'd been standing, she'd been an inch taller than him. Somehow, she'd pictured someone bigger. As if Gabe wouldn't have short friends.

She tilted her head and Rich added another layer. Such a perfectionist. "Don't you have someone who does this for you?"

"I do."

"And yet, you're here with me. Should I be flattered?"

"Jo," Gabe said from his spot in the corner. "Leave him alone."

She gawked. "Yeesh. I'm just asking a question."

"You never *just* ask a question. Every one of your questions is packed with dynamite."

Another layer of cloth was added. "I think he's tired today," Jo whispered to Rich.

"I heard that."

Using her free hand, she flipped Gabe off. The good doctor burst out laughing, one of those hardy, addictive laughs.

"Now that's an awesome laugh," she said. "I still want to know why you're doing this instead of handing me off. I promise I won't sue you if your assistant screws it up."

Rich glanced at Gabe. "She's something else, this one."

Gabe sighed. He knew all too well.

"I'm in here," Rich said, "because Gabe has referred a lot of people to me."

Gabe cleared his throat loud enough to shake the room. What on earth was his problem? "He said you two have been friends a long time."

Another exquisitely placed layer went on the cast. "Yes. And in all the times he's referred patients to me, he's never, not once, come along."

A whooshing noise filled Jo's head and that crazy explosion of heat from the night before happened again.

He's never come along.

She so should have slept with him.

"Oh, Christ," Gabe muttered.

She didn't dare look at him. Nope. Not going there. Instead, she'd park that information in the part of her brain that housed nonthreatening items. "He's guilt ridden because his rookie screwed up and now my hand is broken."

Rich's head snapped up.

"I do feel bad," Gabe said. "But that doesn't come close to my feelings about a certain loudmouthed attorney who doesn't listen when she's told to stay put."

She swung her head in his direction. *Shark Gabe.* "Well, maybe if a certain bullheaded sergeant—"

"Ho-kay, folks," Rich said. "Let's not fight in front of the children."

"And to think," Jo muttered, "he's never been married."

Gabe laughed. "Uh, Counselor, neither have you. What does that say about us?"

"What it says about me is that I'm particular."

"No. It says that we're both pains in the asses who want everything our way and no one could put up with us."

Rich cleared his throat. "So, *anyway,* to answer your question. Yes, I usually have someone do this for me, but since my friend Gabe is here, I figured you must be someone I'd like to meet."

Such a charmer. Who'd have guessed? She waggled her finger at Gabe. "That's how it's done, big boy. I hope you're taking notes."

Her cell phone chirped. Sherry's ringtone. "Ooh, I have to get that." Trying not to move the arm being casted, she bent sideways to retrieve her phone from her purse and hit the button before it went to voice mail. "Hi. Sorry. I'm getting an exceptional cast put on my hand by a charming doctor. It sucks to be me." Rich smiled at her. "What's up?"

"I've been to three vendors already. None of them have that new Konklin watch, but they all said there's a shipment coming in on Friday. *Friday.*"

Jo looked at Gabe. He sensed her excitement and stood tall. "What?"

"They all said that?" she asked Sherry.

"Every one of them."

"What is it?" he asked, getting louder.

"It's Sherry. She's on the prowl for a Konklin. Three vendors told her there's a shipment coming in on Friday."

He snatched the phone. "Sherry? Gabe Townsend."

"Hey," Jo yelled. "Give that back."

She held her hand up, but Gabe grabbed it and squeezed. Not hard. Just enough to keep her from the phone. Or to distract her with how *incredibly* warm and good and cozy it felt to hold his hand.

Bastard.

"Okay," he said, entwining his fingers with hers. "Type that up and email it to me. Right...thanks." After finishing up with Sherry, he clicked off, slipped his hand free— damned shame, that—and dropped the phone back in Jo's purse.

"What'd she say?"

"One big shipment coming in on Friday for multiple vendors."

"That's my guy. Has to be. We need to figure out who he is and how he's getting these huge shipments into the city."

"And we will. My guess is the load is coming in on a container ship. I'll get with someone at the Port Authority. If we're lucky, we'll find the ship." Gabe pointed at the doctor. "Rich, hit the gas. We have work to do."

—:—

So much for his day off. Gabe dropped Jo at her office then hauled ass to the Port Authority to alert Customs about a possible shipment of counterfeit goods.

Next he put the word out with the undercover guys. With all the informants those guys had, someone on the street would know where this shipment would be coming from.

By three-thirty he was heading home to take his mother grocery shopping. His phone rang and he checked the screen. Calhoun. One of the vice guys.

"I just talked to one of my CIs," Calhoun said. "Check out a warehouse in Brooklyn."

Brooklyn. Could be the same place they'd been watching? Jo would have a coronary. "What's up with this warehouse?"

"The CI knows a guy who hijacks trucks. They bring the hot load to this Brooklyn location and get paid for the goods. He said it's a huge fuckin' place."

"Address?"

The detective rattled off an address on First Street. Yep. Their warehouse. Prickling energy shot up Gabe's arms. "Who pays them?"

"He doesn't know. All he knows is what the guy told him. This was a few months back though."

Well, shit. A few months back? Might as well have been years.

"You got a name for anybody at the warehouse?"

"All my guy knows is a street name. Kiki."

Easy to remember.

Gabe swung a U-turn in the intersection and headed back to the Queensboro Bridge. He'd have to get with Bev on this, which meant returning to the city and blowing off grocery shopping with his mother. She'd been waiting on him all day and he hated disappointing her, but this might be months of work finally paying off. "Good enough. I'll check it out. Thanks."

The CI's information, combined with all the surveillance they'd done on the place, might be enough to get them a warrant.

He called his mom to break the news and then reached out to Bev. He got her voice mail and called Jo.

"Good afternoon, Sergeant," she said. "What can I do for you?"

"I got a lead on a warehouse in Brooklyn."

A pause. "My warehouse?"

"Looks like."

"No!"

He grinned. Crazy-assed woman. "Yes. An informant gave it to one of our undercover guys. The intel is old though. Few months at least. We're looking for a guy named Kiki."

"Is he our guy?"

"Don't know, but we might have enough for a warrant. Heading back to see Bev now." He hit a little construction traffic on the bridge. "Damn."

"What?"

"Nothing. Traffic. I was heading home. I promised my mother I'd take her shopping."

"I'm sorry, Gabe."

"Not your fault." A cabbie cut him off and nearly clipped his front bumper. "Hey, asshole! Watch where you're going."

Of course, it was November and he didn't have the windows open, but maybe the guy read lips.

"But it's your day off."

"Yeah, well. You of all people know how that goes. Are you taking the ferry home tonight?"

"Yep. And now I have my new cast that can double as a weapon if I get mugged."

"Not funny, Jo."

"I thought it was."

He snorted. Maybe it was a little funny. "Okay. I'll call your cell if I find out anything. Do me a favor and see if you can track down Bev. I left her a voice mail. You might have better luck. I'm gonna send someone over to Brooklyn to grab a few bags of garbage from the warehouse Dumpster. See if we find anything with the name Kiki."

"Perfect. I'll come by and help you."

"Jo, it's garbage. Forget it. Go home and I'll let you know what we find."

"No, I want to help. It'll go faster with another set of hands. Besides, I'm excited."

Of course she was. She lived for this. "Your call. Let me go. I'll let you know when the garbage arrives."

He tossed the phone on the passenger seat and focused on the traffic ahead. Without getting too ahead of himself, he tried to remain cautiously optimistic about a warrant. He'd been doing this job long enough to not make any assumptions, but something told him they'd be hitting this warehouse in the next twenty-four hours.

Two hours later, Gabe stood in the damp HQ basement with three trash-filled construction-sized garbage bags ripped open on a plastic lined table. Most of what covered the table were reports, invoices, used mailing envelopes, printed emails and a couple of coffee cups. In other words, nothing too nasty. At least the stuff didn't come from a restaurant. That's when things really got interesting.

Across from him, Jo had taken her jacket off, pushed up her sleeves, cut three holes in a clean garbage bag he'd snagged from the supply closet and shoved it over her head to protect her clothes. Latex gloves topped off the ensemble. Somehow, she made a garbage bag sexy.

Unable to resist, he snapped a picture of her with his phone.

She glanced up, saw him with the phone and narrowed her eyes. "Oh, no you didn't."

He tucked his phone away and went back to his garbage. "Oh, yes I did."

"What are you going to do with that?"

He shrugged. "Not sure."

"You're such an ass."

"Yeah, I know." He went back to the load of trash in front of him. "Snag anything with a name. Envelopes, memos, emails. Anything. Kiki is a street name. Chances are we won't find anything with that name on it."

"Then what?"

"Then, Ms. Pomeroy, we check all the names, pull photos of the males and show our pipe wielding scumbag a photo lineup. See if he recognizes anyone."

"He won't tell us."

Gabe unraveled a crumbled sheet of yellow legal paper.

Nothing but stick figures. "The eternal optimist is turning negative on me?"

"Not negative. Realistic. I know these vendors. They're too afraid to talk."

"We'll see. I'll get the A.D.A. to make him a deal he can't resist."

FIVE

On the ferry the next morning, Jo got lucky and only had to share her window bench seat with one other person. A regular she saw most mornings who, like her, took advantage of the extra space on the bench by setting his briefcase there.

Around them, other commuters worked on their laptops, read or fiddled with their phones. Many mornings, Jo did the same. Today though, the lunacy of the week had set in and she simply wanted to watch the sun glisten off the Hudson. If her emails took an extra chunk out of her day, so be it.

From inside her bag, her cell phone rang and she checked the screen. Gabe. Hopefully he had good news. "Tell me you got the warrant."

"Good morning, Counselor."

And oh, the sound of that voice in the morning. Mr. August at his smoldering best. "Good morning, Sergeant. Tell me you got the warrant."

Her bench mate shifted his eyes to her then back to his newspaper.

"I got the warrant," Gabe said. "Kiki is Clarence Hill. Your pipe wielding scumbag picked him out of our photo lineup. Done deal."

"Yes!"

He'd done it. Even when she doubted the vendor would help them, Gabe got it done.

"Take it easy, Counselor. He's not our guy. He's the number two guy. Scumbag doesn't know who Kiki's boss is."

"Darn it."

"Yeah. Anyway, we're gonna hit the warehouse this afternoon. Got a meeting at ten hundred."

A ten o'clock meeting would most likely mean an early afternoon search. She'd have to move her appointments. Assuming he'd stick to his word and let her participate. "I'd like to be there when the search is done. You'll let me know what time?"

"I'll call you. Remember what we talked about."

"Yes, sir."

"I'm not kidding, Jo. Unless I tell you to go in, you stay put. Don't screw with me on this. I'll lock you in the truck if I have to."

Only if you're locked in with me, big fella. "I love when you talk dirty."

Her bench mate snorted. Men.

"Jo!"

"Oh, all right. Don't start yelling. I'll be a good little girl and stay outside until you, and only you, tell me it's safe to go in. Happy?"

"Thank you. You're giving me an ulcer."

He hung up and she smirked. An ulcer wasn't so bad. Could have been worse. Still, she'd try not to aggravate him. She owed him that much. She clicked the end button on her phone and went to her calendar as the ferry slowed for its arrival.

Two client meetings this afternoon. She'd have to postpone those. She hated asking people to rearrange their day for her, but this couldn't be avoided. Not if she wanted a firsthand look at what was in that warehouse.

—:—

Gabe stood at the open door to the warehouse his unit had just hit and waved Jo in. Miracle of all miracles, she'd actually listened.

She walked toward him in a killer pair of high-heeled shoes—designer no doubt—and black slacks. Her red trench coat was cinched tight against the cold November day, but the sun was decently warm and glistening off her blond hair.

Beautiful, sexy and a pain in the ass.

I'm cooked.

He dragged his eyes from her—which completely sucked—and glanced at the precinct guys filtering in through the loading dock doors.

"Did you see anything?" Jo asked when she reached the door.

"Nothing but a few employees and a shitload of boxes. No Kiki."

"How many employees?"

"Just the ones you saw come out. Three of them. They're not talking."

She snapped on a pair of latex gloves. "Let's see what we've got, Sergeant."

He held his hand out. "Lead the way, Counselor."

One of the guys, Delaney, stepped out of an aisle. "Over here," he yelled.

The aisles were alphabetically labeled, the first two being A through G. Delaney stood in the K aisle. Jo glanced up at Gabe and lifted her eyebrows.

"Don't get excited, Jo. We don't know what it is."

"Yeah, but the K aisle is a good omen."

If she didn't find Konklin watch knock-offs she'd be crushed. He didn't want that for her, but with her tendency to go emotionally all-in on these things, it could happen. They walked by two deep aisles filled from floor to ceiling with boxes. Next to him, Jo's long legs ate up the ground in front of her.

They stepped up to where Delaney stood. "What is it?" Gabe asked.

The man pointed to a stack of boxes, five wide from floor to ceiling, labeled KON. One of the bottom boxes had been torn open and on top of it sat a watch. Jo damned near knocked Delaney over lunging toward the box.

She scooped up the watch, studied the face then flipped it over and ran her finger along the edge.

Gabe stepped closer and glanced over her shoulder. "Jo?"

A bright smile lit her face before she turned back to him, went up on tiptoes and threw her arms around his neck. Visions of that smoking hot kiss they'd shared flooded his mind and Gabe froze.

Well, a large part of him froze. The other part, the one between his legs, had hardening issues unrelated to freezing.

Delaney's eyebrows hitched up and Gabe, not knowing what to do with his hands, held them wide. *See, no hands.*

"Okay, Counselor," he said. "Let's try and contain the enthusiasm."

Please freaking contain it.

She leapt back and the stretched look on her face indicated nothing short of horror.

"I'm so sorry." She spun to Delaney. "I—I got excited."

Delaney held his hands up. "I was hoping I'd be next."

"Whoa," Gabe said.

Jo straightened her coat, ran a hand over her ponytail and offered a small smile. "Nice try, Officer, but I've squandered my quota of professional slip-ups for the day."

"Always the way."

Gabe jerked his head toward the door. "Delaney, go do something. Start packing up your gear. *Something.*"

Delaney marched his ass to the loading dock doors. Gabe waited for him to leave the building before turning back to Jo.

"Shoot," she said, shaking her head. "I'm sorry. I saw all these boxes and then the watch and I went on overload." She held her arms out. "Look at this stuff. If all these boxes have counterfeit goods in them—"

Gabe nodded. "It'll be the biggest haul yet."

She pounded her fist in the air. "Yes! The mayor will be ecstatic. *I'll* be ecstatic."

He should take a second and lecture her about the hugging thing. If she didn't want a team of ESU guys speculating, she needed to deep-six the PDA. Seeing her so excited over the watches though, he couldn't do it to her. Maybe later. Right now, he'd let her enjoy the find. "Do you want to stay and go through all this stuff with the search team? I'll talk to the sergeant."

Already, she was pulling her phone from her coat pocket. "Absolutely. I'll clear my afternoon. I want to inventory everything we find related to my clients." Again she stared up at the tower of boxes then shifted her gaze down the long row. "If all this stuff was actually real, it'd be worth millions."

"Yeah. Even being counterfeit, it represents a huge loss to the smuggler."

"Hundreds of thousands of dollars."

She spun to him, raised her open hand and they high-fived. "If this is what I think it is, we did it, Gabe. All these months of working together and finally, *finally*, a huge seizure."

That was true, and his rapid pulse indicated his own sense of accomplishment. But this huge seizure, the one that would make them heroes and give the mayor something to brag about, would also royally piss someone off.

And they had no idea who that someone was.

—:—

Jo's office was fairly quiet the following morning as she read over deposition notes. The only sound came from her television on low volume. The mayor was doing a 10:00 a.m. news conference regarding a new appointment at the Health Department and she was sure he'd go off-script and mention the seizure of counterfeit goods. The task force being his pride and joy, he took every opportunity to mention their successes.

"Finally," the mayor said, "I'd like to thank the members of the Clean Sweep Task Force, including Bev Richards, Sergeant Gabriel Townsend and attorney Joanna Pomeroy, for the flawless execution of yesterday's massive seizure of counterfeit goods. This task force continues to perform above expectations to cleanse our city of a billion dollar a year criminal enterprise."

She raised her hands in victory. "And the crowd goes wild."

The mayor stepped from the podium and Jo broke into a celebratory chair dance. Someone knocked on the open door and she glanced up. Her assistant, Liza, stood there holding what looked suspiciously like a Barelli shoe box.

Another gift from their satisfied client?

Jo grinned like a fool. "What do you have there?"

"It just came for you. I took it out of the bigger box, but figured since it was your gift, I'd let you open it."

Jo waved her in. "I'll tell you what, whatever is in this box is yours."

A huge smile split Liza's face. Good assistants weren't easy to find and Liza was not only good, she was spectacular. The firm worked this young woman like a slave and she never complained. Not once. The least Jo could do was share the riches.

"But it's your gift."

"I just got the boots. You take this one."

Liza bit down on her lip. "Are you sure?"

"Absolutely. Open that sucker up and see what you got."

Rushing to the desk, Liza set the box down and flipped the cover back. This would be good. Jo kept her gaze glued to Liza's face so she could see her reaction.

Only, Liza's smile dropped like the Titanic. Her lips recoiled and she threw her hand over her mouth before looking away. "Aah!"

Jo scooted forward in her chair and tipped the box up. A severed hand slid to the bottom of the tilted box, tumbled out, bounced off her wrist and landed on the deposition notes.

Ohmygod. Jo's eyes throbbed as blood roared in her brain. She raised her hands and slammed her eyes closed as sickening bile filled her throat. *No throwing up.*

Running from the room, Liza screamed for John, the senior partner.

Evidence. *Don't touch it.* With her eyes still closed, Jo realized the hand would have to sit on top of the Alderson deposition until they figured out what to do. *Look at it. Make mental notes.* After one long breath, Jo called the bulldog of a lawyer inside her back to the surface and opened her eyes.

Palm up. That's how the hand sat. It had been severed at the wrist. Cleanly. Whatever the hell that meant when dealing with a chopped off hand. Still, the bones and tendons had been severed, as if by a blade, rather than gnawed. Just one effective swipe had detached it. Otherwise, it was perfect—as perfect as a severed hand could be—the grayish-blue color was even, the skin unmarred, the nails clean.

Nausea swirled and, unable to control herself, Jo gagged. "God, that's disgusting."

She closed her eyes for another second and breathed into the crook of her arm. The clean scent of her laundry soap settled her rioting stomach. She needed to study the thing. Note her first impressions. Anything that might help when the police eventually showed up.

It also appeared to be a female hand. Jo held her left hand in front of her, then glanced at the severed hand. Yes, most definitely a woman's hand.

"Jo." John rushed in. "Don't touch it."

"I haven't. Outside of it falling out of the box."

John stepped closer, gasped and spun away. "Jesus!"

Liza hovered in the doorway refusing to come in. Who could blame her? "Liza, I don't want to touch *anything.*

Would you please call Gabe Townsend and tell him we have a...uh...situation?"

He'll love this one. It would probably launch him directly to yelling mode. Something to look forward to.

Liza swung from the doorway. "Right away."

John stared at the ceiling a second—*yeah, pal, I know*—then his shoulders lifted and dropped as if he'd taken a deep breath.

With one foot, Jo shoved her chair back from the desk. She'd had enough of staring at that disgusting hunk of human flesh that had been sent to her.

In a Barelli box. Oh, that message had been received loud and clear. The cast on her hand should have been her first warning. Her stomach tumbled again and she looked down, shaking her head, willing the bile to go down her throat instead of up. She swallowed a couple of times, closed her eyes and exhaled.

"Are you gonna pass out?" John asked.

Not if I can help it. She opened her eyes, ignored the wayward hand on her desk and zeroed in on John. "I'm okay."

Liza stormed back to the doorway and told her Gabe had gotten called out—a barricaded accused murderer holding his wife hostage.

Jo's severed hand delivery had nothing on that one.

"They're sending the crime scene people over," Liza said. "Don't worry."

Unfortunately, that was easier said than done.

SIX

Gabe stepped off the elevator in Jo's apartment building and spotted Wasco, a guy who'd come to ESU not long after he did, standing guard at her front door. Wasco was still dressed in his tactical uniform from his shift and was probably ready to get home to his family.

"Hey, boss," he said.

Gabe halted in front of him and pointed at the door. "Hey. She okay?"

"Pretty freaked, I'd say, but she was cracking jokes about one-handed women the whole way home."

Gabe snorted. That sounded like Jo. Using off-color jokes to deflect her fear. "I've got it from here. You can shove off."

Wasco glanced over his shoulder, then back to Gabe. "You sure? I mean, you had a long day. I could stay."

A long day was putting it mildly. They stood outside that jackhole's house for six hours until negotiations broke down and they finally had to go in and get him. The guy had beaten his wife to a pulp and the woman had been unconscious on the floor by the time they'd gotten inside.

Sometimes Gabe just didn't understand. But he'd walked away with the suspect in cuffs and his clothes reeking of the chemical agent they'd used trying to smoke the guy out. Nasty shit, that.

At least a shower washed the odor away, but like every other time, the scent lingered in his mind. Now he stood in front of Jo's door wondering what the hell he'd say to her that didn't sound too much like "You're fucking done going on these hits."

She probably wouldn't like that, but he'd had enough of this nonsense. National task force dreams or not, if she wouldn't be responsible for her own safety, he'd do it for her. He'd lock her in a cell if he had to.

"I'm good," Gabe said to Wasco. "Go on home."

"Awright. Tell Jo to hang in there."

The guys knew she was a pain in the ass, but they liked her sassy mouth. Gabe liked her sassy mouth too. For a variety of reasons. He nodded. "I will."

Wasco strode down the hall and Gabe waited for him to get on the elevator before knocking on Jo's door. "It's Gabe."

A minute later, the door swung open. She stood on the other side wearing a pair of those stretchy black yoga pants with a long-sleeved fitted T-shirt. And, once again, the wrong brain in his body took over. There was no denying this woman had one hell of a sumptuous figure. Curves in all the right places.

Places he wanted his hands to be. For a lengthy period of time.

"Hi," she said. "Come in."

He stepped over the threshold. "Sorry about this afternoon."

"It's okay. A barricaded murderer was more important than me."

He shrugged. "Not really, but it's the job."

When he walked by her, she stuck her head into the hallway. "Where's Wasco?"

"I sent him home. I'll stay with you."

She opened her mouth to say something, stared at the open door for a second, then shook off whatever she'd been about to say. When she closed the door, the snick of the lock echoed in the quiet hallway. Whether it was some sort of sign that he should run from the apartment rather than risk being alone with Jo after an emotionally charged day, Gabe didn't know. Either way, he was in now and had no intention of leaving.

"Did you have to come all the way over here? Aren't you tired? And hungry?"

He dropped onto her sofa. "Yes, I did. Yes, I'm tired. Yes, I'm hungry." He flashed a grin. "Not bad. All three of your questions answered. Boom-boom-boom."

She rolled her eyes and marched to the kitchen, her ponytail swinging as she walked and giving her an almost youthful appearance, a sweetness he normally wouldn't attribute to her. He liked it though. This other side of Jo. The reverse Jo.

Over the breakfast bar, he saw her open the fridge and start pulling platters. Might as well see what she had going on there. He wandered to the kitchen and leaned against the support wall. "I didn't come here for you to feed me."

"I know. But I have a ton of leftovers that my mother left me. Some shindig she hosted and ordered too much food for. This is one of the benefits of having parents who are both political consultants. They go to all these fancy fundraisers."

"Both your folks work in politics?"

She shoved one of the platters into the microwave and started it. "Yep. Mom is a democrat and Dad is a republican. Makes for interesting family debates. I refuse to visit them during October of an election year. Filthy drama."

No wonder Jo was so combative. Suddenly, he understood her better than he had seconds before.

She shifted back to him, propped a hip against the counter and loaded him up on eye contact. *Holy hell.* Those blue eyes were laser sharp and focused squarely on him. *Run.* He should hightail it out of there. If she kissed him again, with the mood he was in, his body aching for all the wrong reasons, he'd be all over her. They'd both had a shitty day and he couldn't summon a whole lot wrong with dropping into her bed and working off the stress.

His little brain definitely wanted things his big brain told him were a mistake. Never mind that it could completely annihilate their working relationship and splinter the mayor's pet project.

Except, right now he wasn't sure he cared.

"I was hoping you'd show up," she said.

"You waited for me?"

"I did."

He'd never been accused of being stupid. Particularly when it came to females who green lighted him. All this eye contact? Definite green light. And Jo, at least in his experience, wasn't one to be cagey. Once she decided on a course of action, she went for it.

Typically, her course of action drove him insane. Now? Insanity looked pretty good.

The microwave dinged, but Jo didn't budge. Not an inch.

He pointed. "Microwave."

"I heard it."

"You okay?"

"I'm trying to decide if you'll help me get the picture of that severed hand out of my head. I guess I'm confused. You showed up here after, if the news coverage is accurate, you had a horrendous day. You sent Wasco home, and now I've pretty much thrown you every damned mating signal I can think of and you're still standing there staring at me."

He took a small step back. Yeah, that'd help.

She spun to the microwave. "You can stop backing away, Gabe. I won't tackle you."

Which would be fun.

She set the hot food on the stove and shoved another platter in the oven before poking one of the numbers on the keypad. "This has been—" another poke, "—a truly sucky day." She jammed her finger against the keypad again then hit the start button.

Start button.

He wrapped his fingers over his forehead and squeezed. *Helluva day.* "The crime scene guys are running tests on the hand. They'll...uh...fingerprint it and see if it matches someone in the system."

"Did you see it?"

"Yeah, I stopped by on my way here. Nasty shit."

"It was a woman's hand."

He gave up on retreating and inched closer. "Jo, you've gotta lay low for a while. No more hits. Please."

She glanced down at her casted hand. "What kind of monster does something like that?" She looked back at him and her eyes filled with tears.

Jo Pomeroy.

Crying.

Game over. He took one long stride and pulled her close. Immediately, his body turned rigid. How many nights had he thought about her? About holding her? Running his hands over that amazing body.

Too many.

She grabbed onto the back of his T-shirt and squeezed. "Did I deserve that?"

Ah, jeez.

"Whoever did this is an animal. Nothing shocks me anymore, but this guy is escalating. He had your hand broken and you didn't back off. The fact that he sent a severed hand in a Barelli box? No coincidence. Stay off the streets, Jo. No more investigating. No more hits until we find this guy." He kissed the top of her head and the scent of her shampoo, something clean, like ocean air, bumped his pulse up.

Back away now.

He didn't move. What was the point? They both knew where this was going.

THE MICROWAVE DINGED, but Jo kept her forehead pressed into Gabe's chest. If she could just stand here like this, letting him hold her, maybe the chill, that paralyzing freeze that had soaked into her, would disappear.

Not that she'd ever needed a man to chase away her demons, but this was an unusual circumstance. For one night, she'd like to let someone take care of her. To allow her to be vulnerable without it turning into a power play.

Tomorrow she'd be herself again. She'd be the woman who wasn't afraid to break rules to make a difference. Tomorrow she'd wake up and the person who sent that hand would experience how tough Jo Pomeroy could be. She'd find the sick bastard and make sure justice was served.

Tomorrow.

Tonight she needed a taste of euphoria to even out her fried edges and obliterate the recurring vision of that hand tumbling out of the box.

Tonight she'd allow herself to be weak.

She gripped his T-shirt again. "Are you going to help me forget about that hand or not? I know you want to."

Unless the erection poking her belly was an apparition, he *really* wanted to.

"This is unfair."

Leave it to her to find the one man on the planet who wanted to be a good guy and fight an opportunity to have sex.

She stepped back and held her hands up. "I see what you're doing here. You're trying to be a stand-up guy. I appreciate that, but I know you're not a pig."

He snorted. "Thanks so much for that stunning observation."

"I call 'em like I see 'em, big boy. Here's what I propose. We'll have dinner. A dinner that is probably now cold again, but whatever. We'll have dinner, have a glass of wine, I'll tell you about the lacy red bra I'm wearing—"

"Are you fucking kidding me?" he shouted. "That is *totally* unfair."

"I know. But you're a man, and men are easy when it comes to sex. Trust me, you'll see this bra and you'll give in. Laws of nature." She handed him the platter sitting on the stove. "Take this to the table while I get dishes."

He marched to the dining area grumbling about manipulation and trickery. If he thought this was manipulation, wait until she got him naked. "Sergeant, you ain't seen nothing yet."

From the dining area, he laughed, but not his normal

laugh. This one was low and tight. Frustrated. "You know what? Forget it. You're on, Jo."

He stormed back to the kitchen, pushed her against the wall and kissed her. Her mind exploded, every nerve ending sending signals. Here. Not here. Yes. No. All at once they hit her, but she wrapped her arms around him and held on while his kisses incinerated her. Literally fried her mind. *No more deep freeze, that's for sure.*

Then his hands were under her shirt in search of the red lace she'd promised.

"There it is," he said. He lifted her shirt, pulled it over her head and tossed it on the counter. His gaze zeroed in on the bra and he grinned. *Shark Gabe.* "Nice, but take it off. I want the real goods." He spun her around, unhooked the bra and pressed his body against her, pinning her to the wall. From behind, he clasped her hands and squeezed. "Are you sure you want to do this?"

Still being a good guy. *I'm so gone.* Racing tingles shot down her legs and she caught her breath, held it a second to enjoy the swirling heat consuming her.

Mr. August.

He's so much more.

She eased her body from the wall and slowly turned. He kept his gaze on her face. Oh, she knew he wanted to look at her naked torso, but he waited for her to answer. She went on tiptoes and kissed him. Softly. Not like the last one, or the one the other night that should have set the place on fire. This one was gentle and lingering, and she loved the experience of it.

She backed away from the kiss, hugged him to her. "Yes. I'm sure. Bring it on, Sergeant."

Suddenly she was airborne, a second later landing on his shoulder. All she could do was laugh. She had, after all, teased the monster. He carried her down the short hallway to her bedroom and, along the way, used his free hand to shove her stretchy pants off.

A multitasker. Lucky her.

When the pants reached her ankles she kicked out of them and let them drop to the floor.

He kicked the half-closed bedroom door open, got to the bed and put his hands on her back. Gently, he lowered her and stepped back. The wall sconces from the hallway illuminated him and threw shadows across the room.

Hang on. How the hell did she get ninety-percent naked and he was still fully clothed? Not only that, his dark gaze devoured her. Up and down, up and down, up and down it went.

"I knew it," he said. "I knew you'd be exceptional."

"Thank the surgeon."

His head snapped back. "What?"

She launched herself forward and unfastened his jeans. "The anticounterfeiting guru has fake boobs. Counterfeit ta-tas."

She cracked up. Must be the fatigue, because she'd never found that fact particularly amusing. She'd also only ever admitted it to a handful of people. Two of whom had been men.

"Wow," he said.

She worked his zipper down. "I was always an A cup. Hated it. I wanted boobs, and on my twenty-third birthday decided my A cups needed a boost. Voila. They got a boost."

"Nice boost."

Again she laughed. What a conversation. "Come on, Sergeant. Let's get this show on the road."

He laughed at her and kicked out of his pants. "Shit. Condom."

"On it." She rolled sideways to the bedside table, flipped the lamp on and pulled out the two boxes of condoms she'd bought.

"Jo, should I be concerned that you have two boxes of rubbers in your nightstand?"

"No, dopey. I bought them for you after the insanity known as our first kiss. I figured it was inevitable and wanted to be prepared." She gestured at his protruding erection. "I guessed at the size. And I wasn't sure which ones you'd like. The guy at the store told me he likes these." She pointed to one of the boxes. "But then another guy—a customer shopping in that aisle—said he liked these. So I bought them both. You can pick. I personally don't have a clue. Just be fast about it."

He pressed the fingers of both hands into his forehead. "You are unbelievable. You took a goddamned survey at the drug store?"

"Hey! Forgive me for caring. A little research never hurts and I certainly couldn't call you and ask what size condoms you wear."

He tore open the first box, the ones marked ecstasy—*oh, baby!*—and did his thing while she stripped off her underpants.

"Okay, Mr. August, let's see what you've got."

"*What?*"

She waved it off. "Mr. August, the hottest month on the man candy calendar. That's you. Except in the calendar you're not talking. At all. Come on, Sergeant."

He shoved her backward and climbed on top of her, trapping her against the mattress. The weight of him, so big and solid and *safe,* only increased the urgency.

"Where's the damned fire?" he asked.

"I'm hungry. For many things."

"My kind of woman." He nudged his knee between her legs.

She arched against him, needing the contact, the heat that would drive away the day's demons and let her feel loved. Then he was inside her, gasping in her ear, and she went crazy. Lost her damned mind in a blast of white sparks. She was so *not* in control and, for once, loved every second of it.

They found their rhythm, at first fast and then slower, the easy slide of his body so perfectly suited for her. *Yes. Yes. Yes. Yes.*

He propped himself on his elbows and kissed her. "I knew it. Amazing."

Her core tightened. A squeezing, sensual twisting that urged her to pump her hips harder. Gabe was here. With her. Making her crummy day so, so, so much better.

"I needed this," she said. "Thank you. Perfect."

"Me too." The sound of his voice, the roughened edges so soft and gentle calmed her chaotic thoughts.

She looked into his eyes, ran her fingers down his cheek to his shoulder and held on as their pace increased. A coiling sensation wound through her core and she held her breath until, finally, her world exploded.

GABE THOUGHT a heart attack was imminent. *Someone call 9-1-1. Officer down.* He heaved out a breath, pulled himself free of Jo's delectable body and rolled off her.

No sense crushing her before they were able to do this again.

"Mission complete." She snuggled into his side and he flopped his arm over her.

"Off the charts. I knew it. In fact, I might chain you to

this bed." He caught his breath and rolled to face her. "What do you think? Wanna try it?"

"Only if you're chained too."

He shrugged. "Sure. Why not?"

"Kinky."

"Uh, *fun.*"

She laughed at him, sat up and smacked his leg. "Let's eat. I'm hungry."

But she straddled him and leaned forward so that amazing rack pressed against his chest. "Your body makes me nuts. I'm sending that surgeon a bottle of scotch. The guy's a genius."

"I'm sure he'll appreciate the endorsement." She kissed the center of his chest, then rested her cheek there. "Thank you for scaring off my demons."

Careful here, buddy. Slippery slope. He could tell her he'd chase away her demons on a daily basis, but knowing her independence, her strength, she'd despise that. He tickled his hand over her spine, massaging as he went. "You chased your own demons. I helped."

"Yeah, but you were the one I wanted help from."

He smiled and sat up, holding her in place so she didn't go anywhere and then kissed her. Hard. Like the first time.

"Anytime, babe. Anytime. Now feed me so I can have at you again."

"Oh, my. Ecstasy round two."

She leapt off the bed, walked to her closet and grabbed a red silk robe. The lady liked red. She came back to the bed, grabbed his jaw and dropped a kiss on him. "I'll meet you in the kitchen. Take your time."

Jo left the bedroom and Gabe flopped back on the bed. He could sleep for a month. Right here. Apparently he needed a new mattress, because this king-sized deal Jo had was freaking fantastic.

He glanced toward the two side-by-side windows. Through the crack in the heavy black drapes, the Manhattan skyline winked at him.

"I gotta get up," he muttered.

His aching body needed rest. And food. And Jo again.

He levered himself up and glanced around the room. Not surprising, it screamed of Jo. She'd managed to fit a white loveseat in the corner of a roughly fourteen by fourteen room. Red pillows added a blast of color to the stark white. The walls were a subtle white, maybe a little pink thrown in. He wasn't sure, but it was oddly perfect. He stood and straightened the funky black and white comforter and his gaze zoomed in on the triangular pattern. Eventually, the lines blurred and he blinked.

He retrieved his underwear from the floor and slipped them on. The jeans came next. His shirt was somewhere. He rolled to the other side of the bed and found it on the floor.

Insanity. All of it. The sex. Sex with Jo.

What were they doing? He shook his head. Getting busy with each other might embarrass them both. Worse, it might screw them up on the job. He couldn't be worried about her all the time. Nor could he be arguing with her about laying low. Not with what he did for a living. When hitting a building, he needed to concentrate on the bad guys.

He shoved his arms into his shirt and pulled it on.

Too late now. Whatever this was, they were in it. Together.

SEVEN

Gabe twisted the shower knob and grabbed a towel off Jo's fancy rack inside the oversized stall. This shower would suit him well. He didn't have the room in his midget bathroom, but the multiple body sprays would do wonders when his overworked body ached.

It wouldn't hurt to have Jo join him in there either.

He'd let her sleep though. 5:00 a.m. came early for some. Plus, time was running short and Gabe wanted to be outside the front door before Ramirez showed up for his security detail.

Soon enough, the team would figure out Gabe was getting busy with Jo, but he was in no rush for that.

Containment. That's what they needed. At least until he figured out where this thing was heading. For a guy who lived a relatively simple life, things had suddenly gotten a whole lot more complicated.

He didn't need complicated. He had enough of that on the job. He tossed the towel over his head and rubbed. His short hair only took a few minutes to dry. If he timed it right, Ramirez would see him in the hallway wearing the same uniform from yesterday. What Ramirez wouldn't know is that Gabe had showered and put on the fresh uniform he kept in his car for emergencies.

For insurance, he balled up his pants and shirt to wrinkle them before dressing.

Not wanting to disturb Jo, he slapped the bathroom light off before opening the door. Should he leave, or nudge her and let her know? Damn, he hated to wake her after he'd kept her up half the night.

Then again, he'd look like a jackwagon if he left. If that didn't send a hey-babe-thanks-for- the-stupendous-lay-but-I'm-outta-here message, he didn't know what did.

Say goodbye.

He slipped into the pitch-black bedroom, feeling his way around the bed to where she lay and set his hand on her back. Her soft snoring put a smile on his face. He'd break her chops fierce about that. "Hey," he whispered.

Nothing.

Gently, he ran his hand up her back to her cheek and rubbed.

"Hmmmm."

That moan got the brain in his crotch thinking back on the previous hours of the two of them inventing new sexual positions. His morning erection suddenly did an encore. *Oh, hell.* Now he'd have to face Ramirez with a boner. Not to mention, time was ticking. He checked the bedside clock. Five-eighteen.

He tickled Jo's cheek with one finger. "Honey, I'm leaving. See you later. Ramirez will be outside."

Another moan. He rolled his eyes. Total freaking killer of a decision. He could easily climb back into bed, coax her into getting rid of the boner and head off to work with time to spare.

Except Ramirez would be standing outside.

Jo reached up, her hand hit his thigh and worked its way —*whoa, there babe*—to the waistband of his pants.

"Come back to bed."

"Can't. Ramirez will be here soon."

"Gabe, I'm naked and my sense of touch is one hundred percent accurate. You should come back to bed."

Her voice held the gravel of sleep. Morning phone sex with her would be wicked fun. Forget the phone, he'd take the sex.

He slid his hand down her sheet-covered body, over the curve of her hip. It would be so easy to give in. "If I get back in bed, I won't get out."

"What's your point?" She wrapped her hand around the back of his leg and urged him forward. "Come on, Sergeant, live a little."

Another glance at the clock. How fast could they make this happen?

With the current state of his body, pretty damned fast.

He looked toward the hallway and the silence in the room expanded. If he walked out of this apartment and found Ramirez standing there, forget it, he'd never hear the end of it. The guys would ride him endlessly.

She nudged his leg again. "I don't care about Ramirez."

"Yeah, you say that now." The clock blinked. Five-twenty. He bent low and kissed her cheek. "I'd love a replay, but I don't want my team talking shit. I'll be back tonight. How's that?"

"And you'll bring your erection?"

He cracked a smile. This woman. Total trip. "Usually it comes with the rest of me."

"Okay then. You can leave."

But she pulled him back and kissed his neck, then his jaw. "I have morning breath. Don't want to scare you off."

"After last night? Nothing is scaring me off. Pretty damned incredible, lady."

"I know. Now leave before I make you stay."

He glanced at the door, then back to Jo. The neon numbers on the clock blinked again. Completely unfair. He marched to the living room, shoved his feet into his boots and did a piss-poor tie job. He'd fix 'em later.

He opened the front door. *Crap.* Ramirez. Wearing his tactical uniform and a mile-wide grin. Gabe's stomach lurched. "You're early."

"Five-thirty, dude."

Gabe checked his phone. Yep. Apparently Jo's clock was slow. Maybe she could have mentioned it? Not a break to be had this morning.

He jerked his thumb to the door. "She's asleep."

The shit-eating grin expanded. "I'll bet she is."

The ragging begins. He'd have to shut this down quick. Ramirez was about to find himself on the receiving end of the U-boss death glare. "I hear that from you again and you get an ass-kicking. I hear it from anyone else, I'll figure it came from you and you get an ass-kicking. Either way, you get an ass-kicking." Gabe folded his arms. "You can choose to do the right thing here, Ramirez. Outside of that, I'm still your superior. I got no problem finding you grunt work. Are we clear?"

The grin disappeared. Not a shock. Ramirez was no genius, but he understood chain of command. With Gabe on the track to lieutenant, this was not a difficult decision to land on the right side of.

Ramirez cleared his throat. "Understood."

"Good. Get Ms. Pomeroy to work and report in." Gabe

turned to leave, but shifted back. "And thank you. For volunteering your downtime. She appreciates it. You keeping your trap shut about what you saw here, *I* appreciate."

"No problem. I like Jo. She got a bum deal."

"Yeah, she did. We're gonna fix it for her."

—:—

At precisely 3:00 p.m., Jo followed Bev into the small conference room next to the mayor's office. This conference room held a gleaming mahogany table with deep-cushioned leather swivel chairs. The room even had mahogany chair rails as accents. All in all, it screamed power and money and good taste.

Already in the room was Lieutenant Tom Ross, otherwise known as Gabe's boss. Tom was the fourth member of the Clean Sweep Task Force and Jo, although having worked mostly with Gabe over the months, found him to be just as diligent in the success of the project.

Tom stood when they entered. "Bev, Jo, good to see you."

The normal greetings and small talk were exchanged as they took their seats. All meetings had a set system by which they ran. The process included them all sitting in the same positions meeting after meeting.

It never bothered Jo. It was a rank and file thing. The mayor would take the leadership chair at the head of the table. Bev and Tom, being the next highest in rank would sit next to the mayor and then Jo and Gabe. Jo appreciated the almost ceremonious feel. She always knew what to expect.

And staring at Mr. August never hurt.

"Good afternoon, sir," someone said from the outer hallway. A second later, Mayor Allan Graff entered the room, his stride efficient and determined. He was not only the most powerful mayor in the country, he was the shortest. At five foot seven, Jo stood three inches taller than him and always kept a pair of low-heeled shoes in her office for impromptu meetings such as this.

Call her paranoid, but towering over the mayor didn't seem like a smart move for a woman who'd worked so hard to be welcomed into his world.

They all stood and a variety of "Hello, sirs" followed.

In typical fashion, Jo's pulse kicked up. For two years she'd badgered the mayor's aids to get face time with him, and her efforts had paid off in a spectacular way. Today it was a task force, but by the time she was done, she wanted that nationwide initiative. The man in front of her had the influence and contacts to make it happen.

Height challenge aside, he carried his authority in a way that instilled a sense of don't-mess-with-me in those around him. Maybe it was the prematurely gray hair or his uncanny ability to slice through reporters like a guillotine, but he demanded and received respect.

He glanced at Gabe's empty chair. "We're missing Sergeant Townsend."

In other words, how dare he.

"Yes, sir," Tom said. "He got called out earlier and needed a quick shower. He should be here in a few."

"A shower?"

Tom flicked a glance at Bev and Jo. "Yes, sir. Pedestrian meets subway train. They had to peel the body off the bottom of the train."

The mayor pulled an "ick" face.

Maybe Jo did too. How did Gabe do his job day after day? The *cha-chunk* of the door handle sounded and Gabe strode into the room in a fresh uniform, his short hair still damp.

"My apologies, sir. Got…uh…caught up."

He glanced at Jo and gave her a succinct nod as he came around the table. Business as usual. Not that she expected him to give her a "Hi, honey," but—*jeepers*—something containing a wee bit of warmth wouldn't kill Mr. August.

Then again, he'd just unglued a corpse from the bottom of a subway train.

The mayor shook his head. "Not a problem, Sergeant. Rough one?"

After taking his seat, Gabe flipped his notepad to a clean page and gave his pen a click. "Helluva mess, sir. All cleaned up, but the trains are behind."

"It'll screw up rush hour."

No one bothered to comment. It wasn't the first time a dead body had slowed the city's commuters.

The mayor swung to Jo. "How are *you* today?"

She wasn't quite sure how to take that. The emphasis on "you" went beyond casual inquiry. She sat a little taller. "I'm fine, sir. Thank you."

Gabe rolled his eyes. "You got a severed hand in the mail yesterday. *I* wouldn't be fine after that."

What the hell is he doing? She eyeballed him. "I'm fine. And it didn't come in the mail. It was sent by courier. Just to be clear, because as you know, *mailing* it would be a federal offense."

He snorted and Jo drove her low-heeled pump into the ground. If only she had the spikes on, she'd blast him with them under the table.

"Okay," Bev said holding her hands out. "Don't start."

The mayor laughed—actually laughed—and Jo wanted to crawl away. How humiliating.

"Sorry, sir," she said. "Sergeant Townsend and I tend to bicker. In a friendly sort of way."

Except for tonight when I stab him in his sleep.

"So I see. Let's discuss the situation with the severed hand."

Uh-oh. "Of course, sir."

"I've conferred with both Tom and Bev, and we feel for the time being you should not accompany the men when they execute the warrants."

No. Nuh-uh. No way. She slid a sideways look at Gabe. This was his doing. Every instinct told her he'd gone to Tom and convinced him to shut her down. Inside, a piece of her heart ripped away. He'd sabotaged her.

She cleared her throat. "Sir, I don't think that's necessary. My identity is out there. What does it matter now? The vendors know who I am."

"Exactly why you should stay away. The last thing we want is you getting hurt." The mayor pointed at her cast. "Again."

Horrid. That's what this was. She'd go insane sitting in her office, missing all the action.

Bev turned to her. "I'm sorry, but I have to agree. The risk is too high."

Jo looked at the still silent Tom. Somehow, she couldn't look at Gabe right now. "Were you able to identify whose hand it was?"

Tom glanced at Gabe. That silent communication men did drove Jo nuts. "No," Gabe said. "I called the lab on my way here. The prints aren't in the system. They're working on who sent the package. There were a ton of prints to check. Maybe something will pop. Got a lead on this Kiki, though. The address on his license is old. I talked to one of the undercover guys. They heard he's squatting in Flatbush. We're canvassing."

In the meantime, Jo got benched. Silently she fumed,

her insides literally frying. *One more shot at the mayor.* "Sir—"

Before she'd even launched into her argument, he shook his head. "No, Jo. I'm sorry."

—:—

When the meeting adjourned, Gabe and Tom followed Jo to the elevator and they all waited together in an ugly, nerve-shattering silence. The power in the building could have run on the steam coming off Jo.

The elevator arrived and they all piled on. Tom hit the lobby button and leaned against the far side wall. Gabe stood behind a clearly pissed-off Jo. Well, life sucked. If her being furious with him kept her out of harm's way, he'd welcome the tension.

The only noise was the Muzak version of "Copacabana." He grunted. What a colossal goatfuck of a day.

Tom glanced at Jo, then to Gabe, who slowly moved his head back and forth. *Don't go there.* If the guy had any survival instincts at all—and he didn't get to his rank without them—he'd keep his mouth shut.

"Jo—" Tom said

Survival instincts must be on a union mandated lunch break.

"Forget it," Jo shot. The elevator doors opened and she bolted into a small group of people waiting for their lift.

"Talk to her," Tom said to Gabe. "We can't have her this way. She'll wind up slipping with the press and we're all screwed."

With that, Gabe watched his superior officer abandon him and head toward the lobby doors. Jo had stopped at the desk to drop off her visitor's pass and Gabe hustled to catch her before she ran. She spotted him coming and turned tail. "Don't talk to me," she yelled over her shoulder.

She might have long legs, but his were longer. He easily caught up and grabbed her arm. "Counselor, let me drive you to your office."

She jerked her arm free. "No. Thanks. A cab sounds delightful."

A few of the visitors wandering in and out tossed curious glances their way. Time to get her out of here. He latched onto her arm again. "You want to yell at me, fine. I'll drive you back to your office and you can scream the whole way. The thing we won't do is make a scene in the lobby so you can lose your spot on your precious task force."

Her flaming blue eyes clouded over. *Ah, yes, comprehension.* What a concept. Slowly, she eased her arm free.

"Where are you parked?"

"In the lot." He held his arm toward the back door. "Right this way."

Still bent on ignoring him, she strode to the door, nodded at the guard and pushed through. Once in the lot, Gabe directed Jo to the unmarked cruiser at the end of the row. She didn't bother waiting for him to open the door and hopped in on her own. Yeah. This would be brutal. Fucking bad day all around.

He climbed into the car and no sooner did he have the door shut than she started in.

"You completely undermined me."

Gabe closed his eyes. "I did not."

"You went to your boss and told him to bench me. He listens to you. You could have talked to me first."

Talked to her? Hadn't he done that? Several times? She never goddamned listened. Never. And it was starting to royally irritate him. He breathed through his nose—*don't yell*—and faced her.

"I did talk to you. How many times have I told you to wait, to not go inside until I say? I practically begged you to be smart. And you ignored me and did what you wanted." He poked his finger at her. "Guess what, babe? Now you can't ignore me."

Her face stretched into that open-mouthed horrified look often found in bad B movies. "Babe?" she hollered. "Have you lost your mind? Listen, *babe*, I've worked too hard on this task force to let you decide you're calling the shots. *Guess what, babe?* A few orgasms won't give you the authority to decide what I will and will not do."

Apparently she'd missed the fact the Mayor of New York had told her to cool her jets. He pursed his lips for a second and stared out the windshield. They should leave. The longer they sat there, the more notice they'd bring to themselves. He flipped the key and backed out of the spot, barely sparing Jo a glance.

"Be pissed at me if you want. Bring it on. I had a guy's body parts fall on me today. As tough as you are, you got nothin' on that. I'm done asking you to help me keep you safe." He bullied himself into the afternoon traffic and was the recipient of a few horn blasts. *Screw them.* "If a severed hand won't convince you, then nothing will. Yeah, I told my boss to bench you." He stopped for the red light at the corner and finally looked at her. "And I'd do it again."

EIGHT

"**G**reat," Jo said. "I can see ten months of working together—never mind the smoking hot sex—has truly solidified your faith in my professional abilities."

The light turned green and Gabe shot in front of traffic and slid into the right lane to make the turn toward her office. The man's driving could qualify for the Indy 500. She gripped the door handle.

"Cut the crap, Jo. That's the biggest line of horseshit I've heard. You're pissed that I won't let you have your way."

Searing blood shot to her cheeks. Let her have her way? *That's* what he thought this was? "No. I'm mad because you undermined me. You could have called me and said, 'Hey, either you bench yourself or I'm going to my boss.' You didn't do that. You gave me no respect. And frankly, I expected more from you, Sergeant. You owed me that."

He came to another red light. This one only a block from her office. She tugged on the door handle, but it was locked. "I'm getting out."

Before she could hit the unlock button, the light turned green. "Relax, Counselor, it's only another block."

"A very long block. And right now, I could bludgeon you."

He slid his gaze to her, but immediately went back to the road.

"I could take a tire iron and just beat you senseless, Gabe Townsend. You totally manipulated this situation."

"I tried everything else and you wouldn't listen. My going to Tom was your own goddamned fault. Think about it. How many times did I tell you I was concerned?"

That tripped her up. The man had practically begged her to consider staying in her office rather than going on the raids. "Not that many."

"I call *bullshit*."

He brought the car to a halt at the bus stop in front of her building and hit the unlock button. She gave the handle a yank and jumped out into the slew of pedestrians on the sidewalk. Before closing the door, she spun back. "You could have had a conversation with me. Considering the multiple orgasms and all."

A young guy walking by stopped to check her out. "Whoa, lady. I'll take a few orgasms from you."

"Nice, Jo," Gabe said. He poked his finger at the guy. "You. Keep moving."

She slammed the car door, hurried into her building and waited for the elevator while her brain slowly disintegrated. She'd had enough of bullheaded alpha males for one day. Wasn't this typical? She slept with him and all of a sudden he thought he could control her?

Why were men so stupid when it came to strong-willed women? They just didn't get it. In their ten months of working together, he should have known having her benched would infuriate her. Not only did he have her benched, he did it in an unscrupulous way. He'd essentially flipped her the professional middle finger.

Well, Sergeant Townsend, screw you. Or, in this case, *un*screw you.

"Gah!" she said and the businessman on the elevator glanced at her. The bell rang for her floor and the doors opened. "Men."

She marched through the open suite door and Maggie, the receptionist, said, "Wow. You look fierce."

"I *am* fierce. Hold my calls."

That sounded bad. Maggie didn't deserve to be the brunt of Jo's fight with Gabe. Slowly, she turned back. "Maggie, I'm sorry. That was completely awful of me and it will never happen again."

Maggie's eyebrows rose. Of all the lawyers in this office, Jo was probably the only one who'd ever apologized about anything. What that said about the lawyers in their office, she didn't want to speculate on.

Too much darned thinking today. That was the problem. "Anyway, I'll be in my office. Please hold my calls."

"No problem. And thanks. You didn't need to apologize, but I appreciate it."

"The people in this world need to learn a little civility," Jo called over her shoulder.

By five o'clock she had burned through every last ounce of mad fueling her. The fact that she'd realized she may have forced Gabe's hand wasn't making her too happy, but he still should have talked to her. They were both stubborn. Too much so. He'd asked her several times to be careful, to stay back, to let the P.D. handle the warrants. Each time, she'd resisted.

She simply wanted in on the action. Wanted to feel all

those counterfeit products in her hands so she'd know, without a doubt, the effort had been worth it. Seeing a room full of counterfeit merchandise made the dream of a nation-wide initiative seem within her reach.

She stared down at her bright red cast. He'd warned her she could get hurt. The day before that vendor had taken a pipe to her hand, he'd warned her. And then he'd warned her multiple times after that.

Liza poked her head in. "Hey, I'm heading out. You need anything?"

I need a week in Maui.

Jo shook her head. "No. Thanks."

Not moving from the doorway, Liza narrowed her eyes. "You don't look so good."

"I need to do something I absolutely hate."

A look of concern washed over Liza. "What is it?"

"I have to apologize to a bullheaded alpha male."

—:—

Gabe sat in front of Tom's desk in a too-small, crappy metal chair that had to be forty years old. The office itself was barely eight feet by eight feet and between the bulk of the big desk, the two chairs and the two of them, a sudden bout of claustrophobia had set in.

By the way he sat with his fingers steepled and his eyes focused, Gabe suspected his boss had something on his mind. It couldn't be anything good either. Not with that intense stare.

Gabe had been under Tom's command since his days at the 14th and after he'd been transferred to the Special Operations Division, the parent command of ESU, he'd made sure Gabe came along.

For years, Tom had been his mentor, had helped him position himself on the fast track to lieutenant. Together, they were powerful allies.

Tom finally sat back and dropped his hands. "Jo was steamed today. That's saying something, since she's usually full of piss-and-vinegar anyway."

Gabe shifted in the crappy chair. "Yeah. She's not happy with me. It'll pass."

"You sure?"

He nodded. What else could he do? "I'll handle it. She's smart and knows how to play politics. She won't jeopardize the success of this task force."

Outside the office, an uproar of laughter broke out. A couple of the guys hadn't yet gone home after their shift.

Tom tapped his fingers against his thigh. Definitely something on his mind.

"What's up, Tom?"

"Anything you want to tell me about Jo Pomeroy?"

Like the life altering sex from last night?

Could Ramirez have been that much of a douche to go to Tom?

Ah, shit.

Not a chance. That kid knew where his bread was buttered. Tom was fishing. Something in that meeting today rattled him. Gabe shook his head. "Nope."

"Because I'm getting a sense there's something."

"No, boss. Nothing. Look, I've been hounding her about staying away when we do the hits. All these vendors know her. Right before her hand got busted, I told her to stay away. She didn't listen. I told her again after the hand got busted. Again, she didn't listen. Then after this latest incident, I tried again. I got sick of trying and came to you about sidelining her. She didn't like that."

Tom made an "eh" gesture. "She figures you threw her under the bus?"

"Yes, sir. She came at me after the meeting today. Gave me a bunch of crap about working together all this time and how I went behind her back. Which I did. No problem there."

"Her winding up dead won't do us any good. Fucking public relations nightmare."

Gabe's gut clenched. His boss was worried about PR when Jo could get hurt? Killed? Voicing that would surely earn him a rip—cop talk for getting in trouble. "Sir, I'll take care of it. Jo and I are like-minded. We yell and scream and then we're done. She'll get over it."

"I hope so. The mayor likes her and I won't be the one to piss him off. And neither will you." Tom sat forward and picked up his phone. "We're done here."

"Yes, sir."

On the way to his car, Gabe checked the calls that had come to his cell while he met with Tom. Three missed. One from his mother, one from a number he didn't recognize and—look at that—the Queen of Sheba. This should be good.

He pressed the call back button. Why not? If she wanted to get into it again with him, he was irritable enough to let her.

"Hi," she said, not sounding too pissy.

Didn't that suck?

He hit the unlock button on his key ring, but decided to take the call standing in the parking lot. The cold air might keep him from losing his temper. He drew a deep breath, let it fill his lungs and released it. Totally shit day. "What's up?"

"I'm sorry."

Come on. What kind of schmuck did she think he was? "Nice try. You're still benched."

She laughed. He leaned on his car and pondered the silky tone of that laugh. Not manufactured. That was the real deal.

"I'm not—" she paused. "Gabe, I'm not patronizing you. I was wrong. I'm sorry."

Say what now? "Jo?"

"Yes?"

"You're freaking me out. I can't believe you admitted you were wrong. You're a disgrace to alphas everywhere. We have rules."

Hoping she'd find the statement humorous—after all, he was most definitely a member of the alpha club—he waited for her response.

"Whatever you do," she said, "don't tell anyone."

"Your secret is safe." He cracked his neck. *Damned tired.* "For the record, I *am* worried about you. The severed hand did me in. After that, I knew I'd have to go to Tom. I know how dedicated to this job you are, and I figured it would get ugly between us, but when it comes to your safety, I'll deal with the ugly. I wasn't undermining you. I wanted you safe. That's all."

He stopped talking. Nothing else to do. He'd said his piece.

Through the phone line, he heard her sigh. "I realize that now. Two hours ago, I could have taken your head off."

"I got that message."

"Now I realize you were trying to protect me from myself. I appreciate that. As crazy as it makes me, I get it."

A group of guys came out of the building and hollered to him about getting a beer. "Can't," he yelled back. He had nothing going, but he was dog-assed tired and wasn't in the mood to sit at a bar talking cop talk. "Promise me you'll be careful. That you'll stay away from Tower Street."

"I will."

Her voice was soft, almost defeated. He hated that. Wanting her safe didn't mean he wanted her defeated. What he enjoyed about Jo was all that defiance. Like him, she went to battle for what she believed in, more than willing to piss people off when necessary.

"Just because you promised me that doesn't mean you can't still fight with me."

Dead air. Thinking he'd lost the call, he checked the signal. Nope. Still good.

"Sergeant, are you flirting with me?"

He thought back to their first kiss, the night she'd literally thrown herself at him. "Yeah, I guess I am. In our own twisted way." She got quiet again. "Jo?"

"We are so alike," she said. "It scares me a little. Like there's no counterbalance. Shouldn't there be a balance?"

"Not always. For people like us, balance might be boring. We're adrenaline junkies."

She laughed. "Do you realize how pathetic that sounds? That, if we're not going a hundred miles per hour we might find each other boring?"

"I don't think it's pathetic. I think it's what it is. You don't want a guy who gives in all the time. You wouldn't respect that. You like conflict. In fact, I'll bet it's a turn-on for you."

"You'd win that bet."

"And, as crazy as this thing between us is, I'll be damned if it doesn't work. Our problem is, we've got the nation's most powerful mayor in the middle of it and after what we went through today, arguing over the job, something will have to give or we'll tear each other up."

On the other end of the phone line, he heard a click.

Maybe a drawer closing. Jo packing up for the night. "I know. I don't have an answer though."

"Me neither. Not yet anyway."

Bringing embarrassment to the mayor and his task force by getting distracted and making mistakes would kill his career. He understood enough about politics to know that. Tom had already done him a huge large by sending him a warning. If Tom had noticed a change between Gabe and Jo already, Bev and the mayor wouldn't be far behind.

Somehow, they had to figure this out. Whether the relationship turned into something long-term or not, one of them would have to leave the task force. Working together flat out wouldn't work.

She sighed. "Well, what's happening with this Kiki character? My investigators can't find the S.O.B."

"I hear ya. Nothing yet. The guy keeps moving. We'll find him. Getting close."

"I know," she said. "Anyway, Sergeant Townsend, have you forgotten what you promised me this morning?"

Suddenly—and this was shocking considering the dropping temperature outside—Gabe's face got hot. He tilted his head up to the black sky and sucked in cold air. "About the—"

"Yes, the giant erection you promised me."

He cracked up. "I—uh—no, haven't forgotten."

"Good. I'll tell Carlson he doesn't have to babysit me tonight because Sergeant Townsend is bringing me a giant erection."

She'd do it. He could see it. "Jo, I *will* kill you."

"Gabe, even I wouldn't do that. Now come and get me, big boy."

NINE

In her office the next morning, Jo found herself in a giddy state of exhaustion. She might need a nap to get through the afternoon, but the long night had been well worth it. Her brain disagreed, but her extremely sated body had no complaints.

Without a doubt, Gabe would have to stay away tonight. She needed sleep and him being in the same bed wasn't conducive to slumber.

Her desk phone *bleep-bleeped*. "I have Sherry for you," Liza said. "Line one."

Ooh, might be an update on Sherry's continuing search for counterfeit Konklin watches and the elusive Kiki. Jo snatched up her phone. In the background, she heard music. Car radio. "Hi. Good news?"

"I think so," Sherry said. "I went back to the vendor from the other day. He said the watches are in, but I have to go to their warehouse to pick one out."

Vendors sending customers to a second location wasn't unusual. With the crackdowns on counterfeit goods, the vendors had learned which products Jo and her team were targeting. Sales of those targeted products now happened quietly with whispers instead of open negotiations. For that reason, the vendors kept those goods locked away or off premises.

"Good work. Who's going with you?"

A pause. "Just me."

"No."

"But Mark is in Jersey and can't get back quick enough."

As stubborn as Jo could be about collecting evidence, even she wouldn't go to a second location alone. Add to the mix the severed hand, and Sherry could forget about winning this battle.

Jo tapped her hand against the desk. "As much as I'd love to get my hands on that watch, you cannot go alone. Too dangerous."

Mr. August would kill us both.

The background music disappeared. "This could be another huge get for us. Twice in one week we'll have confiscated Konklins. If we want this, the guy told me I had to be there in fifteen minutes. If I don't show, they'll know something is up. They'll clear out. You know it."

Jo nibbled her bottom lip. With the pressure the NYPD had been putting on these vendors, they'd get spooked and close up shop. They'd take their bundles of counterfeit goods somewhere else and Jo's team would have to start from scratch. Months of work blown. Shot. Incinerated.

If she did this, Gabe would blow his stack in a catastrophic way. After the major battle they'd had, she promised him she'd stay in her office and here she was, at the first temptation, giving in. Breaking promises was never part of her personal operating procedure. Particularly in this situation. Plain and simple, she wanted him to trust her. Doing this run would obliterate any faith he had in her.

She glanced down at her bright red cast and her legs tingled. *Dammit.* They needed that watch. Not so much the watch, but where the watch was stored. With any luck, they'd find Kiki nearby. Whoever this smuggler was, he had the goods hidden somewhere and they suspected the place had to be big because the stream of goods into Tower Street had become an unending supply. If they found Kiki, they might be able to persuade him to flip on his boss.

More than that, she'd be one step closer to a nationwide industry task force. If they went nationwide, she could lobby federal *and* state governments for funding and police support.

"Well," Sherry said. "I'm going. I'll check in when I'm finished."

Promise or no promise, she couldn't let Sherry go alone. Jo would face Gabe's wrath, but on her worst day she couldn't let her employee, her friend, walk into a potentially dangerous situation without support.

Decision made.

"Okay," Jo said. "Where are you?"

"Ha! I'm just pulling around the corner. I knew I'd talk you into it."

"Nice. But you almost didn't. I was benched by the mayor yesterday. We'd better hope this field trip turns into something or I'm going to get my butt handed to me."

The mayor, as mean as he could be, she'd handle. But Sergeant Gabriel Townsend? *He'll kill me.*

She slipped her coat on and shoved her hand in her pocket. Luckily, it was deep enough to hide the bit of cast that stuck out under her coat sleeve. By now, all of Tower Street would be buzzing about the blonde lady who'd gotten her hand broken. The bright red cast would be her tell.

Next came the wig. She'd try red today. It had been a while since she'd donned that one.

Liza stepped into her office with a stack of mail, took in the red wig and halted. "I thought you were staying put."

"I was. Now I'm not. Sherry can't go alone."

"Is it safe?"

"I honestly don't know. Which is why Sherry can't go alone."

"Oh, jeez. When Officer Hottie hears about this, he'll crucify you."

Jo laughed. Liza had been around long enough to hear Gabe and Jo sparring over various topics. "Don't I know it? I'll try to reach him on the way. If he calls here, tell him I'm in a meeting and to try my cell. Don't tell him where I am. I need to do it."

Jo made her way downstairs and found Sherry's car idling at the curb. She jumped into the passenger seat and dumped her bag on the floor. "Here we go."

"It's a building in Brooklyn."

"*Another* Brooklyn location?"

Sherry nodded. "Yep. I guess they like the area. Here's the address."

Jo grabbed the slip of paper and read it. The address didn't sound familiar. "Okay. Well, let's check it out. They're waiting for you?"

"Yeah. The guy said to go to the side entrance and knock."

"I hate these cloak and dagger missions. They give me the damned willies."

"Me too. I've got a feeling about this one though. This could be another huge break."

They cruised over the Brooklyn Bridge and Jo stared out the window at the sun glistening off the East River. The chop in the water only added to the sparkle and she hoped it was a message from the counterfeiting gods that she'd made the right decision.

Except no one knew where they were headed.

Not smart.

She might be brave, but stupid she'd never been. Time to face Gabe's wrath.

From her purse, she grabbed her phone then spread the slip of paper with the building's location on her lap. She dialed and closed her eyes for a second while the call connected. He might be a hothead, but he was also a reasonable man. He, of all people, would understand that she couldn't let Sherry investigate alone. The call went directly to voicemail.

Of course it did.

This would start a war, but she left him a voicemail explaining what they were doing and that she'd text him the address. Then she hung up. It was done.

The GPS led them to Pearl Street and then two more turns onto a block with several ancient buildings.

"There it is," Sherry said. "The one in the middle."

She drove into the gravel lot and parked while Jo studied the unmarked four-story brick structure. On one side were two loading docks. The front of the building had three windows on each side of a thick steel door.

In the far corner sat a minivan, the lone vehicle in the lot. Not unusual if someone had been dispatched to sell counterfeit goods.

Sherry pointed to the far end of the building. "I guess we go around the other side."

Jo's phone beeped an incoming text. No doubt who that was. She refused to look. At least she could tell him she hadn't seen his text until they were done buying the knockoff watch. She shoved the phone into her purse, yanked on the handle and kicked the door open. "Let's get this over with."

"Yep," Sherry said, sounding much too eager.

Typically, Jo would have been right there with her on the eager front. Now though, it felt wrong. All because she'd given her word that she'd stay in her office rather than chase down leads. Guilt, that horrible emotion, landed on her like a crashing plane.

Still, she followed Sherry around the side of the building, her skinny heels wobbling in the gravel. She glanced at the open door ahead. Someone had propped it with a doorstop. Jo kept her eyes on the door and sighed. "He'll kill me."

—:—

Gabe stared down at the address on his phone. *What the hell?* Tom sat beside him in one of ESU's unmarked cars, navigating the streets of Manhattan while they patrolled and supervised various operations.

Why would Jo be sending him an address? Impatient for her response, he called her office and tracked down Liza.

"I'm sorry, Sergeant. She's in a meeting. Try her cell."

"A meeting." Standard stall tactic.

"In the building or out?"

"Um, out?"

Hesitation. Something was up. "Liza, are you asking me or telling me?"

Another pause. "Telling you. She's out at a meeting. Shall I have her call you?"

The fact that she was lying to him was obvious, but beating up on Liza wouldn't do him any good. He'd skin this cat—or Jo—another way. "Yes. Ask her to call me ASAP."

He clicked off and waggled his phone.

Tom slid him a glance. "What's up?"

This was some bullshit luck. His boss, who Gabe had asked to speak to the mayor about sidelining Jo, was sitting next to him while he tried to figure out what kind of trouble she might be getting herself into.

"Jo sent me an address. Not sure why. She's in a meeting."

"Run it."

Gabe checked Jo's text again and punched the address she'd sent into the car's computer.

"Anything?" Tom asked.

"Nope."

"Where is it?"

"Brooklyn."

Tom hung a left. "Let's check it. See what's what."

She'd better not be hunting counterfeit merchandise. And if she was, Tom would see firsthand how she disregarded all their recommendations to stay. The hell. In her office. *Dammit.* "It's probably nothing, but couldn't hurt to look."

Without a doubt, he'd kill her with his bare hands if she'd broken her promise. His voicemail chirped. *Might be her.* He checked the message and Jo's voice came through the phone.

Yep. She'd broken her promise.

—:—

Jo followed Sherry up the building's cement stairs and took note of the chipping white paint in the stairwell.

Asbestos anyone? Even the railing was a disaster. That thing hung so loose that if they were to fall and grab it, it would fly off the wall and impale them.

Don't think about it.

"Hello?" Sherry called.

"Hello," a man yelled back in a thick Asian accent. "Fourth floor. Come."

"Creepyville," Sherry whispered.

"No kidding."

Jo's phone buzzed again. Had to be Gabe. She could sense the steam coming through the phone. It was a wonder the thing hadn't melted.

Don't think about it.

When they made the turn at the fourth-floor landing, they spotted the man in one of the doorways. His body was mostly compact and proportioned to his height. He had a shock of white hair—he'd either gone prematurely gray or had great genes, because he didn't look a day over fifty.

He waved them up. "In here."

A nerve in Jo's jaw pulsed and, hidden behind Sherry, she opened and closed her mouth in an attempt to stop the weird sensation. No luck. If ever there was a sign to run, that might be it. Or, maybe, the guilt was working her over.

Still, she followed Sherry up the last few steps. As soon as Jo stepped into the room, her spastic nerves turned into the sweetness of a blood rush. Before her was a roughly twelve by twelve room stuffed from floor to ceiling with designer—counterfeit of course—apparel and accessories.

Yay, us.

The man studied them for a moment and his gaze lingered on Jo, but he showed no sign of recognition. The wig must have done its job.

On the far right wall, three shelves of Barelli handbags

greeted her. She glanced around, caught more Barelli products, some Gucci, Louis Vuitton and an assortment of other knock-offs.

"You have the new Konklin watch?" Sherry asked."

The man nodded. "Yes. Over here." He slipped behind a glass case and motioned them over. "Gold?"

"Titanium," Sherry said while Jo wandered to the Barelli section.

"You want?" the man asked. "Barelli? I give you good deal."

"Maybe," Jo said.

Forgetting her cast, she reached up, but quickly switched hands. She glanced back at the man, who busied himself searching for the fake titanium watch.

He caught her eye then spotted the cast. Jo's stomach pinched.

"You injured?"

"I fell," she said. "Klutz."

The man slid the drawer closed. "Titanium downstairs. I get it."

He walked from the room, closing the door behind him. Jo watched as it clicked into place with a loud snick.

Double key lock.

She lunged for the door. Another snick. The little turd had locked them in. "Hey," she yelled, yanking on the knob with her good hand. She charged to the window. A minute later, the man ran from the building and hopped into the parked minivan. "He's leaving. The bastard locked us in here and now he's leaving." From somewhere below a piercing, high-pitched alarm wailed. Jo cocked her head. *Oh, no.* "Tell me that's not a smoke alarm."

Sherry cocked her head and listened. "That's not a smoke alarm. Except I think it is."

Jokes? *Now?* Must be inappropriate investigator humor. "Do you smell anything?"

"No."

"Well, I'm not waiting."

Jo unlocked the window and, using her good hand, tried to lift it. Stuck. A slow moving thought took root. If the building were on fire, she wouldn't have to worry about Gabe's wrath.

She'd be dead anyway.

Sherry shoved her aside. "I got it." She gripped the ancient metal handles with both hands and heaved. Nothing.

Jo rushed to the items stacked on the shelves. She needed something to break the window. The purses wouldn't do. One of the shoes? As a last resort, maybe she could use the heels to break out the window. She continued to scan the shelves. Umbrella.

She slid one of her gloves on and grabbed the umbrella. "Okay. Back away." Jo rammed the umbrella through the window. Glass shattered and sprinkled to the ground below. She tapped out the remnants of glass still in the pane until the frame was empty.

Sticking her head out, she checked the bottom floors of the building. Nothing. She looked right and there, from under the crack in the main entrance, thick black smoke billowed.

Like lightning, hot, slick panic engulfed her. *Gotta get out.* She backed away from the window and spun to Sherry. "We're on fire. And not in a good way. We have to get out of here."

TEN

Gabe tapped his foot as they approached the address Jo had texted him. Directly in front of them, a white minivan barreled toward them.

"Ho! What's his hurry?" Tom yelled and Gabe swung his head to see if he could get the tag number.

"Did you get it?"

"Only the first three letters. A-D-L."

Tom turned into the back side of the lot and pulled around the front of the building. "Fire!"

"Oh, shit." Gabe grabbed his radio and called it in, barking out the address while he scanned the first floor. Tom killed the engine, got out and hauled ass around the rear of the building.

A car sat in the corner of the lot, but Gabe didn't recognize it. He jumped from the cruiser and a flash of white in the fourth-floor window caught his attention. A coat hanging over a broken window frame.

One long leg—he knew that leg—came through the window and his heart damn near stopped. "Jo! Back!"

With her legs straddling the frame, she held on and

maneuvered her head out the window. "We're locked in. There's no way out."

Tom flew around the far corner again. "Fire escape," he yelled to Jo. "South end of the building."

"No good," Gabe said. "They're locked in. Jo! Stay put." He sprinted back to the car. "Tom, pop the trunk."

The trunk lid opened, Gabe snagged the shotgun and loaded the door breaching rounds. He took off to the rear of the building, his boots slipping on the gravel, but he focused on remaining upright. No time for wipeouts. He swung around the corner and spotted the rickety fire escape. *Damn.* That thing looked more deadly than the fire.

He tried the rear door. Locked.

An explosion from inside the building rocked the ground and the crash of shattering glass came from the front. He'd love to know what the hell was stored inside this building. By the sound of that explosion, it was something that would blow the place to hell.

Tom tore around the opposite side and halted in front of him. "All exterior doors locked."

No way in. Another explosion, not as loud as the first, came from inside the building and an acrid smell, like burning rubber, reached Gabe.

He raised the shotgun, aimed it between the lock and the handle at forty-five degrees and—*bang*—the boom of the shot pierced the air. The round drilled through and sent the lock flying. Tom pulled open the door.

An enclosed stairwell was behind the door. Gabe stepped in. The burning rubber smell was even more pungent. No smoke. Must still be confined to the front of the building. He hustled up the stairwell, shotgun at the ready.

"Stay outside," he yelled to Tom. "Help them out."

The fire department should be on scene any second, but

Gabe wasn't about to stand around and let this building burn with people in it. With *Jo* in it.

He wanted the opportunity to kill her himself.

A third explosion, loud and ominous and penetrating, literally shook the building. Part of the structure had to have come apart with that one. The penetrating odor stole the oxygen from his lungs and he shoved his face into his sleeve as he hit the fourth floor.

"Jo!" He ran the length of the long corridor, checking doors along the way until he reached the north side of the building. "Jo!"

She banged on the door from the inside. "Here!"

Her voice carried from three doors down. Had to be that first doorway. He got there, checked the handle for heat then jiggled it. Nothing. He knocked on the door. Laminate. The inside frame would probably be soft wood.

"Back away." Gabe shifted sideways, hoisted his booted foot up, leaned his weight into the kick and slammed it next to the doorknob. The door flew off the hinges.

Jo and Sherry stood on the far side of the room, gawking at the now defunct door. The place was packed with what he assumed were counterfeit handbags.

He snapped his fingers toward the hallway. "You waiting for the building to blow? Let's go!" Finally, they got their asses moving and Gabe pointed to the rear of the building. "That way."

Through the broken window, he heard sirens. Fire department.

Jo scooted past him. "Holy cow. You were like the Incredible Hulk coming through that door. I about peed myself."

Scared. People chattered when they were scared. No time for chatter.

"Move!" The women ran down the hallway to the stairs,

their heels stomping and clicking against the cheap floor. "Hold on when you're going down."

Last thing he needed was one of them flying over a step. A minute later, Jo burst through the door at the bottom of the stairs.

"Away from the building," Gabe yelled, and she took off toward the far end of the property. From there, they could make their way to the road and walk to the front.

He tromped to the parking lot, where firefighters went to work knocking down the fire.

Tom glanced at Jo, then Sherry. "Everyone okay?"

"Fine," Jo said.

"Good," Sherry said.

Gabe, though, was pissed. For safety, he handed Tom the shotgun. No sense giving in to temptation and using it on Jo. Considering she'd promised him she'd stay in her office. He'd deal with that later. "How did you get this address?"

"It was me," Sherry explained. "One of the vendors gave it to me. Told me to pick up a Konklin watch here."

An NYPD squad drove into the lot and Tom wandered over to talk to the officers.

Gabe shifted to Sherry. "Which vendor?"

She rattled off the name of the store and he waggled his fingers at her. "Give me your keys."

"What?"

"Your keys. I'm borrowing your car. Tom will give you a lift back."

"Whoa," Jo said. "What are you doing?"

"Nothing to be concerned about." But Sherry wasn't moving. He gave her his best intimidating stare. The one that warned he didn't want to be screwed with. "Keys. Now."

Finally, she handed them over and Gabe strode to the car with Jo on his heels. "What are you doing?"

"Jo, back off. We'll talk when I don't want to strangle you. And take off that stupid wig." He unlocked the doors and jumped into the driver's seat.

Jo slid into the passenger side and dumped the wig on the floor. "I'm going with you."

"Get out."

"No."

So fucking stubborn. This woman tormented him. All he wanted was to keep her safe, and time and again she threw herself into the fray. Every. Fucking. Time.

He dug his fingers into his right eye and rubbed. Massive headache. "You wanna come? Fine. At least I'll know where you are and that you're not getting your other hand broken or, hey, getting caught in a warehouse fire because some asshole wants you *dead*." He punched the gas and stormed out of the lot. "What don't you understand about this not being a game?"

She gasped and he glanced her way. Her blue eyes shot lasers and her long hair had come loose of her hairclip in certain spots. She looked steaming in a twisted way that reminded him how dumb it had been to get personally involved with her.

"I know it's not a game," she said. "But my investigator wanted to do this alone. I couldn't let her do it."

He hooked a left and headed for the bridge. "You have other investigators."

"Actually, Mr. Know-it-all, at the time we didn't. Mark was in Jersey and couldn't get back in time. Lecture and yell all you want. It won't make a difference. There's no way—no way—I was letting Sherry go alone."

"You could have kept trying to reach me."

"Why? So you could scream at me? Besides, for all I knew we were just picking up a watch. My hope was that we'd find another location to pass along to the NYPD. I didn't know it was a setup."

Exactly his point. She wasn't trained to deal with these situations. "You shouldn't have risked it."

She threw her hands up. "No kidding, Gabe. Thank you so much for telling me. At least give me credit for giving you the address."

God, she never quit. "A damned good thing too or you'd be toast right now. And you'd probably still be yapping."

She gasped again and—*whoosh*—all the energy got sucked out of the argument. He shot her a sideways look as they made their way over the bridge, but all he saw was part of her profile as she stared out at the water.

"Now you're just being cruel," she said. "Fine. Be an ass."

He grunted and jammed his palm into the horn at some schmuck who'd cut him off. What was it about Jo that pushed every one of his buttons? Even after the marathon sex last night, he wanted her in a way that made his body ache. He loved the challenge of her, but he didn't want to break her down. All he wanted was to keep her in one piece.

Why did keeping her safe take so much energy? Because she was high-maintenance, that's why. He breathed deep, focused on the road and rolled his shoulders. After counting to ten, some of the tension eased.

"You're right. I'm sorry." He slid his gaze to her, but she kept her head turned.

"I accept your apology."

Then things got quiet. Too quiet where Jo was concerned. He hated quiet Jo. With loud Jo, he always knew where they stood. Maybe they needed the silence though. To regroup.

He turned onto Tower Street where midday traffic piled everything to a crawl. Half a block down, he double-parked in front of the address Sherry had given him. He wouldn't be here that long.

He shoved the car door open.

"Gabe?"

"I'm going inside." He strode to the door, pushed it open and surveyed the interior. Garment racks and overstuffed shelves crammed the small space. Wherever he looked, cheap clothes and accessories greeted him. No knock-offs. Obviously, the proprietor had wised up and kept the counterfeit crap hidden. Probably in the warehouse that Jo almost became kindling in.

A woman behind the counter focused on his tactical uniform then stepped back. She'd obviously seen enough ESU guys to know he was NYPD. A few customers pawed through the garment racks, but nobody looked all that interested.

He turned back to the door and held it open. "Sorry folks, store is closed." The patrons looked up at him and he waved them to the door. "Come back later."

The woman behind the counter took off down a narrow hallway. Probably to summon her boss.

Just as Gabe was about to close the door, Jo stepped in. "What are you doing?"

"Getting information. You staying or going?"

A spark lit her blue eyes and burned right into Gabe. *That's my girl.*

"Oh, I'm staying."

He shut the door behind her and flipped the open sign to closed.

An older man, with thick gray hair and saggy skin came from a room off the hallway where the woman had just disappeared. "Can I help you?"

You sure can, asshole. Gabe grabbed Jo's elbow and

dragged her to where the man stood. "You know this woman?"

The man concentrated on Jo. "No."

"Take a better look," Gabe said. "I think you do."

The man looked again. "No."

Gabe got close enough to the old guy to crowd him. "You sure? Because I think you sent her investigator to a building this morning to buy a fake watch. *I* think you sent them into that building, had them locked in and the place set on fire. That's what I think." He turned to Jo. "How about you?"

She nodded. "Yep. I'd bet he set the whole thing up."

"Yeah, and lucky for him you two didn't burn up in that place. Then he'd be looking at a double murder charge. Not to mention arson."

"Don't forget the conspiracy charges."

Gabe snapped his fingers. "Right. I forgot about those." He turned back to the old man whose veins bulged in his forehead. "At the very least, you're looking at attempted murder. All roads point to you, pal. You're the one who sent them into that building."

The old man's eyes bounced all over the place. Then he shook his head. At first slowly, then as the panic started to build, with more force.

"You wanna tell me anything?" Gabe said. "Or do we lock you up for attempted murder? Ever been in prison? How do you feel about being gang raped in the shower?"

"No," the old man said.

Gabe cocked his head. "No, what?"

"It wasn't me."

"But you knew?"

Silence.

The woman rushed into the front of the store waving her

arms. She was younger than the old man, but her eyes were frantic and her face was tight. She might have aged thirty years in the last five minutes. "They told us to send her there."

Now they were getting somewhere. Jo touched his arm and came up on tiptoes to whisper in his ear. "Mirandize them."

Her words penetrated and he ran some options. What he was doing could get him into a shitload of trouble. Sure, he could say they were simply having a conversation and no, he was not harassing them, but the one thing he always wanted to be was a good cop. And he wasn't sure this made him a good cop.

He didn't regret it because Jo almost got killed, but wanting to protect those he cared about couldn't be intermingled with his job. That was where the lines blurred, and he'd spent years trying to stay clear of blurry lines.

He had to remove himself from this equation. "Here's what we'll do, folks. I'll get a detective down here to talk to you. You're gonna tell those detectives everything you know about counterfeit merchandise, a guy named Kiki and that building my friend here almost lost her life in. In exchange, I'll do what I can to keep you out of prison."

—:—

Jo watched Tom walk into the conference room at police headquarters and drop a manila file folder on the table. He took the seat at the end, rubbed the heels of both his hands into his eyes and let out a breath that must have weighed thirty pounds.

She glanced across the table at Gabe. His shoulders were back and rigid in a way she didn't see all that often. The look of a man waiting to get his butt handed to him by his superior.

Well, she wouldn't let that happen. Even if it cost her a spot on the task force, she wouldn't let him take the plunge alone.

Eventually, Tom dropped his hands and focused on Gabe. "I don't know what you were thinking going into that store."

She slid a sideways glance at Gabe. *Please stay silent.*

"You could have blown this whole thing to hell."

Gabe jerked his head. "I know, sir. Sorry."

"Fortunately, you took your head out of your ass and got a detective down there."

"Yes, sir."

Tom shifted to Jo. "You okay?"

"Yes. Fine. Thank you. And I'm sorry. I should have told Sherry to wait. I got ahead of myself."

"Yeah, you did. And the mayor isn't happy." He turned back to Gabe. "With either of you. We'll do damage control on that later."

"Later?" Gabe asked.

"Yes. Later. Now, we're about to execute a warrant on a building and separate private residence in Queens."

Gabe sat a little straighter and Jo inched forward. This could be it.

The whale.

"What did the man from the store say?"

Tom flipped open the file and passed Gabe a photo. "He gave us a name. Donald Martinson. Apparently Mr. Martinson owns half the storefronts on Tower Street. His name isn't on the deeds though. He's the money guy. Kiki runs the day to day. The vendors pay little rent, but they are forced to sell the counterfeit items Martinson smuggles into the States. According to our witness, the smuggled items are kept in the location where the warrant will be executed."

Gabe handed Jo the photo. Looked like a driver's license photo showing Donald Martinson to be in his mid-thirties. His face held the fullness of someone carrying an extra thirty pounds. Jo studied his half-crooked smile, dark eyes and hair. The tilt of his left eyebrow. All of it, she committed to memory.

This was the person running counterfeit goods through Tower Street.

And they were about to nail his ass.

"So," Tom said to Gabe. "You need to get briefed. We'll do the hits simultaneously. One on Martinson's house and one on the building where the stuff is stored. Jo, I'll let you on-scene at Martinson's house, but you stay across the street. Got it?"

She nodded. "Yes. Thank you."

"And, look, don't screw with me on this. The only reason I'm even letting you on-scene is because the mayor wants a photo op."

Wow. She'd been relegated to photo-op duty. She supposed, after her flagrant lack of following orders, she should be grateful.

Tom stood. "Let's go bust this guy."

—:—

Being a good little girl, Jo stood on the sidewalk one house down and across the street from Donald Martinson's two-story home while ESU entered the residence. The afternoon sun shifted and she moved with it to absorb the miniscule heat it offered.

A couple of hours ago she'd been trapped in a burning

building, yet, she still craved heat. Considering Gabe's attitude toward her, the temperature outside wasn't the only thing dropping. Her own fault. Still, faced with the same set of circumstances, she wouldn't let Sherry, or any of her investigators go on an assignment like that alone.

She understood this about herself and Gabe needed to adjust. Simple as that.

A gust of wind whipped at her hair and she tucked a few loose strands back while she studied Martinson's home. For a smuggler, she expected something more lavish and less, well, *homey*. What she hadn't expected was beige aluminum siding and small windows. This home needed children playing in the patch of yard or someone sitting on the stoop at night chatting with a neighbor. Considering the neighbor's house was barely fifteen feet away, that would be easy.

A man in track pants and a gray wool jacket sidled up next to her. "What's going on?"

This happened a lot. Since she generally stood on the street waiting for the all clear, someone inevitably asked her what the deal was. In a quiet, residential neighborhood like this, the number of rubberneckers increased, simply because people wanted to know why ESU was on their street. The P.D. had barricaded the area and onlookers were forced outside the restricted area.

She glanced at the guy. He wore sunglasses and a black skull cap. His face was lean, but sort of round and his dark hair stuck out of the hat at the neckline.

Something about him was familiar, but with all the people she'd met, he could be anyone.

"I don't know," she said, responding to his question. Only a partial lie because, at this very second, she had no idea what was taking so long inside that house.

She caught a flash of white from the corner of her eye and shifted. A news van had just pulled around the corner. Within minutes there would be more. If she knew the mayor like she thought she did, he'd had someone leak this bust. Thus, why she was allowed on-scene for a photo opportunity.

Politics.

"Wow. Newspeople," the guy said.

Jo rocked forward on her toes. The house wasn't that big, what was the holdup? Or maybe she was antsy and wanted to see Donald Martinson in handcuffs. Who knew if he was even home? "There will probably be more newspeople. They're like ants. See one and there's usually more to follow. Do you live on the block?"

"Yeah." He pointed to the opposite end of the street. "Down there."

"Do you know the people who live in this house?"

"Nah."

Jo nodded, but her attention was on the front door where Gabe had just exited the home. Every ounce of her yearned to step forward, but she remained in her spot, exactly where he'd told her to be.

It completely sucked.

He marched over and removed his helmet. "He's not home."

Jo closed her eyes. Could have guessed. Anytime she wanted something this bad, she had to work hard, then a little harder for it. They'd get him. It would just take longer. She opened her eyes. "Okay. What now?"

In Gabe's hand was a silver picture frame. "This is our guy. According to his wife, he's lost weight since his DMV picture was taken."

Jo looked at the photo and a spark of recognition singed

her. *Son of a gun.* She spun sideways. The man who'd been chatting her up had disappeared.

Gone.

She slapped her hands on top of her head, bashing herself with the hard cast. "Ouch."

Gabe rubbed the spot for her. "Honey, be careful."

"That S.O.B."

"What?"

"He was just here."

Gabe followed her gaze. "Who?"

"Martinson. He must have recognized me and started a conversation. The weasel is taunting me."

Gabe turned and surveyed the area, his eyes sweeping left and right. "You see him anywhere? What's he wearing?"

She rattled off a description while scanning her surroundings. "I can't believe it."

A uniformed cop walked by and Gabe stopped him. "Start looking for a guy with a gray wool zip-up jacket. Black skull cap and sunglasses."

The cop nodded and stalked off. Gabe got on his radio to alert his team and Jo propped her hands on her hips, cursing her rotten luck. He'd been right in front of her. Leave it to her to be chasing a guy on a diet.

She pulled her phone from her pocket just as Gabe finished on his radio. "Who're you calling?"

"Sherry. I want to give her an updated description."

"I've got cops canvassing. He's probably in the wind now." He shrugged. "Never know. Gotta give him credit for having a set of stones."

"I give him credit for *nothing.* He's a thief. And a weasel."

"Yeah, well, that thief and weasel just played us."

ELEVEN

Jo stood in her kitchen with the palm of her unbroken hand pressed into the countertop. If only the cold granite would soothe the boiling under her skin. At this rate, her veins would disintegrate.

So. Incredibly. Pissed.

Donald Martinson, weasel extraordinaire, was now on her list. She had to find him. Had to. This went beyond counterfeit goods.

This was a matter of pride.

And she had plenty of it. Not only had Martinson played her, she'd missed Kiki getting arrested at the other building ESU had raided. At least they'd gotten one of them. That fact was only a small bit of salve on her singed ego.

Someone knocked lightly on her door. *Gabe.* And what was that? Suddenly he had a recognizable knock? Next he'd be moving in.

Right.

Making matters worse, she didn't exactly take her time getting to the door. Getting attached to him was a bad idea. One she should have considered *before* it actually happened.

She checked the peephole and there he was, Mr. August, in all his glory. She swung the door open. The smell of his soap, clean and pure, reached her and she assumed he'd recently showered after this miserably long day. She herself had spent a good twenty minutes scrubbing her skin, yet the smell of a burning building still lingered.

Whether it was her imagination working her over, she couldn't be sure, but she knew she'd never forget the terror involved in being trapped in an inferno.

Donald Martinson, weasel extraordinaire.

"Hey," Gabe said, stepping across the threshold in his spiffy clean jeans and a green sweater.

How the man never wore a jacket and didn't freeze, she couldn't fathom. Freak of nature. That's what he was. Mr. August. The hottest month.

"Hi. Everything okay?"

He dropped onto the couch and stretched his massive body into it. A sight she was getting used to seeing and hardly minded.

"Aside from the extra holes the mayor drilled into me, I'm good."

Jo winced. "Sorry."

"The good news is, I took the bullet—make that *bullets*—for both of us, so you're off the hook."

She perched across from him on the coffee table. "You didn't have to do that."

"I was there and he was pissed. Now we're done. Our task force hauling in close to a million dollars in counterfeit goods this week is saving us. He might have a bug up his ass, but it's a happy bug."

Jo snorted. Shark Gabe grinned at her. She fanned herself. "Now what?"

He sat up and their knees bumped. "We hunt down Martin-son. We're *chatting* with Kiki, but he's not talking yet. Other-wise, the task force has been successful. We continue to do what we've been doing. With the exception of you going on hits. After the fire today, the mayor doesn't want to hear jack about that."

"I figured. It's reasonable."

He backed away. "Pardon?"

She rolled her eyes. "I'll admit it's dangerous. That's all you're getting from me, Sergeant, so lay off."

He grabbed her good hand and pulled her onto his lap. "That's all I'm getting? Really? I saved you from a burning building *and* came all the way to Jersey."

When he started nibbling on her shoulder, she reconsid-ered. "Jersey isn't that far. And you are a civil servant." More nibbling. *Definitely hot in here.* "Well, maybe that's not *all* you're getting. If you're nice to me."

"I'm always nice to you."

"Liar."

The nibbling turned into kisses trailing up her neck. Maybe she'd crack the window. Get some fresh air.

"Hot flash?" he cracked.

"Big one." She shoved him away. "Stop. For one second. Maybe two. I can't think."

"So don't think. It's been a rough day. Let's burn off steam by creating new and exciting sexual positions."

Typical man, but oh, how easy that would be. Aside from the fact that she was bone tired, they needed to figure out just what they were doing with each other.

She scooted from his lap and went back to the coffee table.

"Uh-oh," he said. "I feel like a we-have-to-talk talk is coming. Have I ever mentioned how much I hate talking?"

"Have I ever mentioned that I don't care how much you hate talking?"

He blew air through his lips and slouched back. "Go ahead. Let's get it over with."

"We need to decide where we're going. As much as we can, anyway. Both of our careers are on the line. Are you willing to risk that?"

He folded his arms. Sergeant Townsend body language for *I can kill you.* "And if I said I might be?"

Wow. In her mind, she happy danced. He'd blow his career for her? For good sex?

"Before you say anything," he said. "It's not about the sex. Wait. That's a lie. It is about the sex, but it's also about what happens *with* the sex. I blew it in a big way today. If I weren't emotionally involved, I never would have left the scene of the fire to talk to that vendor. Never. The fact that I'm invested, tells me we shouldn't throw whatever this is away."

"But the mayor—"

"To hell with him. He exacted his pound of flesh today. Outside of the tantrum, he's a happy guy. He's busy telling the media how exceptional his task force is. Which, of course, he's taking full credit for."

Nothing surprising. The mayor was a politician and a master of spin. Mr. August, however, was full of surprises. Like his emotional *investment.* An investment that made the girlie-girl inside Jo a little giddy.

The grown woman, though? She had major problems with this risk. She glanced up at him, the dark hair and eyes, the strength and protectiveness and—*sigh*—the girl was about to flip the grown woman off.

"You're not helping," Jo said. "I'm trying to be rational."

He laughed. "And I'm trying to get laid."

She threw her hands up. "This is serious and you're screwing around."

"Actually, I'm not screwing around, which is the whole point because I'd *like* to be screwing around. See how that works?"

Hopeless.

"Look, Jo, I'm sorry for screaming at you today. That was wrong. And I know this is freaking you out. It's freaking me out too. For the first time, I'm on my boss's radar for all the wrong reasons. Whether I understand it or not, I'm in this. *We're* in this. We might as well see what happens. If we go down in flames, then we've got problems and one of us will have to make a career decision."

"Or the decision will be made for us."

He shrugged one shoulder. "When have you ever been afraid to break a rule? For now, we're okay and for once, I don't mind being emotionally invested. Why not have some fun?"

Fun didn't sound all that bad. He was after all, her intellectual equal and, unlike a lot of men, wasn't intimidated by her aggressiveness.

It might work.

If it didn't, they'd both suffer and it would be about more than their jobs. She'd be heartbroken. Devastated even.

He's worth it.

Using her lone good hand and a sudden lack of common sense, she boosted herself off the coffee table, grabbed his arm and dragged him down the hall toward her bedroom. "Okay, big shot, show me what you've got."

THE EVASION

THE JUSTIFIABLE CAUSE SERIES

His role on an anti-counterfeiting task force earned NYPD Sergeant Gabe Townsend the catch of a lifetime—tough as nails but sexy as hell Jo Pomeroy. The woman has a body that drives him wild and a way of attracting danger that's making him crazy. And her relentless pursuit of an elusive criminal has his protective instincts in overdrive.

Jo didn't get to be a hotshot attorney by giving up easily. Her high-end clients count on her to keep knockoffs of their luxury goods off the streets. Distractions are the last thing she needs. Especially six-foot-three, hard body calendar-worthy distractions.

She failed once, letting a smuggler slip through her grasp. Next time, he'll have nowhere to run. A lead takes Jo and Gabe to a small town where not everything—or anyone—is as innocent as it seems. Making this bust could be the biggest break of her career...but at what risk to her newfound love?

ONE

Gabe rolled sideways in the pitch black of Jo's bedroom and smacked his hand along the night-stand. What the hell time could it be? Still dark out and his damned phone was ringing, which meant he was most likely getting called out rather than once again ushering in a sunrise with Jo—something they'd been doing on a fairly consistent basis and he had no complaints about.

He cleared his throat and snatched the phone before it woke her. "Townsend."

"Hey. DeFiore here."

When an undercover vice cop called at—he checked the blaring red numbers on the bedside clock—four-thirty; chances were, something was happening.

Behind him, Jo shifted. Well, she did more than shift. She scooted right up to his back and pressed that amazing rack against him, skin to skin, all warm and sexy. His mind fast-forwarded to the end of the conversation with DeFiore. Hoping for a false alarm, he'd ditch the call, roll Jo onto her back and put a smile on her face. If their most recent history proved right, she wouldn't mind.

"You there?" DeFiore asked.

"I'm here."

"Your guy is in some Podunk town near Charleston, South Carolina."

His guy? Jo snuggled closer, wrapped her body around his, and something in his chest kicked. Every time she touched him, it brought an explosion of shock, then pleasure, then calm, in perfect order. *Bam, bam, bam.* He didn't understand it and didn't really care to.

Gabe scrubbed his hand over his face, snapped his fingers against his forehead to clear the morning cobwebs—and distract himself from his insane erection—and focused on the moonlight squeaking through the curtains. *Ignore the hot blonde behind you.* "Martinson?"

"What?" This from Jo. *She's awake.* Good.

"Yeah," DeFiore said. "One of my CI's heard it. I don't know how solid the intel is, but this guy is usually good."

For six weeks, with the help of investigators from Jo's law firm, Gabe had been chasing down leads on the elusive smuggler that Jo was bent on locking up. Until now, nothing had popped.

"You know where he is?"

Behind him, Jo levered up and her bare breast connected with his arm. His little brain—the one between his legs—shot to full-scale alert. Jo did this to him, sent his mind and body to overload. Every time. He could barely be in a room with her without a raging hard-on. Which made life fucking uncomfortable considering she was the pit bull intellectual property attorney on the Clean Sweep task force and he was the ESU sergeant on the same team. Together, they'd cleared the streets of New York of more than two million dollars in knockoff designer handbags. Not to mention the other bullshit items women—and some men— had to have.

Yeah, that's it. He'd think about the case and not Jo's hand sliding over his stomach and coming to rest by his hip.

"You found him?" she asked.

Gabe snapped his fingers at her. What the hell was she thinking? His boss already suspected something might be happening between them. Something they'd been trying to hide. They didn't need DeFiore telling a bunch of cops Gabe had a woman in bed with him. The guys on his team weren't stupid. Eventually, they'd figure out who the woman was.

Jo bit his arm. Not hard, but enough to make sure he knew she damned well didn't like him snapping his fingers at her. Hell, *he* didn't like snapping his fingers at her, but what was he supposed to do? Tell her to be quiet?

He sat up, dug out the pen and paper he knew she kept in the bedside table. "Whatcha got? I'll check it out."

"Town is called Leeville. Small. As in population two hundred twenty-five. My guy said Martinson's wife has distant family there and they're staying with them."

"Name?"

"Sorry, dude."

Ach. Well, that sucked. But in a town of two hundred twenty-five people, it wouldn't take long to narrow down the visitors. "I'm on it. Thanks."

He dropped the phone and rolled back to Jo, throwing his leg over her so she'd know exactly what his little brain was thinking. "You bit me."

"You snapped your fingers at me."

He inched closer, tightened his leg around her and nipped her shoulder. "Because I don't want some detective spreading word that the woman I'm sleeping with knows

Martinson." He knocked on her head. "Hello. Wouldn't be hard for my guys to figure out who I'm in bed with."

"Oh. Right. Didn't think of that." She lifted her chin, giving him access to her neck. "Martinson?"

He dotted kisses along her neck and she let out the small moan he'd grown to recognize. The screw-me-now moan. "South Carolina. At least the CI says South Carolina."

"We can go there."

"Someone can."

"*We* can."

"Sshh. Right now we have other places to go."

—:—

Jo sat at her desk staring at the phone that refused to ring. She picked up the handset. Dial tone. Good. Maybe her cell? But that one was right next to her. She pushed the button to make sure the phone hadn't somehow shorted out. Her screensaver flashed—an artist's rendering of the Greek god Apollo, because she couldn't very well put a naked picture of Gabe Townsend on there. Gabe, a.k.a. Mr. August —the hottest month on the Man Candy calendar—with that thick dark hair, olive skin and linebacker build trumped any Greek god.

Hands down.

The warm buzz that always followed thoughts of him settled in her core. Whether it was lust or love, she sure appreciated the gooiness of it all.

She shoved her cell phone away. Greek god or not, he needed to call her. The receptionist buzzed her desk phone. *This is it.* "Hi, Jo. I have Al from Barelli for you."

Not Gabe. "Thank you. If Gabe Townsend calls, would

you please get a number from him and I'll call him back." A second later, her phone rang. "Hello, Al. How are you?"

"I'm good, *Ms.* Pomeroy. How are you?"

She never minded Al. He was one of those middle-aged corporate big shots who thought all women should fall at his feet simply because he was a corporate big shot. But she and Al had quickly gotten to a place of understanding. That understanding being that Jo would not, under any circumstances, no matter how much he flirted and peppered her with sexual innuendos, open her legs for him.

Nothing derailed a career like sex with the CEO of her firm's third largest client. Sleeping with clients would never be part of her resume. ESU sergeants were another matter altogether.

As intellectual property attorneys went, she wanted to be the best. She *wanted* nationwide expansion of the local task force she'd convinced the mayor of New York to form. Her dream was to bust every counterfeiter of her clients' luxury items. Was it feasible to get every knockoff purse, shoe, umbrella, watch and the litany of other accessories counterfeiters copied? Probably not, but she'd damn well try.

And being given that opportunity came with keeping her vagina off-limits to corporate big shots. Besides, she had Mr. August these days and as far as her hormones could tell, he couldn't—wouldn't—be beat.

I so adore that man.

Jo cleared her throat—and her mind. Thoughts of Gabe continually distracted her. Made her look like a flighty female. So un-Jo-like. "I'm great, Al. I wanted to update you on the Martinson case."

"He's the smuggler?"

"Yes. The task force has a lead on his location. We think he's in South Carolina."

"Huh."

That *huh* was loaded. "Something wrong?"

"No. It actually makes sense. Charleston is one of the largest ports in the U.S."

Sneaky Martinson bastard. Things got too hot in New York so he moved his operation to South Carolina. Obviously, the man didn't know just how badly she wanted him behind bars. He'd made an ass of her six weeks ago by pretending to be a curious onlooker while Gabe's ESU team searched his house. The man stood there talking to her —*talking to her*—and she hadn't even known it was him. Foolish on her part, but Mr. Martinson wouldn't get that opportunity again. Being made to look like a dumb blonde turned her into a python.

One that would swallow her prey whole.

"Apparently," she told Al, "Mr. Martinson's wife has family in Leeville."

"You'll be going there?"

Not if Gabe had anything to do with it. He'd been so freaked after her run-ins with Martinson that he constantly feared for her safety. Plus, the mayor had been equally freaked and banned her from being on-scene after the ESU team took down merchants peddling their illegal counterfeit items. According to Gabe and the mayor, she should stay in her office like a good little girl. For the most part—*ahem*— she'd cooperated. "The members of the task force are still confirming his location."

"If you need the jet, Barelli will fly you down there. I'd like to know what this guy is up to."

Jo sat back and slapped her palm over her forehead. The Barelli jet. And Gabe didn't want her to go. Totally unfair. This trip could be a dream come true. No crammed coach seat on the ride down and busting the smuggler she'd been chasing for months. If she could get Martinson, she'd be one step closer to a nationwide task force.

But Gabe worried about her. Insanely. She flexed the fingers of her right hand. The one recently freed from a cast after a shop owner had broken it with a pipe. Her stomach squeezed. Maybe Gabe had reason to worry, or maybe he was just a fatalist. What she knew was her emotional attachment to him was getting in the way of doing her job.

And she couldn't have that. She'd never ask him not to do his job. Day in and day out he faced unimaginable violence. It came with being a sergeant for New York's Emergency Services Unit, more commonly known as S.W.A.T.

"Thanks, Al. I'd appreciate that. Let me talk with my contact on the task force and I'll get back to you."

"Whatever you need, Jo. I want this guy shut down. You've already taken a million dollars' worth of bogus Barelli merchandise off the streets. Imagine how much more he's moving."

Didn't she know it? This guy was her white elephant. And she wanted to bag him—so to speak—with or without the extremely hotheaded ESU sergeant who'd been sharing her bed for the last six weeks.

—:—

After the briefing for their afternoon hit—ESU speak for taking down a location—on a crack house later that morning, Gabe marched into his boss's shoebox of an office, nodded at Tom, who was on the phone, and took a seat in one of the crappy metal guest chairs the city deemed appropriate for lieutenants of the NYPD.

Tom finished his call while Gabe mentally arranged his approach. He wouldn't throw Jo under the bus, but before he left this office, one sexy attorney would not be visiting South Carolina any time soon.

Not that he wanted to stunt her career. He wanted her to have whatever success she could achieve. They were similar in that sense. Ambitious. Dedicated. *Hungry*. They craved professional achievement and used each milestone as a measure of their self-worth. He got it. More than she knew. It was, in fact, the thing he loved most about her.

But it wouldn't stop him from making sure she didn't get herself killed. In her unrelenting quest to nab this guy, Jo had lost perspective. She saw him as prey, but that prey had continually outwitted her. This asshole had locked her in a burning building she'd been lucky to escape from.

Martinson wasn't playing. And Jo had yet to fully grasp that. In this instance, her ambition had blinded her.

Tom dropped his phone into the cradle, rocked back in his desk chair and clasped his hands behind his buzz cut blond head. "What's the word on our rookie?"

"Aside from the fact that, if his ass wasn't attached to him he'd forget it?"

"What'd he do?"

"No wire cutters. On that hit we did yesterday we had gunfire everywhere and were trying to get through chicken wire to breach the back door of the house. Helluva time to figure out he didn't have wire cutters in his go-bag. I gave him mine. Told him to tie them around his neck so he didn't lose them."

Tom winced. "Is he gonna make it?"

Gabe shrugged. "Don't know yet. Might be nerves."

"What else?"

"I got a bead on Martinson."

Tom's eyebrows hitched up. They all wanted Martinson. Bad. "No shit."

"CI says he's in South Carolina."

Still rocking, Tom considered this. "Reliable intel?"

"It came from DeFiore. His stuff is usually good."

Tom sat forward, made a note. "I'll make some calls down there. See if he's on their radar. Anything else?"

"Jo."

His boss eyed him. Tom had been Gabe's supervisor since their days at the Fourteenth.. After Tom transferred to the Special Operations Division, the parent command of ESU, he'd made sure Gabe made the move with him. The man wasn't stupid or blind and had all but asked Gabe if he and Jo were doing the nasty, which Gabe steadfastly denied. Was it a lie? Sure. Was it a lie worth telling? Abso-fucking-lutely.

On looks alone, Jo had grabbed the attention of the men surrounding Gabe. She was one of those tall blondes who immediately sparked carnal thoughts in males. Throw in her smart mouth and aggressive attitude and some guys wanted to tame her. Gabe had no interest in taming her. He liked that she was a pain-in-the-ass. Kept him sharp and mentally challenged.

What he didn't like was the idea of a squad of ESU guys snickering about her. If that pack of animals knew about them, the cat calls would be endless, the off-color jokes even more so. In short, that goatfuck of a situation would embarrass Jo and take Gabe's protective nature to a whole other level.

I'm screwed.

"Where's Jo on this?"

"I spoke to her earlier." *Way earlier.* "She's talking all crazy that she wants to go down there and see what Martinson is up to. We need to bury that. Tell her no, straight away. Before she gets hurt again."

That bit about her getting hurt again had to help his cause. And Tom knew all about Jo's antics, the disguises as she marched down Tower Street—the knockoff capitol of New York City—trying to gather evidence. When it came to busting counterfeiters, her lack of fear strung them all out.

Tom rubbed one hand across his mouth. *Strategizing.* "Let me talk to Bev. She's got a way with Jo."

Bev Richards was the mayor's point person on Operation Clean Sweep. All information regarding task force functions went through Bev and she decided what the mayor needed to be brought up to speed on. After Jo nearly lost her life in that building fire, Gabe's shit-meter roared into the red and he begged Tom to sideline her. Tom agreed and the request went through Bev to the mayor, who also agreed Jo getting hurt wouldn't help their cause. Of course, the mayor, an asshole among assholes, probably only cared about the success of his precious task force. A member of said task force getting killed would send the New York media into a feeding frenzy.

Bottom line, Jo was done playing detective and, yeah, Gabe had suffered her wrath. But he'd do it again—and again if it kept that gorgeous woman intact.

Gabe stood. "As long as it doesn't come from me, I don't care. She fights with me. She won't fight with the mayor."

Tom laughed. "She's a spitfire."

That was putting it mildly. And that fire extended into the bedroom. A bedroom Gabe was having a hard time resisting. For many reasons. The first one being that, at thirty-three years old, he suspected he'd fallen in love. For the first time.

It was his dumb luck that the woman was a total pain in the ass. What that said about him, he couldn't dwell on. God knew he wasn't the easiest man to live with. But he and Jo had a thing. They understood each other. Accepted each other's flaws and their sometimes harsh personalities. For them, twisted as it was, their aggressiveness doubled as foreplay.

Really excellent foreplay.

Tom cleared his throat. "You good?"

Wake up, dumbass. Gabe headed for the door. "I'm good. I'll keep you posted on the hit."

TWO

"The mayor already has concerns about your safety," Bev Richards said via Jo's office speakerphone. "What will this trip to South Carolina do for us?"

Jo sat back in her desk chair, crossed her legs and prepared for the verbal sparring she was so good at. From the minute Bev had answered her call, Jo knew she'd be in for a fight.

"What it will do is help locate Martinson, a man who is ripping off my client. Four million dollars, Bev. That's what Barelli estimates they lose in New York alone." Jo stopped and took a breath. *Easy, girl.* "How about we compromise?"

"How?"

"Let's call the local P.D. down there and I can work with them on locating Martinson. Even if he's laying low and not selling any knockoffs, he's still wanted in New York. All they need to do is get him in custody and we can ship him back up here. It's the perfect plan. And if we can get him wrapped up in a nice little bow, the mayor will be a hero to high-end manufacturers everywhere. He'll be King of Anti-Counterfeiting and you'll be his queen."

Bev snorted. At fifty-eight, she'd spent her entire life in Manhattan. She wouldn't be played unless she wanted to be. "I have no interest in being queen. My interest is for my boss to not yell at me. And if I'm not mistaken, he gave you strict orders to stay out of the action."

"Hang on. That was specifically regarding going with Gabe's team on hits. This isn't a hit. It's a fishing expedition. And I hear fishing is awesome in South Carolina."

On her end of the line, Jo grinned. That fishing line was a winner. She knew it. Felt it in the pit of her stomach. This was why she loved being an attorney. Who said intellectual property law wasn't exciting? In a few hours she'd be jetting south to hunt down a smuggler. When she found him, it would get her one step closer to achieving her dream of a national anti-counterfeiting task force. *Te-he*. Every major port in the U.S. should have the same model as the one in New York. And she'd make sure it happened.

Bev sighed. "You'll stay out of trouble?"

Victory. "Yes."

"Promise me. Because if something goes wrong, I'm telling the mayor you went rogue. Don't think I won't do it."

Jo held up three fingers. Not that Bev could see, but hey, it was the effort that counted. "I promise. I'll stick with law enforcement down there. You may not believe me, but I did learn my lesson after the broken hand and the fire. I'll be careful. I'll stay at the damned P.D. all day so they can watch me."

Maybe.

"Jesus," Bev said. "Mr. August is gonna go apeshit."

Jo laughed. They'd originally given Gabe his moniker and if Bev had a clue about Jo wrapping herself around all that male perfection, she hadn't let on. Unprofessional? Absolutely. But months before Jo and Gabe started their affair, Bev and Jo had secretly commented on the level of hotness contained in that six-foot-three package. To suddenly stop that banter would raise questions and Jo wasn't ready for that.

"I'll take care of Mr. August. I'm not afraid of him."

Not much anyway.

—:—

Two hours later, Jo stepped out of the lobby doors of her office building into the biting cold of a January day. She stopped on the sidewalk and smiled—not hard to do—at the man leaning against his unmarked NYPD cruiser. None other than Mr. August, dressed in his tactical uniform—navy cargo pants, honking big gun strapped to his thigh and a heavyweight NYPD jacket. The jacket alone should have alarmed her. The man was a self-proclaimed furnace who never wore anything heavier than a wind-breaker.

In the back of her mind, something snapped and that something told her his presence wasn't accidental. Not when she was on her way home to pack a few things for her trip to South Carolina. A trip she fully intended on sharing with him.

From the airport.

Seconds before takeoff.

She waited for rushing pedestrians to hustle by and crossed to him. "Hello, handsome."

He gave her that sly grin, the one that hinted of talents she'd recently been made aware of. *Shark Gabe.*

"Afternoon, Counselor. Heading to lunch? Thought I'd treat."

Lunch. *Um, no.*

A gust of wind howled and Jo held the collar of her coat closed. "How long have you been out here?"

"Not long. Ten minutes maybe."

"Huh. Why didn't you come up?"

This time when he smiled, it was the real Gabe smile. The silly, boyish one that turned her into a puddle. "I'm illegally parked."

Cop humor. She rolled her eyes.

"So," he said, "we'd better get moving before I get a ticket." He lurched off the car and opened the passenger door. "Hop in. I'll take you to lunch. Your choice."

"I'm sorry, I can't."

He stepped around the open door and squared off with her. "No? How come?"

Okay. This was a problem. She had never—and would never—lie to him. Not purposely. Then again, was it possible to not purposely lie?

Don't get distracted. With Gabe's intelligence, this conversation would take every one of her brain cells to navigate. She shook her head. "I have a meeting."

Which she did. With an airplane.

Slowly, he nodded. Those dark eyes like focused lasers as he took in her face, looking for clues of deception. *Uh-oh.*

"A meeting."

Jo stood still. *Don't react.* If she moved, he'd sense her discomfort. He was brilliant that way, every little nuance of her personality had been figured out. After months of working together and, more recently, enjoying a personal relationship, he'd identified all her signals: happiness, sadness, anger. He knew all the cues.

"Fine. I'll drive you. Get in." He waved her into the car. "Get a move on. Don't want you to be late."

And then she caught it, the quirking smile. *He knows.*

She marched right up to him. Even with her wearing heels, he looked down at her. Terrible position of weakness. Still, she squeaked out a few more millimeters by holding her head high. If he wanted to play, she'd let him. But she wouldn't make it easy.

She walked two fingers up his jacket to his collar and tugged. "What are you up to, sergeant?"

"Me? *You're* asking *me* what *I'm* up to?" He stepped back, clearly wanting to break the contact. "That's classic, Jo, considering you're trying to bullshit me right on the goddamned street. You are *busted.*"

A few pedestrians glanced their way, spotted the giant man wearing a gun and kept going. *My heroes.*

"Why are you yelling?"

He shoved his hands in his jacket pockets and leaned toward her. "Because I'm upset. I'm *communicating.*"

Jo made snoring noises. Communicating. Funny man. Two weeks ago they'd argued over something—who knew what—and she'd scolded him for failing to communicate. "Okay, smartass. Fine. You've communicated. Now I have to go."

She made a move to step around him, but he blocked her path. Not in an aggressive way, just a minor hindrance that she could avoid if she wanted. She glanced up at him expecting to see the normal ferocity and tight skin that were so much a part of him. Instead, his mouth sagged and his eyes—those were the killers—his eyes didn't have that normal heat. He looked...sad.

"Gabe?"

"You were going to fly off to South Carolina and not tell me?"

He knows.

She grabbed his arm and squeezed. "No. I'd never do that."

"I just caught you."

"You caught me going home to pack. I planned on calling you from the airport."

"So I couldn't get there in time?"

"Yes."

"And somehow that should make me feel better?"

Now that he'd mentioned it, she supposed not. She *supposed*, she'd be furious and more than a little hurt if he'd done something like that to her.

Damn, Jo. This was the problem with them. They were stuck in this loop of her trying to do her job the only way she knew how and him trying to keep her out of harm's way. If she had any issues with their relationship, this was it. In order to give Gabe peace of mind, she'd have to be sidelined. Being sidelined, in many ways, meant giving up her ambition.

And she couldn't do that.

"No. It shouldn't make you feel better. This was horrible of me." She squeezed his arm again. "I'm sorry. My mind got ahead of my common sense. It's not an excuse. I'm just telling you what happened. I was so focused on doing my job, I didn't think about the collateral damage."

"I asked you not to go."

"You *told* me not to. Big difference."

He huffed. "Either way, you knew where I was on this. This guy tried to make kindling out of you."

"I know, but—"

"No buts."

Time to convince him. If he'd even let her. When he dug in, chances were slim he'd change his mind. "I took precautions. I've spoken with the sheriff down there. They'll do the leg work. I'll stay behind. I need to see if Martinson is moving product or if he's just hiding. That's all. I promise you, I'll stay out of the way. You don't have to worry about me."

"I always worry about you."

"I know."

He gestured to the still open car door. "Get in."

"Why?"

"Because we have a plane to catch."

Jo opened her mouth and he gently laid his fingers over her lips. "No talking. You didn't think Bev was gonna let you go down there alone did you? The minute she hung up with you she called me. *We*, honey, are taking a trip. Romantic, don't you think?"

"Bev double-crossed me?"

Shark Gabe grinned. "You bet your life. Now get in."

—:—

Gabe stood in the bright afternoon sun on the tarmac at Teterboro, an airport twelve miles outside of Manhattan that catered to private planes. Frigid January air slapped at his cheeks as he gazed up at the gleaming Gulfstream G550. He glanced at Jo. "There's our ride."

And if he were in a little bit of awe, too bad. Being a middle-class kid from Queens, not to mention a cop, didn't offer the luxury of a spin on a private jet. Particularly one in the $55 million dollar price range. Yeah, this city boy would enjoy the ride, even if he had to come to Jersey to get it.

A pilot stepped around from the aft side of the aircraft. A good six inches shorter than Gabe, he wore a pressed blue uniform, no cap on his thinning gray hair. His body was lean. Fit. Gabe pegged him at around fifty.

"Afternoon, folks. Great day to fly."

"I bet you say that to all the girls," Jo cracked.

Leave it to her. Always breaking balls. He loved it. Gabe grinned. "Sweetheart, let's not scare him off."

She held her hands out. "I'm just saying."

The pilot laughed. "I'm Hank Stearns. Climb aboard. I need to check a few things." He gestured to the fold-down stairs on the plane's door.

Gabe held out a hand for Jo. "Let's go get this guy."

"I hear that."

With Jo ahead of him, they climbed the steps into the plane and the rich scent of leather and polish alerted Gabe's senses.

"Gabe, quit pushing me."

He glanced down. "I'm not." But, yeah, he was damned near on top of her.

"You're hovering. And you're a big guy, so hovering is... well...hovering."

"I'm sorry. I'm...I'm..."

She dumped her briefcase on the shiny wood table centered between four plush seats. Opposite the table sat a long credenza—and behind all that, toward the back of the plane were two very comfortable looking sofas. Wood grained walls with a tie-back curtain separated the front seating area from the sofas. Something told him those sofas had beds inside them.

He glanced down at Jo, who'd stripped off her long coat and set it on one of the chairs. She still wore the gray slacks and silky button-down blouse from earlier. She could stand to give a guy a gift and undo an extra button.

She tilted her head, gave him that smile that told him she knew his mind had gone to the gutter. "What?"

Admission time. He could blow off the question. Let it

hang there. A lot of guys would. Not him. He had no issues pertaining to being on a $55 million dollar plane with Jo Pomeroy. "I'm excited."

Apparently she liked that answer, because she grabbed his hand and linked her fingers with his. "Are you?"

"Yep. I've got you, no cell phones and a ride on an outstanding private jet. My life is good."

She glanced around, twisted her lips. "It is pretty cool, isn't it?"

"It sure is, baby."

The pilot stepped onto the plane and pulled the door closed. Ten minutes later he'd gone over all the flight safety instructions with them and gave them a tour of the galley. There'd be no cabin service, which was just as well. Gabe shot Jo a look. He had things in mind they didn't need a flight attendant for.

"Sit back and enjoy the ride," old Hank said. "Flight time is a little over an hour."

Gotta love flying private. This trip on commercial, between parking, security and flying time would take five to six hours.

"Thank you," Jo said, already pulling files from her briefcase.

Gabe stayed quiet while he analyzed the sofa.

"Let's talk about our plan when we get there," Jo said.

Plan? He checked the cockpit door. Closed up tight. "I have a plan. As soon as we take off, I'll fill you in. You're gonna love it."

AFTER TAKEOFF, Jo unbuckled from her single seat across from Gabe's and moved to one of the sofas toward the rear. She brought two file folders with her and although Gabe was distracted and experiencing that childlike joy he sometimes let slip, it made Jo smile. She simply adored this side of him. The big bad ESU sergeant, who, on a daily basis faced depravity that would drive most insane, somehow was still able to allow himself moments of silliness.

She gestured to the seat next to her. "Come sit with me and we'll figure out what we're doing when we get there."

He dropped onto the sofa and turned sideways, stretching one arm across the back and fingering her hair.

Uh-oh. She knew that horndog look. He had to be kidding. "Absolutely not."

Feigning ignorance, he held his free hand out. "What?"

"I know what you're doing. And the answer is no. I'm not messing up my clothes."

He inched closer, right next to her ear, as that free hand wormed around her waist. "Come on, Jo."

She smacked him with the file folders, zinging him on the side of his face.

"Ouch! You've deafened me. How will you ever make amends?"

Such a horndog. "That has to be the worst line you've ever tried."

The hand at her waist inched up and he made a move toward her neck. "Usually I don't need a line. *Usually* you're extremely willing."

Out of habit—*right*—she angled her chin up and he licked the spot behind her ear. The one that drove her mad. *Don't let him do this.* She smacked him again.

"Allow me," he said, grabbing the folders and tossing them on the floor.

"I need those."

"Not right now you don't. We're negotiating."

"Negotiating my ass. We have work to do, and I'm not

having sex with you on this plane." She poked her finger toward the cockpit. "The pilot is right behind that door."

"Pfft, he won't come out. He's flying."

"Auto pilot," Jo shot.

"I'll close the curtain. We'll be quiet."

She rolled her eyes. "When have we ever been quiet?"

"That's true. We do tend to enjoy ourselves."

He dipped his head, got close to her ear again while his fingers skittered over the top two buttons of her blouse. The normal eruption of heat slammed around inside her, knocked her a little sideways. Damn this man. Every time he put his hands on her she went up in flames. Every time.

She grasped his fingers, the ones that had just unfastened two buttons and dipped into her cleavage. "Stop. We can't do this."

He ran his tongue over that spot by her ear again—*rowr*—and she let go of his hand.

"I've always wanted to do this," he said. "The Mile High Club. If I can do it with you, in this particular plane, my life is made."

"That's a little sad you know. That sex in an airplane is on your bucket list."

"I also have running with the bulls on the list. This is safer. And a whole lot more fun."

She rested her head back, let the heat of his fingers on her breast sink in. How she loved when he touched her.

"Jo," he whispered, "you know you want to. I can feel it. You're body gets all tense. You're about to snap."

"I have to finish reading a deposition. And the notes on Martinson."

"Screw that. Make my dreams come true instead. I'm a cop on a $55 million dollar plane with a woman I can't get enough of. In every way. Let's live a little."

He pushed his hand further into her shirt, then kissed her neck. "Come on, Jo. I'll take you places."

Places she loved to go. With him. Because, as much as she didn't want to admit it, she'd fallen in love with Gabe Townsend. A man who continually worried about her and hindered her attempts to do her job. All out of concern.

Which she appreciated, but his over-protectiveness and her need to take risks had caused plenty of arguments. Arguments she didn't see ending in the very near future.

She glanced down to where he'd worked every button loose and her blouse hung open. *Master*. "Damn you."

"I know. I suck." He rolled sideways, reached for the curtain separating the two cabins and whipped it closed. "Get naked, Jo. You're about to make my dream come true."

HE HAD to hand it to her, she'd put up a bigger fight than he'd expected. When it came to sex, there weren't a whole lot of mixed messages between them. They both wanted it. All the time.

And as Gabe watched Jo shimmy out of her slacks, her long legs gliding along the fabric, his need for her exploded. She did this to him. Every movement, every touch sent him to an immediate erection. In the office, it had become treacherous territory. Nothing like sitting in a meeting with Jo and the mayor of New York and trying to figure out how he'd get out of the room without his boner waving hello to everyone.

Sexual connection aside, Jo filled his mind throughout the day. What they'd have for dinner, if they'd sneak off to a movie in a town where no one would know them or if they'd stay at her place. She'd never been to his home yet. Considering his parents lived in the apartment two floors below him in the three-story house he'd grown up in, they'd avoided going there and igniting his mother's interest.

Now it was time to meet the folks. He wanted Jo to be part of his life. All of it. And that included his parents.

When a man fell in love, it was time to move on it. Stake his claim.

That's what he'd do.

Jo set her clothes neatly on the other sofa and turned back to him, her amazing body free of any clothing, and he sucked in a breath. She was no waif. Her hips and ass rounded nicely and the rack—*yoi*—that thing made him howl.

"I love how you look at me," she said. "I'll thank the surgeon."

He grinned. She liked to joke about her fake tits, but down deep he knew it made her happy that he couldn't get enough of them. She'd been flat-chested into her twenties. Being Jo, she decided she wanted an A-list set of knockers and made it happen. "Thank him for me too."

"I will do that."

And then he was on her, moving fast and reaching her in two strides, running his hands over said rack and down around her waist to her ass, pulling her closer. A naked Jo against his fully clothed body was one of the thousand things that did it to him every time. This was the dance, her slowly removing his clothes after letting him watch her get butt naked.

He dug his hands into her hair and kissed her while she worked his belt loose. "I love you," he said. "You know that, right?"

Her hand tensed at his waist. *Uh-oh.* Could be he'd misread this.

Needing to see her face, gauge the expression, he backed

away from the kiss, but kept his hands cupped around her head. Her blue eyes were on him, focused, studying, but her expression remained neutral.

"Do you?" she whispered.

She wanted to play. "I do."

Finally, her lips spread into a slow, wicked smile and she tipped her head up to kiss him. She ran her tongue along his bottom lip and he groaned, deepened the kiss, brought his hands back to her ass and squeezed her against him. Letting her see just how much his body craved her.

She stepped back, finished unfastening his cargo pants and shoved them to the floor. He kicked out of them. His shirt went next and she let her fingers glide over his chest, laid her palm flat over his heart where the pounding increased.

But she hadn't responded to the whole I-love-you thing. Nothing. Was this how it should go when a guy told a woman he loved her? Somehow he didn't think so and a spark of panic flicked at that back of his neck. He might have just blown this whole relationship. *What did you do asshole?*

She kissed his chest, right smack in the middle, letting her lips linger there before looking up at him.

He tipped her chin up, took in the tears filling her eyes. Crying. *Jesus.* He'd driven her to tears. What could *that* mean? "You okay?"

She blinked a couple of times. "I thought it was just me. Or lust or whatever, and it scared me. I don't want either of us to have to give up jobs we love. We have to figure it out."

What the hell was she talking about? Women. No wonder men went insane. "*Now* you want to talk about this?"

"No. I love you too. That's all. I love you."

Finally. She'd said it. He shoved her backward onto the sofa and she pulled him down with her, laughing as she hit the seat.

He sat next to her, turned sideways. More than ready for her. "You're beautiful, Jo. Every crazy-assed inch."

"Even my smart mouth?"

"Even that."

"Good." She pushed him back against the chair. "I want on top."

"Yes, ma'am."

She straddled him and, with her eyes on his, lowered herself onto him. The explosion of heat hit him and he bucked his hips, grabbing her, holding her down. Damn, he loved this part. That first second inside her.

Turbulence shifted the plane and Gabe grabbed her, held her in place as the ding of the seat belt sign sounded. "A little chop," the pilot said. "Seat belts on, folks."

Jo burst out laughing. "Now that's funny. I think we should listen."

If Gabe knew anything about her, he knew she was breaking balls. When they were together like this, she craved it as much as he did. No way she'd stop now. "I'll save you."

On her knees, she slid up, and that same explosion of heat fried him. Reading his signals, she picked up her pace, rocking her hips, driving him to the brink while his hands roamed. Breasts, belly, ass, everywhere he could find, he touched her.

"It's so good with you," she said.

And that did it. The sound of her voice, that low raspy tone that meant she was close to orgasm. He knew this woman. Wanted her. Loved her.

She arched, threw her head back sending her hair flying

and exposing the long column of her neck. He sat up, devoured it, nipped and kissed as she continued to rock her hips through the shattering orgasm, and then she went quiet. But those hips—those amazing hips kept moving—and his world tilted. The tension in his body built, climbed higher and higher, and then—*snap*. The wave assaulted him, just pummeled him and he held her, digging his fingers into flesh, praying she wouldn't move. Wouldn't do anything to take these final seconds from him.

Slowly, she eased forward, rested her head against his heaving chest. Hell of a way to join the Mile High Club. Helluva way.

After a minute, he brought his hand up, set it on her head and rubbed. "Amazing. Total bucket-lister."

Jo shifted off him, dragged her hand across his still heaving chest. "Now, Mr. August, we have work to do."

Gabe parked the rental car on the street across from the sheriff's office in Leeville, South Carolina. Stuck in the grass of the house next door was a red and white re-election sign. Sheriff Connelly, the sign said, the man for us. It didn't take a creative genius to come up with that campaign slogan. Gabe slid out of the car, enjoying the blue sky and fifty-nine degree temperature that welcomed him. Winter in South Carolina.

The sheriff's office was actually a converted church, one of those old brick deals complete with scrollwork over the red double doors at the entrance. Maybe they had a confessional inside. Talk about multitasking. Bad guys could step into the box and make things right with God and the law all in one stop.

Wait until I tell Tom. "Un-frigging-believable."

The passenger door slammed and, unable to resist his habit from home, he hit the lock button.

"Listen, city boy," Jo said walking around the car, "we're in someone else's town. They do things differently here. You'll need to dial it down."

He met her at the rear bumper and assumed the I-am-Officer-Townsend stance of squared shoulders and folded arms. "What does that mean?"

She circled her open hand in front of his chest. "All of this. It works at home, but we need to play nice with these people. They probably don't like Yankees. You're definitely a Yankee. A big one. You need to get smaller."

Smaller. That made him laugh. A good, deep rumbling one that made Jo smile. "Should I go in on my knees?"

She grinned up at him, waggled her eyebrows. "No. But maybe later."

Damn, he loved this woman. "Oh, honey."

She threw her hand up. "Zip it. I know I started it, but sometimes you don't have to take the bait."

"You know better."

She spun to the road and took three steps, but a sound—the not-so-distant hum of an engine—made Gabe reach for her—grab the back of her blazer. She stopped, glanced over her shoulder, her eyes questioning. Gabe turned left and all at once, as if fast-forwarded, a black pick-up tore around the corner, its tires shrieking as it swerved and the driver over-corrected. Probably a teenager screwing around.

He glanced back at Jo, in the street, transfixed by the charging truck. A horn blared and Gabe's chest squeezed. Blood filled his head like a battering ram. "Jo! Back!"

Get her. He gripped the back of her blazer tighter, checked the oncoming truck—ten yards—and hooked his free arm around her. *Now.* The explosion in his head droned on as he plowed her against the car and pinned her there.

The truck roared by, the driver still sitting on the horn. He glanced at the rear of the truck. No plate. He ticked back a few seconds, replayed what he saw. Front plate. Had a P in it. PC something.

Damn. For a cop, he'd just done a shit job of capturing the details.

Jo pushed away from the car, her body pressing into him. He stared straight ahead into the square where a statue wobbled. *Dizzy*. He shook his head, closed his eyes, focused on controlling his breathing.

"You okay?"

"For God's sake! He almost killed me. Don't these people know how to drive?"

"Did you see the driver?"

"Not really. All I saw was that big grill coming at me."

Gabe rested his forehead against the back of Jo's skull and let out a soft grunt. One way or another, she'd do him in. "Damn kids."

"Okay, sergeant. Let me up."

"Sorry."

"Don't apologize, big boy. You just saved me from being a tattoo on the street." She turned and faced him, patted his chest and went up on tip-toes for a quick kiss. "Thank you."

"Scared the crap out of me. You need to watch, Jo. Even down here, you gotta look before you step into the street."

"I know. I'm sorry. I got caught up and wasn't paying attention."

"It's okay." He pointed across the street. "Let's find the sheriff."

After checking traffic—thank you—they crossed the street and climbed the brick steps to the church—ah, sheriff's office—and tried the door. Locked.

Gabe snorted. Nobody home.

Jo marched back down the stairs, waving her hand at him. "Don't start. They knew we were coming, but maybe they had an emergency. Let's take a walk through town. See what's what. I'm starved anyway. We'll eat and come back."

"You're the boss."

"Ha! I'll remember you said that."

—:—

After finding a café for an early dinner, Jo waited outside for Gabe, who had ducked—literally—into the men's room. Everything about this town, the doorways included, screamed casual and cozy. A softer way of life so unlike New York and the frenetic pace that intimidated some, but Gabe and Jo thrived on. Still, this way of life offered possibilities in terms of vacations and down time. Short bursts of it she might enjoy.

Behind her, the bells on the door jangled and Gabe came out of the restaurant, his stride, as usual, determined and with a commanding grace that never failed to attract attention.

On the plane, he had changed into his favorite pair of broken-in jeans, a black T-shirt she'd bought him at Eddie Bauer last weekend, and sneakers. Dressed like this, he could have been an average guy out for a meal with his girlfriend.

Could have been.

Anyone with eyes saw he wasn't any average guy. Gabe's presence, that relaxed, confident stance that came so naturally to him, screamed power and strength and the ability to rock a woman's world if she'd let him.

Mr. August. In the flesh.

"You've got that look, Jo."

She knew the look. The one that set both their sexual engines purring. "Can't help it."

He grinned. "We can head to the hotel if you'd like."

"Later, big boy."

A woman loaded down with bags left the dress shop beside the restaurant and Jo perused the items behind the plate glass window. *Well, lookie here.*

Gabe waved a hand in front of her face. "Jo?" When she didn't respond, he followed her gaze. "Oh, shit."

She took two steps, only to have a giant hand grip her arm. "Forget it."

"Let's just look. Could be the real thing."

She doubted it. Her hand over Gabe's, she walked backward toward the window. "Let's play tourist. You can be my soon-to-be-hubby. I'll hang all over you. I'll even undo a couple of buttons for you. Whaddya, say? Deal?"

"I say nuh-uh. We both know that's a knockoff Barelli and you're trying to bullshit me into letting you go in and buy it."

Jo gasped, but it didn't pack the wallop of authentic shock.

"You're full of crap, Jo. The deal was that the sheriff would handle this and you'd stay out of it. You haven't been in this town two hours and you're already saddling up. Our only job here is to offer support to local law enforcement and hopefully escort Martinson back to New York. Getting into our own investigation is a giant no-no."

Of course, she knew all that, but she didn't see any harm in confirming the bag was counterfeit. Wasn't that what they were here for?

Yes.

All she needed to do was convince Gabe to let her take a teeny-tiny step over the line. Teeny step. Not all of her knowledge regarding Gabe Townsend involved creating sexual positions. No, she knew exactly how his mind worked on a professional basis too, and it was time to put that knowledge to work.

"You're right. I'm sorry." She turned toward the window, feigning wistful. "I guess I just don't see how it would hurt to go in and buy the bag?"

"An hour ago you were telling me we were in someone else's town. These small town sheriffs don't like us city folk busting into their business. Trust me."

Now he's getting mad. She leaned in, walked two fingers up his chest and rested her head against him. Just a couple in love enjoying the fading sunlight. "We could use it as evidence for the local authorities. Think about it. If we score a counterfeit Barelli bag, we have proof someone, probably Martinson, is moving fakes through this area. And they're probably coming through the Charleston Port Authority. That'll be it. I promise. We'll just hand the bag over to the sheriff."

He breathed in. Not once. Not twice. Three times.

Come on, big boy, come to the dark side. Stroking his ego couldn't hurt.

"Please? You're with me. I'm safe. What could go wrong?"

He slid an arm around her shoulder, dipped his head and nuzzled her ear. "You are a pain in the ass."

Gotcha. "But you love me."

He pulled her closer, snuggled in and bit her ear. "I'm seriously rethinking that. Let's go buy you a purse that will probably haunt me for years."

She patted his chest. "Thank you, honey."

"Screw off."

"Your love language is truly wonderful."

He opened the shop's door with enough force that the glass panes should have shattered.

"Helloooo!" a tiny brunette with giant hair called from behind one of the clothing racks stuffed into a shop barely bigger than Jo's office.

The saleslady wore a light blue, long sleeved dress tailored to fit her reed-thin body. A well-dressed woman who understood the benefits of good clothing. Excellent. Jo entered the land of hopefully forbidden fruit and waved. "Hi."

The woman eyed Gabe and glanced back at Jo. "My, my, my, he's a big one."

Sister, if you only knew. "Don't let him fool you. He's a giant teddy bear."

"Honey," Gabe said, "you're killing me here."

That would be the warning to get this fiasco rolling. Jo spun to the front window. "I saw that lovely purse. Could I take a look at it?"

"Of course. I'm Ellie, by the way. I own the shop. Are y'all visiting?"

Gabe settled himself against a shelf packed with sweaters, his gaze shooting around the shop. She'd known him long enough to know he'd be taking in the details—the oak wall units, the strategically placed clothes, the jewelry and handbags—and mentally cataloguing the items.

"It's a Barelli," Ellie said. "They're such beautifully crafted bags."

Not this one. This one was a piece of crap. "Yes, they are."

Jo dragged her hand along the front of it. The buckle would pop after the second use. A Barelli buckle weighed enough to give someone a concussion. This thing would fall apart on the first swing. "What's the price?"

"One twenty-five."

For a so-called Barelli. Please. The purse Jo held in her hand, if authentic, would retail at eight hundred dollars. She turned to Gabe still leaning on the wall unit, and that beautiful mouth of his dipped into a frown.

"Baby? What do you think?"

He offered up an eye roll. Calling him baby might have been pushing it, but, hey, call it method acting. And she was trying to bust a counterfeiter.

"If you want it, buy it."

"Oh, I want it."

"Wonderful," Ellie chirped.

Jo ran her hand over the cheap leather again, eyed it with what she hoped were lustful eyes and held the bag back to Ellie. "I'm terrible with impulse buying. Let me think about it."

Ellie glanced at Gabe. Without even trying, the man looked like a badass. Excellent method acting from him as well. Only he wasn't acting.

"Well," Ellie said, "I don't usually do this, but that item is scheduled to go on sale next week. I want you to have it. How about seventy-five?"

Seventy-five. For a bag that cost less than five bucks to make. Criminal. Literally.

Jo shoved the crappy bag at Ellie. "In that case, I'll take it. Thank you so much."

Ready to close her sale, Ellie swung to the register and Jo waggled her eyebrows at Gabe. Mission accomplished. She now had the evidence she needed to get the sheriff fully on board. This would be easier than she'd thought.

—:—

"Happy now?" Gabe said when they reached the sidewalk.

"Ecstatic, sergeant. Now we have proof that someone is moving counterfeits through this area. Counterfeits with my client's name on them. With your informant's lead and now this, it has to be Martinson. I want this guy. Bad."

"I love it when you talk dirty."

Jo poked him in the chest. "Save it, buddy. Let's find the sheriff."

Gabe climbed the church—uh, the sheriff's office—steps while staring at Jo's exceptional ass. Why not? It was right there and her slacks fit in a certain way that wasn't tight, but showed off the rounded fullness. If they hadn't been in public, he'd smack his palm right over that gorgeous work of art.

At the top of the steps, Jo turned the handle on the huge arched door. If that thing fell off its hinges, it'd crush someone. "Ooh, it's open."

Oh, goodie. Gabe crowded behind her to push the door open and caught the lingering citrus scent of her soap. He inhaled, thought about all the distractions she created and —sure enough—the little brain came alive, tightening his jeans in the crotch area.

Focus here, dumbass.

Before too long, one of them would have to flinch and give up the task force. And it would most likely be him. He was okay with that. Jo wasn't. She wanted each of them to be able to keep their task force positions. By her way of thinking, they should be able to bend their task force jobs to fit into their personal lives. Nice thought, but unrealistic. What she didn't understand was that working together messed with his mind, and a guy who did what he did for a living needed all brain cells in working order.

The task force work gave him a rush, no doubt. Work wise, it had been a solid move because it put him in direct contact with the mayor of New York, a man who could fast-track Gabe's career. Right now though, he wasn't sure if he liked the assignment because it was good for his career or because it let him hang around Jo.

Later. He set his hand flat on the door and pushed. "Let's see what's what."

A bell jangled as the door swung wide.

"Afternoon, folks." A barrel-chested, balding guy—mid-fifties easy—came around a desk tucked into an alcove on the right side.

Career cops, wherever they came from, had a certain way of moving. A self-assuredness that became a defining factor easily recognized by other cops.

Gabe glanced around at the cavernous space. Church pews had been replaced with desks and metal cabinets, but the marble floors and ceiling fresco of angels and a robed woman remained. The idea of processing a murderer or a junkie under a ceiling depicting what looked like a woman's ascent into heaven was just plain bizarre.

Jo strode toward the man and extended her hand. "Hello. I'm Jo Pomeroy. Are you Sheriff Connelly?"

Like most red-blooded men, the sheriff took in Jo's long legs and the silk blouse she'd buttoned back to a professional level, as opposed to the screw-me-stupid level Gabe enjoyed. This might be fun to watch. If this sheriff didn't cut the crap, Jo would hit him with a remark sharp enough to slice his balls off.

One at a time.

On cue, she circled her finger around her face. "Right here, Sheriff. Come on now, up you go."

Atta, girl.

The man's head snapped from the middle button on her shirt to her face.

"Much better," she said.

Gabe puffed out his cheeks because, damn, it was hard not to laugh.

"Sorry, ma'am." The sheriff grasped her hand but

released it quickly. No lingering after she'd made that first nick into his balls. "Welcome."

Gabe held his hand out. "Gabe Townsend."

The sheriff shook his hand. Not too hard, but enough to exert some power. "Sergeant, right? Emergency Services?"

"Yes, sir."

"That's gotta be somethin'"

"It's not dull."

The sheriff waved them to his desk in the freaky alcove. Damned sheriff's office in a church. The whole thing gave Gabe the willies. He needed white walls, cracked ceilings, linoleum floors and interview rooms that held secrets most people couldn't comprehend.

"Have a seat."

"You alone here?" Gabe asked.

"I am. Deputy is out on patrol. Receptionist leaves at five. We have a regional S.W.A.T. team here. Men from different towns in the area. Don't have much call for them, but they train hard."

Gabe didn't see a need to respond. His only job here was to make sure the sheriff had whatever he needed and not get into a pissing match over who the better officer was. Really, he just wanted to capture Martinson and go home.

Without preamble, Jo flung the counterfeit Barelli on the desk. It landed with a *whap* and the sheriff jumped.

And here we go...

The sheriff glanced down at the bag, then back to her. "Well, that sure is a nice bag."

Prepare to lose a nut, pal.

"Actually, no, it's not," she said. "You may recall from our earlier conversation that I'm an intellectual property attorney. One of my clients is Barelli Incorporated. Are you familiar with them?"

"Heard the name."

"Yes. They're a huge fashion company." She tapped the knockoff bag. "This is a counterfeit Barelli. Whoever made this bag is responsible for copyright infringement. We need to stop them, Sheriff."

Connelly pulled a notepad from his desk drawer. "Right. You mentioned you're looking for a fella."

Gabe sat forward. "Donald Martinson. He's wanted in New York."

"And you think he's here?"

"We do. An informant indicated Mr. Martinson has family here and is hiding."

Connelly rolled his bottom lip. "Haven't seen anyone new." He made a note. "Let me check around."

As expected, this good ol' boy wasn't in a rush. He'd be losing his second nut any time now.

"Thank you, Sheriff. We'll also need to question the owner of the boutique across the square. She's breaking the law by selling fake goods."

"Oh, hold on here. That's Ellie. She's a good girl. She probably doesn't even know."

Gabe leaned forward. "That could be true, sir. Either way, she's got to shut it down. Ms. Pomeroy is an expert on identifying counterfeits. She'd be happy to relieve Ellie of any illegal items."

The sheriff gave him a look. And it wasn't friendly. Nope, this was more get-the-fuck-outta-my-town. "I'll talk to her. See where she bought it. I'm sure she's been duped."

"If that's the case," Jo said, "it's unfortunate. She could be charged with a crime."

"Now hold on here. This is my town."

Jo blew that off. "Unless, of course, she's willing to cooperate and help us catch the smuggler. Then she'd be a hero."

Gabe grinned. *My girl.* The sheriff didn't look too good though. He'd gone straight-out green.

"Give me until morning to get into this. *I'll* talk to Ellie."

Gabe studied the sheriff, who obviously didn't want Jo stomping through his playground. Maybe he'd help the guy out and convince her to let the man do his job.

"Of course, sir," she said. "It's getting late anyway. Sergeant Townsend and I have an appointment at the Port Authority in the morning."

They did? Gabe shot her a look. So much for her laying low and letting the locals handle this.

"Hey, now. Let's not get too crazy here, little lady."

Little lady. Gabe sighed.

The sheriff stood—a clear announcement that this meeting was over. "You let me handle it. I'll let you know if we need help. You folks at the hotel?"

Jo pulled her card and a pen from her briefcase. "We are. I'll give you my number so you can reach this *little lady* anytime."

Second nut, gone. She wrote her number on the back of her card and handed it over.

Gabe stood, smacked his hands together. "We're all set here then."

"We are indeed," Jo said. "Thank you, Sheriff. I'm sure we'll get this wrapped up quickly and you'll help us put a smuggler behind bars. I have no doubt."

She charged down the church—sheriff's office—steps and hooked a right. "Come with me." Jo was already twenty yards in front of him and picking up speed. "We need to get over there before he calls Miss Ellie."

Gabe hustled to catch up. "You're gonna piss this guy off. What's this about an appointment at the Port?"

She stopped walking and faced him. "I lied about that.

And I don't care if I piss him off. Staring at my boobs is one thing. Little lady? *That*, I won't tolerate. The sooner we get on this, the sooner we find Martinson and get home."

For once, in the interest of expediency, he wouldn't argue with her about wanting to be involved. Investigating on their own would land both of them in hot water. Something neither of them could risk after the lambasting they'd received six weeks ago when their investigation ended with Jo stuck in a burning building and Gabe threatening a witness. Not a stellar day that one.

Gabe held his hand up. "I'm all for busting this guy and getting the hell out, but we need to be careful, do it quietly."

"Excellent. We need a plan."

"Lucky for you, I'm a quick thinker. Follow my lead."

Two minutes later they re-entered Ellie's store. The doorbells jangled and she wandered from the back room.

"Hello again. Back so soon?"

"Yes, ma'am." He glanced down at Jo, brushed his fingers over the back of her neck, stroked the warm skin with his thumb and made goo-goo eyes at her.

Ellie let out a little sigh. "Y'all are so sweet."

Figuring he'd laid it on thick enough, Gabe gave up on goo-gooing. "I adore this woman." Not a lie. "She is, in fact, the love of my life." Also, perhaps not a lie. "And I think she needs another Barelli bag. In a different color."

He glanced around, knowing from his earlier study of the premises, there weren't any other bags in the front of the store.

"Oh, I'm sorry. That's the only color I have."

"Oh, shoot," Jo said.

Gabe gave her neck a squeeze. "Don't worry. Something tells me Ellie will get you another." He turned back to Ellie, offered up one of the smiles that, more times than not, helped him score with a woman. "How about it? Will you make my girl happy?"

Ellie bit her lip. "Well—"

"I'll make it worth your while. As you can see, my girl is well dressed. She enjoys shopping. A lot. Just ask my credit card company."

She seemed to consider this a moment, staring at him as his meaning drifted, drifted, drifted and—bull's-eye—her eyes flew open. "Let me make a call."

Cha-ching. You do that, sweetheart.

In a rush, Ellie spun and headed for the cash register toward the back of the store. The two of them followed and watched her flick through her Rolodex, one of those old circular ones with cards busting out all over. Jeez, they still made cards for that thing? After finding the card, she picked up the cordless and dialed.

Jo stared up at Gabe and blew him a kiss. *Heh.* She seemed to be enjoying all of this PDA, considering they didn't get to do it in New York. Not if they didn't want the old ladies on Gabe's team talking shit all day. And one thing Jo didn't deserve was a bunch of guys making crude comments, ribbing Gabe day and night because he was banging the sexy attorney. Plus, he'd wind up killing someone and that would be bad for both their careers.

Ellie clicked off the call. "There's no answer at my supplier. I got the recording. How about I try them in the morning? Maybe y'all can stop back?"

Gabe nodded, but he wasn't leaving yet. Not until he got a look at that number on the phone. "That's too bad." He gave Jo another squeeze. "Ellie has been so gracious, why don't you look for something else while we're here."

Jo made her eyes dumb-blonde big. "Really?"

That was him. The sugar daddy. "You bet. I rushed you

earlier. Maybe you'll find something special." He dragged his hand across the upper part of her chest, where a modest amount of skin peeked out. His body fired and her eyes went berserk in that what-the-fuck way she was so good at. "Ellie," he said, "got anything naughty my girl will like?"

Town like this didn't have a lingerie store. If they did, the church ladies would probably boycott it just to prove they didn't have impure thoughts. Of course, this would all occur after their husbands dressed in leather chaps and smacked a whip against the headboard. Yeah, town like this, they kept the smut in the back room.

"How naughty?" Ellie wanted to know.

He turned to the shop owner. "Make me howl."

The woman's gaze dropped to his crotch and Jo made a gagging sound. How funny was that?

"I have just the thing."

Jo tugged his T-shirt. "You've lost your mind."

"Not yet, I haven't."

"Right this way." Ellie stormed through a curtained doorway. "The fitting room is in the back. I'll get you settled and bring you some things to look at."

As soon as the women were out of the room, Gabe snatched the phone from the desk and hit redial. Come to daddy. The number scrolled on the screen and he swiped a piece of scratch paper and a pen from the counter.

Gotcha.

What he had, who knew, but that had never stopped him before. They'd have to fly under the radar or his buddy the sheriff would be pissed.

Ellie emerged from the back room just as Gabe tucked the phone number in his pocket. Good timing, that.

"I found some lovely things for her to try. I think you'll be happy."

Little did Ellie know Gabe's favorite outfit on Jo was her birthday suit. Call him crazy but sexy to him was just plain naked.

"Y'all passing through?" Once again, Ellie eyed him. Not a big deal. Women did shit like that all the time. He'd grown used to it, used it to his advantage.

He smiled. "How'd you guess?"

"The accents give it away some. New York?"

Sorry. No dice. Ellie might have that southern charm going for her, but she was certifiable if she thought he'd tell her where they were from.

"We needed a vacation," he said, ignoring her inquiry. "We're road-tripping. Not sure where exactly we're going, but here we are."

"Oh, that sounds fun. To just up and leave."

The curtain separating the back room from the store flew open and Jo stepped through wearing her regular clothes.

"What? No fashion show?"

"Relax. You'll get a fashion show." She set something red, silky and skimpy on the counter. "We'll take this one."

But when she dug into her purse for her wallet, Gabe stepped up. Maybe they were playing a role or maybe it was a turning point in their relationship, but they'd spent so much damned time hiding from their bosses that he'd never bought her lingerie. Suddenly, he wanted to.

He put his hand over hers. "I've got this."

"No. I want to."

They'd never discussed their personal finances in detail, but any idiot would know a lawyer of her caliber made more than a cop. He gave her *the* look. The one that sent the guys under his command scattering. "*Honey*, I'm buying."

She stared up at him a minute, clearly contemplating an

argument because that's what she did. Argued, debated, challenged. All good things generally. Between the two of them, they were goofy that way. They got off on the conflict. Their own brand of wacky foreplay.

Jo backed off. Physically took a step away from the counter. "Okay, sailor. You got it."

Whether she understood his wanting to buy her a gift or simply chose not to do battle, he wasn't sure. Either way, he'd chalk it up to a win. Where Jo was concerned, he didn't win very often.

"Thank you," he said.

"Anything for you, *honey*."

And God help him, she batted her eyes, completely charming Ellie. Maybe that fluttering thing worked for some women. Jo? Not a chance. He hated it on her. He wanted her tough and clawing.

What kind of freak was he? *Not exploring it.*

Ellie rang up the lingerie and he grabbed the bag. Holy smokes, his budget couldn't take too much of that. Another thing he'd have to get used to—Jo probably made as much in one day as he made in a week. She could afford to pay a hundred bucks for lingerie. Him? No way. *Suck it up, pal.* "Thanks for your help, Ellie."

"Y'all come back and see us again."

Oh, we will, Ellie. We will. It just wouldn't be to purchase lingerie.

FOUR

"You sneaky devil!" Jo grinned at Gabe after he admitted to scamming the supplier's number from Ellie's phone.

I adore this man.

Hand in hand, they strolled down Main Street, passing the closed pharmacy and bakery on their way back to their rental car. The evening air was thick and moist and heavy and for some reason, Jo liked it. Maybe it was the lack of chaos and noise. Small town quiet versus screaming sirens and traffic.

Across the street a couple had taken over a bench by the huge pond in the town square. In the center of the pond was a brass statue that poked at Jo's curiosity. She'd have to wander by to see who the statue represented.

Her curiosity also went to the couple on the bench. The man was stretched flat, his head in the woman's lap. Jo considered steering Gabe in that direction. Why not? At home, they didn't have the luxury of holding hands and stretching out on a bench. Too much risk of getting caught.

Now that she'd had a taste of freedom when it came to their relationship, she resented all the secrecy.

"I needed something to do while you were in the dressing room," Gabe said.

Jo focused on him, watched his lips move and in her mind replayed where they were in the conversation. Ah, the phone number. "I'd say you made good use of your time, sergeant."

He squeezed her hand and she glanced down, took in his long fingers. Fingers that, before today, she only held behind closed doors because they were too terrified—yes, the big, bad ESU sergeant was terrified—their bosses would toss one of them off the task force.

For now, they were in tiny Leeville where only the sexist sheriff knew their identities and, damn it, Jo wanted to hold her man's hand. Wasn't a lot to ask. She lifted their joined hands, kissed the back of his. There. Affection in public. The horrors.

"Careful," Gabe said. "I might start to enjoy all this domesticity."

As usual, their thoughts had aligned. Amazing how that happened. Even when they disagreed about work, their minds were in perfect tune. "Exactly!"

"What?"

"I was just thinking I never get to touch you unless we're in private. I like holding your hand. Makes me realize what we don't have at home. It bothers me. Like we're doing something wrong. What we have together isn't wrong."

"I agree. But there's not much we can do about it."

Unless one of them left the task force. And they weren't deluding themselves. If one of them left, it would be Gabe. Jo was the driving force on project Clean Sweep. She'd been the one to badger the mayor into forming the task force. She had the manufacturer contacts. And she had the passion for it. Not that Gabe wasn't dedicated, but he didn't live and breathe Clean Sweep like she did. He just wanted to be good at his job. At least that's what he told her.

If it came down to it and they had to choose, he'd be the one to leave the task force. She knew that. He'd give up a position that put him in the mayor's path every day. A position that showcased his excellent tactical and management skills and would earn him a promotion to lieutenant in the not-so-distant future. In the land of goals and dreams, Jo knew Gabe wanted to make lieutenant by the time he was thirty-five.

But she also knew he'd walk away. He'd do it for *her*. Some would call him a fool. She'd call him an honorable man. A man willing to sacrifice for his loved ones.

I adore this man.

And yet, she couldn't let him give up the task force. Not when it could catapult his career. If the roles were reversed, she wouldn't want to make that decision and she didn't want him to either. Stuck. That's what they were.

"You look like you're thinking. That always scares me."

She shrugged, held their joined hands in front of them. "It just bugs me that we can't do this at home."

"I can leave the task force."

"No."

"Then why are we talking about this? There's nothing we can do except catch this Martinson asshole."

Right. She waggled the fingers of her free hand in front of her. "Let me have that phone number. I'll get one of the firm's investigators on it. See who that phone is registered to."

"I was going to call Tom with it."

"It'll be faster if I have one of my people do it. Besides,

you're the one who wants to do this quietly. Tom will ask questions."

He stopped walking and still holding her hand, squared off with her.

"Gabe, you know I'm right. Tom will have a million questions."

He let go of her hand, dug the number from his pocket and handed it to her.

"Thank you. By the time we get to the hotel, we'll know who that phone is registered to. Count on it."

—:—

Gabe parked the rental car in the small lot behind the hotel and stared up at the back of the old Victorian. In his world, this facility would be called a bed-and-breakfast. A hotel meant a Marriott or a Hilton and would be forty stories high with long, door-lined hallways. This *hotel* was a big ancient house dropped on the edge of town next to other big ancient houses.

"Wow," Jo said. "How fun is this?"

He glanced at her, ready to jump in with an equally snide comment, but she stared out the windshield with a quiet sense of wonderment he didn't always see on her. Conclusion: her comment wasn't meant to be sarcastic.

He sighed. "I hope our room has a king-sized bed."

Christ, he hated those midget beds that his giant feet hung off of.

"Don't be such a worry wart. I requested a king and the owner said it shouldn't be a problem. I mean, how busy can this place be?"

She didn't sound too convinced and just as he was about to share that thought, her phone rang.

"Ha!" she said. "That's Sherry's ringtone. Told you we'd have an answer fast."

Sherry, one of Jo's investigators, scared the hell out of him even more than Jo with the risks she took. These women thought nothing of entering back rooms and basements of stores in their never ending quest to find counterfeit merchandise. As a cop, Gabe understood their motivation, their need to conquer the bad guy and all that crap. He got it. No problem. But as a man with street sense, he couldn't wrap his mind around it.

Jo took the call, rummaged in her purse for her notepad and made notes. A minute later, she punched off. "Okay, Mr. August, that phone number you stole belongs to a business here in town. TBR Industries. I have the address. We should check it out."

Gabe checked his watch. Almost nine. He could get Jo settled in and do a sneak-and-peek. He wouldn't actually go into the building since they were already pushing the boundaries of investigating on their own, but maybe a drive-by and a look in the windows.

Keeping silent, he eased out of the car.

"Gabe, did you hear me?"

"Sure did."

"Oh, come on."

This would make, what, the eight-hundredth time they'd had this argument? The one where he told her to keep that beautiful ass of hers inside and out of danger while she let him do his job. No matter how many times she agreed, she never could resist the pull of action.

He didn't blame her. If he had to sit at a desk all day, he'd take his service weapon and blow his brains out. Adrenaline freaks, the two of them.

This sneak-and-peek, he supposed, was kindergarten

stuff. If he took her along, he might score points for the next time he threw his weight around. *Yeah, that's a plan.* He'd take her, but insist she stay in the car. Which she'd debate. No doubt there. Whether she'd realized it or not, they'd fallen into a rhythm. He'd give a little, remind her that he'd given a little and she'd give some too. Perfect harmony in their fucked up world.

He closed the car door and headed to the trunk for their gear. "Here's the deal. We get checked in and then we find this address. See what's what. When we get there, if I think it's safe to take a look, you wait in the car while I go in."

She folded her arms, watching him retrieve the bags. "If you're with me, why can't I get out?"

"Uh, because someone might shoot us?"

"Oh, stop it. Nobody knows we're here. Who's going to shoot us?"

Stranger things had happened and he wasn't risking it. That sheriff could be in bed with any number of people. "I'm not kidding. I could lock you in the hotel room. And you know I'll do it. Take what you can get, Jo, and live with it."

"You wouldn't dare."

"Yeah, I would. My guess is this big Victorian has a nice, heavy bed I can cuff you to. I'm not talking for sexual reasons either, although, we should definitely explore that." *Definitely explore that.* "That's my offer, Counselor. Take it or leave it."

She bumped her fist against her leg. "I wouldn't put it past you to confine me. You're mean that way."

"If it keeps you out of harm's way, you bet your ass I am."

Jo stood back while Gabe, being the macho man that he

was, unlocked the hotel room door. Why not? This minor stuff gave him a sense of control and let him feel like a gentleman. Down deep, under her I'm-an-independent-woman attitude, she kinda liked having a man to rely on. Not that she'd ever admit that to anyone. Her inner feminist was already preparing to launch the first stone.

Plus, there were other perks. Standing back like this gave her an exceptional view of Gabe's equally exceptional jean-clad butt. Not to mention the way his rock hard shoulders angled into narrow hips and long legs. She focused on his right shoulder. Hidden under his shirt was the tattoo of an eagle, wings spread, holding a submachine gun in one talon and a lightning bolt in the other—the unofficial S.W.A.T. insignia that members of Specials Operations Groups often wore. They were a proud bunch, and no matter how they ribbed and argued, they always took care of their own. In many ways, they were a family.

He shoved the door open and stepped in to do his little surveillance sweep.

"There's a king bed. As they say in the South, 'thank you, Jesus!'"

She entered the room, spotted the brick fireplace first, then the huge sleigh bed. And lucky her, or depending on how one looked at it—unlucky her, there were no posts to cuff her to. "You're safe, sergeant."

Gabe didn't fuss over much, but not having the right bed did him in. In his line of work, the man needed solid sleep. Thankfully, it seemed he'd get it in this room.

If she didn't distract him, which she'd most certainly do.

He tossed her suitcase on the bed and swung around. "Nice room."

She waited, as she always did, for him to complete his inspection. The law enforcement officer in him wouldn't let him enter a room without giving it a visual sweep. Instinctively, she never moved, preferring to stand just inside the doorway until he finished.

His gaze slid to the fireplace, then to the tall dresser, the cute drum table in the corner where a large gift bag sat. There, he halted.

"What—the hell?"

He rushed to the bathroom, cleared it and then went to the table. Angling his head this way and that, he checked either side of the bag before peering inside.

Jo huddled beside him. "What is it?"

"Can't see. There's a load of tissue paper. Were you expecting something?"

"No."

She reached for one of the handles and he stopped her. "Don't touch it." After snagging latex gloves from his go-bag, he inched the mouth of the bag open. "Son of a bitch."

"What is it?"

He turned back. "Well, shucks, honey, it looks like a knockoff Barelli bag."

"Stop it."

Crowding even closer, she looked in the bag. "Is there a note?"

"In addition to the knife rammed through the purse? Yes, there's a note."

Sharp, spidery pricks traveled up her neck. "There's a *knife*?"

How could this have happened? The only people who knew they were down here were the sheriff and the other task force members. Could they have a leak somewhere?

Gabe held the bag wider, gestured with his chin for her to look. "Got tweezers? I'll dig the note out."

"In my toiletry bag."

Tweezers retrieved, he lifted the note—a flat piece of stationary folded in half—out of the bag and nudged it open.

The message couldn't have been more simple. *Welcome to South Carolina.*

—:—

Gabe hauled ass down the creaky wooden steps leading to the lobby-slash-parlor below.

Don't yell, don't yell, don't yell. But—*son of a bitch*—this asshole Martinson was not going to terrorize Jo. And if someone's ass needed to get kicked to make that happen, well, Gabe would get the job done. No question.

"Don't start yelling," she called from somewhere behind him.

At the landing, he strode to the giant reception desk and banged—*ding, ding, ding*—on the obnoxious bell.

"Gabe, calm down. You going off won't help us."

He held his hand up, shushing her, knowing goddamned well that she'd hate that and give him an earful, but he'd deal with it later. More pressing matters to handle now.

Hello? Was no one going to answer this fucking bell?

He smacked it again just as Jo came up beside him and set her hand over his. "Please calm down."

No. He would not calm down. Not when someone got into their room and left a taunting message. And the only person who supposedly knew their true identities was that backwoods sheriff. From this moment he'd been renamed Sheriff Dead Meat.

Dead. Meat.

Mrs. Jenkins, the hotel's owner, entered the reception area from the door on the far corner. "Is there a problem?"

"You bet there is," Gabe said. "There's a bag in our room. A gift bag. Who put it there?"

The woman slid her eyes to Jo and back. "I did."

She did. Terrific. "And you got it where?"

"Um..." She looked at Jo again. Came back to Gabe. "It was delivered earlier."

"By who?"

"Whom."

What. The. Hell. Harsh, brutal pounding filled his head, the strain so intense his eyes might be bleeding. He turned to Jo with his—*is-she-fucking-kidding-me?*—face. Jo grabbed his wrist and squeezed—code for *don't yell*—and that small touch, the connection of warm skin, released some of the pressure.

"Mrs. Jenkins," she said her voice even and direct, "was it a messenger service that delivered it?"

The woman glanced at him again, then shifted her body to Jo. "In a way."

Right there, Gabe thought his head would shoot straight off. Just bam! He clenched his muscles. *Don't yell, don't yell, don't yell.* Jo squeezed his wrist again. He inhaled a massive breath, hoping the overdose of oxygen would settle his temper.

"It was little Timmy Thompson," Mrs. Jenkins said. "Though, that boy isn't so little anymore. No, sir, he's a grown man now. Got a baby on the way too."

Gabe slapped his hand over his face and the sound cracked the air. *Don't strangle her.*

"Is there a problem?" Mrs. Jenkins asked.

He dropped his hand. "Big problem. I need to talk to Little Timmy."

"It's rather late now."

Nine o'clock?

Done deal. Time to go to guns. He reached into his front pocket, slid the leather case out and flashed his badge.

The woman's eyebrows shot high. *Yeah, thought so.*

Jo cleared her throat and gave Gabe the stink-eye. "Mrs. Jenkins, would you please get us Timmy's phone number? We have a quick question." She pinched her thumb and index finger together. "Teensy question."

After eyeballing that badge, the woman checked the phone book she kept behind the desk. "If you're sure it can't wait—"

"It *can't*," Gabe half hollered.

The woman dialed the number, spent a good two minutes on the hello-how-are-you routine—apparently with Little Timmy's wife—before turning the phone over to Gabe.

"Calm," Jo said.

Sure. Right. On it. "Timmy, this is Sergeant Gabe Townsend from the New York City police department. You delivered a gift bag to the hotel this afternoon. I need to know who paid you to deliver that item."

"Yes, sir. I understand. But I'm sorry, I can't share that with you. It's confidential."

Oh, Timmy. Gabe cracked his neck. Organized his thoughts. "Do you have a lawyer?"

"Sir?"

"Preferably a criminal lawyer, because by the time I get through with you, you'll be walking into a prison shower. Alone. Are you getting my drift? You *feel* me, dog?"

Beside him, Jo threw up her hands. *Sorry, babe.*

"Sir?" Timmy said again.

What was with this kid? "You want to stay out of jail, right?"

"Uh."

"That bag contained an illegal item. Are you an accessory to this crime?"

"Oh, shee-it," the guy said, his voice high enough to crack glass.

"All I need is a name. Give me that name and I don't call the sheriff. Or a prosecutor." The threat couldn't hurt.

"Okay, okay. No need for that. I was hired to deliver it by Thelma."

"Thelma who?"

"I don't know. She has an office on the edge of town. I do deliveries for her every now and again. Just local stuff. She called me tonight, maybe six-thirty, paid me double to deliver the bag ASAP."

"What's Thelma's address?"

"I don't know the exact. It's at the corner of Chamberlain and Hedge. The Canary building."

"The *Canary* building?" Gabe shot a look at Mrs. Jenkins, who nodded. "Thank you, Timmy. That's all for now."

"Am I in trouble?"

"If this turns out to help apprehend a fugitive, probably not. I may need to talk to you again." Gabe handed Mrs. Jenkins the phone and started for the stairs. "Chamberlain and Hedge," he said to Jo. "The Canary building. I need car keys."

Her heels clacked against the wood as she ran up the stairs behind him. "You didn't need to scare the crap out of the poor guy."

"Yeah. I did. Chamberlain and Hedge, babe. You stay here."

"Wait. Chamberlain. The address Sherry gave me is on Chamberlain."

"There you go. How convenient."

She tugged on the back of his shirt. "I'm coming with you."

"No. I'm not screwing with you on this. I don't know what's in that building."

"Yeah, but then you have to leave me alone here. After someone left that threatening package."

He reached the hotel room, shoved the key into the door—he sure as hell wasn't gonna leave that door unlocked after their delivery—and pushed.

She's got a point there.

"Fine. Let's go. But you do exactly as I say." The minute the words left him, he held his hand up. "Scratch that. You won't agree to it anyway. I know this. Why do I bother?"

He grabbed his sidearm and holster out of his duffle and shoved them both under his T-shirt.

"We should call the sheriff," Jo said.

"Sure. From the car. I want to get there before he does. If he even decides this is worthy of him rolling out of bed." Gabe stopped, heaved a breath and looked down at her. "I don't trust that guy."

FIVE

The cruise around the Canary building—aptly named for its neon yellow color, turned out to be a bust. And not the kind of bust Gabe liked. All they'd found was a locked, two-story unit that, in his citified opinion, didn't measure up to being called a building. That thing was no wider than a convenience store. Half of it was occupied by an insurance guy and the other was marked TBR industries.

TBR Industries, whatever the hell that was, had him all kinds of pissed off. And when he got pissed, he didn't sleep. Thus, he'd spent the last minutes ripping off pre-dawn push-ups beside the bed where Jo slept, her soft breathing timed perfectly with every other push-up. After this, he'd do crunches, maybe some squats. A few pull-ups if he could find something in this room to hang from.

He'd love a run. A body-pounding, mind-numbing one that would clear him of the mutilating rage. But after finding that knife in the Barelli bag, leaving Jo alone down here, maybe anywhere, would never happen. He pushed up. *Not.* Lowered himself. *Gonna.* Pushed up again. *Happen.* It would be a debate, as usual. As convincing as she could be, the idea of that knife sticking out of her chest, which Gabe felt one-hundred percent, rock-solid sure, was the implied message, rocked him like nothing ever had. Even seeing her trapped in a burning building hadn't ignited this fury in him.

That was weeks ago. Before they'd spent nearly every free moment of their time together. Then was then, now was now. He loved this woman and with all his experience, he'd repeatedly failed to control her, to keep her safe.

"Hey, Mr. Atlas," Jo grumbled.

She rolled to her side, rested her head and the wild blond hair against his pillow, and that same fire he'd felt the moment he'd first seen her tore into him. *Should have known then she'd drive me bat-shit.*

Gabe busted off the last push-up and switched to crunches. "Morning. Sorry to wake you."

"You were muttering. Something about a dumb ass. What's on your mind?"

"Aside from that knife sticking out of you?"

"Don't get dramatic on me."

He stopped mid-crunch, gawked at her and went back to burning through his anger. "Maybe someone needs to get dramatic. In a few hours, we pay Ellie another visit."

"The sheriff said he'd talk to her."

"Great. Then we both can. Either way, Ellie will tell us who her supplier is."

Jo propped her head on her hand and the sheet slid off her bare shoulder. "You think Ellie is involved in the knife thing?"

"Don't know. We'll find out."

"How long are you going to be killing yourself here?"

He glanced up at her as he crunched. "As long as it takes for me to not feel homicidal."

"Ooh, given your foul mood that might be a while. I'm going back to sleep. Unless there's anything I can do for you."

Ha. Sex with Jo didn't take a lot of convincing. "Twenty more crunches. I'll need a shower. We always have fun in the shower."

She grinned at him, all sly and wicked and so completely Jo. If he hadn't known it before, he definitely knew now—he wanted to marry this woman. She'd put him in an early grave, but he'd enjoy the ride while he could.

—:—

"Morning, Ellie," Gabe said, striding through the door to the shop.

Jo latched onto one of his back belt loops and tugged. "Take it easy, sergeant."

Ellie glanced up from whatever she was doing behind the register. "Well, good morning folks. How are y'all today?"

"We're doing great," Gabe said. "Well, maybe not great considering we had a package waiting in our hotel room last night."

"Gabe," Jo said.

"A package?"

"Yeah. A Barelli purse. A fake one."

"I'm sorry?"

For God's sake. What was he doing? Jo eased forward, hoping Gabe would take the hint and shut up. "Ellie, has the sheriff contacted you this morning?"

"No. Why would the sheriff contact me?"

Jo took a business card out of her purse. If she could keep the madman next to her at bay, she might have a shot at convincing Ellie to tell them where her supplier stored their stock. "My name is Joanna Pomeroy, I'm an attorney from New York. One of my clients is Barelli Incorporated."

Ellie took the business card, ran her fingers over the gold embossed letters. "Oh."

"I'm an intellectual property attorney. I help crack down on the sale of counterfeit items."

"Oh," Ellie said again, but this time that *oh* was packed with a whole lot of understanding. *Yes, Miss Ellie, you are running illegal items through your shop.*

Jo held her hand to Gabe. "This is Sergeant Townsend. He's from the New York City Police Department. He's part of the Clean Sweep task force. We're here looking for a Donald Martinson. He allegedly runs a multi-million dollar counterfeiting operation and he's wanted for questioning in New York."

"Yeah," Gabe said. "He also *allegedly* conspired to kill two women by locking them in a burning building."

"Oh, my God!" Ellie said.

Jo shot Gabe a look and he shrugged. "Them's the facts, ma'am."

"Ellie," Jo said, "Sergeant Townsend and I received a tip that Donald Martinson is in the area. The package that was left for us at the hotel last night, in our experienced opinion, confirms he's here. Now we have to find him. Can you help us with that?"

If any of what Jo said had registered in Ellie's apparently frying mind was anyone's guess. The woman's partially open mouth and rapid, shallow breathing definitely indicated a level of nervousness.

Beside Jo, Gabe tapped his fingers against his legs, that

limitless, primal energy filling the empty shop. *He's going to snap.* Almost a year of working with him taught her the warning signs. The stiff posture, the focused intensity. When Gabe took over a situation his already large body expanded, his presence saturating the room.

"Ellie," he said. *Here we go.* "You are going to be arrested for selling counterfeit merchandise because the bag you sold us yesterday is most definitely counterfeit. So, right off the bat, we're talking conspiracy and trafficking charges. The conspiracy charge will get you a max of five years in prison. The trafficking? For each count, that's somewhere around ten years. Then there's the fine you'll get. That could be in the millions." He turned to Jo. "Am I right, Counselor?"

Jo stayed silent. No sense interrupting when he was on a roll. Seriously, she could bludgeon him right now. She'd been doing fine easing Ellie into talking to them and then —*wham!*—Mr. August throws his mighty weight around.

"Last guy we busted got 40 years," he said to Ellie. "You up for that?" Poor Ellie's face stretched long, the color fading to a putrid green. "Or—and I think you're gonna like this option—you can be a cooperating witness and never see the inside of a cell."

"C-c-cooperating witness?"

Jo crowded closer to the desk, sending Gabe the definite message that he should back off. "Yes. If you agree to provide information about the counterfeit goods we can help you stay out of prison."

"I have young kids. A husband. I didn't know I was breaking the law."

"Copyright infringement," Jo said.

"I didn't know. I swear."

With all the cases Jo had dealt with, she didn't doubt Ellie didn't fully grasp her crime. Most people who sold counterfeit goods didn't understand copyright infringement. Or that they were literally taking money from companies that paid enormous amounts to build their brands.

"Can you help us, Ellie?"

She bobbed her head. Three times. "He's new to the area. He came in about a month ago and showed me samples. He's also working with some of the vendors at the outdoor market on Sundays. He sells me the bags wholesale and I mark them up by fifty percent. They've been selling like crazy."

Of course they have. "I'm sure. How much inventory are you carrying?"

"I'm fresh out. You bought the last bag. I've been calling for three days begging for more. They told me I'd get more on Friday."

Friday. And today was Wednesday. Which meant Martinson was getting a shipment sometime this week.

Jo slid Martinson's picture from her purse. "Is this the man?"

"Yes. That's him."

The bells on the shop door jangled. Jo and Gabe turned to see the sheriff looming in the doorway, his lips puckered, his nostrils as wide as his big chest that rose and fell. A bull on the attack.

Oops.

"Sheriff," Ellie squealed. "I swear I didn't know."

The sheriff patted the air. "Now, now, now. You just settle down." He swung a vicious glare at Gabe and Jo. "Did I not make myself clear?"

"Crystal," Gabe said. "Except, Ms. Pomeroy received a gift at the hotel last night. And it wasn't what I'd call a nice one. You'd know that if you answered our call."

"What gift?"

"We'll bring it down to your office, let you see it. Your crime scene people can check for prints."

"Boy, what are you talking about?"

Oh, jeez. Calling Gabe *boy* would likely send Mr. August into overload. He'd need another hundred push-ups after this. He stepped forward, his long body a head taller than the sheriff's.

Make it two hundred push-ups.

"Sheriff, I'm playing nice here. I really am. You are harboring a fugitive. A man wanted for not only trafficking counterfeit goods, but more importantly, conspiracy to commit murder. Now, you will either help us or I get on the phone with the mayor of New York and tell him we've found our guy but the local sheriff isn't cooperating. I'll *tell* him we need the FBI and maybe the Department of Justice. They're not particularly fond of counterfeiters."

And, wow, Jo loved this man. He might have driven her crazy with Ellie, but the way he handled this sheriff? Poetry.

At the mention of the Justice Department, the sheriff straightened. "Don't go gettin' above your raising. We don't need any feds. I can take care of this. I don't have crime scene techs here. We use the regional lab."

"Fine." Gabe said. "You tell me where it is, and I'll deliver the items to them. Because, no offense, Sheriff, I don't trust anything about this town."

—:—

Driving to the Gilfroy Laboratory hadn't been on the daily to-do list, but Jo couldn't blame Gabe for wanting to hand-deliver their evidence. With the sheriff's permission of course. Even if it did take a wee bit of strong-arming.

One thing about her man, when he wanted something, he found a way to make it happen.

After dropping off their bag of evidence, Jo stepped out of the lab's front door into the afternoon sunshine and glanced at Gabe holding the door for her. "I have a plan."

"Can't wait."

"Hardy, har, sergeant."

He smiled at her in that way that made the crappiest of crappy days instantly transform to something light, fun and worthwhile. *Crazy in love with this man.* "First, I'm starving. The prints will take a while, so let's eat lunch."

"That idea I can get behind."

As they walked, she held up two fingers. "Second, if Martinson told Ellie she'd have new stock by the end of the week, he must have a shipment coming in either today or tomorrow."

"A safe assumption."

"If he has a shipment coming in, how's that shipment getting here? We know from his activities in New York that he brought items into the States via container ship. Stands to reason that he's down here, conveniently twenty-ish miles from the Charleston Port Authority—one of the largest ports in the country—to expand his criminal empire."

They reached the rental car and Gabe leaned on it. "If I know you, you want to talk to someone at the Port Authority."

Jo batted her eyes. "Am I so predictable?"

Laughing at her, he drew his phone from his pocket and scrolled his contacts. "This is one for Bev. She'll throw the mayor's name around and get us someone to talk to. Then we eat."

Lunch on the run and a schlep across two huge counties brought them to the Charleston Port Authority where Bev, the make-things-happen queen, had found them a Customs and Border Patrol inspector to speak to.

Gabe parked the car and turned to Jo. "All we have is TBR Industries? No other name?"

"Not unless we can somehow tie Martinson or his list of family members to something."

"Doubtful. After we busted his New York operation, he's probably not shipping this stuff in under TBR. He's flying under the radar."

Jo thought about it a second. *Think like him.* How would Martinson do this? He'd use a new company name for sure. Something not flagged in the system. And what about the sender? He'd need a new one. But he'd still be using the same supplier for the counterfeit merchandise. They'd most likely have a different name to avoid discovery.

"Jo?"

She squinted at Gabe. Reviewed the angles in her mind.

He sighed. "I hate that look. That look is always trouble."

"Not this time. We need to have the Port Authority look at any shipments coming from the same general region as Martinson's other shipments. Also which shipping companies he uses. He may not have changed suppliers, but he wouldn't risk them using the same name as last time. If I were a betting woman, I'd say same supplier, different name and same shipping companies."

Gabe whistled. "Good work, Counselor. They'd have to crosscheck any cargo from shipping companies Martinson has used in the past. If he uses big companies—that could be a lot of shipments."

"But it's worth a try, right?"

He pushed open the car door and slid out. "It's all we've got. Let's hope he's using a shipping company that's not so popular."

SIX

Forty-five minutes later, after leaving all pertinent—and some not so pertinent—information about Donald Martinson's prior activities with the CBP inspector, Jo and Gabe were back at their rental car. Gabe glanced up at a clear blue sky and decided he'd like to find a place along the harbor where he and Jo could be still. Have a drink—him a beer, she a dirty martini—and just be a regular couple. Which they weren't. Not in the sense he wanted them to be.

The short of it? He didn't like sneaking around at home.

Next to him, Jo tugged on his shirt to get his attention. "With all the information I gave them, I should have just left my laptop."

"Please. That poor schmo was already crapping his pants with the info dump you left him. The laptop would have meant psychiatric care."

After said crapping, the inspector assured them he'd have answers in the next couple of hours. He'd also warned them that if Martinson had a shipment coming in using alternate names and shipping companies, they'd be trying to find a needle in a haystack.

Gabe didn't give a shit. He'd risk it. Hell, he'd search those containers himself if he had to.

"Where to now?" she asked. "Sooner or later, the sheriff is bound to hear about our excursion to the Port Authority. Well, I did tell him we had an appointment there."

Gabe's stomach pinched. If this went bust, Tom would chew him up. Sanctions would be sure to follow.

If it went bust.

Which meant he couldn't let their investigation go bust.

"We're back to Ellie. She needs to help us figure out where Martinson is storing his stuff."

From Jo's jacket pocket, her phone rang. She dug it out, glanced at the number. "Ooh. This might be the lab." She hit the button. "Hello?" She nodded at Gabe. "Right... Really? Can you email it to me? Thank you."

She punched off and tapped the phone against her lips.

"That was a fascinating conversation."

"Sorry. Should have put him on speaker. It's partial good news. The only print that came up in AFIS is that of one Hillary Hodges."

"And she's who?"

Jo flopped out her bottom lip. "Beats me. She has a rap sheet. Mostly petty crimes. Basically, she's a grifter. He's emailing me a report."

"Where do we find her?"

"You'll love this, Mr. August. Her last known address is in New York."

Gabe squeezed his eyes closed. Those hours of sleep he'd lost last night would come in handy now. He shook it off. Caffeine—lots of it—would be his next stop. "So, we've got a dead end?"

"We do. Unless someone in town knows Hillary Hodges. We can show Ellie the photo coming over by email."

"And Little Timmy. Maybe the woman who sent you the purse is Hillary, but she's using Thelma as an alias."

Jo smacked him on the arm, the tips of her fingers stinging his bare skin. "Yes! We should start with Timmy. Show him the photo and if he identifies her, you can do your..." she cleared her throat, threw her shoulders back, "...'you-can-go-to-prison-or-be-a-cooperating-witness' routine."

Gabe had to laugh. She did a hell of an impression of him. *Never admit it.* "I don't sound like that."

She poked him in the arm. "You did this morning, hot shot."

A breeze blew in from the harbor sending a few strands of Jo's hair across her face. He hooked his finger around them, dragged them back the way she liked it. "Hey, I was pissed. We're down here, supposedly on an assignment that should have kept you out of the action, and on day one, we're burned. If Bev or Tom knew, they'd order us back to New York. *Today.* No argument."

"I agree. That's why we're not telling them. We're close to this guy. I know it. We just have to keep working."

Gabe glanced beyond her to the docks. Sunny day like this, the water would sparkle, reminding him of being a kid and crabbing with his father. He'd hated crabbing back then. Now? He might like to try it again. Might force him to slow down every now and again. With his job and squeezing in time with Jo, the days ran together.

Order of the day: work, go to Jo's, have dinner, shower, collapse in bed, sleep. Next day, same thing. Not that any red-blooded male would consider it a bad routine. Not with Jo anyway. Still, it left him...unsatisfied...somehow cheated.

"We need to go on a date."

She glanced up from studying her phone. Probably waiting for that email. "Pardon?"

"Us. We need to go on a date. All we do is work, go to your place, eat, have sex and sleep."

"Whoa, fella." She dropped the phone back in her pocket, stepped closer and tugged on his T-shirt. "Is this a complaint or a statement? Because it hasn't seemed to bother you before."

"It's not a complaint." He tilted his head, thought about it a second. "Maybe it is. I don't know. I want more. It would be nice to take a weekend and go somewhere. Take day trips, I don't know."

Jo blinked a couple of times. He'd surprised her. Good. Sometimes she needed surprises.

"Well, Gabe Townsend, I never figured you for a romantic."

"Neither did I. Suddenly, it's important. I want us to slow down once in a while.

He ran a finger under her chin, back and forth, back and forth, and those beautiful eyes of hers sparked. Amazing. He dipped his head, kissed her, lingered longer than usual because, hell, they were in public and he didn't get to do that too often. After a few long seconds, he backed away, dropped another quick kiss on her lips. "I want you to meet my parents."

He studied her reaction, took note of the cues, the slightly raised eyebrows and barely puckered lips. "Is that a problem? Considering the whole 'I love you' thing?"

"No," she said. "It's not a problem at all. Of course, you'll have to meet my folks too. And you might run screaming from that freak show."

Jo's parents were political consultants. One a democrat

and one a republican. He laughed and his body went loose. "I'll tell them I'm an independent."

"For the love of God, don't say that. They'll eat you alive."

"I have a gun."

She snorted. "There is that."

Another gust of wind blew her hair and he peeled the stray strands back again. "Settled then? Next week, you'll come over and meet my folks. You've never been to my house. That's nuts."

"Yes. Next week. I'd like that."

As a tried and true Queens boy, Gabe saw his folks once a week when he took his mom grocery shopping and they all had dinner together. If they all got lucky, maybe he'd see them a second time.

But his mom had spectacular radar. When he had a woman in his apartment, she sensed it and hoofed up three flights of stairs, making up some bogus excuse to bust in. Given her heightened perception skills, he'd avoided bringing women around unless he intended them to meet his mother.

And *that* hadn't happened much.

At least until now.

Jo's phone beeped. She reached into her pocket, but stopped, glancing back at him. "Can I get this? It's probably Hillary's rap sheet coming through."

"We're good. Go for it."

"It'll take a second for the photo to load, but we'll need to stop somewhere so I can print it."

She punched the screen a few times and came back to him. "Gabe?"

"Yep?"

"I'd like a weekend away with you. Being down here

makes me realize we miss out on a lot. My folks have a house in the Hamptons. We should go there. Even in the winter it's beautiful."

The Hamptons. Jo Pomeroy was so far above his pay grade he didn't know what to think of it. "Is there a king-sized bed?"

"Two of them."

"Sold. Get some dates together and I'll work it out."

"Good." She squeezed his arm; let her hand stay there, skin-to-skin. Just how he liked it. "I'd like that. A lot."

—:—

"Okay, Tim," Gabe said after Little Timmy had requested not to be referred to as Timmy.

Jo resisted an eye roll. Whatever. All they needed was Little Timmy—Tim—to look at the picture and give them a thumbs-up or down about Hillary being the one who'd hired him to deliver that package.

She slid the mug shot she'd printed, complements of the office supply store that doubled as a pharmacy, across Tim's kitchen table. "Do you recognize this woman?"

"That's Thelma. She's the one who had me deliver the package."

Behind her, she heard the rub of fabric that was Gabe shifting around in the tiny kitchen. Heaven help them all if the man's overactive system would let him relax for a full five seconds. There couldn't have been ten feet of space and his presence managed to claim every inch of it. "You're sure?" he asked.

"Positive. Her hair is darker now, but that's her. No doubt."

Jo nodded. "Thank you, Tim. One more question. How

about this man?" She passed him the photo of Martinson. "Recognize him?"

Tim analyzed the photo, tilted his head left then right again. "I don't think so."

Huh. *Doesn't sound confident.* Jo inched the photo closer. "You seem hesitant. Which is okay, I just want you to be sure."

"I've never met him, but he kinda looks like a guy I saw coming out of Thelma's office last night. He came out as I went in. I didn't pay him too much mind though. That's why I'm not sure."

Jo didn't bother looking back at Gabe. She didn't need to. His hyper-awareness flooded the room and the surge must have been rising to epic heights.

Time to go.

"Thank you, Tim. You've been extremely helpful."

She slid her chair back and stood. Timmy's gaze tracked her then moved to Gabe. "So, am I in trouble?"

This poor guy. All he wanted was to raise extra money for his growing family. Jo leaned forward, patted his hand. "I don't think so. If you are, I'll help you. Don't worry. Okay?"

He glanced at Gabe, who remained stoic, arms folded, face revealing nothing—zippo. The man was a New York City cop. One couldn't expect him to have reactions to every situation. With the horrors he faced on a daily basis, continually getting emotional would get him locked in a psych ward.

She turned to Gabe. "Sergeant? Shall we go?"

"Oh, we shall," he said.

—:—

Jo stood behind Gabe in the hallway of Thelma's-slash-

Hillary's office building while the big man banged on her door. No answer. She checked her watch. Three-thirty. Apparently Thelma kept banker's hours.

After trying the handle and finding it locked, Gabe backed up a step, staring at the door. "Damn."

"Plan B. Lawyers always have a plan B."

"Let's hear it, Counselor."

She swirled her index finger and held it up. "We visit Ellie. Maybe the sheriff too and show them the photo. In a town this size, someone will know where she lives."

"Yeah, and then the sheriff will be all kinds of jacked-off that we're running rogue. If we don't find Martinson, we'll both get our asses handed to us for investigating on our own."

"We're not running *rogue*. We're assisting his investigation."

Gabe made a strangled sound. "Sure, the sheriff and my boss'll buy that. No sweat." He grabbed her elbow and ushered her to the front porch, where a second door led to the insurance office next door.

"Should we check in there? See if they know where she lives?"

"I thought about it. But if she has a friend in there, the second we leave the office, she makes a call and Thelma is in the wind."

"Good point."

He scratched the back of his head, scrunching his face. "Our best bet is to figure out where she lives and ambush her at her house."

Working with Gabe for the past year had seasoned her for his moods, his ability to make a plan and attack a situation. Regardless of where he stood on an issue, he never—ever—appeared apprehensive. Regardless of his emotional state, what he showed the world was a warrior, unafraid and ready for battle. What she hadn't been seasoned for was this Gabe, who, for the first time on a work-related assignment appeared...anxious.

She touched his arm. "Hey, if we have issues with the sheriff, I'll take the bullet, so to speak. Everyone on the task force knows I'm a wild card. I also don't work for the NYPD. They can't fire me and I promise you, they won't fire you. I won't let that happen."

"I'm not worried about getting fired."

"What then?"

He waved his hand. "This. All of it. We're in a strange place. I know nothing about how things are done here. In New York, if I need something I know where to go and when. Everything about this place feels...wrong."

"You're overthinking."

"Hell, yeah, I'm overthinking. What else is there to do? We're completely on our own here."

Jo's phone rang. Why did it ring every damn time Mr. August decided to open up to her? *Ignore it.*

Gabe waggled his hand. "You need to get that. It might be the Port Authority guy."

Point taken there. Third ring. She fumbled in her pocket and managed to hit the talk button before the call dropped. "Jo Pomeroy."

"Ms. Pomeroy, this is Chuck Davis."

She glanced at Gabe. Nodded. "Hi, Chuck."

"You might be the luckiest woman alive."

Not likely. She latched onto Gabe's wrist and squeezed. "Why is that?"

"Because Martinson's container—at least we think it's his—is here. Scheduled to be picked up tomorrow. It was x-rayed, then subsequently searched, and it's loaded with counterfeit items. Shoes, purses, watches, you name it. We've seized it."

Got him. The rat bastard. They got him. Jo slapped a hand on top of her head and blew out a long breath. "That's great news."

"What?" Gabe asked.

Jo held the phone away from her. "The container is there. Scheduled to be picked up tomorrow. They searched it and it's stuffed with knockoffs."

"Well, holy *shee*-it," he said, doing his best imitation of Little Timmy. "Put him on speaker."

She brought the phone back to her ear. "Chuck, Gabe is here. I'm putting you on speaker. Hang on." She pressed the speaker button. "You there?"

"I am."

"Chuck," Gabe said, "we've *got* to let them pick up that shipment. If we alert them it's been seized, our guy is in the wind. If we *don't* alert them, we have time to saddle up S.W.A.T. and hit the final delivery location. That way, everyone's surprised and Martinson doesn't have time to run. Assuming he's at the delivery location. Either way, we'll get a bead on him and we'll still have the shipment."

As good as that argument sounded, Jo bit her lip. A whole lot of politics would have to be played to pull this one off.

"Sorry, man, that's not my call. I had to kick it upstairs."

Gabe glanced at her and shook his head. The fastest way to reach Chuck's boss was through Tom or Bev.

And they needed to do it fast.

"Thank you for the update," Jo said. "We appreciate all you've done. We'll be in touch."

Before she disconnected, Gabe was jabbing at his own phone. "I'm calling Tom. You call Bev."

Perfection. That's what they were together. Sharp minds, sharper instincts. No matter how much they disagreed about her risky behavior, when they worked together, they made magic.

"I got voicemail," Gabe said.

"Me too."

So much for magic. They both left messages then stood on the street staring at each other. Back to plan B that might actually be plan C now.

"We need to find Thelma's house," Gabe said.

"Start with Ellie?"

"Or the sheriff."

Jo scrunched her nose and Gabe laughed. "We're in it now, honey. Either way, the sheriff is going to find out. Might as well face it."

SEVEN

Of course, because shit luck ran parallel with the Martinson case, the sheriff was, once again, out of the office. They stood on the steps while Jo left a voicemail for him to call her or stop by the hotel ASAP.

"Hopefully, he'll call soon."

Ever the optimist, this one. Her phone—the one that never stopped—rang and she checked it. "It's my office. Hello?...Hi." She glanced at Gabe. "It's good. I'll fill you in later, but we're making fantastic progress...The Moore case?...Sure...I think I have a copy on my laptop. *Now?*...Uh, okay. I'll run back to the hotel and send it to you." She paused, gritted her teeth and looked up at the sky. "Ten minutes? I haven't prepared."

It sounded like this Moore thing was about to bust in on their day. Gabe stuffed his hands in his pockets and waited while Jo smacked her free hand over her head, her universal signal for great or crappy news.

"Okay," she said. "Give me a few minutes to get to the hotel. Right." She punched off. "Damn it!"

"What happened?"

"That was *my* boss. I'm helping on a case he's handling and they want me on a video conference in ten minutes. He knows how important Martinson is and he's pulling me into a conference? Really?"

Gabe held his hands up. "It's okay. We're in stand-by mode anyway until we figure out where Thelma lives. While you're on your conference, I'll run over to Ellie's shop and see if she knows anything."

Leaving Jo at the hotel alone would suck. Martinson knew they were here. He could be watching and that didn't sit right. And Gabe couldn't even ask the sheriff to keep an eye on the hotel because then he'd have to explain why he was trampling all over a case he was supposed to be staying out of.

Shitstorm. He had to do it though. "I'll only be gone a few minutes, but you gotta lock yourself in that room. Martinson knows we're here and poking around. Wait'll he figures out his container was seized. We have to get to Tom and Bev, get them to talk to someone who can release that shipment."

"Don't panic. By the time you get back to the hotel, we'll have heard from Bev or Tom. Hopefully. That's all we can do. Just keep moving."

He hesitated.

"Gabe, you'll be gone fifteen minutes. I'll be fine." She tugged on his shirt. "I promise I won't leave the room."

As much as he wanted to believe she'd keep that promise, when it came to Martinson, Jo sometimes lost all track of her sanity. If catching Martinson meant breaking promises, she'd do it. He knew this about her. And maybe he hadn't reconciled that with himself yet, but if nothing else, he understood her passion for the job. He poked his finger at her. "You stay in that room. Door locked."

She waved him off. "I've got it. I said I would and I will."

"Then let's roll."

Five minutes after Gabe left, Jo's boss called back and told her the client cancelled the video conference.

Seriously? After making her drop everything, they bailed on her. Now she'd be stuck in this room until Gabe returned, because going outside for air would send Mr. August to fits.

She adored the man, but his overprotectiveness made her insane.

The scraping of a key sliding into the door lock drew her gaze. He must have forgotten something. She took two steps. *No.* Gabe would have called out, alerted her. The door swung open, one smooth arc that she tracked until the door bumped the wall.

In front of her stood Donald Martinson. With a shiny silver key in his hand. *Gabe's key?* Something jammed in her throat. No. Couldn't be. Gabe would pummel the much smaller Martinson. Plus, he was armed with his giant .45mm. Between Gabe and that gun, Martinson didn't stand a chance.

She glanced at the white key ring she'd never seen before. *Not Gabe's key.* Bursting air flew from Jo's mouth, the relief so intense she missed Martinson's approach, his coal-black eyes on her. Her prey had once again spun things around, made her the vulnerable one.

Get out now.

She dodged right, swung an elbow and connected with

the meaty part of his bicep. He grabbed the back of her shirt, his fingers gouging her skin.

"You're not going anywhere. I almost got you in the street, but Sergeant Townsend continues to get in my way. Not this time."

The black truck. Martinson had been driving. *Bastard.*

"That was you in the truck?"

Martinson laughed. "Stupid woman. Your sergeant isn't the only one with contacts in the police department."

A leak. As careful as they'd been, someone on Tom's staff was a traitor. She'd deal with that later. Now, she had to save herself.

"Help!" Jo screamed.

She kept her eyes on the door. *Get there.* Few more steps, that's all she needed. She swung again, hauled her elbow across his cheek, and the *thunk* of bone against bone echoed in the quiet room.

"Goddammit," Martinson said. A second man about Gabe's height appeared in the doorway. In his left hand, he held a gym bag. "Don't let her out."

I'm trapped. The man entered the room, closed and locked the door, then gently set the gym bag down. What was in that damned bag?

Not waiting to find out, Jo backed toward the window and the roll top desk with the ladder-back chair. If she could get to the chair, she'd at least have a weapon. Something to swing. All she'd need was a whip and she could join the circus. God help her. This life.

But Martinson anticipated her move and slid into the corner behind her. Slowly, the two men advanced, sandwiching her between them. She shifted her gaze left and right, searching for any escape. Nowhere to go. Still, she wouldn't stand there and make it easy.

No chance.

The bed was directly in front of her. It would slow her down, but if she could get there, she'd scramble across it and head to the door.

Do it. *Now*.

She leaped, landed in the middle of the bed and gripped the far edge, pulling herself across. A huge weight bore down on her, not Martinson, the other guy. Something pinched in her ribcage. Jo kicked backward, the heel of her loafer connecting with her attacker's leg.

"Crazy bitch. Don't make me hurt you."

"Help," she yelled again.

Panic, deep and raw, scraped at her and she clutched the edge of the bed tighter. Where was Mrs. Jenkins? The other guests?

"Don't bother," Martinson said. "No one is here and the owner is cooling her jets in her office. We took care of that."

Oh, no. All Jo could hope was that they'd confined her and swiped her master key. Anything else would be too horrible to consider.

But Gabe and that man-stopper .45mm would be back any second. *Any second.* Jo focused on breathing, on keeping the panic from flooding her brain. *Work the problem.*

"Help!" Her voice cracked with strain from the ape on top of her.

A screech came from near the window and she swung her head to find Martinson dragging the chair across the hardwood.

He set it next to the bed and smacked the top rung. "We got something special for you, Jo."

EIGHT

abe climbed the hotel's porch, thinking the twenty-minute visit with Ellie was a bust. She'd seen Thelma around town, knew her from their merchandise transactions, but didn't know where she lived. The sheriff, she'd suggested, he'd know. Sure, if Gabe could find that son of a bitch. For kicks, he stopped at the sheriff's office on his way back to the hotel. Once again, it was locked. Another voicemail. All he could do.

He supposed he could call 9-1-1, but being an officer, abusing that system wouldn't fly. Nor did he want it to. Dispatchers and cops got seriously pissed at bogus 9-1-1 calls. Besides, he and Jo were doing just fine in the pissing people off department.

From the street came the sound of a purring engine. A familiar one. He turned back. A black pick-up, suspiciously similar to the one that almost ran Jo down, made a left at the corner. Too bad he wasn't closer or he'd have chased that bastard.

He turned back and pushed the hotel's front door open. The bells jangled and he glanced around the parlor. All quiet. No one behind the reception desk either. The very tips of his fingers tingled. He stood for a second, cocked his head, listening. Each time he'd entered the hotel, one of two things generally happened. Either he heard kitchen noises from the back end of the first floor or Mrs. Jenkins entered the reception area from her office.

Gabe waited. No noise. He angled back to the door. *Black pick-up.* More tingles shot down his arms into his hands and he flexed his fingers. *Not right.*

"Mrs. Jenkins?"

He waited another second. No answer.

The entire building was quiet. And it wasn't normal quiet. This was quiet that came with danger and fear and panic. His body tingled, his senses on full alert.

Jo.

He drew his weapon, sprinted up the stairs, his gaze focused on the upper landing. Clear. At the top, the hallway was empty and he did a visual sweep of the hallway. Nothing out of place. All doors closed and looking unharmed.

Maybe his nerves were fucking with him. *I'm too keyed up.* But something made him stop. Stop and listen. *Nothing.* .45 drawn, he sidestepped to their door and wrapped his hand around the crystal knob, the cold surface a shock against his sweaty palm. He turned it. No movement. Good.

At least she'd locked it.

He slid his key into the lock and turned. Before shoving the door open, he moved to the side, using the wall as cover in case a bullet roared through the opening.

Four, three, two, one. No noise. *Where is she?*

"Gabe?"

Jo's voice. He bent forward, breathed in and out a few times to settle his hyper nerves. What the hell was wrong with him? *Too amped up.* Laughing at himself, he straightened up, threw his shoulders back, stepped into the room and froze.

Jo sat in the desk chair, a thick rope circling her body. Each of her ankles was tied to the chair legs.

"Oh, shit."

"Gabe?" Her body trembled, a small but deadly motion.

"Don't move." He moved closer to inspect the device. A single, six-inch steel pipe with capped ends had been secured to the chair leg on the opposite side of Jo's leg. From where he stood, he couldn't see the other components.

In all his training, he and his ESU counterparts had learned one thing: when faced with a bomb, they were to run.

Run fast, run hard, run long.

But this time he couldn't run. Not with his hopefully future wife—when had he decided that?—tied to a chair with a bomb riding shotgun. No running. He was thoroughly stuck in this Podunk town where the fucking sheriff left his office unmanned and the nearest bomb squad was at least, *at least* an hour away.

I got this.

"He came here," Jo said, her voice gruff, shaky. "Martinson. It was him and another guy. The door was locked. I swear I locked it. They had Mrs. Jenkins's key."

That explained the quiet. And if they had the woman's key, they must have gone through her to get it. Jesus, he could have a dead body somewhere. *Later.*

"Okay," he said. "Stop talking. Let me see what we're dealing with."

As if he'd know? He didn't know jack about bombs. That's why they had bomb techs. *Run fast, run hard, run long.*

He got down on his belly to inspect the device. Most

definitely a pipe bomb. The ends had been capped and a wire, along with a trip line, ran from the timer through a hole in one end cap. *Son of a bitch.* He glanced at the timer and the seconds disappeared like ice on a scorching day. Fifty-nine minutes, three seconds.

Not much time for a man who'd never been within two feet of one of these things. *Get her out.* Gabe waited a few seconds, let the whooshing in his head subside while he focused his mind for the task ahead. *Gotta roll here. Think, think, think.* When the only sound became the hum of the ceiling fan, no whooshing, no slamming heart, no racing thoughts, he breathed in. *Ready to go.*

He scooted backward, got to his feet and found Jo staring up at him. All the time he'd known her, those baby blue eyes always held paralyzing and laser sharp directness. Today, for the first time, he saw none of that.

And he despised it.

"You will walk out of here."

"He said if I moved, it'll blow. We have sixty minutes to get his cargo released. If we call the police, he'll blow it before then. He left a phone on the desk. He'll call us."

Sixty minutes? The timer just went to fifty-eight. "When did they leave?"

"Maybe ten minutes ago. He was the one in the truck. The one that almost hit me."

They're watching. Or at least one of them was because they knew when he'd returned to the hotel and triggered the timer, probably using a cell phone. "I just saw the truck downstairs. They waited for me to get back and started the clock."

A remote controlled *and* trip-wired bomb. Terrific. He ran a hand over his face. *Think.*

"I'm gonna call 9-1-1." *And pray the energy from the phone won't trigger this fucking bomb.* "But I think it'll take longer than sixty minutes for the bomb squad to get organized and get here."

"Oh, God." She dropped her chin to her chest.

"Jo, don't move. Please. Once I deal with this trip wire, you can move. And believe me I'll deal with this trip wire."

How the hell he'd do that, he didn't know, but part of his ESU experience meant dealing with any scenario.

He dialed 9-1-1 on his cell.

"I love you," she said.

"Which makes me the luckiest guy alive. But we're not gonna talk about that now. We're gonna talk about getting you out of this chair."

"9-1-1, what is your emergency?"

Lady, you'll love this. It took four precious minutes for the operator to figure out it would require a small miracle—or Santa—to get the regional bomb squad on scene in an hour. Gabe hung up and tried the sheriff again. No go. He left a voicemail letting him know they had a problem. An enormous one that might blow apart the man's town.

"What now?" Jo asked.

"Now I call Tom."

"What can he do?"

He scrolled to Tom's number. "He can get me someone from our bomb unit to walk me through disabling this trip wire."

"*You're* going to do it?"

He didn't believe it either, but, hey, plenty of shit happened—barricaded maniacs, wacked-out crackheads, subway jumpers—in his line of work that he didn't believe. Why should today be any different? "You got a better idea?"

"Yes. Leave me here."

Speaking of crackheads, when had Jo become one?

That'd be the only explanation for her believing he'd walk out. "Yeah. I'll get right on that."

"I'm serious. Please. Don't do this. It's too dangerous."

His boss's line rang for the third time. *Please, no friggin' voicemail.* The ringing stopped and—*oh, yay, Skippy*—voicemail.

"Tom? It's Gabe. We're in a shitstorm. Call me. Pronto." Next up, Tom's secretary. She always knew where to find him. Gail answered, heard the word bomb, put Gabe on hold and within three minutes tackled their boss.

Love that woman.

Gabe gave Tom the shortened version of how Jo ended up with a bomb strapped to her leg. Of course, there'd be a fair amount of yelling and threats to be dealt with later, but Gabe was connected to Reese Claymore, a bomb tech who'd been in his academy class. These days, they ran into each other at various crime scenes, but Gabe wouldn't call him a friend. Right now, they were two guys who had forty-eight minutes to separate Jo from that bomb holding her beautiful body hostage.

"Whatcha got?" Reese said.

The cell phone Martinson had left chirped. *Goddammit.* He needed to get this bomb dealt with.

"That's him," Jo said.

"Reese, sit tight. This is our guy on the other line."

Gabe grabbed the phone before the ringing stopped. All the fucking electronics in this room and the bomb hadn't gone off. Thank God for the advancement of technology. He hit the speaker button on Martinson's phone and held it in front of him while eyeing Jo. "Gabe Townsend."

"Sergeant Townsend, this is Donald Martinson. Get my cargo released. A truck will pull up to the Port Authority. If my cargo is ready for me, I'll tell you how to deactivate the bomb. If the cargo is not ready, Ms. Pomeroy is dead. If anyone follows my truck, Ms. Pomeroy is dead."

Click. Gabe spun to Jo, took in the spooked look in her eyes and went to work. He and Jo, they needed constant action. Sitting in that chair must have been destroying her. If he had his way, he'd fix it quick. "Where's your phone and the card from our Port Authority guy?"

"Outside pocket of my briefcase."

The briefcase sat on the floor beside the desk and Gabe rifled through the outer pocket. *Got it.* Keeping Reese on hold, he used Jo's phone to call Chuck Davis. Voicemail. Nothing but voicemail today. If Gabe wasn't careful, all the blood rushing into his head might cause an explosion of another kind.

"Chuck, Gabe Townsend here. Call me ASAP."

He clicked off and tossed the phone on the bed. *Screw this.* He went back to Reese. "I need the Port Authority to release a shipment and I can't reach our contact there. Can you get someone to help on that? Call Tom. He'll know what to do."

"I'm on it. Tell me what you've got there first."

Right. Bomb. "It's a pipe. Roughly six inches long and one inch in diameter. Timer and a trip wire. And it's wrapped around a woman's leg."

Reese let out a low whistle. "Six inches. That'll have a kick. Trip wire spring loaded?"

Gabe put the call on speaker, got down on his belly again and followed the wire to where it was secured to Jo's leg. "No idea. It leads inside the pipe."

"How much time you got on the timer?"

He checked it. "Forty-two minutes, thirty seconds."

"I'd like to get eyes on this thing. Can you send me video?"

"My laptop," Jo suggested. "We can video conference."

"That'd work," Reese said. "Let me get into the briefing room for the big screen. I'll call Tom on the way. Meantime, you got your wire cutters in your go-bag?"

Wire cutters. Hell no he didn't have wire cutters. Dumbass that he was, he'd forgotten to restock his go-bag after his rookie scrounged through it and took his because *he* didn't have wire cutters.

Being met with silence was all Reese needed. "Seriously? You don't have them?"

What a completely stupid mistake. How many times had he berated his team for not being adequately prepared? Sure, people forgot things—gas masks, vests, a weapon— but for Gabe to do it? Unacceptable. Particularly now.

"On our last hit, my rookie didn't have his so I gave him mine. Then I jumped on a plane here and didn't have time." *Bullshit.* "I'll check with the owner."

Jo in an attempt to keep her body still, bugged out her eyes. "You can't. Martinson might be down there. You said he had to be close. They did something to Mrs. Jenkins or they wouldn't have her key."

Slowly, using controlled movements that wouldn't bump the chair, Gabe rose from the floor. "I'll be fine. They probably tied her up and one of them is somewhere close. Someone definitely saw me enter the hotel. The timer told us that much." He headed toward the door. "I'll be right back. Don't move. Not an inch."

"I'm trying, Gabe, but my legs are asleep."

He turned back, fought the urge to waste precious seconds by going back to her and...and...what? Offer comfort? The woman had a fucking bomb strapped to her leg. Comfort from him meant getting her free of said bomb. "I'll have you out of there soon. Do *not* move."

"Be careful. We don't know…"

Gabe didn't wait for her to finish. Time was literally ticking. He tore down the steps, .45 aimed and at the ready. At the bottom, he cleared the parlor, sticking close to the far wall as he made his way to Mrs. Jenkins's office at the end of the hallway. Closed door. He halted, listened. From behind the door came a muffled cry. *Alive.*

He shoved the door open. When a hail of bullets didn't fly at him, he peeked in and spotted Mrs. Jenkins gagged and tied to her desk chair. Surveying the room, he swept left to right. Nothing. *Go.* Gun raised he checked behind the door. Clear. Under the desk. *Go.* No Martinson. He re-holstered his weapon, went to work on Mrs. Jenkins's gag and the half-hitch knot keeping the woman hostage. "Are you hurt?"

"No."

"Good. They're gone. Do you have wire cutters?"

Mrs. Jenkins rolled her shoulders, rotated her hands to loosen the tight muscles. "I don't know. The tool box is in the shed out back."

Gabe worked the remaining ropes loose. "Show me. Fast. Jo has a bomb strapped to her."

"What?"

He grabbed the woman's elbow and helped her out of the chair. "No time to explain. Let's roll."

Four minutes were lost searching for the wire cutters, but they found them buried at the bottom of a rusty toolbox in the even rustier shed. In Gabe's estimation, that shed should have been condemned. And if he didn't get his ass moving, it might get blown to bits. "Stay out front. As far away from the building as you can get. If the sheriff or the bomb squad arrives, send them up. Everyone else stays out."

He hauled ass back upstairs, found Jo sitting, staring at

him with wild eyes that screamed of fear and panic. Like him, Jo always, without fail, wanted to do something, anything, to move an operation forward. Being bound was slowly destroying her.

"I'm back," Gabe said to Reese, who was hopefully still on speakerphone.

"Okay. Jo gave me her email address. I'm dialing you up for video conference now."

Jo's laptop sat on the desk and Gabe stood in front of it, waiting for the call to connect. "How do I work this thing?"

"The little phone icon will pop up, just click it."

Yep. Phone icon. He clicked it and Reese's red hair and freckled face appeared onscreen. Gabe squatted so he'd be at eye level with the computer. "Can you see me?"

"Yeah. Show me what you've got."

We're on. Moving fast, Gabe unplugged the laptop and dropped to the floor again.

"Hang on." Reese said. "Right there...Okay...move it to your left and up. I gotta see where the wires lead. Don't bump anything."

That's all he'd need and—*boom!*—they'd both get blown away.

"Who put this thing together?" Reese asked. "Amateur?"

"Not sure. We're chasing this Martinson guy. He's into trafficking counterfeit goods. Bombs are new. Why?"

"Because if he's an amateur, chances are the trip wire isn't spring-loaded. Amateurs don't know what the hell they're doing and won't mess with unintentionally releasing the spring-loaded pin. They're afraid they'll blow themselves to shit. Problem is, he could have concealed the spring inside the pipe."

Gabe didn't dare look at Jo. Not a chance. He lay on the floor, the muscles in his shoulders and neck coiling as that damned timer ticked down. Every muscle, every instinct honed from years of tactical maneuvers begged for action.

"Tick, tock, Reese."

"With this setup, I don't think it's spring-loaded. That's a guess though, bud."

Gabe wrapped his fingers around his forehead and squeezed, let the pressure build for a second while considering his options. "If it's not spring-loaded, all I need to do is cut the trip wire, right? That'll at least let me get her out of the chair."

"Yeah, but if there's a pin against the cap and it's spring-loaded, the pin will release and..."

"Ka-pow," Jo said.

The room went quiet and Gabe gave Jo his best hard stare. Commentary he didn't need. "Really?" he said to her.

"Pretty much," Reese said.

Before he lost his shit on both of them, Gabe checked the timer. Thirty-three minutes. *Crap.*

Not willing to waste any more time, he sat on the bed far enough from Jo that he wouldn't accidentally bump her. She liked her bad news like a good shot of whiskey. Fast and furious.

"Talk to me," she said.

He held his hand out, wanting that hand on her, massaging every inch, but he wouldn't risk it. Not now. If they reached critical mass, and he couldn't get her out of that chair, he'd do it, but they weren't there yet. "You know where we're at on this. If we get the cargo released, Martinson tells me how to deactivate this thing. If we don't release the cargo..."

"Do it," Jo said.

"What?"

"Cut the wire. It's not spring-loaded. Call it intuition, but I can feel it."

Gabe shook his head. "It's not just us. This whole building could go and it might take the buildings on either side. Who knows?"

Jo closed her eyes and sat for a few seconds. When she opened them, tears bullied their way free. Crying wasn't part of her repertoire and he could count on a couple of fingers how many times he'd seen her well up. Tough stock, his girl.

He ran his thumb under her eyes, wiped them dry for her. If this wasn't some kind of bullshit situation, he didn't know what was. At thirty-three years old, he finally finds a woman he wants to put in front of his folks to say, "Yes, she's the one we've been waiting for," and now they might both get blown away. Screw that. Neither one of them would die in this Podunk town. "I'll get you out of here."

"I want you to cut the wire. Just do it. We're wasting time."

Roger that. He got back on the floor. Now or never. "Reese, fuck it. Let's just do this and hope to hell the thing isn't spring-loaded."

"I'm guessing it's not. Especially if he's going to tell you how to deactivate it."

"What do I do?"

"Just snip the wire, dude."

That simple. Gabe squeezed the wire cutter handles a few times to get the feel of the motion. Light rust coated the blades, jerking the movement. *A few more tries.* He needed to do this in one smooth motion, no hesitation. *Got this.*

"Hey."

He glanced up and she mouthed, "I love you."

"Ditto," he said.

Slowly, he positioned the wire between the blades, hesitated long enough to throw out a prayer that might save both their asses, and squeezed.

He held his breath while the blades slid, connected with the wire—so far so good—and met resistance. *Damn it.* Energy whipped around him, charging the air, closing in. *Cut it.* One more squeeze would do it. Go time. *Let's roll.*

Snip.

Gabe waited, his pulse jackhammering, making him sweat. He checked the wire to be sure. Two ends lay on the floor. He dropped his head, rolled it around as the bunched muscles in his shoulders released.

"Did you do it?" Jo asked.

Sure did. "We're good."

"Yay for us. That seriously sucked."

Maybe it was the stress, maybe it was their combined caustic humor that most didn't understand, but he laughed. Couldn't help it. "You're still attached to the bomb." He checked the timer, thirty minutes. Crap. "Reese, where are we on getting the shipment released?"

"Tom's on it."

"Okay. Can I untie Jo from this chair?"

"Yeah, but be careful. No jerky movements. I don't know what that thing is made of."

Gabe's phone rang—Tom—and he propped the phone at his ear while he went to work on the ropes. "What's up?"

"The mayor is on with the Port Authority now."

The mayor? They were so fucked. They were supposed to be down here lending support to the sheriff and they'd gotten themselves into the middle of a PR nightmare.

"Hang on," Tom said and music suddenly came across the phone line.

Sure, boss. Got all the time in the world. Gabe managed to get Jo's hands loose while Barry Manilow sang in his ear. Could this get any worse? She kept her lower body still, but worked her fingers in and out. *Must be numb.*

"They'll do it," Tom said. "They're releasing it now. "They're putting an unmarked car on the truck so we don't lose it."

Thank you. "Roger that. But tell them if the driver spots a tail, we're fucked. Martinson said no tail or he blows this thing."

"I'll take care of it. What's Jo's status?"

"I just cut the trip wire. I'm getting her free and then I'll deal with the bomb."

"Go. Call me when she's safe."

Gabe dropped the phone and set his sights on the knots at Jo's ankles. Right foot first and then the one with the bomb. *I got this.*

The cell phone on the desk chirped. Martinson again. Jesus, he had three phones and a computer going while trying to get rid of a bomb. Gabe had always been a great multitasker but this might break him.

"That's him," Jo said. "The truck must be there."

An inch at a time, making sure not to jar the bomb, he rose from the floor and snatched the phone from the desk. "Gabe Townsend."

"Sergeant," Martinson said, his voice cool, unfazed. "My truck is at the Port Authority."

I will beat this fucker into the ground. A child's squeal sounded from Martinson's end. *Outside.* Gabe still believed he was somewhere close. Maybe the park adjacent to the square? He'd find him. Sooner or later, he'd find him. "They're releasing your shipment."

"Excellent. When the shipment has been released, I will call you."

"Hey, asshole, we don't have time for that. Down to twenty-one minutes."

"You'd better hope they move quickly."

Click. Fighting the urge to hurl the phone, Gabe used deliberate care to press end. *Gotta move.*

"Gabe?" Reese said.

"Yeah, we're here. About to get royally fucked by this guy." He squatted again, went to work on the last knot. "How do I diffuse the bomb?"

"With the time you have, you don't. You get it to an open area and let it blow."

An open area. *Think.* In his mind, he pictured the layout of the town, the stores lining Main Street, the small parking lot behind the hotel, the square—not enough room. No matter how he sliced it there was no room anywhere. Not for a bomb.

"That won't work. How about a Dumpster? Would it contain it?"

"Yeah, but the lid could fly off and decapitate someone. If you leave the lid off, the blast would go straight up."

"The pond," Gabe said.

He unwound the last knot on Jo's ankle and pulled the rope away from the bomb still secured to the chair leg by electrical tape. *She's free.* For a moment, he let the thought sink in. The two of them could run the hell out of here and just let the place blow. They'd be safe. They'd be free to go on with their lives, get married—if she'd have him—and have babies. They could do all that. Together.

Run fast, run hard, run long.

"There's a pond?" Reese asked.

Who was Gabe kidding? He couldn't walk away from this thing. Let it blow away half this block? Not if he could contain it.

Jo stood, shook out her legs. "In the square. Right across the street."

"How big?"

He rolled out his bottom lip, visualized the pond he'd walked by on his way back from Ellie's shop. "Roughly fifty-by-fifty-feet wide. Five or six-feet deep, I'd say."

"Dude, clear the area and throw that bitch in there."

NINE

"Seriously," Jo said, "that's the plan?"

Gabe and the bomb wizard had to be kidding. They were going to blow up a pond in the middle of town. The pond with that big, honking brass statue that would probably become a giant projectile and kill someone. Although, she supposed it was better than blowing up the hotel. And the surrounding businesses. *I cannot believe this.*

Gabe was still focused on the bomb and probably hadn't even heard her protest.

"Reese," he said, "the tape is only around the pipe. Can I pull it off? If not, the whole chair is going. I just don't want to bump anything along the way."

"Yeah, you're good. As long as there aren't any wires stuck to the tape, go for it."

To keep the chair still while Gabe pulled the tape, Jo set her hands on the seat and leaned in. "How much time?"

"Eleven minutes."

For the first time, she noticed the beads of sweat dripping down his face. He rolled his shoulder, trying to dry the moisture with his sleeve. Jo cupped her hand around one side of his face, held it there while she took in the tiny lines around his eyes and the bunched skin between his eyebrows. His look of concentration when working—one that was so much a part of this man she'd fallen in love with.

One who was about to risk his life by carrying a bomb across the street. She dragged her hand down both sides of his face and wiped the sweat on her slacks. She couldn't think about losing him. It had taken years of failed relationships to find him. They'd accomplished so much together, as co-workers *and* lovers, and she wasn't ready to let him go. Not now. Not ever. "You're doing great," she said. "Thank you."

He jerked his head toward the laptop on the floor, an obvious message that they still had Reese keeping them company. She didn't care. All the hiding, she didn't want it anymore. What that meant for the task force and their careers, she couldn't think about. Not now.

Gabe held the bomb in place with one hand and peeled back the last piece of tape with the other. "Got it. What now?"

"You have anything you can put it in to absorb some of the blast? Paint can, garbage can, anything?"

"Reese, minutes to dump this thing and you want me to do a scavenger hunt?"

"Hey, it's a thought."

Propped on his elbows, Gabe hesitated.

Jo bent low and touched his shoulder. "Should I look for something?"

"No. We don't have time. I'm going."

Give him room. She stood and held her hands out. "Let me hold that while you get up."

"I've got it."

"Come on, sergeant; what happens if you bump that

thing when you're getting up? Let me hold it for you. I'll stand here like a good little girl and won't move."

"She's right, Gabe. Let her hold it. Jo, whatever you do, don't drop it."

Cop humor. Terrific.

Jo snorted. "I'll do my best."

"I'll wait here," Reese said.

More cop humor. Later, she'd smack him. After she kissed him square on the mouth. She bent low, took the pipe from Gabe and held it by both ends. Tiny pricks ran the length of her arms, but she kept her hands still. *Don't move.* "I've got it."

Reese cleared his throat and Jo shot a look at the computer where he shifted around, his head looming on the screen. "Come back and give me an update. Jo, record the blast for me."

Now that was pushing it. They were about to blow up the town square and he wanted video? "Oh, my God! Are you serious?"

"Bet your ass I'm serious."

Gabe jumped to his feet, gently took the bomb from her. "Get the doors for me."

"Right." She lunged for the door and yanked it open. "I'll go down with you."

Their eyes connected for a small second as he strode to the door. "No. Just get the door downstairs. Stay here. I have no idea what the blast will bring. This thing could blow before I even get there."

And in that second, she thought about him once again marching toward a task most people wouldn't even consider. She thought about Reese sitting in front of his computer, listening to them, and as much as she didn't want to dwell on it, she thought about these being the last moments she'd spend with Gabe. A man she had an intense love for but had kept that love hidden for fear they'd be reprimanded by their bosses.

Suddenly, their jobs seemed so meaningless. She could lose him and no one would know what he meant to her. That she'd never survive the loss of him. That kind of love didn't deserve to be buried under office politics. She shifted back to the laptop where Reese sat, now leaning back, arms folded while he waited.

And then she turned back to Gabe who was almost out the door. "Gabe?"

"What?"

"I love you."

"Come on, Jo, don't do this to me." He kept walking, but shook his head, frustration obviously tearing at him. "You're a lunatic, but I love you too. Reese," he said, "you didn't hear that."

Jo followed him down the stairs, swung around him in the parlor and opened the front door. "Let me at least make sure there's no traffic. I can help clear the area."

And, as if on cue, the sheriff pulled into the empty parking space in front of the hotel. Gabe took his eyes off the bomb for a millisecond and glanced at the sheriff. "Priceless. Now he shows up."

"Sheriff," Jo yelled, "clear that square. Gabe is about to dump a bomb in your pond."

"Sweet Jesus, what are you talking about?"

The man was just told a bomb would be detonated in his town and he wanted the backstory? "We'll explain later. You should probably get your residents out of the area. It's an election year after all. You wouldn't want a bunch of bodies shooting through the air."

Gabe made a noise. Tried to hide a laugh by grunting, and she smiled. Another thing they shared, twisted humor.

Still, the comment earned her a sharp look from the sheriff. Well, she had that whole stress paralyzing her brain thing going on. And, anyway, her sarcasm motivated the good sheriff to start yelling at his citizens to evacuate.

Gabe slowly ventured down the porch steps. "Stay put, Jo. Don't step off this porch."

"Please, sergeant. Someone has to play crossing guard and stop traffic so you can get across the street."

"You're pissing me off. I don't want you out here."

As if that tactic had ever worked on her before? "Somehow I think you'll *forgive* me after I keep you from getting *flattened* by a *car* while you're *carrying a bomb*."

He drew deep breaths through his nose and out his mouth. "You are the most stubborn, frustrating woman I know. One way or another, you're gonna kill me."

"Love you too, honey."

Enough of this arguing. She marched into the street, held her arms wide and stopped the two cars cruising along. Pre-rush-hour traffic on Main Street.

Gabe passed her, alternating his gaze between the bomb and any impediments he might trip on. A woman walking in front of the hotel pushed a stroller into the street, clearly wanting to take advantage of the crossing guard. "No, no, no," Jo said. "Ma'am, you need to get out of this area. *Now*."

"Why?"

Why? *Um, because you're about to get blown up?* How was she supposed to answer? "Ma'am, please. We're working on a training exercise. The bomb squad is detonating a bomb in the pond."

"What? In the middle of the afternoon? Are they crazy?

We paid good money for that pond. And what about the statue?"

"The county is reimbursing the town."

Mark of a good lawyer. Fast on her feet.

"Well, in that case. It's a shame though. We just got that statue."

Jo sighed and waved the woman along before planting herself on the curb near the square. The sheriff would have to deal with the fallout of Jo's lie, but someone dying would be a lot harder to explain.

A second police cruiser screamed around the corner, lights flashing, and a young—really young—deputy screeched to a halt in the middle of the street.

"You'll need to barricade this street," Jo said.

"Ma'am, you need to move."

She patted her hand in the air, but she wasn't moving until Gabe got rid of that bomb and came back with his big, beautiful body intact. "I know, Deputy. I know."

In the square, the sheriff moved from bench to bench, clearing pedestrians. The last two were occupied, one by a couple, the second by a dark-haired man. Did they not see the sheriff shooing people? Or the giant man carrying a pipe bomb?

"People," she hollered. "You need to leave this area!"

The couple looked at her and she pointed at Gabe moving closer to them. Their heads slowly swiveled and stopped. Any second now it would sink in.

Any.

Second.

Now.

And they're off. The couple bolted off the bench and ran like hell. *Finally.* Staying behind was the dark-haired man, who apparently had a death wish and wanted to watch Gabe blow the town square to smithereens. Unbelievable. Jo took two steps and he turned, facing her dead on.

Him.

Her chest locked up, the pressure building and building until the squeeze in her ribcage cut off her air and her heart damn near burst.

Martinson fast walked to the opposite end of the square. *Nuh, nuh, nuh.* Another three feet and Gabe would be at the pond. That timer had to be close now. Could Martinson even get out of the square before it went off? If he did, they'd be left hunting him all over again.

She tore into the square, running harder than she had in a long time, the sound of her loafer heels smacking against the bricks. Her gaze bounced between Gabe and Martinson. *Get him, get him, get him.* Just as she reached the edge of the pond, Gabe swung his arm, sending the pipe sailing.

Not much time. *Don't get distracted.* Martinson cleared the opposite end of the square. Adrenaline kicked in, giving her an added push as her long legs devoured the space between her and Martinson. She'd never been a runner. Or any kind of an athlete for that matter, but this? Too much. This maniac had to pay.

Martinson glanced over his shoulder—catastrophic mistake. It slowed him down enough for her to get within a couple of feet.

"Jo," Gabe shouted from behind her. "Get out of—"

Boom!

Huge flumes of water shot straight in the air, the blast knocking her to the ground with enough force that her loafers flew off her feet. When the wave broke, the weight of it landed like bricks pounding her back, over and over, making her gasp. Crushing pain swept through her. She opened her mouth but only sucked more water. *Drowning. Help me.* After a long span of time that could have been a minute or five seconds, the water stopped. She lifted her head, opened her mouth again and gagged, her chest and stomach wrenching as the trapped water gushed from her throat.

Her ears clanged and she shook her head, took stock of the sudden pain in her elbow. She'd fallen on it. Didn't matter. One at a time, she waggled her feet, shifted her legs. All working. Nothing broken. Just the ringing. She scanned the space in front of her where Martinson lay, moving slowly but pushing himself to all fours. One of her shoes had landed beside him. Ferocious blast.

Get him. Jo lunged, one giant leap to her feet before he could get away and she dove on him.

"Crazy bitch!"

He rolled and she countered by shifting to the side, forcing him back down. Height-wise he only had an inch on her but he definitely outweighed her. Could probably pin her if she let him, which she wouldn't do because this jerk had humiliated her, made her look like a fool in front of the mayor of New York.

And he'd almost blown Gabe up.

You're so dead.

Martinson rolled again and knocked Jo off balance, her body half on him, half off. Her shoe, the Barelli loafer with the solid wood heel, lay inches away. She'd like to mash his skull with that heel. Just beat him senseless.

And why not? The man had terrorized her by locking her in a burning building *and* strapping a bomb to her.

She picked up the shoe, held it with the heel out and squeezed, let all her rage—the fire, the bomb, Gabe in danger—funnel into her hand. *Bastard.* She raised the shoe over her head, swung wide and the heel connected with a sickening *thunk* to the back of Martinson's head.

"Ow!" he hollered.

Ow? *Ow*. He had no idea the pain she'd cause. No idea. "You think this hurts? You could have killed us. Stupid bastard."

Bam! She smacked him again, and then again. "You're going to prison. I don't care how long it takes." *Bam!* "I love that man and you almost killed him."

Bam! Martinson lifted his hands to protect his head and she smacked the shoe against his knuckles. After what he'd put them through, she wanted him to feel pain, like fangs tearing at his skin, she wanted him to feel it. *Bam!* She hit him again.

A second later, an arm—Gabe's—came around her waist and she went airborne, kicking out but failing.

"Relax, Counselor."

Jo inhaled long and deep and an enormous pressure slammed against the back of her eyes. *I'm insane, right now.* Her vision blurred into hazy white lines and she exhaled, tried to focus on something, anything other than killing Martinson, now getting to his feet.

"He's going," she yelled.

Gabe set her down, reached across and grabbed Martinson by the shirt before shoving him to the ground and planting his knee in Martinson's back. "If you move I'll shoot you."

"Shoot him anyway," Jo muttered, breathing hard as the ringing in her ears clanged on. She stooped low and—*bam!*—whacked him again.

"Ow!"

"What the hell is wrong with you? Smuggling counterfeit merchandise is one thing, but you could have blown half this town away. Idiot." She smacked him on the non-bloody side of his head and he lifted his hands to shelter himself from another attack.

She may have looked like a lunatic clubbing him with a shoe, but by the blood seeping from the back of his head, she'd gotten her point across. Martinson, his hands still hovering, lowered his cheek to the ground.

"Okay," Gabe said. "Crazy blonde lady, you need to back off." He shooed her back. "Go on."

Seeing the hard look in his eyes, recognizing it as the one that happened right before his famous temper blew, she obliged. He wasn't fun when mad. A shout came from behind and she turned, taking in the destruction. Instead of gently swaying water, only a giant, muddy puddle remained. The edge of the pond, amazingly enough, remained mostly intact. Thankfully, the blast had been contained. The sheriff stood in the street, where the brass statue she'd admired had landed on his deputy's cruiser, the impact crushing the roof.

Holy moly, that was a sight.

Somehow, they'd managed to get through the explosion with no injuries. Her ears might ring for days, but she was alive.

And so was Gabe.

"Sheriff!" Gabe shouted "Handcuffs!"

They'd finally caught Martinson and didn't have anything to cuff him with. At some point she might find it funny. "Seriously? No handcuffs?"

"They're in my go-bag. I had a bomb in my hands and was busy saving your life. What was I supposed to do?"

Point there.

Under Gabe's knee, Martinson squirmed.

"Keep wiggling," Jo said, "and I've got another shoe begging for a crack at you."

Gabe grinned. So she was crazy. *Sue me.*

Across the expanse of the square, the sheriff got his mojo on and did some kind of quasi run-walk thing. Really, she didn't care. She just wanted a vision of Martinson in cuffs.

As he approached, the sheriff spotted Martinson's bloody and matted hair, halted and gave Gabe a heated look.

Oh, no. Jo wanted credit for this one. "He didn't touch him." She reached down, pulled her shoe off and waved it. "That was all me."

"Jo, stop talking. Now."

Said the hot sergeant to the lawyer. *This is a switch.* "No. He's not going to blame you for this."

The sheriff stared up at the sky and shook his head before signaling Gabe off their prisoner. "Let me cuff him."

Gabe rose to his feet, let the sheriff step in. "All yours."

She flapped her hand. "Sheriff, don't give that slippery bastard an inch of room."

Not appreciating her comment, Gabe shushed her. "Swear to god, if you hadn't just escaped death, I'd kill you."

What? "I'm just saying."

The sheriff grunted. "Both y'all need to pipe down."

Within seconds, the sheriff hauled Martinson to his feet, Mirandized him and glanced back at them, his face an array of interesting colors. "I should wrench y'all with a hosepipe."

Gabe's bottom lip curved out and he tilted his head as the sheriff pushed Martinson toward the street, where a crowd of rubberneckers gathered.

Hosepipe. What the heck? "What do you suppose he means by that?"

"How should I know? They speak a different fucking language down here. It's like being in a foreign country."

She stepped closer, linked her arm through his and snuggled in as she swept her gaze over the crater of mud where the pond had been just minutes ago. Slowly, the full force of what they'd done sunk in and the cold punch of a fist rammed her in the chest, trapping her air. She opened her mouth, rasped out a breath.

They'd almost failed. Almost lost it all.

Gabe freed his arm, slid his hand over her waist to her back and squeezed. "You okay?"

At the entrance to the square, the sheriff angled Martinson toward his car—the undamaged one. She watched him load his prisoner into the vehicle and for the first time, wondered if nabbing Martinson had been worth all they'd almost lost.

What's wrong with me?

Six weeks ago, she'd have risked anything to catch the elusive smuggler. Now? Looking at Gabe, hero that he was, the man that fit her better than Barelli loafers, she wasn't sure how far was too far.

Mr. August had ruined her.

"Jo?"

She nodded. "I'm good. I love you. That's all."

He dipped his head low and kissed her. Soon they'd go home and all this PDA would be tamped down, locked away again. Pity that. But they'd agreed to make changes. To go out more, take weekends outside of the city. Meet the folks.

Progress. Even if it was small.

Gabe pulled back from the kiss, ran his hand over her hair and gently tugged. "I love you too. Let's go home."

TEN

"You were damned lucky, that's all."

Tom was well into the ten-minute mark of a scathing lecture. Gabe and Jo sat in front of his desk, absorbing the reprimand like bad children in the principal's office. With the way Tom speared his index finger at them, that digit might require physical therapy when this was over.

Less than twenty-four hours ago, they'd captured Martinson, who was now caught in a dogfight between the states of New York and South Carolina over whose justice system would have the first crack at him.

For Gabe, it didn't matter. All he knew was Martinson, along with his assistant, Thelma, was behind bars, their huge shipment of counterfeit goods seized and their smuggling operation brought to a halt.

Not bad.

"It was my fault," Jo said.

Gabe shot her a look. With Tom, there were times to speak and times to shut the hell up. This would be one of the times to shut the hell up.

"Your fault?" Tom mocked.

Yep. Here we go.

"Well, Joanna—*Ms.* Pomeroy—I appreciate that, but let's analyze this. My sergeant, an appointed member of a mayoral task force, escorted you to South Carolina. The two of you were supposed to *assist* local law enforcement. I believe that was fairly clear."

Ouch. This getting reamed by the boss was starting to get old.

"Instead," Tom continued, "the two of you went off on your own, investigating, threatening witnesses, blowing up a town square, destroying police property and, for your final act, almost getting killed."

Maybe Gabe was too close to it, but threatening witnesses might have been extreme. But he sat still, tapping his fingers against his thighs, mentally willing Jo to go against her instincts and keep. Her trap. Shut.

"Tom—"

So much for mental will.

"Quiet!" Tom's eyes bulged and the veins at his temples throbbed, the greenish-blue tint coming through his skin.

Tom. Was. Pissed.

In his head, Gabe began counting. Nothing else to do. They just needed to get through this initial meltdown. The guy had one of those tempers that flared and raged and tore things up. Then he'd be done. Unfortunately for them, this tantrum had lasted longer than usual.

He ripped a file from his desk drawer, slapped it on the desk, the *thwack* filling the small office and making Jo flinch.

"And somehow," he said, "you managed to not completely screw this up."

Hell to the yeah on that one. They caught the guy.

Tom shifted to Jo. "Your guy Martinson isn't much for jail cells. Their closed-in nature makes him talk."

"Seriously?"

Of all the bad guys Gabe had encountered, Martinson ratting surprised him. And that was saying something. Not much shocked him anymore.

Tom nodded. "Martinson has a boss. In Los Angeles. He's running networks in every major port in the U.S. He had a guy on the inside at the Port Authority who told Martinson the shipment had been seized."

Gabe whistled. He'd love to know who that son of a bitch was. And who the leak in Tom's circle was. For now, Gabe would sit on that one. No sense going there when his boss was already fired up.

Tom glared at him, one of those icy stares that severed limbs. He went back to Jo. "You, Ms. Pomeroy, in a completely back-assed way, have achieved your goal of expanding the task force. You're about to help the mayor of Los Angeles duplicate Clean Sweep."

Well, shit. Suddenly unconcerned about his boss's reaction, Gabe looked at Jo, studied her profile. She slid him a sideways glance, but beyond that, he couldn't read her. Although he was damned sure her mind was laying down some serious rubber.

She swallowed once, then a second time. "L.A.?"

"Yes. At 9:00 a.m. tomorrow, the three of us are meeting with Bev and the mayor. Right after, we'll have a video conference with the mayor of Los Angeles. I'm assuming you're available."

Now she turned to Gabe, her mouth slightly agape. Tom had silenced the mighty Jo Pomeroy.

"Hey," Gabe said. "It's the start of what you wanted."

Part of him was proud of her. More than anyone, she

deserved credit. She'd spent countless hours making this happen. The other part of him hated it. Los Angeles wasn't a hop-skip. And forming the Clean Sweep task force had taken months of planning before they'd rolled it out. Would she leave New York for months?

And if so, would they survive a bicoastal relationship? A sick feeling gripped him, made his shoulders ache.

Jo's eyes were on him, holding his stare—questioning. *She's not sure.* And that, he knew, was his fault. Two months ago, she would have pissed herself over this. Now? Now she had guilt because he loved her and was a selfish prick who wanted her in New York. With him.

Tom sat back in his chair, the springs shouting from the strain. "9:00 a.m. tomorrow, people. We're clear?"

"Yes, sir."

"Of course," Jo said. "I'll be there."

They filed out of Tom's office, Jo in front of him. In the hallway she stopped and two patrol officers angled around her. Gabe kept moving. *Not in here.* "I'll walk you out."

Keeping his gaze on her, he slid her coat from her arm and held it while she maneuvered her briefcase and put the coat on.

On the sidewalk, the biting cold caught him up short. *No jacket, dummy.* His balls would turn to ice, but some things were more important. He veered away from the building to the corner where they'd find a cab.

"Gabe?"

"Jo, it's good. You've worked for this and I'm proud of you. The rest of it we'll figure out."

"I'll have to go to L.A. You know that."

"Yeah, I know."

"It won't be forever."

"I know that too."

He stopped walking and faced her, blocking her path to the corner so he'd have her full attention. "Whatever needs to happen, we'll make it happen. We'll be bicoastal if we have to."

"With your schedule, how would we do that?"

"I don't know, but we'll figure it out."

"I could say no. If you asked me to, I would. I'd walk away."

And didn't that slay him. *Say no.* It'd be easy. Just to tell her he wanted her here with him. Something deep in his gut twisted. From the day he'd met her, she talked about a nationwide initiative against counterfeiting. And he wanted to take it away from her. Selfish prick.

Resisting the urge to touch her because someone inside the building would see them, he folded his arms, pressed his fingers into his biceps trying to draw heat. "You need to do this. It's the start of everything you want. As much as I want to tell you not to go, that I'll miss you and worry about you, I'm not doing it. I'm not taking on that responsibility. I love you and this is your dream."

Finally, she smiled at him. "You're a good man, Gabe Townsend."

"Don't spread that shit around."

Jo waggled her eyebrows. "If I get lonely out there we can send each other dirty pictures."

"Uh, not happening. Just don't go getting busy with some other task force guy. That'll piss me off."

"Not a chance."

A gust of wind ripped into his bare arms and he hunched against the cold. "Besides, I'm sitting on three weeks' vacation. California in January sounds pretty good. Are you in?"

She grinned up at him. "Oh, I'm in, Mr. August. I'm in."

THE CAPTURE

THE JUSTIFIABLE CAUSE SERIES

Sun, fun, and Jo Pomeroy, the sexiest, most-driven attorney around, await
NYPD Sergeant Gabe Townsend in Los Angeles. A trip to the West Coast
is the perfect vacation—he won't have to hide his relationship with Jo from
the New York anti-counterfeiting task force, and he can finally enjoy some
overdue time-off with the woman of his dreams.

Jo makes undercover deals for fake merchandise, but her feelings for Gabe
are all too real. Unfortunately, she isn't the one on vacation, and while she
can't wait to get her heartthrob alone, she also can't say no when the
mayor of Los Angeles asks for her help in ridding the city of illegal
knockoffs.

Being too dedicated for her own good backfires when Jo ends up on a
killer's hit list. Gabe wants Jo to back down; she's not about to. As the
danger escalates, so do their feelings for each other. All Jo's ever wanted is
to expand her task force nationwide. Now, with her life on the line, Jo must
decide if heading the taskforce is worth sacrificing it all, including a future
with the man she loves.

"How much for the shoes?"

Jo eyeballed the clerk standing behind the glass counter in yet another crappy store selling counterfeit goods in Los Angeles's Fashion District. How many of these stores had she been in over the past couple of years? And how many of them had she confiscated merchandise from?

Merchandise Jo's high-end clients wanted off the streets because it took money from their bottom line and—oh, right—was a trademark violation. By now, her purchasing the goods and turning them over to the PD had become routine. At one time, the chase, the intrigue, and the occasional danger in her effort to see justice done had lit her fire.

Now? Eh. The endless stream of bogus items exhausted her, left her feeling she'd never get ahead of it.

Giving up wasn't an option though. So she stood in front of the display case containing earrings, wallets, key chains, and every other small counterfeit item she could imagine. Behind her, another case was stuffed with more knockoffs and Jo seethed, the tension shooting straight up her back to the base of her skull. At least those items didn't have her clients' logos on them. Even the shelves lining the walls in the long, narrow building were full. This merchant was making a small fortune selling knockoffs.

So far, she hadn't spotted any Barellis, but those shoes were definitely Dansens, a client Jo had signed just before coming to California. A client she wanted very badly to make happy. Which the middle-aged, dark-haired woman in front of her might involuntarily help with by selling Jo this crummy pair of shoes.

"Sixty," the woman said. "All the shoes are sixty."

Kudos to the sales clerk—obviously a negotiating pro— for making Jo wait for an answer on the price of the shoes, but what she didn't know was Jo excelled at waiting out her opponent. In the world of cut-throat negotiations, the first to flinch lost. In this case, Jo didn't care if she lost. She *needed* to lose. Needed to tuck those knockoffs in with the rest of her stash collected over the last two hours, all of it evidence of the illegal selling of counterfeit merchandise within LA's Fashion District, and take them to Lieutenant Wes Palermo of the Los Angeles Police Department.

The bells on the front door jangled and Jo glanced over her right shoulder. A big, beefy man with a long beard and stringy, long hair lumbered through, carrying a large box with a familiar cigarette logo on the front. The box may or may not have contained cigarettes. Cigarettes that may or may not have been counterfeit. No way to know without seeing them. But, while here, she'd ridden shotgun on multiple S.W.A.T. activations—raids—that procured over two-hundred-thousand dollars' worth of knockoff cigarettes. She'd reported this to Sergeant Gabe Townsend, aka, Mr. August, aka her current squeeze, back in New York, letting him know that Operation Clean Sweep, the task force Jo helped create, needed to pay more attention to cigarette sales.

But that had to wait until she got back home in two weeks.

For now, she needed to concentrate on Los Angeles and helping them get their own version of Clean Sweep organized. Which included standing in this store, haggling over cheap shoes while this beefy guy, more soft than hard around the middle and wearing a leather biker-gang vest adorned with patches, gave her the once-over. She'd been in Los Angeles long enough to know that when a man wore those patches, more often than not, it meant something. Something not good.

Something criminal.

Slowly, not wanting to show fear or interest in this man, she pulled her gaze away. Gabe would have a fit if he knew she was even in the place, doing the exact thing he'd asked her a hundred—maybe two hundred—times not to. But LA was different. The vendors here didn't know her, and unlike in New York, wouldn't consider her a threat.

At least not yet.

Two feet from her, the biker swung a right, leaving his body odor in his wake—bathe much?—as he headed down the hallway behind the sales counter. The name on the back of his vest read 12th Street Crew, and although Jo didn't know a lot about that particular gang, she'd heard enough to know they were bad news.

The tension in her neck barked and Jo tapped her fingers against the glass case. Whatever the biker guy was doing, she didn't want any part of it. She'd simply procure her evidence and get out.

She puckered her lips, tapped the case again. "I'll give you fifty."

The woman turned, pretending to study the shoes that her boss had probably paid three dollars for. In the world of high-end fashion, those shoes would go for twenty times what Jo offered.

"Fifty-five," the woman said.

For crying out loud. Really? *Whatever.* "Fine. Fifty-five."

As long as it got her out of here with her evidence, she didn't give a rip. Jo dug exactly fifty-five dollars from her wallet and handed the cash over.

"Great," the woman said. "If you like them, come back on Tuesday. We get new shipments every Tuesday and Friday."

Wasn't that handy information? "I sure will," Jo said.

Only next time, she'd be accompanied by a team of hot S.W.A.T. guys who would shut down this illegal enterprise *and* make Jo a rock star to her clients.

Win.

Win.

The woman scooped the bills off the counter. "I'll get you a fresh pair of shoes from the back."

A fresh pair? Gee. Thanks. But losing the sales clerk to the back room would delay Jo's departure, and she couldn't have that with Gabe's plane landing in an hour.

Although, she could surreptitiously watch where the woman went and pass the info on to Palermo for when they took the place down. Jo wandered to the end of the display case, faux-enthralled with a pair of gaudy gold earrings. Quickly, she peeked around the doorway into the long corridor with peeling wallpaper. The woman disappeared through another door and voices erupted, filling the narrow hallway with angry yelling. Two men. And the woman. Jo checked her phone. 3:31. *Darn it.*

On a good day, assuming she didn't get lost, an airport

run from here took a good thirty-five minutes. Forget about if she hit the insanity known as LA traffic. And one thing Jo didn't want after almost three weeks of waking up in a cold bed that had a definite lack of Mr. August's hotness was to be late picking him up. Being late because of one of her shopping excursions that he despised so much would certainly fire that temper.

Seconds later the woman re-emerged, but angled back to flip someone off—aww, just like home—before tromping back to Jo.

But the yelling continued in the back room, getting louder even through the closed door and that snicking tension on the back of Jo's neck went full blown. *Get out. Now.*

Jo waggled her fingers as the woman tried to shove the shoe box into a half-inch too small bag. "I don't need a bag. Thanks."

The woman shrugged, set the bag down, and handed over the shoes. "How about some jewelry? Fifty percent off since you bought the shoes."

Any other time, she might have jumped on that. But the yelling continued with someone dropping an f-bomb along with a few other choice words that would make the S.W.A.T. guys envious, and every alarm bell Jo possessed urged her to get out. Whatever this was, she wanted no part of it. She tucked the shoes under her arm.

"No. Thanks. I need to get going."

"Come back and see us again. Don't forget. New merchandise on Tuesday."

Excellent. "I guess I'll see you Tuesday then."

—:—

Gabe stood at the luggage carousel between two women, alternately scanning for his bag then checking his surroundings for Jo. The place was a madhouse—people everywhere bumping each other, jockeying for a better spot at the belt cranking out bags, and limo guys holding signs. He breathed in and counted to three after the short guy behind him shoved through. All the way on the other coast and somehow it all seemed similar. If Gabe weren't on vacation, he'd let this prick know to be a little more courteous. Instead, he locked his shoulders back and cracked his neck.

Vacation.

With Jo.

Finally.

The douche-bag—make that double-douche bag—who'd just pushed through hefted his luggage off the belt, nearly hit the older woman standing beside him.

Now I'm done. This guy was bigger than a douche-bag. What Gabe had here was a douche canoe.

"Dude," Gabe said. "Take it easy. You almost took that woman out."

The guy swung back, clearly about to mouth off and came face-to-face with Gabe's chest. Gabe kept his gaze glued to the top of the guy's head. Slowly, that head inched up. Up, up, up—*hello, douche bag*—until he finally made eye contact.

"Uh, sorry," the douche canoe said.

Vacation. Barely on the ground thirty minutes and he didn't need to be losing his shit on someone. Gabe side-stepped, jerked his head for the guy to move on. Which he did. Without speaking. *Thank you.*

The brunette next to the older woman eyed him with that *I'm interested* look. Being male, he appreciated her full lips and killer body, and a few months ago, he'd have been happy to oblige her in some recreational activity of her choice. Right now, he had a thing for a loud-mouthed, blond attorney who made him howl like a wolf separated from his pack, and although beautiful, the brunette didn't stack up. Not even close.

Gabe had come to believe no female in his lifetime would compare to Jo. Which meant things were getting serious. Plunge-worthy serious.

Speaking of the loud-mouthed blonde, she'd texted him ten minutes earlier from the wrong airport garage and it made her a few minutes late. No shock there. Plus, as much as he adored her, respected her intelligence and her determination to get shit done, her driving sucked. Good thing she took mass transportation everywhere in New York or he'd never get any sleep from worrying about her.

He nodded at the brunette, friendly, but not enough that she'd think getting busy was an option, and shifted to the luggage belt that finally spit out his bag. He grabbed hold of it, wheeling it to the doors that would lead him to the perfection—at least from the perspective of a guy who'd left thirty-five degrees in New York—of LA's March sun. The winter had been a bitch-and-a-half and being an ESU—New York's version of S.W.A.T.—sergeant meant dealing with all kinds of nonsense in freezing temps, snow, and ice. Yep, all he wanted on this trip was Jo, mostly naked, and some sun and quiet time to explore a city he'd never been to. Hell, maybe he'd even take the bus tour. Why not?

People whizzed by him, heading out to grab taxis or rides and he pulled his phone to see if Jo had texted again. From behind him, someone—he knew who—slid her arms around him and her scent, the light, musky soap she'd taken to recently, instantly sparked that crazy feeling. The killer combo of lust and protectiveness and power he always got around her. Describing it had become a useless endeavor since he'd never experienced it before. But pretty much, with Jo, everything just felt like home. And he liked it.

"Hello, Mr. August," she said in her playful sex-line operator voice. "I've missed you."

He studied her hands sliding over his shirt, across his belly, those long, elegant fingers as perfect as ever and he smiled because, yeah, even in an airport with a fucking bazillion people around, his mind went straight to the gutter.

She kissed the back of his shoulder then pressed her forehead against the spot. "God, it's good to see you."

Still in her arms, he turned sideways, brought her in for a hug and buried his face in her hair, lingering there a few seconds. *Home.* "I missed you, too. Crazy missed you."

Then he kissed her, dragging her close so she'd know just how much. She let out a soft moan and his body, as usual, responded. A man could only take so much, as evidenced by his growing chubby, and they both laughed. One thing they never had issues with was a lack of sex.

She nipped at his bottom lip, then backed away. "This might have been the longest three weeks of my life."

"I hear ya, babe. It's not the same without you. Even my guys are asking when you'll be back."

As the force behind Operation Clean Sweep, the team responsible for clearing millions of dollars in counterfeit merchandise off the streets of New York, the men in Gabe's unit had gotten used to Jo and her sassiness. She'd badgered the mayor relentlessly until he finally gave in and dedicated a team to battling trademark infringement in the city. Gabe's boss had once told him the mayor had gotten so beaten down by her constant attention he gave her a task force to shut her up.

In an odd way, Gabe understood. When Jo got her mind wrapped around something, she did whatever necessary to make it happen, including helping the mayor of Los Angeles replicate what they'd done in New York. As much as he hated her being around a bunch of horny S.W.A.T. guys on the other side of the country, her dream was to form a nationwide task force and getting the city of Los Angeles on board with that initiative would only help her.

"It's past your dinner time," she said. "Are you hungry?"

Oh, he was hungry. For many things. "I am." He nuzzled her neck again. "If you're done for the day, I'm thinking room service. You can get naked and feed me."

"Ha. That'll be the day."

"You won't get naked?"

"I'll get naked, but I'm not feeding you." She stopped, went on her tiptoes, and got right next to his ear. "Unless you're licking something off of me."

And the chubby became more painful, pressing against his jeans and making his eyes cross. "Careful what you wish for, Counselor. I'm a man who hasn't gotten laid in three weeks."

"Well, Sergeant, I'm a woman who hasn't gotten laid in three weeks. I guess we're eating in tonight."

"We sure are." He pulled her closer and kissed the top of her head. "Damn, I missed you."

"It's crazy, isn't it? We've spent so much time together this past year and then all of a sudden nothing. I hate that."

They reached a door and Jo pointed. "We're going this way."

"Okay." He held the door open and watched her step through. "So, you're not staying in LA?"

And how pathetic was he? She'd been gone a few weeks

and suddenly he's some pansy, wondering if his girl was going to dump him and switch coasts.

"Heck, no." She stopped, turned to him and gripped his T-shirt in her fist. "Are you seriously worried about that?"

Apparently so. *Pansy.* He shrugged. "If you like it out here, what's to stop you from moving?"

"Um, you?"

He shook his head. "But that's what I don't want because one day you'll look at me and wonder if you should have gone."

Jo gawked, her jaw literally flopping open. "Listen up, Sergeant. LA is nice, but it's not New York. Everything I love is in New York. That includes you. It's fun to visit and help with this new project, but I should be wrapped up here in a couple of weeks and I'm heading home. I might even fly back with you when you go."

Well, all right then. She'd pretty much made her intentions clear and his newly appointed pansy status gave him permission to feel no small amount of relief. The truth of it was he'd spent the last weeks prowling around New York in a pissy mood, screaming at his subordinates, and as much as it surprised him, he knew, without a doubt, the lack of Jo Pomeroy was the cause. He just wasn't sure how to control it.

Aside from dragging her back to New York.

"Sounds good to me," he said. "Now take me back to your hotel and make me howl."

—:—

Jo's phone rang, the obnoxious *bling, bling, bling* of her law partner's ringtone destroying the quiet inside the hotel suite.

Not now. Please.

Go away, go away, go away.

Underneath her and groaning, Gabe opened his eyes and gripped her hips in his giant hands. "Answer it and I'll kill you."

She smiled down at him, as usual, loving the view of a naked Mr. August after they'd just finished one of their mad dashes to make love. At times, their lovemaking was slow and exquisite. At other times, well, they needed what they needed, and after weeks away from each other, this was one of those times. "I won't answer it. That's a promise."

"Thank you."

Twenty floors below, a siren wailed, reminding her they were in the city, just not their city. Which was fine too. As long as she had Gabe close, it didn't matter where they were. At least until a knock on the door mixed with the siren, and Gabe's eyes lit up. Dinner had arrived and he was starved.

She slid off of him, and in one fluid move, he got to his feet, his big body showing that odd lumbering grace only a man possessing immense self-confidence managed to pull off.

Mr. August.

So hot.

From his suitcase, he grabbed a pair of shorts and a mismatched T-shirt off the top of the stack and slipped them on.

"I'll wait in the bathroom," Jo said.

No sense letting the room service waiter see her lounging in bed. Naked.

Gabe waggled his eyebrows. "That was a helluva way to kill time while waiting for dinner."

On her way to the bathroom, she dug through her suitcase for her silk robe and toiletry bag so she could put a brush through her hair and tie it back. Might as well get comfy. Without a doubt, they'd be hopping back into bed after they fueled up. A pleasant thought any day.

Two minutes later, Gabe rapped on the door. "You're good. Let's eat."

Which they did. Heartily. Halfway through the meal, Gabe waved his fork at her. "Let's talk about this room. I know the L.A.P.D. doesn't have digs like this in the budget. What gives?"

When she'd switched rooms, she'd anticipated this, and like any good lawyer would, prepped for it. As an attorney, Jo's salary was triple what Gabe made as a police officer. It had come up when she bought him clothes or refused to take money from him for picking up takeout. The salary issue, although not often verbalized, bugged him. What he couldn't get through that stubborn skull was that he took care of her in the most important ways. He loved her and protected her. Physically *and* emotionally. But being a proud man, he didn't like her spending her money on him.

And upgrading to a suite wouldn't fly.

She'd play it off though, totally nonchalant. Even if he didn't like it, she wasn't moving. Gabe would have to adjust to her wanting to pamper him a little bit. "Nothing gives. I upgraded us. The room I had was the size of a closet. I barely fit in it myself. The small mountain known as Gabe certainly wouldn't." Mirroring him, she waved her fork. "And I'm not arguing about this."

He eyed her and she set her fork down, readying for battle. This time, she didn't care. He worked hard and deserved a nice room for his vacation. As much as he'd complain about her spending the money to upgrade, she'd known he wouldn't be comfortable in the smaller room. Not for two weeks. She wanted her hardworking man to enjoy this break.

"I'm not arguing either. That being said, I don't want you spending your money on me. You didn't have to do this for me."

"I didn't do it for you. I did it for us. This is your vacation, one you told me you hadn't taken in a while. I wanted it to be special. For us to have extra room. To snuggle on a couch or eat a meal at a table. Or soak in that giant whirlpool tub in there. We wouldn't have been able to do any of those things in that shoebox of a room I had."

"Then I'll help you pay the difference."

Oh, whatever. "Okay, Sergeant. You can help me pay the difference."

Not that she'd take money from him, but he didn't need to know that.

He laughed. "You are so full of shit. I know you and you're gonna be a pain in the ass about this."

Holding back a laugh, Jo twisted her lips. "A pain in the ass? I'm insulted."

"No you're not."

He stood, walked over to her, propped one hand on the table and one on the back of her chair then he kissed her. Whammo. Just laid a scorcher on her—tongue and all—and Jo curled her toes.

Whew. Mr. August. So hot. If only she had a fan.

He backed away, taking those amazing lips with him and the agony of that might just kill her. "Leaving so soon?"

"Only for a minute. Thanks for taking care of me all the time."

She gripped his T-shirt, scrunching it in her hand. "Ditto, big boy. I know you hate when I spend money, but I can afford it and I love you. Why shouldn't I splurge on you?"

"Maybe because I don't want to be the guy whose girlfriend supports him."

As if. "You're not. And you never will be. You just happen to be a civil servant where I work in the private sector. That's all. Now shut up and go soak in the whirlpool before I have my way with you. *Again*." She let go of his shirt, cracked a smile, and gave him a light shove. "I swear my work is never done."

"Yes, ma'am. I gotta admit I saw that tub and my beat-to-shit body damn near groaned. You should come in with me."

And that fan was where? "I will." She glanced at the clock on the table. Almost time for the news. "We've been watching a storefront all week that we identified as selling knockoffs. S.W.A.T. was supposed to hit it this afternoon and I'm hoping it made the news."

Gabe nodded. "What's the latest on this guy?"

The guy Gabe referred to, one Andre Theo, was the leader of a smuggling ring responsible for flooding the West Coast with billions in counterfeit goods. Goods that bore the name of some of Jo's clients. Months of work on the East Coast had resulted in the arrest of Donald Martinson, Theo's number-two guy, who'd squealed the minute hand-cuffs hit his wrists. Andre Theo had been arrested, his ware-house seized, his accounts frozen, and now the smuggler awaited trial while out on bail. But Jo knew he still operated his illegal business by flying just under the radar. If nothing else, the man had an astonishingly large set of balls. She'd give him credit for that much, but she wanted to catch him, once again, and secure a nice long prison sentence for trade-mark violation.

She'd get it done. No doubt about that. *Look out, Andre Theo.*

"We're getting there," she told Gabe. "Cigarettes are huge

out here. I think we need to really focus on that when we get home. I've been so dialed in to finding knockoffs of my own clients' items, I haven't been looking at the big picture."

"Well, yeah, but your clients are paying the bills."

Which couldn't have been a truer statement. When Jo had finally convinced—er, badgered—the mayor of New York into starting the Clean Sweep Task Force, part of the agreement was her clients would help pay the massive cost of the operation. If she wanted to expand into cigarettes, she'd have to get one of the tobacco companies to pony up.

"I know. As soon as we get back, I'll get on it. This problem is massive. Manufacturers lose billions!"

Gabe held up his hands. "Whoa, Counselor. I'm on your side, remember? When we get back, let's talk to the mayor about it. If your clients are footing the bill, he's not gonna care what products we go after. All he cares about are his morning press conferences when he tells the city how great he is at cracking down on criminal activity. No matter what form it takes."

He smacked a hard kiss on her lips. "Now, I'm gonna soak in that badass tub you got me. Make sure you come in after you watch the news. I'll make you happy."

"You always do, Sergeant. You always do."

She flipped the television to the local news channel and sat back, propping her feet on the ottoman while she watched.

The blonde—was everyone blond in LA?—stared straight into the camera, her face completely neutral as she gave an update on a shooting in the Fashion District.

Jo sat up. The Fashion District. Wow. She grabbed the remote and tapped the volume button as the anchor went to an on-scene reporter standing in front of a store. Jo's gaze zoomed in on the bright-red store logo and—*holy, holy God.*

She gasped, holding her breath until the pressure built behind her eyes.

She watched the blonde's mouth moving, but...what was she saying? The words sounded distorted, slow motion maybe, and Jo shook her head and took another breath.

"The shooting," the blonde said, "occurred at approximately 3:40 this afternoon. At the time, the only ones in the store were the owner, Maurice Cummings, and an unnamed female employee. Mr. Cummings and the woman were pronounced dead at the scene. According to police, pedestrians in front of the store heard gunshots, but the assailant appears to have fled through the rear door of the building into the alley. So far, no witnesses have come forward."

The anchor took the reins again, leading into another story and Jo collapsed back in her chair, paralyzed for a few seconds, her body buzzing.

Dear God.

Gabe. She scrambled from the chair, running to the bathroom, her bare feet sinking into the thick carpet until she reached the doorway. Gabe sat in the giant tub, unbelievably dwarfing it, his head back against the wall, eyes closed. This might be the most relaxed she'd ever seen him. The man worked harder than anyone she knew. The atrocities he saw on a daily basis were enough to drive the sanest of people to an asylum. But he did it. Every day. Sometimes for sixteen hours a day. This was supposed to be his vacation, one he hadn't had in years.

And she was about to ruin it.

"Gabe?"

He lifted his head and gave her that shark grin she loved so much. "Make my night and tell me you're coming in. We can do fun things in this tub."

"I think I witnessed a murder."

Of all the fucked-up things Jo had ever said to him, and there'd been plenty, this was tops on the list.

Gabe sat up, stared right into those blue eyes of hers and saw something he'd only seen once, maybe twice before. Gone was the usual intensity and the fixed focus, the single-minded stubbornness that sometimes fired his temper and caused one hell of a fight. Right now, he didn't see any of that. What he had here were wide, spooked eyes that screamed of fear.

Jo. Afraid. What. The. Fuck?

He reached behind him, grabbed the towel from the rack and stood. "What are you saying?"

Jo flapped her hands, paced back-and-forth, which—hell, no—he'd never seen this hand-flapping-pacing thing either. Never. His girl was coming unglued.

He toweled off enough to stop dripping and stepped out of the tub, securing the towel at his waist. Grabbing hold of her, he pulled her into a hug. "Babe, slow down. I can't help you if you don't talk to me. Take a deep breath and tell me what happened."

She rested her forehead against his chest and sucked in a huge breath. "Before I came to pick you up, the S.W.A.T. guys were on a call so I had time to kill."

And, goddamnit, he knew what this was. Every time she was bored, no matter how much he begged her not to, she went shopping for knockoffs. *Don't yell, don't yell, don't yell.* He ground his teeth together, locked 'em tight before he lost it on her. That wouldn't help. Considering her current state of whatever the hell this was.

She turned her head, rested her cheek against him, and nuzzled into his neck. "Don't freak out. I have a job to do."

Yep. Shopping for knockoffs. Probably alone. *Focus here, guy.* "I know that. Just tell me what happened."

"I can't believe you're not yelling."

Ha. It was still early in the conversation. Anything remained possible. "If you don't start talking, I will be. Spill it."

She marched out of the bathroom, flipped open the suitcase he'd set on the luggage rack and rifled through it. When Jo got nervous, she stayed active. Right now, active meant digging clothes out for him. Whatever. As long as he got the whole story, she could dress him in a butler uniform.

"I went into a store," she said, "in the Fashion District. There's a ton of knockoffs being sold there, Gabe. It's really crazy. As bad as when we first started in New York. Tons of opportunities."

He closed his eyes, concentrated on staying calm. *Calm, calm, calm.* "Jo."

She gave up on tearing apart his suitcase and tossed her hands up. "Okay, I'm sorry. I went into a few stores, but the last one—" She stopped. Put her hands over her face, burst into tears, and dropped onto the bed. "Oh, my God," she shrieked, "it was on the news!"

And, holy, holy shit. This kind of panic from a woman who chased down bad guys and beat on them with her shoes didn't compute. Not at all. Mission critical. Handling this in a towel would suck the motherlode, so he snatched up the first pair of boxer briefs and shorts from the suitcase and slid them on. He squatted in front of her, ran his hands under her silky robe and over her bare thighs. Ice cold. Yet another first. "Just tell me. You'll feel better once you get it out and we'll deal with it." He pulled her hands away from her face and ran his thumbs over her wet cheeks. His chest hurt. A plunging pain that went right through him because Jo, strong, solid, fearless Jo, had one hell of a freak-out going. "Whatever it is, we'll deal with it."

She nodded, drew three deep breaths and let the last one out in slow bursts. "I was in the store. I was the only customer."

Shit.

"And someone else came in. A biker guy. The biker guys are big out here."

They sure were. And the sons of bitches were mean. Violent too. "How do you know he was a biker?"

She patted his chest just over his heart. "Patches. He had on a leather vest with patches. And the back had a rocker. You know that patch on the back in the shape of an arch?"

"I know. Go on."

"It said 12th Street Crew. He creeped me out a little bit. You know, typical jerk, checking me out. Staring at my ass, that kind of thing."

Now Gabe was the one breathing deep, keeping his temper in check. Men noticed Jo. Simple fact. Kinda hard not to with the long legs and the great rack and a face so perfect he figured some angel dropped it straight outta heaven. Most of the time, he didn't worry about it. Men were men. They looked. Lately though, he'd gotten territorial and the more men looked, the more it pissed him off.

"Did he say anything?"

"No. He walked to the back of the store. A few minutes later, I heard arguing."

"From the back?"

"Yes."

"I'd just bought a pair of shoes and the woman helping me—" She sucked in another breath, slammed the heels of her hands into her eyes. "Oh, my God. I was irritated because she was taking so long."

He squeezed her legs, gently, but enough to get her attention. "Jo, you gotta focus here. Tell me what happened."

And, cripes, she grabbed his hands in a grip tight enough to crack a few digits. *Ow.* "Okay, tiger. Try not to break my fingers."

"Sorry." She let go of him, shook her hands out and started talking again. "She went into the back room to get me another pair of shoes. A fresh pair. And they were all still yelling."

"The woman too?"

"Yes. I was impatient because I knew you were landing soon and I didn't want to be late. But she came back out and I got the weirdest feeling."

Now this was a serious problem. As much as he fucking hoped for it, begged for it, because maybe, just maybe, if some internal sensor went off inside her, she'd hightail it out of whatever situation had spooked her. No matter how much he hoped and prayed and begged, Jo never got weird feelings. Her instincts went the other way. The way that told her to charge in and not worry about the bad shit that could happen. "What feeling?"

"Like something wasn't right. I knew it and wanted to get out of there. Before that biker guy had walked in, I didn't feel it. It was him. He had rotten energy."

"And then what?"

"That's it. The clerk gave me the bag and I left. That was right after I checked the time. So maybe 3:32 or 3:33. I got out of there fast, cut across the street, walked down the next block and got to my car in probably less than five minutes."

Okay. Now, she'd just told him she'd left the store without incident. Maybe his S.W.A.T. brain had already slowed to vacation mode, but he wasn't seeing where she'd witnessed a murder. "And then you came right to the airport?"

"Yes."

Welcome to confusion land. Please stay seated until the captain turns off the seatbelt sign. He held his hands up. "Uh, where was the murder?"

"I didn't actually see it."

Can we say twisted? He cocked his head. "Seriously, babe, are you on something?"

"What? No!" She flapped her arms. "You ass! I just saw on the news that a woman and a man were murdered in a store in the Fashion District. At 3:40 this afternoon."

Ah, shit. He sat back on his heels, dropped his chin to his chest and cracked his neck. "Tell me it wasn't the store you came out of."

She bit her lip and nodded.

"You're sure?"

"I'm positive. The reporter was standing right in front of the store. She said there were no witnesses. Only people who heard the shots and that the killer ran out the back door." She squeezed his hands. "I have to go to the police. Tell them about that biker guy."

"Just hang on a sec."

Goddamn squatting killed his knees. He stood, shook out his legs, propped his hands on his hips. Back home, he'd already be on the phone with his boss, figuring out how to do this without putting Jo in danger. Out here? All he knew was LA bikers were notorious for their brutality. Gang rapes, murder, assault—none of it was off-limits. And Jo might now be able to identify one of them in relation to a double murder. *Jesus.* "If we were in New York, I'd call Tom. What about the lieutenant you've been riding with. Palermo?"

"I can call him," she said. "He's my day-to-day contact. I ride with him when the guys do hits and he lets me go into the stores after they clear them. He's basically you here in LA. Well, not you, of course, but you know what I mean."

Yeah, he knew. For weeks now she'd been talking about him, chattering on about how he was LA's version of Gabe. Only *he* was a lieutenant. Not that Jo said that. She wouldn't. They'd been together long enough for her to know Gabe wanted to make lieutenant and comparing him to this Palermo guy would only irritate him.

But right now, he was their go-to guy.

"Okay," Gabe said. "Start with him. He'll know how to handle this."

—:—

Jo scrolled to Wes Palermo's name, tapped the little green phone icon and placed the call on speaker. With her shattered nerves, having Gabe listen in would only help in case she missed something. She glanced to where he stood, feet spread wide, arms loose at his sides, so in control and commanding that she said a silent thanks for every blessing that had this man in front of her. If this had happened yesterday, she'd have been alone. *Don't think about it.*

She waggled the phone. "I want you to hear in case I miss something."

"Good idea." He sat next to her on the bed and dropped a kiss on her head. "Don't get ahead of yourself. Could be it wasn't the guy you saw."

Wes's ringing phone blared from the speaker. "You think someone else walked into that store within five minutes of me leaving and committed two murders?"

He shrugged. "Hey, I'm trying."

"I know." She kissed him quick. "And thank you."

On the third ring, one away from voicemail, Wes picked up. "Hey, Counselor."

Next to her, Gabe's shoulders flew back. Oh, she knew what this was. From the moment they'd met, she and Gabe had a sarcastic way of communicating. When it came to humor, they shared the same wit and in those early days thrived on one-upping each other. In an attempt to rattle her, Gabe would call her *counselor*. She retaliated by calling him *sergeant* and the whole thing became a game. Now, it was part of their love language and often, when in bed, the dirty talk included use of counselor and sergeant. A playful reminder of how far they'd come.

At least until her beloved heard Wes Palermo use her moniker. Suddenly, Gabe was all tense and his stony face had the look of a man bent on war. Being the most self-confident, commanding man she knew definitely had its limits. But, really? Now he decides to get jealous?

She squeezed his thigh, then gave it a *please-don't-do-this-to-me* pat. "Hi," she said into the phone.

"I thought you had a friend coming in," Wes said.

A *friend*. Great. Gabe would love being referred to as her friend. In the last ten minutes, her terrific day had not just disintegrated, it had been blown out of the atmosphere. Pow. Gone.

As expected, Gabe shot off the bed, prowled to an open spot on the wall, leaned against it and folded his arms. The go-to stance when he didn't like the way a conversation progressed. She didn't necessarily blame him. If the roles had been reversed and she'd heard him refer to her as a "friend" when talking to another woman, one who Jo might feel the teensiest bit professionally competitive with, it probably wouldn't sit well.

But telling Wes she had a friend coming in seemed the only way to go. Back in New York, she and Gabe kept their relationship quiet. No use in flaunting it when they were both part of a task force that could make—or break—their careers. Chances were, if news of their relationship spread, the mayor would make one of them leave the task force. And neither of them wanted that. So, yes, in order to preserve their privacy, she'd told Wes she had a *friend* coming in.

And Gabe obviously didn't like that.

"I did. Do. Whatever. He's here."

There. She'd said it. Put it right out there. Sort of. She locked eyes with Gabe, forcing him to acknowledge she'd made it clear her friend was male.

"Then why are you calling me? It's Friday night. Take a night off, Counselor."

And, again with the counselor nonsense. Why didn't Wes just shoot a flaming arrow at her? Gabe propped a foot against the wall and tapped his fingers against his extremely large biceps. This just kept getting better.

"I think I have a situation," she said to Wes. "I may need

your help."

"Sure. What is it?"

"I'd rather not talk on the phone. Can we meet some-where? I know it's Friday night and you're probably headed home, but it's important. I wouldn't ask—"

"Jo, it's okay. I'm still packing up at work anyway. Are you at your hotel? I could swing by."

Gabe switched feet on the wall, and if Jo wasn't in the midst of a full-blown crisis, she'd have laughed. The sex god of the century had finally revealed a weakness. Gabe hated weakness. His job pretty much dictated that weakness was a flaw. The man was always so confident and powerful she'd begun to wonder if he actually had any insecurities. In everything he undertook, even when she had a bomb strapped to her, he had never faltered.

Until now.

"Hang on, Wes." She put her hand over the phone and locked eyes with Gabe again. "I love you. Whatever is going on with you, I need you to stop. We can talk about it later, but I need you now, Gabe. Please."

She went back to Wes. "I'm back. Sorry. Yes. The hotel is fine. We'll meet you in the lobby. I'll see if they have a small conference room we can grab. I'd like to talk in private."

"Affirmative. Be there in twenty."

"Thanks."

She disconnected and faced Gabe, making sure to keep her body still. Assertive but not combative. A fight right now wouldn't help. But, dammit, he had to pick now to turn into an ornery teenager?

Alpha males. Unbelievable.

"Seriously," she said. "I can't believe you're suspicious."

"I'm not suspicious. Jealous maybe. Not suspicious. Never that. I trust you. More than anyone. You've also been here three weeks and I've missed you. I guess I don't like other men being so *familiar*."

"Because he knows where my hotel is? That's familiar? For God's sakes, he picked me up my first morning here. That's why he knows. And, Sergeant, if you remember, *you* called me counselor the first day we met. Frankly, if I walked into any courtroom, someone would call me counselor. You don't have the market on it."

His eyes widened. *Haza!* Rational Gabe back in the house.

He scrubbed his hands over his face. Shook his head. "I'm an asshole."

"Right now, yes. A little bit."

"Crap. I'm sorry. I'm...worked up."

And, wow. That, she knew, took every bit of his monstrous strength to admit. What a damned night. "I'm sorry, too. I shouldn't have agreed with you on that asshole thing. You're not." She moved closer, gently wrapped her hand around his forearm. "This is all new to us. Being apart for weeks, me working with other men without you, this murder... It's all hitting at once. And we're out of our environment. It's okay to be rattled. You don't have to be in charge this time."

"But I hate that."

"I know. Out here though, you're way out of your jurisdiction. You know that. It's okay because we have other people to call on."

"*Lieutenant* Palermo."

Of course the man would be a lieutenant, a status Gabe worked his body into the ground for, but hadn't yet achieved. "Yes. Palermo. He'll know what to do. And believe me, Gabe, Wes is a nice guy, but he's not you. Never will be. Not even close. Got it?"

He pushed off the wall and wrapped her in a hug that she realized she desperately needed. For a minute there, strong, solid Gabe had gone a little cuckoo. Maybe they were both a little cuckoo.

Maybe?

Who was she kidding? No maybe about it.

—:—

The second Lieutenant Wes Palermo stepped into the hotel lobby, Gabe tagged him. Cops, S.W.A.T. in particular, had a swagger about them. A do-not-mess-with-me confidence that let everyone in a two hundred yard radius know that he was a badass.

His tactical uniform—cargos, button-down shirt and a pair of side-zip boots that looked a hell of a lot like the ones Gabe wore—was also a dead fucking giveaway. Yeah, he looked like a badass. A badass who had good taste in boots *and* spent his days with Jo. Didn't that just suck?

Gabe slid his gaze to Jo, sitting across from him in the leather lobby chairs. The good news for Gabe was she seemed completely unfazed by Palermo's arrival. What Gabe thought she'd do, he wasn't sure, but that niggling jealousy, that clawing on the inside of his gut, didn't want to let up. But, hey, at least her tongue hadn't rolled out at the sight of the guy. He nudged his head toward the door. "Guessing that's him?"

She glanced over. "The uniform gave it away, huh?"

Gabe smiled. "Something like that."

He stood, held his hand out for Jo, and she latched on, giving him a squeeze. Usually, he was the one doing that squeezing thing, but like everything else on this damned trip so far, things had gotten sideways. He hooked his finger under her chin and eased it up. "You okay?"

She nodded. "I'm good. You?"

"I'm good. Let's roll."

Palermo spotted her through the tourist group saddling up for a nighttime tour of the city. Had to be fifty of them crowding the lobby. Not exactly a bad thing when trying to downplay the beautiful blonde who might have witnessed a murder.

He got close, maybe two feet away and stopped, giving Gabe a better look at him. He appeared older by a few years. Maybe late thirties, which explained the few lines around his eyes. Those weren't a surprise. Men who did their jobs, a lieutenant to boot, were entitled to lines. He wore his dirty-blond hair in a classic high and tight and his arms hung loose at his sides. He may have looked relaxed, but that was all bullshit. If necessary, he'd spring like a cat. Guys like them were wired and ready for action 24/7.

Palermo turned to Jo. "Hey."

"Hi," she said. "Thanks for coming." She tightened her grip on Gabe's hand. "This is Gabe Townsend."

Palermo, a few inches shorter than Gabe—who's counting?—studied his erect posture and thrown back shoulders. "You on the job?"

Sure am, dude. Gabe held his hand out. "ESU. New York. Good to meet you."

"Thought so. You're the friend?"

"Right again."

Jo gestured to him with her free hand. "Gabe is the sergeant on the New York task force. He's the U-boss."

Palermo made an *aha* face, his eyebrows bolting straight up. He swung his index finger between the two of them. "You two a thing?"

And here we go...

The debate on how to handle outing themselves had been raging with no real answers to be found. They'd talk about it, determine it might risk their roles on the task force since the mayor wouldn't want them working together, and that would be the end of the conversation. At least until the next time.

Now, Jo loaded him up on eye contact, looking for a hint on how much to say. That was her call. In the cop world, she'd be the one called a badge bunny. A house mouse. And one thing she'd been determined not to be labeled as was a woman who got off screwing cops.

Gabe held his hand palm up. "Your call, Counselor."

After their discussion over Palermo's use of the word counselor, she awarded him a massive eye roll—looked damned painful too—before turning back to the lieutenant. "We are," she said. "For a few months now. We're discreet about it."

"We'd like to keep it that way," Gabe added. "The mayor likes to tout our wins. Two of the task force's key players being *involved* wouldn't be good PR if you get my meaning."

Palermo held his hands up. "I get it. Trust me." He went back to Jo. "You said you needed help with something?"

"Yes. I'd like to talk in private though. We found an empty ballroom. It's a mess from a function today, but until the staff comes in to clean, it'll give us a place to talk."

Palermo shifted his gaze to Gabe, then went back to Jo, making hard eye contact that, if Gabe guessed right, questioned whether the ESU guy should hear whatever it was she had on her mind.

"Everything okay?" he asked.

"I don't think so," Jo said. "Gabe can hear it. He knows anyway."

Sorry, guy. I'm staying.

Jo gave his hand another squeeze, maybe to prove the point that he could hear the personal details of Jo's life, or maybe to boost his apparently lame ego. Either way, he didn't care. Wherever Jo went, he went. Case closed.

They ushered Palermo down a long corridor, past the first floor elevators to the conference center. Three sets of doors lined the one side. The first set led to a partitioned ballroom they'd discovered before meeting Palermo in the lobby. Gabe held the door open and the three of them moved to the far end of the room so no passersby would overhear their conversation. They parked at one of the large, round banquet tables still littered with a few coffee cups.

Gabe held the chair out for Jo and then sat next to her, stretching his legs out but giving her plenty of space.

On her other side, Palermo spun one of the banquet chairs, straddled it, and propped his arms on its back. "So, what's up?"

Summoning full-on lawyer mode, she pushed her shoulders back and folded her hands in her lap. "Remember I left a little early today?"

"Yeah. You said you wanted to do some shopping."

Gabe snorted and Palermo shot him a look. The good lieutenant was about to learn a vital lesson in dealing with Jo. That lesson being she was a sneaky, yet amazingly effective, woman.

"Yes, I was shopping."

"For knockoffs," Gabe offered, cutting to the chase.

Jo shifted and gave him the business-as-usual scowl she was so good at. "Don't start. I'm allowed to go shopping. And if I choose to do my job while shopping, so be it. It's the reason I'm good at this."

She knew he didn't like her doing these half-assed

excursions, so she tried an end run, hoping he wouldn't give her a hard time. *Nice try, Jo.* But he knew her, better than she wanted to admit. He'd accepted a long time ago that their minds worked in the same twisted way. They wanted justice, in whatever form, and would get it however necessary. And for that reason, complaining about her so-called shopping trips never did him a damned bit of good.

"Hang on," Palermo said. "You went by yourself?"

Sure did, guy.

"Yes, but, fellas, you don't have to gang up on me."

"All I was doing," Gabe said, "was stating the facts. If you want his help, you need to give it to him straight."

"Yes, *dear*."

"Jesus," Palermo said. "Are you two this way all the time?"

"Pretty much," Jo said. "It works for us."

"Meaning, she doesn't take my shit and I don't take hers. Excellent combo."

"Wow." Palermo scratched his forehead then gave his head a hard shake. "Okay. Let's stay on point. You went shopping for knockoffs and what?"

Over the next five minutes, Jo gave Palermo every detail she could remember. Right down to the patches on the biker's leather jacket and the logo on the box of cigarettes. He listened intently, occasionally clarifying a point, but otherwise remained silent, his face stoic, cheeks hard until she finished talking. He hadn't taken one note and Gabe suspected he didn't want to distract her with his note taking. He simply listened.

As Gabe would have done.

And, shit, he did not want to like this guy. Not for one second.

Because something—like the drawling way the man said

the word *counselor* when on the phone with Jo—told him Palermo, prior to putting eyes on Gabe, thought maybe he and Jo would get naked and spend the next two weeks tearing up the sheets before she went home. Yep. When it came to calling Jo counselor, Palermo said it the way Gabe said it. Sarcastic but packed with a whole lot of innuendo.

Gabe needed to shut that shit down fast.

And—hold on. He thought back to that hand squeeze when she'd introduced them. *She knew.* Son of a bitch. Jo knew, or at least sensed, Palermo might be warming her up to take a shot at her. So all that PDA in the lobby did two things for the brilliant Jo Pomeroy. It made it clear to Palermo that Gabe was her guy, and it made it clear to Gabe, after his pansy-assed hissy fit up in the room, that he was most definitely her guy.

And now they were all clear on the situation.

Bravo, Counselor. Shit on a shingle he loved her.

"Okay," Palermo said. "I'm guessing you want my input on who to call?"

"I do," she said.

He stood, slid his phone from his belt, tapped the screen a few times and scrolled. "Let me see who caught this case. Then we'll go talk to him. Or her. They'll probably have a sketch artist do a drawing. Have you look at some mug shots. See if you recognize anyone."

Jo nodded. "Fine. I expected that."

Gabe pushed out of his chair. "We need to keep her name out of this."

Even though he lived on the opposite coast, Gabe understood the violent history associated with this particular biker gang. If someone leaked her name, this crew would hunt her down.

And kill her.

"I'm well aware of that, Sergeant." Palermo stopped scrolling and punched the screen a couple of times. "Laughlin is the detective assigned to the case. He's good. His partner is Wells. She's young, but Laughlin likes her. Let me make a call. You might want to get whatever you need from your room. They're gonna want to talk to you."

—:—

Rather than stand around an LA police headquarters with his thumbs up his ass while Jo gave her statement, Gabe wandered outside for the double whammy of fresh air —minus the thirty-five degrees he'd left in New York—and privacy so he could work his contact list in an attempt to figure out who the hell Jo's biker guy might be.

He stood on the sidewalk in front of the corner building and scoped out a spot along the half wall adjacent to the stairs leading into the building. Only two cars filled the open parking spaces in front of the building, but Friday evening traffic on the main block kept things moving at a steady clip. Also on that main block were a group of home-less guys settling in for the evening under a darkening sky.

Right across from the police station.

Just like home.

Gabe settled against the wall and scrolled through his contact list for his buddy DeFiore. DeFiore, an undercover vice cop, had helped him out a few times, including locating Donald Martinson, the smuggler Gabe and Jo had tracked to South Carolina six weeks ago. What he needed from DeFiore now was a name. Someone in DEA who had intel on motorcycle gangs.

Two rings in, DeFiore picked up. "Hey. What's up? I thought you were on vacation."

Not wanting to make it obvious he'd be spending his time off with Jo, he hadn't given the locale of his impending vacation to his co-workers. When they asked where he was headed, smart man that he was, he'd deflected and told them "on vacation." Short, sweet, and decidedly lacking detail. Being the easily distracted bunch his team was, they'd moved on to other topics. The tough one was Tom, his boss, and the man who already had an inkling Gabe and Jo were bumping uglies. Tom never asked, but he'd made it damned clear he suspected.

The old "don't ask, don't tell" policy.

When Gabe had put in for two weeks' vacation time, he'd gotten ahead of any questions Tom might ask by stressing it was as good a time as any with Jo, a crucial member of the Clean Sweep Task Force, being out of town too. Nothing would get done with her gone, so it made sense —perfect sense—that Gabe should take vacation now.

"I am on vacation," Gabe told DeFiore. "You got anyone in DEA?"

"DEA? Jesus, Townsend, what are you into now?"

Gabe would have liked to laugh at that, but lately, he and Jo had gotten into some interesting dust-ups. None of which could be considered funny. "I need info on a motorcycle gang. 12th Street Crew. I figure the best way to find that info is to go to the feds."

"You in trouble?"

"Not me. A friend."

"Must be a good friend. Maybe a blonde who likes to chase smugglers?"

Gabe sighed. "You about done?"

"Hey, just saying. I heard she was in LA and suddenly you're on vacation asking about a biker gang based out of LA."

Gabe tilted his head back, breathed in the sixty-degree air and stared up at a winking star. Being on the downlow was becoming a pain in the ass. Honestly, he didn't know how criminals led lives filled with deception. Fucking exhausting.

I'm done with that. Probably. He should discuss it with Jo. Probably. But, well, she'd told Palermo, so technically, she'd let the horse out of the barn first. And, right now, she was busy.

"Here's the deal," Gabe said. "You keep this to yourself."

"Oh, goodie."

"Fuck off. Jo and I are…"

What? A couple? Involved? *Banging* each other? Jesus, not that. Definitely not that. Way more than that.

"Yeah, genius. I get it. You think half the department hasn't figured that out? I knew it that night I called you about Martinson and heard her voice in the background. At four in the morning. I didn't squeal because that's your business, but people aren't stupid."

"Once again I'll ask if you're about done?"

DeFiore laughed. "Yeah. I'm done. What happened?"

The overhead street lights flashed on and Gabe glanced around, checking behind him and across the street and anywhere else someone could be sitting and possibly overhear. Nothing. No pedestrians, no cops hanging around, no one leaving the building. All quiet. Still, he walked another twenty yards away from the building entrance and spilled it all to DeFiore. The knockoff shoes, the biker guy in the store with a box of cigarettes, Jo having a bad feeling.

The murder.

When he was done, Gabe sensed something. Not about the current Jo mess though. This was different. A lightness he'd been missing for the better part of almost four months.

Finally, he'd confided in someone, his friend, about Jo and the relief poured over him. Damn it felt good to not be hiding.

"Christ," DeFiore said. "How does she manage this shit?"

Good question. "I don't know. Wait. I'm lying. I do know. She's like us. She never gives up. Plus, she's an adrenaline junkie."

"Does anyone on this end know?"

Gabe stopped near the corner, saw two people walking up the side street and turned back, heading the direction he came so they didn't overhear him. "Nada. Just happened this afternoon. I'm trying to keep it quiet. If I have to, I'll tell Tom. Or she will. Right now, I wanna see if we can identify this guy."

"Easy, my friend. The detectives are probably on it already. You think they want you stomping in their sandbox?"

"Hell no. But if you have someone with the feds out here, maybe we nudge this thing along."

From the other end, DeFiore made a you're-a-dumbass grunting noise. "It's your ass, pal."

"Sure is."

"I'll make a call. I've got a guy I went to the academy with. He's DEA in Newark now. He may know someone. I'll holler at ya."

"Thanks. I owe you one."

"You owe me, like, twenty, Townsend. Just invite me to the wedding. What a pisser that wedding'll be."

"Shit," Gabe said. "I'm out."

Disconnecting, he laughed at the thought of a Jo/Gabe wedding. The guest list alone, considering she was a lawyer, her parents were political consultants, and he worked special operations, would be scary as hell.

They could probably take down a small nation.

But a wedding. He should be so lucky. And hey, he'd admit that wasn't the first time he'd thought about Jo being Mrs. Gabriel Townsend. The last month or so, when he rolled out of bed at oh-dark-hundred and she'd try to coax him back—most times succeeding—or when they crawled under the blankets at night, it had all become…comfortable and he could picture it, a ring on her finger, the two of them popping out a few babies. She wanted kids. He knew that. And so did he. All in all, he liked the thought of it.

And *that* had never happened before.

The sound of voices behind him refocused him and he shook his head. *Later.* Plenty of time to consider marriage— and maybe clue Jo in on his thoughts—later.

He marched up the front stairs and through the lobby area where the desk sergeant waved him back. In the hallway he found Palermo leaning against a wall, talking to a uniformed cop. The cop broke away, nodded at Gabe, and moved on.

Palermo eyed him. "Where were you?"

"Outside. Catching up on calls."

"Un-huh."

Gabe eyed him right back, almost begging the lieutenant to say something. "Yeah. Un-huh."

"Look, Gabe, we've got this. Okay?"

He rolled his bottom lip out, pondered that a second. "Sure."

Clearly, that answer didn't sit well because Palermo boosted off the wall, keeping his arms loose at his sides, but squaring off with him. "You think I'm stupid? Your girlfriend is in there trying to identify a possible murderer and you want me to believe you were outside, where no one in here could listen, catching up on casual conversation? Whatever you're up to, we can handle it. Don't get into the middle of it."

Refusing to let this guy rile him, Gabe mimicked his stance—feet wide, arms loose at his sides. Unthreatening and threatening all at once. He had no interest in pissing off the Los Angeles Police Department. That was pure stupidity —something he'd never been accused of—but if he could move this along, cut a few corners that might get them a good end result, he'd do it. Zero hesitation.

Palermo didn't need to know that though.

"She can't testify." Gabe jerked his head toward the conference room where Jo was giving her statement. "If the guy she saw murdered those people, he has to take a plea deal."

"I know."

A plea deal would mean no trial. No trial meant Jo wouldn't testify and, if they did this right, the biker would never know her identity and she could go back to New York without looking over her shoulder every minute.

"Good. Because if she testifies, they'll find her and kill her."

THREE

Jo closed the mug book in front of her just as the door to the interview room opened. Wes stuck his head in, nodded at Detective Laughlin and then turned his attention to Jo. "You need anything?"

Ha. She needed a lot of things. The first being to get out of this windowless room with its blinding white walls and stale smell. As an intellectual property attorney, she didn't spend much time in rooms like this and being here made her chest hurt, made her feel closed in. Suffocated.

Locked up.

Even in the frigid, artificial air-conditioned air, sweat beaded down her back. What she needed was a shower and a shot of something strong. Tequila? Why not. Considering she didn't do shots—at all—it might help her at least get a good night's sleep.

Really though, it sounded disgusting and would probably make her sick.

Gabe. That's what she needed. A good dose of Gabe in all his sexy, alpha male glory. She shoved the mug book away and glanced back at Wes. "I'm fine. Is Gabe out there?"

"Yeah." He pointed at the mug book. "Anything?"

"No. Sorry."

"It's all right. Still early. We'll find him. Are you good with the sketch?"

When she'd first arrived, they'd called in a sketch artist who'd sat with her for almost two hours, two long, tedious hours, trying every shape of nose, mouth and eyes possible until they got something that seemed close. At least a little close. As tired and bleary-eyed as she'd become, Jo wasn't even sure of that right now. She'd definitely know the guy if she saw him again, but the sketch didn't seem quite right, and in her current state, she didn't know how to fix it. If only the artist could crawl into her head and see what she saw. It would be so much simpler.

She reached for the photocopy of the sketch the artist had left. "I'm as good with it as I'm going to get. If I think of anything else, I'll let you know. Would you please send Gabe in?"

"No problem. If there's nothing else we need tonight, you should get out of here. Go sleep."

That made her snort. Sleep. If only. After this, she'd probably never sleep again.

Detective Laughlin stood and gathered up the mug books spread across the table. "We're good for now. I'll call you with any updates."

"Thank you, Detective."

Wes put his hand against the door and pushed it open before stepping back to let Laughlin through. "She's all yours," he said to someone—apparently Gabe—in the hall.

And then Gabe stepped into the room, his big body filling the space, and Jo's shoulders released, just *foom*, the tension let go, dismantling that aloneness that had settled on her. His dark eyes zoomed in on her, held for a few seconds, and the immediate spark he always brought knocked the chill right out of the room.

"I promise you," she said. "I will never go into another shop looking for counterfeits. I'm done."

He squatted next to her, ran his fingers over her cheek and lightly pinched her chin. "Jo, if I believed that, my life would be made."

"I'm serious."

"I know you are. But I also know when this is over you'll get the itch again. We're alike in this way. The second we get bored, we crave action."

Bastard. She angled her head up and out of his grasp. "Believe what you want, but I'm done. I can't take this anymore."

Still squatting, he settled his elbows on his knees. "You'll be okay. I promise you. We'll do whatever we have to here and then we'll go home. I'll stay with you until it's done."

"How can you do that? This could go on for weeks or months. Even after I go home, if there's a trial, I'll have to come back here. Are you going to leave work for that?"

"If I have to. Right now, my goal is to make sure there's no trial."

Wasn't this typical? Gabe trying to control everything, trying to take command like he always did. As much as she appreciated the effort, it would take a lot more than just him to fix this one. "You think we'll get that lucky? That I won't have to testify?"

"Yep." He flipped her hair over her shoulder and stood. "Palermo and I are of the same mind on that front."

"Well, that would be fabulous, but let's not count on it."

"I've got a call in to DeFiore."

Straightaway, this was not good. "Your undercover friend?"

"Yeah. He knows someone at DEA. He might be able to hook us up with someone out here who might know this guy."

Perfect. Gabe going rogue. In a strange city. God help them both. She popped out of the chair, got right into his space. "Listen up, Sergeant. Do not screw up your career over this. Over *me*. Please. The way you know me, I know you. And you want to make lieutenant in the next two years. Running roughshod out here won't get you there."

"I'm not worried about it."

"Well, you should be." She spun around, paced the interior of the small room then stopped, faced the wall, and pressed her forehead into it, the cold surface reminding her of the chill she'd had a few moments ago. "We've been so careful about protecting our careers. Don't blow it this way."

"Jo, you're worried about something that hasn't happened. I'm poking around. If something comes of it, I'll turn it over to Palermo. That's all."

Someone rapped on the door, a quick, staccato knock and Jo stepped back, straightening her shoulders.

"Come in," Gabe said.

Wes stuck his head in. "We're good here. I'm heading out. The detectives will check in with you over the weekend. Or before if something comes up." He glanced at Gabe, then brought his gaze back to Jo. "I'll call you tomorrow. See if you need anything."

"I've got it," Gabe said.

Oy, these two. An alpha pissing match. Just what she needed. She tilted her head, considered the two men in front of her. Lions, both of them—as similar as they were. Maybe that was the problem, and two leaders never worked; she imagined that before this was over, they'd be at war.

—:—

The following morning, his body still on East Coast time, Gabe rolled out of bed at five-thirty and busted off an hour of push-ups, planks, squats, and whatever other torture he could inflict on himself while Jo slept. Before last night, his plan had been to get up early, hit the gym in the hotel and drag Jo out for a walk on the beach. Maybe spend the day exploring a city he'd never been to. Now, he didn't want to take her outside the building, much less explore.

And he sure as hell wasn't leaving her alone. Jeez. Only they could go on vacation and land smack in the middle of a murder investigation.

Sweat poured down his neck as he focused on the last seconds of a six-minute plank, ignored the raging fatigue in his core and checked his watch. In a few seconds he'd be done. Finished. Even the thought made his arms quiver so he stiffened, determined to gut out this last five seconds. *Four, three, two, one.* Done. Refusing to give in to fatigue by collapsing, he lowered himself to the ground, rolled to his back and stretched his abs. Holy shit, if he'd had any food in his belly, he'd have puked it up by now.

Before his workout, he'd snagged a water bottle from the stocked fridge and now chugged half of it. He set it on the thick carpet and scanned the sitting area of the suite where a night light in the far corner threw shadows across the plush furniture and fancy art. This room had to cost a friggin' fortune. One he knew she wouldn't let him kick in for.

As usual, because God knew every time the subject of money—Jo's money—came up, his right eye throbbed. He pressed his fingers into his eye socket until the pain subsided. He didn't mind that she made more than him. What he minded was her stubbornness when it came to spending her money on them. She wasn't his sugar-mama and she needed to get used to that.

He sat back against the wall, watched Jo flop to her back in the massive bed while the strap of her tank top slid down her arm, making his libido rise up and howl. Some things were just ingrained. Wanting Jo was one of them.

But today, he'd let her sleep. Today, she'd get whatever she wanted.

He rose to his feet, wandered to the bed where her long hair fanned over the pillow. He ran his fingers over the silky strands, thought about how normal it suddenly felt to touch her. Any part of her. Something he'd spent months denying himself. At least until she'd been attacked by one of the merchants they'd busted and it unleashed something in him. Something feral, protective, and—yeah—possessive.

Blame it on falling in love. Why not? Sometimes though, like last night when he watched her come apart, watched fear dismantle the hardened lawyer in her, it hurt him. Physically ripped into his chest. A hot stab that shouldn't feel good, but somehow did because he knew he loved her enough that he felt her pain. Agony mixed with immense pleasure.

So screwed, Townsend.

On the bedside table, his phone buzzed. He'd turned the ringer off when he'd woken up and the thing now rattled against the wood, causing a pretty good racket. He hauled ass around the bed before the warbling woke Jo and hit the button.

"Hang on," he whispered into the phone, moving to the bathroom where he shut the door. "What's up?"

"DeFiore here. I got you a guy. Well, my guy got you a guy who got you a guy."

"Whatever that means," Gabe said.

"Nah. It's good. You'll like it. He's DEA in LA. Cole Bardin. He's their go-to on bikers. He's a motorcycle freak, so he's able to ride and talk the talk. He did a UC assignment with a biker gang last year."

"He might know this guy then?"

Now that would be golden. If Bardin could ID Jo's guy, they'd pass the name along to the detectives and be done with this whole flipping mess.

"Maybe. I got his number. I'll text it to you. Give him a call."

"I owe you a giant steak when I get back."

"Yeah. I know. Stay safe, my man."

"We will. Thanks, bud."

Gabe disconnected and leaned against the sink to await the incoming text. Given it wasn't even seven a.m.—on a Saturday—he'd wait another hour to call Bardin. Then maybe he'd give them a meeting where they'd show him the copy of the sketch Jo had asked for last night. Gabe had smuggled it out of the PD without Jo or Palermo realizing it, which would probably get him in hot water, but hey, wasn't his fault the thing leaped right off the table into his pocket.

Besides, what Palermo didn't know wouldn't hurt him.

Let's hope it doesn't hurt me too.

A knock sounded on the door and he pulled it open. Jo stood there, that strap on her tank top still struggling to stay put, her blond hair a tangled mess and looking so unbeliev-ably hot that Gabe's little brain decided now would be an excellent time to cause a hard-on.

"Damn," he said.

Her sleepy eyes roamed across his face, down his sweat-soaked chest to his shorts—morning, sunshine—and a slow, wicked grin inched across her face.

She squeezed into the bathroom with him. "You were doing your Mr. Atlas routine again?"

"Yeah. Sorry I woke you."

"You didn't. I have to pee."

She reached into the shower and turned the faucet, her eyes still on his and if Gabe knew anything, he knew Jo had one thing on her mind. The woman's libido howled just like his did.

"You taking a shower?"

"I am," she said. "And so are you. With me. And, in case you were wondering, naughty things will happen while said shower is taking place." She looked down at his painfully expanding crotch. "Any issue with that, Sergeant?"

"There never is, Counselor. There never is."

—:—

At exactly 11:00 A.M., Gabe and Jo walked into The Burg, a dump of a burger joint near downtown LA. At this early hour, the lunch crowd—if there was a lunch crowd in this place—hadn't started yet and the ten or so tables were empty. Gabe suspected Bardin picked this place for just that reason. Low traffic meant less opportunity to be seen. Simple fact.

He turned to Jo who, despite her long day yesterday, looked amazing in a denim skirt, flats and a lightweight navy sweater that made her blue eyes sparkle. She'd pulled her hair into a low ponytail and Gabe gave it a tug.

"Have I mentioned you're insanely beautiful?"

She rolled her tongue around her cheek and eyeballed him. "Thank you, Sergeant, but just so you know, when it comes to you, I'm easy. You may have noticed you'll get some even without the awesome compliments."

Damn, he loved when she was playful. "Nothing wrong with a little insurance."

She linked her arm through his and leaned in, her right breast making contact with his arm and the little brain dinged again. *Easy there.*

A beat-up menu, one of those old deals with the plastic letters that had to be hand-placed, hung over the counter and Jo studied it, her eyes scanning for something she might like. "Are you hungry? We should probably order something."

"I could eat."

No shock there. He didn't remember a time he couldn't eat.

After ordering, they grabbed a table near the back of the small restaurant. Away from any windows. For all they knew, Bardin could be working a UC assignment and if so, staying out of sight would be a better option. Speaking of Bardin...

A short—short next to Gabe anyway—man with strawberry-blond hair and hunched shoulders entered the restaurant. Could this be their guy? This non-descript beanpole screamed cop as much as Gabe's crazy Great Aunt Suzie.

But as he said he would, he wore a Florida State sweatshirt.

Gabe nudged Jo. "That's him."

"Really?"

Even she didn't believe it. Then again, she'd spent the last year surrounded by a team of aggressive, filthy-mouthed ESU guys who walked into a room, their dominance obvious by cold self-control rather than loudmouthed bullying. S.W.A.T. guys, by nature of what they did for a living, possessed a sense of superiority. Some found it arrogant.

Oh.

Well.

Because in order to do what S.W.A.T. guys did for a living, to see the crap they saw, face the violence they faced, they had to believe their own brand of bullshit. Believe, unflinchingly, they could conquer whatever hot-ass mess lay on the other side of the door about to be blasted open.

So, yeah, his men needed to believe they were better than everyone else.

"That's him," Gabe said. "Unless some other random person is wearing khaki cargo shorts and a Florida State sweatshirt."

"He's not what I expected. He looks so…"

"Innocent?"

"He looks like a dentist."

A *dentist*. How the hell she got there, he couldn't figure, but he'd mull that later. Bardin spotted them, gave a slight nod and headed to the counter to order. While waiting on him, their food arrived and Gabe dug into his burger. Might as well. His metabolism, thanks to the workout this morning, had mowed through the eggs they'd ordered for breakfast and his body needed fuel again.

Two minutes later, Bardin slid into the chair across from them. No shaking hands, no nice to meet you, no nothing. What he wanted here was to be a regular guy out to meet a few old friends.

"Thanks for coming out," Gabe said.

"No problem." He glanced at Jo, shook his head. "You stepped in some shit here. I'm sorry." He went back to Gabe. "These guys are animals. If one of them did what you think he did, I'd love to put him away."

The young girl who'd delivered Jo and Gabe's food set a tray with a sandwich, fries, and drink on the table in front of Bardin and snatched the number out of the little holder.

Good timing on her part. Now they'd talk without interruption.

Gabe handed Bardin the folded copy of the sketch he'd lifted from the PD. "It's a sketch of the guy," he said, keeping his voice low. "They brought in an artist last night. Jo thinks it's pretty close."

Bardin partially unfolded it and took a peek.

"Ringing any bells?"

"He looks like every guy I hung with last year. Long, stringy hair, beard. Just a general mess." He checked the sketch again. "How tall?"

Jo leaned in. "Maybe five foot ten. I had low heels on and was as tall as he was. And he was carrying a box of cigarettes that he took into the back. I suspect they were counterfeit."

"Yeah, a lot of these guys make their money selling counterfeit—or stolen—goods. Cigarettes are easy. Last month Customs seized twenty-five thousand cartons of counterfeit cigs. Street value over a million dollars."

Gabe let out a low whistle. "They came in on a container ship?"

"Yeah. There were hidden inside a bunch of other stuff. The manifest looked suspicious so Customs nabbed it."

Jo turned to Gabe. "I wonder if that's our guy."

He shrugged. "Could be."

"Who?"

"Andre Theo, big-time smuggler out here. Jo is an intellectual property attorney. She's the brains behind an anticounterfeiting task force in New York. In January we busted Theo's number two guy for selling knockoff Barellis. We nailed Theo too, but he's out now. Awaiting trial. We think he's still running his business under a different name."

"So," Jo said, pointing at the sketch, "maybe he's associated with Theo."

"Could be. If your guy's a major player, he could be the one distributing the bogus stuff to middlemen who then sell it to the assholes—pardon my language—like you saw in that store."

"Alleged assholes," Gabe cracked.

"Amen, brother." He glanced at the sketch again, studied it. "Did you notice if he had a tat on his left forearm. A skull?"

Tilting her head back, she stared at the ceiling in that way she did when recalling something. *Come on, Jo. Whatcha got?*

"I didn't notice." She turned to Gabe. "But wouldn't it be something if Theo could be linked to this murder."

Something? Yeah, it would be something. Something like an epic nightmare. He couldn't even comment on that statement. The possibilities were too vast and disturbing. Then again, this was Jo. If anyone could find this kind of crazy-assed trouble, it'd be her. Didn't that just shrink his balls?

He flicked at the sketch. "You don't know our guy here? Or maybe?"

"Maybe. If he has the skull tat it's a guy they call Jimmy Jax. I met him a couple of times. He's never done time, so he won't be in the system. That doesn't mean he doesn't deserve to be in the system. He's just avoided it. His crew hangs out at a couple of places in East LA."

"You got a list?"

"Sure."

"Text it to me?"

"Not a problem. These are badass places though." He jerked his chin at Jo. "You stay clear. A woman who looks like you has no business in there. You'd be horrified at the shit that goes on. They're misogynistic animals. Fights, harassment, rapes. I was UC for about four months with another gang and it made me sick. We busted a bunch of them though. That's something at least."

Jo sat back, leaned into Gabe a little, and clasped his hand under the table, but her eyes were still on Bardin. "Thank you," she said. "For what you do. I know it's not easy."

"It's the job. Just be careful. Both of you."

—:—

Three blocks from the hotel, Jo's phone rang. She felt around for it in the rental car's door cubby and snatched it up before the call went to voicemail. *Wes.* From the corner of her eye, she saw Gabe glance over from the driver's seat. "It's Wes."

"My buddy," he cracked.

"Relax, tough guy." Jo tapped the speaker button. Clearly, Gabe had insecurities about Wes, and wasn't that just insane? She didn't get it. Not for one second. She couldn't be in the same room with Gabe without touching him. He'd brought out in her a sexual desire that hinged on excessive. She simply could not get enough. Ever. And it wasn't just the sex, although that was certainly worship-worthy. But no, she loved curling up with him to watch a movie or snuggling under a blanket while he took in a game and she read. All of it, she'd never tire of.

"Hey, Wes."

"Hey, Jo. Listen, where are you?"

"Gabe and I are just on our way back—"

Gabe cleared his throat loud enough to start an avalanche and she shot him a look. As if she'd announce to Wes that they were chasing down a murder suspect.

"—to the hotel," she continued. "Why?"

"I'm at headquarters. There was some activity this morning so I came by to check things out."

Gabe turned left a block from the hotel, bullied his way into the right lane and earned himself an enthusiastic flip of the bird from a cabbie. Unfazed, he waved the guy off. "What activity?"

"A couple of guys got locked up last night. Bar brawl in East LA."

East LA. How very interesting.

"And," Gabe said, sounding bored.

But they both knew what was coming because he'd locked his jaw and refused to even shift his gaze her way.

Just ahead, the traffic light turned red and Jo kept her thoughts from running wild by focusing on it. "You want me to look at a lineup, right?"

"Yeah," Wes said. "One of the guys has the look and his alibi isn't checking out."

"Shit," Gabe muttered, still refusing to spare her a look.

"We just need her to take a look," Wes said. "In and out."

Jo reached over. Patted his thigh. "That's fine, Wes. What time do you want us there?"

"The sooner the better."

They came to a stop at the traffic light that had just been Jo's mental savior and Gabe finally looked over at her, the already honed angles of his face sharpening enough to slice cement. He held up his hands. "It's up to you."

Everything in his body language—the stiff posture, the vein in his neck popping—told her he didn't want her doing this. But Gabe was a smart man and knew her temperament. The minute he told her not to do something, she'd do it. She couldn't help it. In her lifetime, her relentless will had gotten her in more trouble than she'd like to admit. It was also the thing that made her a damned good lawyer.

A lawyer who couldn't, in good conscience, refuse to view a lineup. "We're on our way, Wes."

"Thanks, Jo."

She disconnected, dropped the phone in her lap and rested her head back. The light turned green and Gabe went straight, driving past the hotel where the two of them should be enjoying a fun weekend together.

"Jo, you sure you want to do this?"

"Do I have a choice?"

"Babe, you always have a choice. Say the word and I put you on a plane home."

"Says the cop."

"Says the cop who loves you and doesn't want anything to happen to you. That trumps all."

As dedicated as he was to his job, he had no problem helping her walk away from this. And she knew why. After he'd gone to sleep the night before, her mind had refused to concede and she'd slipped out of bed to troll the Internet about the 12th Street biker gang. And, oh, the articles she'd found. According to her research, ninety-nine percent of motorcyclists were honest, law-abiding citizens. The other one percent? Well, the 12th Street Crew fell into that category. Those were the ones who took pride in the violence they subjected their victims to.

And what Gabe probably knew, and she suspected, was that the lineup she'd be viewing contained a couple of one-percenters.

"I know about the one-percenters." She hit him with a faux cheery smile. "I did research."

"Terrific. As much as I'd love to find the son of a bitch

you saw in that store, I don't want you looking over your shoulder for the next twenty years."

"And if I have to testify, that's what will happen."

"Maybe."

The light changed and he gunned the gas in his typical, crazy New Yorker fashion. Or maybe he was simply frustrated. Nervous. That alone, coming from this fearless, capable man, should have scared the hell out of her. But she wouldn't live her life that way. Hiding from a criminal, constantly wondering if he'd find her. No. Justice needed to be done. "I can't walk away. I'd never forgive myself."

"Yeah," he said. "I know."

Ten minutes later, Gabe pulled into a spot in front of the squat brick building and parked. He reached behind him into the backseat, grabbed his baseball cap and dropped it in her lap. "Put this on. It won't completely cover your hair, but it's better than nothing."

"I bet right now you'd like me to have one of my wigs you hate so much."

Back in New York, she kept an assortment of wigs for shopping trips to the vendors on Tower Street, knockoff capitol of the city. During their first few months of the task force shutting down businesses selling counterfeit items, the owners began to recognize Jo's blond hair. Thus, she adopted disguises when on the hunt for knockoff merchandise. Now, even the disguises didn't work and her wigs sat in a closet in her office, virtually untouched.

"That's where you're wrong, Counselor. I don't mind the wigs. I just don't want you wearing them to conduct covert missions."

She pulled the hat onto her head. "Oh, right. I suppose you'd like me to save the wigs for the bedroom." She clicked her tongue. "A little stripper role-playing, big boy?"

Even to her, the joke fell flat. So much for her go-to coping mechanism of cracking jokes under stress. He couldn't blame a girl for attempting to lighten the mood.

Gabe patted her hand and gave her a wilting half-grin. "Nice try. Let's do this and then we'll talk about that role-playing thing."

FOUR

Gabe leaned against the wall outside the room where Jo had just gone in to view the lineup. He hated this. The standing around with his thumbs up his ass. Before she'd entered the room, she'd had that weird look on her face again, the un-Jo look of pinched lips and tight jaw and none of it—not one effing thing—resembled her usual smart-mouthed, determined, and confident demeanor.

Gotta fix this.

His phone buzzed and he drew it from his pocket. His mother. Wasn't this perfect? Chatting with mom while Jo potentially ID'd a killer. *Jesus H. Christ.* Ten feet from where he stood a door led to the back parking lot. Being the closest exit, he headed that way. "Hey, Ma. Everything okay?"

"Hi, honey," she said. "I wanted to tell you I put your clean shirts in your closet."

Um, okay. Wasn't this a pisser? His mother calling him in LA to tell him she'd done his laundry. Mom guilt-speak for she missed him. Living in the third-floor apartment above his parents had its perks. The most important being he was always close if something happened or his dad needed help. Then there was the constant stream of home-cooked meals in his fridge so he had a meal when he got home and—case in point—his shirts being not only clean but ironed.

Maybe he could skip her letting herself into his apartment when he and Jo were in the shower together, but that was pretty much the only disadvantage. And the main reason he spent so much time at Jo's rather than the reverse.

"Okay," he said. "Thanks."

He pushed through the door to the cement stoop and propped his hip on the handrail, glancing back to make sure Jo hadn't come out yet. The afternoon sun blazed and he squinted against it despite the baseball cap he'd reclaimed from Jo. He unhooked his sunglasses from the neck of his shirt and slid them on.

From the street, Gabe heard the loud roar of an engine. One that didn't sound like a car. Suddenly, with this biker mess, he'd gone on hyper-alert for motorcycles. A second engine revved, joining the racket for a few seconds and then —bam—nothing. Silence. What the hell? He glanced back through the doors. Still no Jo. And now he was insanely curious about those bike engines. If they'd been passing, the noise would have faded, a gradual decrease rather than an instant kill. He hopped down the back steps and strode to the edge of the building toward the street.

"How's the vacation?" Mom wanted to know.

Vacation. Ha. "It's good. Haven't seen much yet, but the weather is great. You and Dad should come out here."

"As if I'd get your father to fly."

True. The old man hated planes. The fear of being trapped inside with no way to get out at thirty-five thousand feet made him twitchy. "Right. Sorry. Did you get my text with the hotel info?"

"I did. Thank you."

"How about Joanna?" Mom asked. "Does she like LA?"

Joanna. Someone referring to Jo by her full name always hit him weird. It didn't fit. An interesting thing considering it was her given name, but still, she'd always been Jo to him and to those who knew her well. He'd mentioned it to his mom a few times before their joint dinners, something they did every couple of weeks so his folks could get to know Jo —didn't that trip the Gabe-is-serious-about-this-one radar —but Mom was a tough nut and always fell back to Joanna. Jo didn't mind and he didn't have the patience to keep on her so they let it go. Eventually she'd get it.

"I think she's ready to come home," he said. "Are you okay?"

"Oh, I'm fine. I don't think I like you being so far away though."

She let out a long sigh and Gabe whipped out his imaginary rusty knife, slicing it across his neck. Jesus. If the massive wave of guilt that had just broken on him didn't kill him, the imaginary blood spurting from his jugular would definitely do it. He stopped at the edge of the building and swung his head in both directions. *And, hello, assholes.* On the corner to his left, two men sat on motorcycles, seemingly shooting the shit. What were the chances of that in front of the PD?

He'd see about that by wandering their way. Just a guy taking a walk while on the phone.

"What are you doing today?" he asked his mother.

"Your father and I are going to the movies."

"Good. Have dinner out while you're at it."

"I don't know. Maybe I should cook."

And maybe I should stab myself in the eye with that rusty knife that didn't get the job done the first time. He had Jo inside looking at a lineup, his mother moaning at him, and a bunch of bikers giving him that amped-up, itchy feeling that only happened when busting in on stoned crackheads who were as predictable as a hormonal woman.

He got to the corner where the bikers, total scumbags with their greasy beards and dirty jeans, sat in a fucking no-parking zone. In front of the police department. Total ball breakers. The bigger guy—bigger as in thick around the middle—wore his stringy, dark hair under a bandanna and his beard might have been a year overdue for a trim. His buddy, the younger one, appeared to be about thirty and much leaner. This one wore a sleeveless T-shirt under his leather vest and obviously spent time in the gym. Okay. So one in shape, the other he'd drop like a stone.

"Mom, just eat out."

One of the bikers snickered and Gabe shifted his gaze right where the two men eyeballed him.

The bigger one smacked his buddy on the arm. "We got us a mama's boy here."

And, holy fuck, these guys were going to give him a reason to go apeshit. *Don't do it.* Still, he wasn't gonna run from them either. Casually, he flipped the guy off as he turned the corner, his stride the easy stroll it had been three seconds ago. He shot a look over his shoulder, making sure the assholes were still on their bikes.

"Gabe?" his mom said. "Did you hear me?"

He headed for the far end of the block. And...*shit.* Straight ahead on the opposite corner sat two more bikers and his blood pressure went to double-red zone. Adrenaline poured into his body, a massive rush that made his head pound and his vision blurr. And yet, everything slowed, the cars moving past him, the bus whooshing, all of it blurry and muffled. *Control it.* He breathed in, held it for five seconds and let it out again.

"Ma, I need to call you back."

"Is everything okay?"

"Yeah. I'm in the middle of something. Call you back."

Before she could argue, he committed the deadly sin of hanging up on his mother. But these bikers being here while Jo was inside viewing a lineup could not be a coincidence.

He continued to the far end of the block where the bikers gave him the hard stare but kept their traps shut. At least they were smarter than their counterparts on the other end.

Once he turned the corner, having made it all the way around the building, he hauled ass back inside where Palermo had claimed his spot across from where Jo had gone in to view the lineup. *Still in there.*

Palermo lifted his chin in Gabe's direction. "Where'd you go?"

"Houston," he said, "we have a problem."

Palermo straightened up. Instant warrior mode. "What?"

"We got bikers on both sides of the front entrance."

"Get the fuck outta here."

Gabe jerked his thumb toward the front entrance. "They're parked right on the corners. Two of 'em are in the no parking zone."

"Son of a bitch. They know she's in here."

"Which means either you have a leak in this building or those assholes know one of their buddies is in a lineup and they want a look at the witness. Someone in that lineup is guilty of something."

"Son of a bitch," Palermo repeated. "They're trying to scare her."

"Yeah. Trying to spook her before she gets to the stand. And *fuck* that."

"Where'd you park?"

"Out front."

"They'll see her leave."

He whipped his baseball cap and glasses off. "My ass they will. You got a transport van here? We slap some cuffs on her, tuck her hair under the baseball cap and sneak her out the back. If we're lucky, they won't see her. If they do, she'll look like a prisoner being transported."

Hands on hips, Palermo tilted his head to the ceiling. "Hang on."

He marched off, leaving Gabe standing in the hallway wondering how the fuck he'd get Jo out of here without the bikers spotting her.

Two minutes later, Palermo stuck his head around the corner again and waved Gabe over. From the looks of him, he'd worked out the transport van.

"We got this," he said. "One of our female detectives worked a prostitution sting a few weeks back."

What this had to do with anything, Gabe couldn't figure. "And?"

"She's got her getup in her locker. Wig and all."

What the? He held his hands up. "Whoa. You're gonna dress *Jo* up as a *prostitute*?"

She'd go ballistic. Beyond ballistic. Not so much the disguise because, hell, she did that at home all the damned time, but the prostitution thing. No good. Gabe let out a frustrated laugh. "No way."

"You got a better idea? We need to hide that blond hair and your cap won't do it. I know she'll hate it—"

Gabe straightened up. How well did this guy think he knew her? *Can't think about that now. Fucking idiot.*

"—but it could work. To make it look good, we put her in cuffs, load her in the van and shuttle her out. We'll get a couple of guys to go outside and bust balls with the bikers. While they're busy you get in your car, follow the van a ways and then grab Jo. Even if they see her out back, she'll be a redhead dressed like a street walker."

Gabe propped one hand on the wall, leaned into it and considered the plan. With the front entrance basically shot, they'd have to take her out the back. Without the disguise, the bikers, from their position on that corner, would see a blonde and Gabe's guess was the guy Jo saw yesterday, if he was behind this whole thing, probably told his buddies to look for a blonde. He bumped his fist against the wall. *Goddamn.*

"You're right," he said.

Palermo held his hand to his ear. "I'm right? I know that had to hurt."

Fucker. "Dude, you have no idea. Let's roll."

FIVE

The lineup was a bust.

Detective Laughlin had given Jo eight men—all with long, straggly, reddish-blond hair and scary looking—but not one of them remotely resembled the man she'd seen in the shop yesterday. A tad frustrating, but she knew what she saw and the men who'd just filed out weren't it.

She turned back to the detective who stood behind her in the small room, giving her enough personal space as to not pressure her. The overhead track lights shined down on him, giving his face a weird glow. Wasn't this experience creepy enough without the detective looking like something out of a horror movie?

The door opened and Wes poked his head in. "We're good out here. Everyone is cleared out."

Meaning the men she'd just failed to identify had gone back to wherever they came from and she could enter the hallway without being seen.

Detective Laughlin nodded. "Thanks."

"Slight problem though."

"Oh, come on," Jo said, flapping her arms.

He held up his hand, came into the room and shut the door. "We got company outside. Gabe saw four bikers, two on each corner."

"Oh, come on!" Jo said again.

Detective Laughlin propped his hands on his hips, his face stretched long, incredulous. "Now?"

"Yep."

Even for her, this was a new one. Prior to being on Operation Clean Sweep, she'd never—not once—faced threatening situations. In the last few months, her life had turned into a series of threatening situations, and with the addition of this nightmare, the whole blasted thing had gotten old. Fast. Each time before, she could—at least a little bit—accept partial responsibility. Admittedly, she'd put herself in potentially dangerous situations by hunting down a smuggler. But this? All she'd done was walk into a store and buy a pair of knockoff shoes.

"They're waiting for me to come out," she said.

"That's our working theory. Don't panic."

"Ha!"

And they wondered why witnesses refused to testify. Case in point. Right here. Witness intimidation.

Wes marched over to her and gently touched her elbow. "We have a plan. A good one."

Something about his stance, shoulders back, feet spread and the steady, deep tone of his voice made her think of Gabe when he went into mission mode. So alike these two men were. No wonder they both worked special operations.

Wes went through the plan, carefully outlining each element of how they'd get her out of the building. Including dressing her like a hooker. *Oh. Goody.* Her entire career she'd worked hard—enormously hard—to not be just a leggy blonde. She worked hour upon hour, keeping her legs closed and her mind sharp so the men in her field saw a brilliant lawyer. One who'd fight for her clients as rough and hard as any man. She'd used her brain to succeed.

At least until now.

Now, she'd have to dress like a whore.

Wes cocked his head, drawing her back to the conversation. "Are you comfortable with that, Jo?"

Not one bit. Not that it would stop her. No chance. A bunch of thugs would not make her cower. Even if intimidated, she'd never give in to it. For her, it'd be easier to throw herself off of a building. A very high one. "I'll deal with it." She pointed to the door. "Is Gabe out there?"

"Yeah."

"I'd like to talk to him for a second. In private."

"Sure."

The detective and Wes filed out, and a second later, Gabe strode through the door, his usual I-will-kick-your-ass posture in place. "Jesus, Jo, I'm sorry."

She waved that off, made sure to keep a good two feet between them, letting him know she didn't want to be babied. No time for it now. What she needed from him was Sergeant Townsend. Not her boyfriend. Sergeant Townsend would think strategically. Unemotionally.

"This plan," she said, "what do you think?"

"It works. As much as I hate putting you through it, I think it's your best option. The get-up sucks though. You might as well be walking out naked."

And in a building full of cops, male cops who were used to badge bunnies—as Gabe called them—lifting their skirts for men in uniform, that would be humiliating. "I'm focusing on the big picture here. I am. I know I have to do this."

"But?"

"Can I get out of here without half the men in the building seeing me?"

"Way ahead of you." He gestured to the door. "I talked to Palermo. He said you can change in here. Then you walk out, hook a right and not twenty feet down is the back door. We'll put him in front of you and me in the back and Laughlin'll keep the horndogs out of the hallway."

She dropped her head into her hands, let the relief, silly as it was, clear her mind. Her man. He'd known what to do. Which wasn't a surprise given all the recent experience he'd had saving her butt. Such a good man. One who didn't deserve the chaos she inflicted on him. She went on tiptoes and kissed him quick. "Thank you. I love you."

"I love you, too. And I'll get you out of here. Trust me on that."

Five minutes later, Jo stood in the middle of the room wearing an electric blue micro-mini that barely—barely!—covered her rear and a white halter top with a neckline that dipped to her belly button. Not for the first time she thanked the surgeon who'd given her a bang-up boob job because there'd be no bra-wearing in this getup. Obviously, the woman who'd worn this outfit was shorter and thinner than Jo, what with the skirt doubling as sausage casing and the surgically enhanced boobs refusing to be contained.

Dear God.

The only upshot? No mirror for her to stare at her reflection in. A mewling formed deep in her throat and she swallowed because, no way. Nope. Not happening. As humiliating as this was, she would not cry.

A knock sounded on the door. "Jo?"

Gabe.

She cleared her throat, let out a bursting breath. "Come in."

The door swung open and he stepped in, took one look at her and—whoopsie—froze. Terrific. She plopped her hands on her hips, which might have been a mistake because her boobs bounced and well...so did Gabe's eyes.

"Come on!" she hollered.

But the man had been struck stupid. His gaze traveled down her body, of course pausing at her chest because he was a self-proclaimed breast and leg man. But, seriously? *Now* he wanted to do this?

"Sergeant," she said. "You *have* seen me naked."

He shut the door, puffed his cheeks and blew air. "I know, but this is—" He waved his hands. "—different."

What a flaming idiot. "Don't tell me you like it."

He made a half-hearted attempt to shake his head and she rolled her eyes.

"I know." He pounded his fist against his forehead. "I'm the biggest fucking liar walking. I can't help it. The horny part of me likes it. My brain though? That part of me doesn't."

At that, Jo laughed. What else was there to do? "Thank you for your honesty, at least."

"You ready to do this?"

"I guess. I'm not wearing those crazy shoes though. That would put me over the edge. I'll wear my flats."

He reached behind him and retrieved a set of handcuffs from his back pocket. "Honey, in that getup, no one is looking at your feet."

One thing about men, simple creatures that they were, everything came down to sex. And Gabe was no exception. He was as red-blooded as the rest of the probable horndogs outside that door.

She held her hands out and Gabe secured the handcuffs. The clink of metal pierced her ears and she stiffened.

As usual, he picked up on the tension and met her gaze. "You're fine. Okay?"

He ran his hands up her forearms, the heat from his hands seeping into her skin. "I know."

"Besides, we can use these cuffs later."

Flaming. Idiot. "You know you're a pig."

He twisted his lips to hide a grin. "Couldn't resist."

Before leading her out, he checked the hallway and moved into it. As soon as she reached the doorway, Wes fell in line in front of her, giving her a quick perusal—simple creatures, all of them—along the way.

"Eyes, forward," Gabe shot. "You might be a lieutenant, but you're not my lieutenant and I'll kick your ass."

Wes snorted and Jo figured she must have turned aquatic because the surrounding level of testosterone should have drowned her by now. But thankfully, as promised, they'd cleared the hallway and gave her an easy walk to the waiting van parked just outside the rear entrance.

"We're heading straight out the door," Wes said over his shoulder. "The officer will drive a few miles, then pull over and you can hop into the car with Gabe. Townsend, you'll have to haul ass out to your car so you can follow them."

"I'm on it. If I lose them, Jo'll call me and give me a location."

They hustled her outside and she climbed into the waiting van knowing—absolutely positive—her rear was hanging out the back of the micro skirt.

"You're good," Gabe said, right on her heels, blocking the view of anyone who tried to sneak a peek from inside.

"Thank you."

She settled onto the bench seat of the van and glanced out as Wes slid the door closed, the lock catching with a ka-chunk.

Let the games begin.

—:—

Gabe strode through the front doors of the PD, jogged down the steps, and shot a glance at both corners, and yep, there were his buddies, still on their motorcycles, still harassing pedestrians. In seconds, the desk sergeant would come through the side door of the building and start jawing at them, busting balls in an attempt to create a diversion.

During the ball busting, the van would pull out, and if there was a Save-Jo's-Ass god, he—or she—needed to throw some good vibes their way.

Speaking of asses... From the corner someone yelled something about moving one. Gabe glanced over. *Hello, Officer.*

Appeared Jo's savior was right on time. Gabe hopped into the rental, fired it up and backed out quick enough to see the van merge into traffic. At the light, they made a right and Gabe let one car squeak between them. Might as well at least try not to look like Captain Obvious.

He checked his rear view and—shit on a shingle—the bikers turned the corner two cars behind. All the goddamned rotten luck. The desk sergeant must have chased them off and now they were right on him. He grabbed his phone, dialed Wes because Jo being in handcuffs would make answering her phone damned hard.

"What's up?" Wes said.

"I got company."

"Seriously?"

"Yeah." *Because I was dumb enough to engage these assholes while on the phone with my mother.* If ever he'd made a bone-headed mistake, flipping that guy off would rank right up there. "I don't know if they're following me or the van or it's just crappy luck they turned this direction."

"Why would they be following you?"

Great. Now he had to admit it. To fucking Wes. A guy he sort of liked, but hated at the same time. Call it professional rivalry, but Wes, being a lieutenant, had what Gabe wanted. "When I walked outside before, they were jawing at me. I may have—"

"Shit."

"Yeah. I'm gonna peel away, see if they follow me."

"Fuckers," Wes huffed. "I'll hook up with the van, keep Jo on the move until we sort this out."

Gabe disconnected and scanned the area just ahead. A four-way intersection. Pick a side, any side. He hooked a right—no turn signal—and checked the mirror. *Goddamnit.* His guys followed. Good work, Captain Obvious. Now he had to lose them in an unfamiliar city or lead them straight to Jo, who they probably wanted in the first place. *Congratulations, boys, you got a two-for-one!* His best guess was the other two bikers were still back at the PD waiting on their witness to come out and these guys thought they'd have some fun with Gabe. *Well, assholes, bring it on.*

Half a block ahead, what looked like an alley came into view and he floored it, hoping to get a jump on the bikers. He checked his rear view again. *Still there.*

At the alley, he braked hard, squealing the tires as he turned left, his body in a full explosion of energy that he only felt on the job, and damn, he loved that feeling. The killer combo of fear and excitement. Total adrenaline rush. On the back end of the turn, the rear of the rental swung wide and took out two garbage cans that spilled into the alley. Gabe checked the mirror, spotted the bikers following. The first guy swerved—major mistake—to avoid the trash can and—bye-bye—dumped his bike over.

One down.

One left.

At the end of the alley, Gabe sailed around the corner—oncoming car. *Shit.* He floored it and the car bolted, barely missing a collision with the approaching car. The driver screamed to a stop in the intersection, sat on his horn and flipped Gabe off. Whole lotta flipping off going on today.

"Sorry, dude."

He checked the mirror again, found his biker buddy still with him. But the odds were even now. One on one. Advantage Gabe. His phone rang. Wes. *Now he wants to chat?* He snatched it up as he barreled through another intersection and hit the speaker button.

"Hey."

"You okay?"

"Yeah. How's Jo?"

"She's fine. Hang on."

"Are you there?"

Jo's voice. On speaker. And, damn that was a relief. Just hearing her slowed his heart rate. "I'm here. Are you all right?"

"I'm fine. Wes met up with the van and got me. We're cruising around. Where are you?"

"I lost one of them. He's ass over elbow in an alley picking through garbage."

"Nice," Wes said.

Gabe grinned. Maybe Wes wasn't so bad. "The other one is behind me. I'm about to pull over and have a talk with him."

"Come again?" Wes said.

"Gabe, please don't," Jo added.

Gabe blew right over whatever their concerns might be.

"Wes, you got anyone on patrol you can send to check on a couple of guys about to throw down? They delay this jackhole and I move on my way."

"I like it," Wes said. "Keep driving until you hear from me."

At the next block, Gabe rattled off the cross streets then promised to stay on the current road and disconnected before Jo could start arguing. He tossed the phone on the seat, checked on his tail and hoped like hell those patrol officers showed up.

After the next light, he pulled into a bus stop, the only open spot on the street. A bus showing up would be the least of their problems. No one sat on the bench waiting, so chances were if a bus did show up, the driver would keep going. Gabe jammed the car into park, hopped out and stormed the biker who'd pulled behind him.

"What's your problem, dude?"

"Hey, mama's boy. I'm gonna fuck you up."

Ya think? He swung his leg over the bike—*now*—and Gabe launched forward, shoving him backward over the bike. The guy, surprisingly nimble for someone that fleshy, hopped to his feet and the sun glinted off something in his hand—*knife!* Another burst of energy slammed Gabe and he kicked out, sending the switchblade flying. Biker boy scrunched his face and roared, a seriously primal howl, before plowing into Gabe, the full force of that extra body weight knocking him back a few steps. *Whap, whap, whap.* Gabe popped off a few jabs. The guy staggered a few steps and Gabe cracked him again, sending him to the ground. *Jesus, where's that squad?*

As much as he'd like to beat the ever-loving-shit out of this guy, he was still a police officer and a street brawl wouldn't help his chances at a promotion.

A wailing siren mixed with the honking of horns and shouts from passing cars. People sure loved a show. The *whoop-whoop* of the siren grew louder and the patrol car swung around the corner. Two cops jumped out.

Finally. Gabe threw his hands up, turned to the two officers.

"On the ground. Now!"

Flesh-boy jumped up, his face a bloody mess, but Gabe had to give him points for stamina because he made another move toward him. Lunging as Gabe sidestepped.

"On the ground!" both officers hollered, their voices sharp and seriously direct.

Gabe made eye contact with the officer closest to him, a young guy with sandy hair and a baby face, but this kid was all business as he jerked his head sideways. "You. Against the car."

"Whose knife is this?" the other cop asked.

"His," Gabe said. "I kicked it out of his hand."

The cop pointed at the biker. "You. Over there. My partner will talk to you."

Which meant the older officer had gotten the 411 from Wes. Or at least from someone in contact with Wes. Gabe strode to the car, his hands at his sides where they could be seen.

"Townsend, right?" the officer asked.

"Yeah." Gabe checked his name tag. Wilson. "Thanks for the help."

He nodded. "No problem. These biker gangs are a pain in my ass. Let's stand here a second, pretend we're deep in conversation and then you'll hop into your car and leave.

We'll keep your friend here busy. The knife alone gets him a ride to HQ. Palermo said you're ESU out East."

"Yeah. A sergeant. On vacation with my girl."

And, yikes, he'd said it. Freely admitted to a stranger that Jo was his girlfriend. Stress did that to a man. Made his lips looser. Or maybe, being royally sick of hiding, he didn't give a shit anymore.

"Helluva way to spend a vacation."

"Amen, brother."

Wilson glanced right, checked on his partner cuffing the biker. "Turn around. I'll pat you down to make this look good and you're on your way."

"Roger that."

Gabe put his hands on his head while Wilson did a cursory patdown that avoided the crotch area. *Thank you very much.*

"You're good," he said. "Take it easy."

The biker stood on the curb in cuffs, glaring at him, and Gabe would have loved to smart off, but no sense poking that bear again.

At least not until they switched out their rental car, because if this biker had any kind of street smarts, which Gabe figured he did, he'd have already memorized the license plate. If numbnuts fell into the category of enterprising criminals, he might have connections that could secure an address for the car. In this case, they'd have to get the rental car company to give them the name of the hotel where their customer was staying. No easy task, but the Save-Jo's-Ass god could only be expected to do so much. Why take a chance? They'd play it safe and return the rental.

First, he needed Jo.

Fast.

SIX

The second Wes dropped Jo at the hotel—yay on walking through the lobby dressed like a prostitute—she went straight upstairs, aiming for a good, long shower. The entire experience left slimy, ugly filth—even if she couldn't see it—plastered to her skin.

She twisted the faucet to hot and adjusted the spray on the shower head to just short of bash mode. What she needed was a good scrubbing with her own body wash. Lawyer Jo body wash with its subdued lavender scents that relaxed her.

Stripping out of the clothes, she folded them and set them on the sink. She'd like to toss them into a heap on the floor—or burn them—but they weren't hers and she supposed the officer they belonged to would eventually need them again. And God bless that woman for her service. For being willing to risk getting hurt or possibly killed by walking the streets in that getup. In the past year, Jo had spent a lot of time around cops, mostly men, and could not imagine, not even when she opened her mind to its full expanse, the nerve it took to lure johns. So, no, she'd fold the clothes nicely, have the hotel launder them and return them to the officer herself so she could thank her.

For the clothes and for her service.

Steam filled the bathroom and she propped the door a few inches. As much as she wanted the heat, suffocating didn't seem like a great option. Under the spray, she squeezed a massive amount of body wash into a washrag—could really use a loofah—and scrubbed until pain pricked at her and the pressure turned her skin a raw pink.

She stared at the spot on her wrist where the handcuffs had cut into her, focused on it and breathed in. What a day. All of it. The lineup, the bikers, the getup. But she needed to remain calm. Lawyer mode. In lawyer mode, reason outweighed emotion, but even this was too much.

All because she'd walked into a store to buy some knockoff merchandise. Gabe was right. She needed to stop. Harmless as it might have seemed, if she hadn't been in that store, she'd not be a potential witness to a murder. Simple fact. One added to the other simple facts that in the last few months she'd had her hand broken by an enraged store owner, got trapped in an intentionally set fire, and had a bomb strapped to her. And each time Gabe was left to help her get out of it. They could have both been killed.

All because she wanted to chase counterfeit merchandise.

"Some life, Jo," she muttered.

Her breath caught and she squeezed her eyes closed, forcing herself to concentrate on the mundane task of bathing. Of scrubbing the filth away. Crying would not help her. *Crying.* Please. She'd cried what, maybe three times in the last year? She certainly wasn't going to do it now.

No. Everything was fine. She was safe. *Gabe* was safe. She needed to get through this shower, stop the insane little meltdown, and hit reset. Be the strong, in-control Jo who'd convinced the mayor of New York to trust her. The fucking powerhouse of intellectual property attorneys.

That's who she needed to be.

She raised her head and let the hot, needling spray batter her face. *Forget the pity party.* But, damn, that was getting harder and harder. An intellectual property attorney shouldn't face life-threatening scenarios. With what Gabe did for a living, yes, but not her.

And worse, she'd done it to herself. Every shop she walked into searching for knockoffs, every lead she chased, every smuggler she investigated caused this. *She'd* caused this.

The water continued to pound on her, a storm of drops smacking, stinging her raw skin and she stared down at her brutalized arms. What a mess. *What have I done?*

She didn't know.

Somehow she'd been blind to the series of mini-nightmares her life had become and now they stacked up, crushing her, reminding her it was her fault.

And now, another mess. A murder investigation. With Gabe in the middle of it.

She squeezed the washrag in her hand, raked it against her thighs, scrubbing, scrubbing, scrubbing, but the dirt, she felt it, sticking to her skin, taunting her. *Dammit.* The fucking dirt wouldn't come off and she pounded her fists against her legs, opened her mouth and a gulping sob erupted.

No. No crying. No crying.

But the tears came, flooding her eyes, mixing with the shower spray and she swiped at them. Coming unglued in the shower. *Terrific, Jo. Just great.*

Her heart slammed and she bent at the waist, pushing

her hands against her chest, pressing in, wanting all the pain and agony and fear to cease. Just stop, right there in the shower because she couldn't take it anymore. Not one thing more.

"Jo?" Gabe called

Oh, no. Don't let him see this.

And, God, the sound of his voice triggered something. Something wild and desperate and weak that she'd been so close to tamping down. She shot straight, sucked a huge breath through her nose, held it.

"I'm here," she croaked.

Dammit with the soppy hysterics. Who the hell was she right now? Not the mighty Jo Pomeroy. The woman who never backed down, the so-called powerhouse, had turned tail and ran, leaving behind a sniveling lump of useless tears.

The shower curtain whipped open and she flinched. Gabe stood there, his eyes slightly narrowed as water bounced off of her and hit his shirt. Ignoring the spray, he grabbed her, pulled her against him, her soaked skin rubbing against his clothes as he wrapped her in a back-crushing hug. She buried her face in his neck and held on— *so need this*—squeezing hard enough to pull strength from his huge body. Her breath hitched and she shuddered because Gabe was here. Solid and strong and immovable. The steel structure to cling to when the walls blew apart. That was Gabe. Even when she made him crazy, he kept her safe.

"Just breathe," he whispered, his soft voice drilling right into her chaotic thoughts. "It's okay. Crying doesn't make you weak."

And that did it. All the anger and fear and trapped

emotions shot right up her throat, clawing their way, ripping free in a wail.

God, how humiliating. Not just crying, but wailing like a demon.

"I was so scared," she sobbed. "For you. For me. I didn't know what to do and I had to wear those fucking clothes and they made me feel so dirty and I feel like everything I've done since yesterday afternoon has been wrong. I can't do this anymore."

He kissed the top of her head and stepped back, holding her at arm's length. The man was soaked. His hair, his shirt, his shorts. Even his sneakers were probably ruined. "I'm so sorry," she said.

"Listen, crazy blond lady, don't apologize."

Crazy blond lady. The moniker he leveled on her when she got on a roll. She laughed...well...a quasi-sob-snort-laugh that came out as a honk. Extremely attractive, that.

He hit her with *the* smile. The sexy shark Gabe smile that turned her a little gooey. "I'm sorry," she said again.

"You're apologizing for apologizing?"

Yes. As nutty as that was.

But he hugged her again, running his big hands over her back, dotting kisses down her shoulder while water continued to flood the place. "We're both okay. No harm done. The bikers never saw you. The two that followed me, I took care of."

She nodded. "Wes told me. They arrested the one guy, right?"

"Yeah. He'll be out soon enough, but we'll deal with it. As soon as you're done in here, we're swapping out the rental."

"Why?"

"A precaution. In case he got the plate number. I don't put anything past these idiots. We'll get ahead of it."

Good. She needed that. Getting control back, at least some of it, would settle her. She eased her arms from his and turned back to the falling water so he wouldn't see the damage she'd inflicted on herself. "I'm almost done. I felt...dirty."

"It's okay to feel dirty. Why do you think I sometimes take three showers a day?"

He knows. She thought back on all the times she'd teased him about using too many towels and instantly regretted it. Before today, she rolled her eyes at his sudden announcements that he needed a shower. Somehow, she'd never made the connection that those multiple showers came on days when the depravity he faced had been particularly brutal.

She was so dumb. The showers were his coping mechanism. He didn't talk. He *bathed.* Tried to wash it all down the drain. Just as she'd done. "I never realized," she said.

"Some people disassociate, I take showers." He stepped back, glanced down at the flooding floor and his soaked clothes. "I'm gonna get this cleaned up. Take your time." He waggled his eyebrows. "Unless you want me to scrub your back?"

Reset button. She'd just had a world-class meltdown, showed more vulnerability than she'd known she'd ever had, and had done it in front of Gabe. And she didn't feel...embarrassed.

She felt safe and nurtured and loved.

So this is what it's supposed to be.

She twisted the shower off, stood in the tub naked and dripping while Gabe stared at her, clearly wondering what she was about. Rather than keep him guessing, she grabbed his soaked shirt and went up on tiptoes, kissed him in that aggressive way he liked and he slid his arms around her, lifting her out of the tub.

Reset button. Jo and Gabe style.

They devoured each other. Feasted like never before as he carried her over to the bed, and her pulse slammed in anticipation of world-rocking sex from a man she adored and loved beyond reason.

If she had anything to say about it, the big, bad ESU sergeant would be in a wheelchair by the time she got done with him.

He set her on the bed and went to work ditching his wet clothes. He sat down, got rid of his shorts and Jo shoved him backward, straddling him and discovering, without question, Mr. August was ready for her.

"I'm in a hurry," she said, hoping they were on the same page there.

"Yes, dear," he cracked.

He gripped her hips as she slid over him, as always loving the feel of him inside her. She shifted her hips, silently begging him to move with her, to pick up the damned pace already because, wow, her body ached for this. He closed his eyes again, angled his head back and let out a soft breath.

Then he flipped her. Just like that—*bam*—she was on her back with Gabe still inside her, but moving oh-so-oh-slow and it drove her to madness, her mind absolutely frying from the tension. But she knew what he was doing. Sure did. This was Gabe's own little brand of torment so he could make the euphoria last.

He kissed her neck, nibbled the skin there, that extra sensitive spot and... *I'll kill him later.* He'd discovered that little secret their first night together and had since been using it against her. She'd never complain though.

She loved this man.

Maybe too much. If that was even possible. All she knew was it hurt, a physical ache that bore into her and swarmed when they were apart. If he broke her heart, he'd need more than his ESU team to save him from her wrath. She reached up, ran her fingers into his hair. He'd let it grow an extra half inch since she'd left New York and the strands glided over her fingers.

"Speed it up, Gabe."

"What? You're still in a hurry, Counselor?"

Fwap. She smacked his bare back. Hard. But laughed too because this was them. The interplay. The annoying, playful banter. The challenge. "You're such a smartass."

"Ow," he said, his voice flat, almost taunting in that twisted way that amused him.

But enough of this slow quasi-punishment that made her want to beat on him, just throttle him senseless. From under him, she bucked her hips. If he wouldn't pick up the pace, she would. "We can play later. Now, I need this. *Sergeant.*"

And still, he moved at his maddening pace, his big body surrounding her, consuming her, *loving* her in ways that, before him, she hadn't known someone could. He propped himself on one arm and inched his free hand down her thigh before hooking it around her knee to push her leg up.

Oh, that's good. "There you go, fella."

This had become the game. One of them offering up torture in the most exquisite form until the other begged for mercy. And then, invariably, their greed took over and they couldn't resist the lure of an astounding orgasm.

Gabe exhaled sharply—*now*—his cue that he'd given in.

He pumped harder and she moved with him, faster and faster until her mind splintered and her body did the reverse, somehow coiling and tightening and...so close. She brought her hands up, slid her fingers over the perfect curve of his cheek, down the column of his neck and over the bunched muscles in his shoulder, letting the warmth from his body sink into her. He met her gaze, holding it for a few long seconds until his body tensed up. He was right there. That perfect edge he loved to ride as long as possible.

She loved these seconds, those precious few blinks, before the explosion tore through him. Magic. A drug-free high that came with loving each other. So beautiful. Him, the lovemaking, the way their bodies fit together, all of it brought calm and a wistful happiness.

He pushed her leg higher, getting so deep inside her she gripped the sheet, yanking it right from the edge of the mattress because—*wow*—it had never been quite this intense before. Never. She focused on that feeling—so perfect and extraordinary. Familiar and...well...different.

"Gabe?"

"What?"

A dozen thoughts swirled in her head, each of them smothering whatever naughty thing she was about to say. *Forget it.* She slammed her eyes closed. "So close," she said.

There. The incredible squeeze happened low in her belly and stole her breath. She fought it, exhaled sharply, then pulled air back in again, slowing her body down, forcing the little explosions of light behind her eyes to last. She glanced up at him and ran her hands over his massive chest, along the hard curves he worked so hard for.

The orgasm ripped into her and her body stiffened for a split second before everything broke apart.

Blown away. Completely.

This was life with Gabe. Everything to the limit. Pure totality. She reached up, held onto his shoulders, her gaze on him as he threw his head back again, gritted his teeth and focused on his own body's release.

"I love you," she said.

And that did it. He gave in and let go, crying out, allowing himself to finally lose control as she braced herself for the collapse of two hundred and thirty pounds of muscle on top of her. Wham. He dropped, their bodies, still joined, sinking into the mattress. Eventually, he'd worry about crushing her and would roll off, but she held on an extra few seconds, letting him know she was okay.

Too late.

His weight lifted and a shock of cold air hit her, all that amazing heat gone.

Snuggling in to recapture the heat, she kissed his shoulder. "I hated being gone from you these past weeks. I'll try not to do that anymore."

"That'd be good. Otherwise, Counselor, I'll be trailing you."

"I wouldn't mind that, Sergeant."

Not in this lifetime would she mind that.

—:—

After swapping rental cars, Gabe's body reminded him he needed fuel. They hadn't eaten since that crappy burger five hours ago and Jo always said he ate like a dinosaur so he might as well chow down.

He pulled into the underground parking for their hotel and contemplated food options. After the day they'd had, he didn't necessarily want Jo traipsing around outside. Staying inside, out of public, might be the better option. Paranoia aside, he was damned tired and could use a nap.

"How about we order room service?"

From the passenger seat, she shook her head. "I knew you'd bring up food before we got back. Your body is like clockwork and you didn't have your afternoon side-of-beef. Ordering in sounds good though. I'm beat after my ugly freak-out earlier. I don't know how drama queens do it. All this emotional upheaval is exhausting."

"You're a force, Jo. A strong woman who takes no crap."

"I must have been a man in a prior life."

"Hokay, then. I don't need that picture in my head. Thanks though."

He found a spot close to the elevator, parked, and did a quick scan of the area before getting out. As soon as this incident got cleared—whenever that might be—they were going somewhere. Somewhere warm and away from LA where they could have a real vacation. At this point, he'd rent a damned island and make sure there were no stores there. No threat of knockoffs. Anywhere.

They rode the elevator up to their room where Jo perused the room service menu while Gabe took a call from Bardin, the DEA agent they'd met with that morning. Just in case, he wandered out to the balcony to avoid Miss Big Ears listening in.

"Hey," he said into the phone. "What's up?"

"I just saw one of my informants. Figured I'd ask him if he had anything on that 12th Street Crew."

Gabe swung back to check on Jo. She was out of sight. Bathroom maybe. He leaned one elbow against the balcony wall and gazed up at the sun throwing shadows over the surrounding buildings. "And?"

"They've been hanging out at some place called the Last

Chance. One of their members owns it. Apparently the guy's mother left him money and he sunk it into the bar so he could run a legitimate business."

"You think it's a front?"

"I'm sure. But who knows? The guy is in his fifties, so he may be outgrowing his violent ways."

Hmmm...maybe he'd hop over there. See if their guy with the skull tattoo showed up at the bar. If so, Gabe would call the detectives to get over there. That might be a plan. Might also get him in hot water.

Eh.

His antics today already had him partway there and he wasn't one to do things half-assed.

"I'll do that," he said. "Thanks. You got an address for the place?"

"Not exact, but I'll text you the cross streets."

Gabe ended the call, looked up and—*hello, gorgeous*—Jo stood in the doorway eyeballing him. *So fucked.* "Hiya."

She nodded at the phone in his hand. "Who was that? And don't lie. I heard you say something about a front."

There went plan A. Unless he could come up with a reason his mother had an interest in fronts. Plan B. "It was uh, Bardin. He had some info on a new biker hangout. He figured I'd want to pass it on to the detectives."

"Excellent. Why don't we do that right now? Because if I know you, which I'm fairly confident I do, you've got it in your head that you'll get this thing moving and head over there yourself to check it out."

A few months ago, he'd have talked his way around this. Easily. Now? He was toast. After all the months he'd spent railing on her about hunting knockoffs on her own, she'd give him a good beat-down if he went rogue.

His phone beeped. Incoming text. Must be Bardin. "Jo, relax. It's nothing."

He pushed by her and headed toward the bathroom, tossing his phone on the table on his way. *Yeah, hide in the bathroom, chickenshit.*

Leaning against the sink, he ran options. If he tried to leave the hotel for any reason, she'd be on him. And lying—Plan A—was definitely out.

Rather than admit she freaking terrified him when she got into this hyper-aware mode, he flushed the toilet and washed his hands. *Just taking a piss, honey.*

He swung the door open, found her sitting on the arm of the sofa, hands at her sides, fingers tapping and those fierce blue eyes pinning him. "What are you up to, Sergeant?"

Screwed. No way would he get out of this. He held up his hands. "Okay. Here it is."

"Can't wait."

"Hardy, har. You stay here and I'll cruise by the place. Maybe sit on it awhile and see if our guy shows up."

"No."

No? At that, Gabe snickered. She was dreaming if she thought that'd work. When had *that* ever worked in their relationship? For either of them.

"What if the bikers from this afternoon are there? They'll recognize you."

"Nada. I had a hat and glasses on and the only one who got a decent look at me was the one who got pinched. Besides, I just said I'd stay in the car."

"And you think I believe that?"

This blowout, and it would be a blowout, would have to wait. They didn't fight a lot. Maybe they got loud and disagreed, but they didn't consider that a fight. A fight for them would be full-on war, complete with searing sarcasm, a lot of yelling, and Jo occasionally slamming shit. That didn't happen all that much. When it did though, neither of them feared it. The tension spinning in his gut told him this would be one of those times.

Gabe waved her off. "I don't care what you believe. And I'm not arguing about it." He grabbed the car keys and his phone off the table. "I'm gonna make this quick run. You stay here."

Assuming she understood, he nodded. "No argument. Excellent."

She turned away from him, stared out the balcony door. "I try to avoid arguing with bullheaded people. Do what you want, Gabe. You will anyway."

Please with the drama. As if she didn't do what she wanted all the time? How many times had he warned her about shopping for knockoffs on her own? She was not pulling this bullshit on him.

"Jo, I'm not doing this. Later, we can discuss all the crap you pull when I specifically ask you not to."

She scoffed. "Nice, Gabe."

He waggled his finger at her. "I know what you're doing. You figure you'll keep me talking and I won't go anywhere. It's not working." He turned back to the door, ripped it open. "Lock this behind me. And stay put." He spun back to her. "Jo, I swear to God, if you leave this room, I'll go crazy on you."

SEVEN

Gabe walked into the Last Chance bar, no grill, just your basic shot-and-a-beer joint, and found the place surprisingly clean. Damn near tidy. He'd expected scarred paneling and chipped floors. What he got was freshly painted walls in a dark tan and gleaming hardwood. Even the brass fixtures on the bar had been polished. The few high-top tables were empty, probably because of the dinner hour and customers leaving to find food. In the back corner sat a pool table. Three guys wearing leather vests and looking like they hadn't bathed in months stood around it. Two of them leaned against stools and held cue sticks while one bent to take a shot.

The guy took his shot and walked around the table, flashing Gabe the back of his vest. The upper rocker on the man's vest read 12th Street Crew and the lower one California.

Right place. Bardin had nailed it. But, shit, aside from the bikers, it didn't exactly look like the dump he'd expected.

One of the bikers leaning on the stool stared at Gabe, a

hard, threatening stare meant to engage. *Nice try, ace.* Gabe met that stare long enough to let this asshole know he was aware of him and then squatted on a stool near the middle of the bar. Not too close, not too far from the three men. All he needed to do was nurse a beer and listen.

The bartender, a guy in his fifties with a long beard, more gray than brown, nodded at him. His dark hair was slicked back into a pony tail and he had the burned-out, ruddy-cheeked look of a biker. Well, a semi-cleaned up one. The crew playing pool? They were a mess. Long, greasy hair all over the place, stained T-shirts, and ripped jeans, and even from Gabe's spot at the bar, he breathed in someone's disgusting body odor.

A cardboard coaster landed in front of him courtesy of the bartender. "How you doin'?"

"Good," Gabe said.

He ordered a bottled beer. The place looked more than decent but he wasn't taking a chance on drinking from a tap. Who knew where the beer had come from and the last time the tap was cleaned. The bartender set the bottle in front of him.

"Thanks."

"Sure. First time here? I haven't seen you before."

"Yeah. Figured I'd stop in. You the owner?"

"Yep. Name's Gus. Been here three weeks. Totally remodeled the place."

Gabe looked around, banged his knuckles on the bar. "Looks like it. Nice job."

"You live around here?"

"Nah. Out East. Visiting my sister. She lives here."

Whoops. This would be one of those less is more times when giving as little information as possible would only help. On the way over, he'd put together a piss-ant cover story that included Jo being his sister. If questioned too much, his cover story wouldn't hold up. At all.

Telling these people he was from out of town though worked and explained why he didn't know the area. DeFiore would shit if he knew the ESU guy was test-driving an undercover gig.

To Gabe's left, one of the bikers threw some bills on the bar and Gus poured three more drafts. "You assholes better slow down. I don't want no trouble in here tonight. You bust this place up and you're paying for it."

The biker, the B.O. one, reached across and smacked a hand on Gus's shoulder. "Relax, man. We're chill."

Gus hefted a tray of dirty mugs and walked through a swinging door while Gabe took another slug of his beer. The mirror behind the bar gave him a nice view of the guy waiting for the next game eyeballing him. But Gabe? He'd sit tight and attempt to give Gus his wish and not have the place busted up. Three against one, even as a skilled operator, did not present good odds. He'd still rise to it, but he'd have to break a sweat and really, he wasn't in the mood.

Someone slid onto the stool next to him and he glanced over, nearly pissing himself at the sight of Palermo.

Shit on a shingle. How the fuck? Gabe ticked back his conversation with Bardin. Maybe he'd somehow gotten Palermo's name and number and called him?

Nah. How would that happen so fast?

Gabe took in Palermo's same faded black T-shirt and jeans from earlier. He'd swapped out his sneakers for black boots, but with the high-and-tight hair and thrown back shoulders, he still screamed cop. "Hey."

"You look surprised to see me."

"Fuckin' ay, pal. How the hell?"

Gus pushed through the swinging doors again, spotted

his new customer, and offered up the "how you doin'?" star treatment Gabe had received. Palermo ordered a draft—brave guy—and as Gus poured it, he slid a sideways glance at Gabe.

"Friend of yours? I thought you were from out of town."

Gee, thanks, Palermo, for loading the man up on suspicion. "I am. He's seeing my sister. Just met him yesterday." Gabe reached over, gave Palermo's shoulder a squeeze that would have dropped a weaker man. "We're gonna bond. Aren't we, buddy?"

Gus snorted, apparently understanding the underlying message that Gabe was about to give Palermo the rules about dating his imaginary sister. All Palermo had to do was keep his mouth closed until Gabe could give him the cover story.

Two of the idiots at the pool table popped off at each other and Gus wandered to the end of the bar. Most likely, he had a bat—or shotgun—tucked under the bar to deal with these fuckers. Guys like them were too volatile, too unpredictable, too violent, and if Gus wanted to run a clean place, he needed to bust that shit outta here.

With the bartender occupied, Gabe spun to Palermo. "How'd you get here?"

Palermo held up his mug and grinned. "Jo called me. She read your texts."

Gabe cocked his head, twisted his mouth and replayed his discussion with Jo. The bathroom. When he'd gone into the bathroom, he left his phone on the table and sneaky, brilliant witch that she was, she read his texts. All along, she'd known exactly where he was heading and had probably decided to call Palermo before they'd even argued.

Gabe laughed. "She is brilliant. A pain in the ass, but brilliant."

"Yeah, well, you two can fight about it later." Palermo leaned in, kept his voice low as not to be overheard. "She's worried about you. What are you thinking, doing this by yourself?"

Gabe shrugged. "Hey, I didn't think you'd be interested in a sneak-and-peek. You could get yourself a rip for being here."

"I know. Thanks for that, asshole."

But, would you look at that? Tight-ass Palermo grinned. The guy was having fun. Maybe he wasn't the King of Douche-Bagery Gabe wanted him to be. Which sucked. Royally.

Palermo scanned the place while sipping his bear. "What have we got?"

"Not sure yet. Those three are part of the 12th Street Crew. My story is I'm from out East. Here visiting my sister."

"Jo's the sister and I'm the boyfriend? I like that."

Refusing to rise to that obvious bait, Gabe grinned. "My DEA contact says the guy in the sketch looks like some asshole named Jimmy Jax. He sells counterfeit cigarettes."

"Which was why he was in the store that day."

Gabe rang an imaginary bell. "Ding, ding. Jimmy Jax has a skull tat on his left arm. The goal here is to see if he's hanging around any of the normal haunts. None of these guys are even close. Figured I'd wait an hour, see if he shows up. Or maybe I'll hear something from these mopes."

"Heads up. Company on your six."

Meaning he had one of said mopes coming their way and needed to put his acting skills to work.

"Yeah," Gabe said, raising his voice. "None of this bullshit of not showing up when you're supposed to. I'll kick your sorry ass."

The biker—not the smelly one—shoved the stool next to Palermo sideways and rested one arm on the bar.

Palermo spun around, his back to the bar so he could scan the room while talking. "What's up?" he said to his hovering guest.

"You a cop or military?"

Dammit.

"Military. Retired Marine. Got a problem with that?"

Whether or not Palermo was actually a Marine was anyone's guess, but he had the look so why not? Gabe took another slug of his beer just in case he might have to waste it by cracking the bottle over someone's head.

The biker nodded. "Nah, man. No problem. Thanks for your service."

He stuck his hand out—well, holy shit—for Palermo to shake. This was one crazy-assed scenario.

"Thank you," he said. "Appreciate that."

The guy nodded, started to turn away, but Palermo wasn't done. "Hey, listen, I'm looking for a guy who runs with 12th Street. Name's Jimmy."

This information was met with a cold stare that gave Gabe the *ah, shit* feeling just as his phone buzzed. He grabbed it from his pocket and glanced at the screen. Jo. *Not now, honey.*

Palermo obviously didn't get the *ah, shit* feeling because he dove right in. "Someone told me he sells wholesales cigarettes. I'm up for buying a few cases, see if I can make some fast cash."

"Who's your buddy?"

"He's not a buddy. I've seen him around, talked to him a little bit. Guy named Dougie."

"And how does he know Jimmy?"

"Do I look like the Internet? How the fuck do I know how he knows him? Is he around or not."

And...here we go. Gabe set his beer on the bar, ready to hand out some ass-kickings. He spun around, checked on the other bikers, two of whom now moved closer. If Palermo wanted to nuke the place, he could have at least waited until they'd gotten out.

"Hey," Gus yelled. "I don't want no trouble in here!"

Gabe held up his hands. "No problem, Gus. We're good."

The biker Palermo was jawing with turned back to his buddies. "Get Jimmy on the phone. Tell him there's a guy here, wants to talk to him."

Jimmy showed up twenty minutes later carrying two good sized boxes in each of his beefy arms. Counterfeit cigarettes, most likely, since Palermo had told him that's what he was interested in. Gabe sure hoped Palermo had cash. He'd been so pissed at Jo before he'd left that he'd forgotten to grab extra cash. Forty bucks was all he had to offer to this transaction. And Jimmy didn't look like he took credit cards.

Jimmy did, however, resemble the man Jo described and Gabe glanced at his forearms where a long-sleeved T-shirt covered all skin to his wrists. Crap.

"You Jimmy?" Palermo asked.

"Yeah. You the guy looking for me?"

"Sure am."

Jimmy set the large boxes on the bar and Gabe slid a sideways glance at the other bikers.

"Here you go." Jimmy tapped the box with one knuckle. "You got twenty-five cartons here. These are my best sellers. Give me $300 for all twenty-five."

Gabe swallowed. Yeah. He hoped Palermo had cash.

"Three hundred? Steep, isn't it?"

"You'll sell them for twenty a carton. That's an eight dollar profit on each."

And then Jimmy made Gabe's little heart go pitter-patter by hiking up his shirt sleeves and revealing one very large skull on his left forearm.

Game over. Mission accomplished and all that shit. All they needed to do was either follow Jimmy out of here or get someone from the PD to tail him and haul him in for questioning. Bam. Hello, vacation with Jo.

Gabe stood, dropped a twenty on the bar and waved at Gus.

Palermo glanced up at him. "You good."

"I'm good," he said.

Palermo turned back to Jimmy. "Let me think about it. I don't have that kind of cash on me."

"Whoa," Jimmy said, grabbing Palermo's arm. "I just hauled my ass down here and now you want to think about it. I'm running a business here. I don't have time for this shit." Jimmy stepped closer, got right into Palermo's space. "You're buying cigarettes."

Behind them, the bikers, like sharks to blood, sensed tension and stood. Three on two. Plus Gus—wherever he'd fall. Decent odds.

"Look," Gabe said, "we don't want a problem."

"Then your boy here buys cigarettes."

The bikers stepped closer, puffing up their chests, angling for a dust-up. Gabe sighed. "Too bad you left your cue sticks at the pool table."

"We don't need no cue sticks," the smelly one said, ripping a knife from under his vest.

These fuckers and their knives. Gabe had had enough of it. The third biker stepped closer and—voila—another knife appeared.

Three on two. Plus the knives. *Shit.* Palermo darted his eyes to the smelly one and back. Code for "he's mine."

No problem. Gabe cocked his head, measuring the other two. And then, like hell itself had opened up, the bikers rushed them. Palermo ducked, dropped to his knees and drove a fist between Jimmy's legs. He grabbed his crotch, staggering while his eyes rolled back.

Smell-boy lunged at Gabe, knife whipping and Gabe shifted left—boom—blasted him with an overhand right, flattening his nose.

Palermo leapt for the third biker, but glass shattered behind them and Gabe angled toward the pool table before Jimmy and Smell-boy rebounded. Gus—in a truly fantastic and *oh-fuck* move—stood on the bar with a broken whiskey bottle in his hand. "Cut it out!"

The distraction was all Palermo needed. He grabbed a bar stool, swung it, and knocked the third guy's legs out from under him, sending him crashing into the bar.

Smell-boy launched himself up, throwing wild punches and catching Gabe with a hard right and—whew—that rang his bell. Smell-boy charged, his shoulder plowing right into Gabe's gut, shoving him backward, flat on his back onto the pool table. Gabe wheezed, coughed out a breath just as the guy charged again and leapt. The eight ball sat by Gabe's right hand and he grabbed hold—whack—slammed it into the big man's temple. The man went slack, but holy shit, half the guy's weight pinned him to the table.

At the end of the bar, Palermo and a now recovered Jimmy squared off.

"Knock it off!" Gus hollered. "I'm calling the cops!"

Palermo faked a left, stepped right, and drove a fist deep into Jimmy's ribs. Jimmy winced, grabbed Palermo by his waist, and tossed him onto the bar. He landed hard and groaned as his car keys and wallet flew from his pocket and slid down the bar. Well, shit. The man had serious strength.

"You sonofabitch," Jimmy screamed, pulling a gun from his jacket and pointing it at Palermo. He cocked the hammer back just as Gus scrambled for the wallet.

Ah, fuck.

"Wait!" Gus hollered. He held the wallet open, showing a badge. "They're cops."

EIGHT

Gabe sat in a chair with two of the bikers standing over him, one with a knife, the other with the bad news end of a .38 pointed at him. The second that .38 made its appearance, their odds plummeted. And with Palermo half-conked out, well the fight turned from a bar brawl to survival. And at the moment, survival meant letting Palermo get his head straight before they took another run at these boys.

Gabe shifted his gaze to Palermo, who faced similar circumstances with Jimmy and another knife. Palermo had taken a pretty good beating. Blood poured from his nose and left eye and streamed down his face.

"Stand 'em up," Jimmy said. "Search them."

They were hauled to their feet and held at gunpoint while the two bikers grabbed Gabe's wallet and phone and set them on the bar next to Palermo's.

"Fucking cops!" Gus yelled. "You sons of bitches. I told you three weeks ago I was running a legit joint here."

Then Gabe's phone buzzed, rattling against the solid surface of the bar. *Crap, crap, crap.* He shifted his eyes left, prayed it wasn't Jo calling. If it was, her picture would be stretched across the screen of his phone. Right next to Jimmy, who couldn't resist looking.

"Whoa," Jimmy said. "Ain't she pretty."

Gabe's mind exploded. A full-on panic he'd never experienced, even on the job, and something roared inside. He jumped from the chair, felt the barrel of a gun pressed against the back of his head, and stopped. Halted right in his goddamn spot.

"Sit your ass down," Smell-boy said.

The gun pressed against his head again and Palermo jerked his thumb, urging Gabe to sit. Probably his best option because losing his shit and getting killed wouldn't help Jo.

He sat.

For now.

The phone buzzed again and Jimmy picked it up, studying the picture. "Hold up, here."

Goddamnit.

Then Jimmy burst out laughing, a demented cackling that scraped right up Gabe's spine.

"What's funny?" Smell-boy wanted to know.

Jimmy pointed at Jo's picture then swiped at the screen. "That's her. Huh. Hang on." He looked at Gabe, a shit-eating grin tearing across his face. "This your girl?"

Gabe continued his silence.

"That's okay. I'll figure it out. Oh," he said, laughing a little. "Look at this. You texted your mother your hotel and room number. Such a good boy."

Palermo let out a frustrated grunt. As if Gabe knew their alleged murderer would get hold of his phone.

Jimmy shoved the phone in his pocket, scooped up the boxes of cigarettes and headed for the door. "Gus, you're closed. Lock up behind me. You boys keep an eye on these two."

"Wait," Smell-boy said. "Where you goin'? What are we doing with them?"

"Nothing. Yet. I need to find this blonde and then I'll take care of them."

"Hey!" Gus yelled. "You're not doing this shit in my place!"

Smell-boy turned the weapon on him. "Shut the fuck up." He nodded at his buddy. "Lock that door and unplug the sign."

The lackey hustled after Jimmy, flipped the lock and then yanked the plug on the sign while his buddy stood guard over Gabe and Palermo. The odds though, they'd gotten infinitely better. Two bad guys, one armed, the other with a switchblade. And Gus. Who didn't want any trouble.

"Gus," Gabe called.

"Shut up!"

The guy with the .38 nudged the gun closer to a still seated Gabe. "What? You're gonna shoot me? You got two S.W.A.T. guys here. You know the shitstorm that'll rain down on you?"

"Shut up!"

"Gus? You got a nice place here. I know you're trying to go legit. These boys killing two S.W.A.T. operators is not gonna make that happen."

Smell-boy swung his head toward Gus, and Gabe and Palermo, like a choreographed dance, leapt from their chairs, each of them tackling one of the bikers. The gun went off, a bullet whizzing past Gabe's head and his ear shattered from the pressure, the ringing muffling any other sound. Whoa, close.

Shit, shit, shit. Juicy adrenaline flooded his body and he dove on the biker. They crashed to the ground, the gun flying and Gabe came up swinging, pounding on him, right, left, right, left again until the guy's face split open on both sides. Beside him, Palermo slammed his guy's head into the floor then hopped up, kicking the knife away as the biker groaned, his head lolling back and forth.

The tips of cowboy boots—had to be Gus—filled Gabe's peripheral vision. He rolled Smell-boy to his stomach, glancing up at Gus, who stood there, baseball bat at the ready. Apparently, he'd distracted the bikers with that bat.

"Gus," Palermo said, reaching for his phone. "I'm calling 911. I'll help you out here, let the PD know you did us a huge large. You got any zip-ties? The big ones?"

"Yeah. In the back."

"Go get me a handful."

Gabe watched him go, jammed his knee into the biker's back and looked up at Palermo. "I gotta call Jo. Get her the hell out of that hotel."

—:—

After thirty minutes of pacing the hotel room, her phone in hand, the damned thing finally rang. Jo jabbed at the screen. "Wes, for God's sakes, I've been calling Gabe for forty-five minutes."

"It's me."

Gabe's voice. On Wes's phone. Thank God. She lowered herself to the couch and ran her palm up her forehead. "I've been sick worrying. You could have texted me."

"As painful as this will be for you, I need you to be quiet and not hit me with a stream of questions. I'll explain later. You need to leave that hotel room. Now."

"Where are you?"

"Goddamnit, Jo!"

She inhaled a sharp breath that tore down her throat. Gabe yelling wasn't uncommon. Him yelling in that growling, aggressive tone? At her?

Definitely uncommon.

Whatever was happening, it was nothing good. She shoved her feet into her loafers. "I'm putting my shoes on. Just tell me while I'm walking."

"I'm on my way back. Be there in ten. Maybe less. We found Jimmy Jax—Wes and me—and he's on his way there. He got hold of my phone, saw the hotel and room number from my texts. You *need* to leave that room. Fast."

She reached the door and stopped, her pulse pounding so hard it might burst through her skin. "What?"

"I'll explain later. Just get out of there. And make sure the safe is locked. My weapon is in there."

The line went dead. Wait. What? She checked the screen. Call ended. He must have lost the signal. *The safe.* Not wanting to lose time, she ran to the closet where the safe door hung open from when they'd returned to the room earlier. Inside, his giant handgun sat already tucked into the holster. A burst of panic flooded her body. Trembling, she reached in, grabbed the weapon, flexed her fingers around the hard polymer and—holy smokes—the weight of it stunned her. Like solid lead in her palm. Had to be ten pounds. Maybe a little less, but not much. And Gabe walked around with that thing strapped to him all day.

Focus. After fiddling with the holster, she secured it to her waist, practiced sliding the gun out and rushed to the door, checking the peep. Nothing. She inched the door open, peeked as far as she could—still nothing—and stepped into the hall, swinging her gaze left then right. Two doors down a maintenance cart sat in front of a doorway indicating someone might be there. If she screamed they might help. The door bumped her rear—wait. She'd forgotten her key.

Need it. From the far end of the hall, the elevator dinged, and instinctively, she stopped, just halted right in the doorway.

"I'm here," a man said. "Call you back."

And, oh no, she might know that voice. *Not sure.* Forget the key. She had to get out. Now. She flipped the security bolt so the door wouldn't latch.

But if the man at the elevator was Jimmy Jax, her escape was blocked and he'd be turning that corner any second. She doubled back, sprinting to the room with the maintenance cart, but the door was closed.

Dammit. No time to knock. *Hide.* Five feet away, a small table was centered in an alcove with a house phone. She ran to it, squeezing her body between the wall and the table, so she'd be out of sight. On the phone, she pressed the button for security. *Come on, come on. Answer.*

"Security. May I help you?"

"I'm Joanna Pomeroy. Room 1342 and I need help. Come now."

"What's—?"

Jo gritted her teeth. "Please. There's a man coming. I need *help.*"

She hung up, her elbow bumping Gabe's giant handgun resting at her hip. All the help she needed might be hooked to her body. But could she do it? Could she fire that weapon?

She sure hoped so.

Jo stayed quiet, listening for any noise in the hallway. She peeked out just as a man with stringy, reddish-blond hair—*Jimmy Jax*—pushed her hotel room door open.

"Honey," he called, his voice light and laced with sarcasm. "I'm home."

Once he discovered the room empty, he'd realize she couldn't be too far with the door unlocked like that and he'd come looking.

Move. She glanced at the maintenance cart. *Get it.* Sliding from her hiding spot, she ran back to the cart, latched on, and charged down the hallway, shoving the cart in front of her. The wheels caught on the carpet, lurched, and her stomach crashed into the thick plastic handle. Pain shot clear to her back, but she gave a good shove and the wheels gained traction again. A few more feet and she'd be there.

Her hotel room's door closed, clinking against the security latch. *Gotcha.* In seconds he'd realize the room was empty and he'd come out. Maybe running. One last push and the cart would block the doorway. Perfect.

At worst, it would buy her time. At best, he'd trip over it and give her even more time.

Cart aligned, she stepped sideways and then everything blurred. The door opened, its bottom edge slowly scrapping against the carpeting. *Run.* But her feet wouldn't go. *Run.* Finally her left foot came up as the door slowly peeled back. Her skin caught fire and she sucked a breath, inhaling the pungent air-freshened air that made her stomach roll.

The man's eyes narrowed, focused in on her and a smile seeped across his face. "Hello, Jo."

Nuh, nuh, nuh. He set one of his big, meaty hands on the cart and she squared off with him, holding it in place. Her elbow bumped Gabe's gun—*gun!*—and she let go of the cart, ripping the weapon from the holster. Hands trembling, she stepped back, pointed the gun straight at his chest. Center mass, Gabe called it, but with the way her hands shook, who knew if she'd hit her target. Or even have the nerve to pull the trigger. Jimmy shoved the cart away, sending it sailing and it tipped over, its contents spilling to the floor as he lunged for her.

"No!"

She pulled her index finger back, missed the trigger and a low cry squeaked in her throat. Again she moved her finger and the trigger rubbed against her skin. Too late. He was on her, shoving her backward, grabbing onto her wrist.

Boom!

The shot ripped into the wall and Jimmy, trying to knock the gun free, spun into her, landed with his back to her, her arm trapped in his grasp as he dragged her into her room.

Control the gun. Short on options, she kicked him in the back of the knee and he howled, but hung on. She kicked again. This time, he let go, spun and slammed that meaty fist into the side of her face. For a second there was numbness and the only sound a slow-motion roar—*rowwwwrrrrr*—over and over again.

And then pain tore into her cheek, ripped straight up to her hairline as if someone had reached in and wrenched the skin apart. Agonizing, bone-shattering pain. Dear God that hurt. She moaned and stepped back, reaching for her face and clocking herself with Gabe's ten-pound gun.

God. Help me.

She closed her eyes, resisted the tears, and breathed through the second jolt of crushing pain. Bile backed up in her throat and she swallowed. *Don't throw up.* And then she flew backward, slamming into the wall with enough force to bounce her head off of it. *Gun.* She rebounded off the wall, her body literally springing from it and sailing to the floor, but the gun had skittered away and she spotted it, just a foot from her. *Where is he?* Head pounding, she swung around, found her attacker just above her, arm cocked back, giant fist ready for round two. From all fours, Jo scrambled for the gun. *Please, please, please.*

Knees scraping the carpet and fingers digging in—so close—she waited for the blow, anticipated its punishing force, but still reached the gun. *Yes.*

A thud sounded and she covered her head with her hands, waiting, waiting, waiting but...nothing.

Gun in hand, she rolled right, pointing in the general direction of the thump, finger on the trigger, ready to fire.

Gabe.

"Don't shoot!" he hollered.

Two feet from her, standing over her attacker, he drove his giant foot into him. Jimmy hitting the floor must have been the thump she'd heard.

He grabbed Jimmy by the shirt and—*wham*—slammed his fist into his face. Oh, ouch. With the belt she'd just taken, she knew that had to hurt. Easing her finger off the trigger, she got to her feet. The room shifted, the carpet bending this way and that and she swayed.

Jimmy kicked out, knocking Gabe off balance and sending him stumbling back and—nuh-uh—this was *not* going to happen. She would not let this asshole get to his feet.

She swung the gun right, her hands amazingly steady and aimed. *Center mass.* "I'll do it," she said. "After what you just did to me. I'll do it."

The man stared up at her, his eyes locked on, measuring. Before he'd put his hands on her, she'd been afraid. Now?

Not so much.

Now she'd fire.

And wouldn't miss.

Movement near the door distracted her and she slid her

gaze left. A security guard swung into the room, saw a blonde with a gun and halted.

"Stay there!" Gabe shouted.

And the guard started screaming, hollering something about the police and Jo went back to Jimmy, still on the floor, eyeballing her, ready to pounce. The shouting guard grated her last nerve and she breathed in, readied herself for the shot.

But then Gabe was beside her, placing his hand over hers, his warm skin, as usual, gentle on hers as he eased her hand back, taking control of the gun.

"Step away, Jo," he whispered, his calm voice penetrating the panicked roar in her head.

She slid behind him, resting the untouched side of her face against his shoulder. "I'm so happy to see you."

He reached one arm back while still holding the gun on his moaning prisoner. "That makes two of us." He let out a soft laugh. "Damn, Jo. You finally listen to me and stay put and still wind up nearly giving me a heart attack. I swear you're going to put me in an early grave."

—:—

Jimmy sat up and leaned against the wall. Gabe had minutes, if that, before the cops showed up. Minutes to convince this guy he was cooked.

"Hands where I can see them," Gabe said. "Because listen up, Jimmy. Your life just got worse. We can we put you in that shop when those people were murdered."

"Bullshit."

"Call it whatever you want, but you're cooked. After that show you put on in Gus's bar, detectives are on the way here to pick you up. And when they arrive, I'll tell them to search your car where they'll find counterfeit cigarettes."

Jimmy shrugged.

"You know, the LAPD has a task force cracking down on trafficking counterfeit items. Even if you don't wanna talk about this murder charge, they'll wanna know who your supplier is on those cigarettes. You're definitely doing time on those bogus cigs. Bet on it. They'll find every charge possible. Hell, they'll probably get you twenty years on those cigarettes alone. Right, Jo? By the way, Jimmy, Jo here, the one you just assaulted, is a lawyer. She's working with the PD. You're fucked all around, pal."

"Ah, Christ," Jimmy said.

Still standing behind Gabe, Jo inched sideways. "That's right. The tax revenue lost on counterfeit goods is in the hundreds of millions. Then there's the lost jobs. This city doesn't take that lightly."

"Whatever," Jimmy said. "I'll pay a fine,"

The guy had assaulted two police officers plus Jo and he thought he'd walk? Good luck. Even if the DA couldn't get that murder charge to stick because, technically, Jo hadn't seen Jimmy pull the trigger, he'd still be in a shitload of trouble.

But Jimmy didn't appear to be the brilliant sort, and more than anything, Gabe wanted Jo not to have to testify against him.

Which meant, when the detectives questioned him, Jimmy had to confess.

On it.

"Let me tell you how this works," Gabe said. "First thing they'll do is search your house. There's probably a warrant happening for that right now. If they find any counterfeits in your residence, they'll seize your house and everything in it because that property was used in connection with distributing illegal goods. Oh, and your car, too. That's gone. And if you're married, they might even be able to snag your wife's car. Then you're looking at conspiracy charges. If they find you moved these bogus cigs across state lines or had them shipped in from a foreign country, they'll nail your ass on that."

"Yes," Jo said. "Transporting illegal goods across state and international lines is huge. You could get five to ten years in prison. *Minimum.* Then, well, there are fines. Those could be half a million dollars."

Jo snapped her fingers, really getting into it now. "And you know what? If the manufacturer wants to bring a civil suit against you for trademark infringement, that's another issue. But you won't have to worry about that lawsuit from prison. That'll be your *wife's* problem, right?"

Gabe whistled. "Damn, that's poetic."

"Bullshit!" Jimmy Jax yelled.

"If you say so," Gabe said. "You got kids, Jimmy? You wanna risk it? Making your kids homeless?"

"Fuck you! Don't talk to me about my kids."

Flashpoint. Got him.

Obviously inspired, Jo circled her hand. "Let's get down to it here. I'm not your lawyer, but I'll tell you what I think will happen. The DA will make a case on the cigarettes and you'll take a plea. That's easy. But this murder charge will stay. If you don't give them anything on that, you'll go to trial. Or you can save everyone a lot of time and aggravation, not to mention tax payer money, by admitting what you did. If you do that, maybe they'll cut you a deal so you won't die in prison. Your kids might appreciate you getting out of prison before you die."

Two officers, weapons drawn, swung into the room. "Freeze!"

Game over. And they were just getting warmed up. Gabe lowered his weapon. "Think about what we said, Jimmy, and maybe you won't die in prison."

NINE

efusing to sleep in the room where she'd been attacked, Jo shoved clothes into her suitcase, not even bothering to neatly stack them. As soon as Gabe got back, they were switching hotels. She needed to leave this hotel. This city. All of it. Just get out.

Gabe had brought her back an hour ago after she'd been questioned and then he returned to the PD to monitor the situation with Jimmy Jax while an officer stayed outside the room with Jo. The detectives felt sure that once Jimmy's lawyer talked to him, they'd make a deal and Jo prayed that came to fruition. Testifying against a member of a violent gang was not on her wish list.

She was done. Finished. As of an hour ago when she'd called the mayor and told him, given the circumstances—and the attempt on her life—she needed to go home. Back to her life.

And the mayor had agreed.

The lock on the suite door clicked and she spun, her heart slamming from fried nerves. Gabe, all six foot three of him, stepped into the room and instantly, the sight of him, brought her surging blood pressure down. He did this to her. Gave her comfort just by showing up. Every time.

"Hi," he said, latching the door behind him. "You okay?"

"Better now. How'd it go?"

Gabe tossed the keys to the rental on the side table next to the suite's sofa. In his other hand, he carried a manila envelope and he set that next to the keys.

"They're still talking to him." He angled around the table and dropped onto the couch. "I could sleep for a month. And we're supposed to be on vacation."

He pressed the heels of his hands against his eyes and rubbed. She'd known this man over a year, had seen him break into buildings and take down murderers; she'd seen him reprimand a careless rookie and deal with the volatile mayor of New York. She'd even seen him after peeling a man's body from the bottom of a subway train. What she hadn't seen and definitely saw now, was slump-shouldered fatigue. Even on his worst days, when more than a tad crabby from pulling an eighteen-hour shift, he still carried the command presence that scared the hell out of people.

Tonight, he didn't have it in him. And the blame sat squarely with her. She gave up on packing and sat next to him, running her hand over the back of his head where his short, thick hair easily absorbed her fingers. He rested his head back against her hand and closed his eyes.

"I'm so sorry," she said. "I keep putting you through these traumas with me. I'm done. From now on, I stay in my office and leave the investigating to everyone else. When we get back, with your permission of course, I'm going to meet with Tom and Bev and the mayor and come clean about us. If it means I leave the task force, then I leave the task force. After this experience, that damned task force is not what I'm worried about. I want a life with you, a normal life where we go to functions or aren't afraid to go to a restaurant together. That's what matters. And, I called the mayor of Los Angeles an hour ago and told him I was done."

He opened his eyes and stared straight ahead for a few seconds before turning to her and patting her knee. "Okay."

"You don't believe me?"

"Not for a second. I love you and I'm sick of hiding too. That I'm totally on board with. We'll go home and have that meeting with our superiors. Face it together. For the rest of it? The staying in your office? In two weeks you'll be bored."

"I don't think so."

"We'll see."

Here she was trying to give him the one thing he'd always asked for, and now he wanted to be a smart ass. "Whatever, Sergeant. Tell me about Jimmy."

"He's chatting like an old lady at a gossip fest."

"Thank God."

"Yeah. He gave up your smuggler. The D.A. said they'd offer a plea bargain if he confessed and gave up some intel on the smuggling operation. As we suspected, Andre Theo is operating under a new name. Crazy-assed fucker is awaiting trial and he's still at it. Anyway, Palermo and his men are about to take down the warehouse location Jimmy gave the detectives. Jimmy said the place is huge. Cigarettes, shoes, purses. It's stuffed with counterfeits from overseas. Either way, he confessed. No trials."

No trial. Jo bowed her head, let out a huge push of air, all the tension trapped in her muscles letting go.

Gabe leaned over and kissed the side of her head. "It's over, Jo."

"Thank you. As an attorney, it's been hard to admit I was scared to testify. I didn't want to worry about some gang coming after me. I would have done it, absolutely, but it gives me a whole new perspective on how witnesses feel. I think it'll make me better at my job. So that's how I'll think of this entire ordeal."

"Good." He set his hand on her leg and drummed his fingers. "I need your opinion on something. Actually, it's more of a question."

"Whatever it is, the answer is yes."

He slapped his hands together and shook them. "Finally! I've broken her."

"Hardy-har, Sergeant. But I don't care. I love when you ask my opinion." She poked his arm and grinned at him, feeling like the old Jo, the self-assured, ball-busting Jo she'd been before this ordeal started. "You don't do it nearly often enough. Now, what's your question?"

He shifted sideways, grabbed the envelope off the table and slid a brochure out. "Take a look at this. I snagged it from one of the detectives. What do you think?"

The cover of the brochure pictured a sunset beach with chaise lounges and those huge beds that were popular at beach resorts. Didn't those look heavenly? She flipped it to the back and read the address. Hawaii. "Please tell me you want to go there."

"I totally want to go there."

"When?"

"Uh, now? Because all I've thought about for the last three weeks was sitting on a warm beach with you. I want that. And let's just say LA, at least for this trip, hasn't exactly been the vacation I envisioned. I was thinking, if you're okay with it, we could jump on a flight. I mean, I wasn't sure you'd go for it since you were supposed to be out here another two weeks, but hey, you just said you drop-kicked this assignment. The way I see it, we've got two weeks to bum around."

Two weeks of Gabe on a beach in Hawaii. *Can we say heaven?* "Yes."

He jerked his head back. "Seriously? You don't want to think about it?"

"Nope. I think going to Hawaii with you would be perfect. I've never been."

"Me neither. I didn't check flights, but there's gotta be something."

"Pfft," Jo said. "Trust me. If we can't get a flight out, I will use every one of my contacts to find us a private jet or a charter to get us there. We're in LA. Everyone has a private jet here. And before you moan about charters being expensive, for what we'd pay for a last-minute flight to Hawaii, we'd get a what-a-deal on a charter."

"For once, Counselor, I won't argue with you."

"Please. What fun is that?"

"I know. Tragic."

She leaned in, rested her forehead against his shoulder, breathing in the scent of him. After the day they'd had, his shampoo still lingered and made her thankful because anything having to do with Gabe settled her. Made her feel safe.

"There's something else," he said.

Great. What now? She sat up and looked at him through squinty eyes, letting him know it better not be bad news. "Is it better than Hawaii? If not, forget it."

He tilted his head one way, then the other, thinking it over. "I hope it's better. You'll have to decide that one."

Now he wanted to be mysterious?

He grabbed the pen out of the drawer of the side table, jotted something on the envelope he just whipped the brochure out of and held it out to her.

"What are you up to, Sergeant?"

He pointed at the envelope. She hated when Gabe got cagey with her. But, for a change, she'd be a good girl and cooperate. She snagged the envelope from him and looked down to where he'd written her name. Just her name. What the? Except...*oh.* She drew a soft breath and her thoughts scattered. *Yes, yes, yes.* Her hand trembled and she squeezed the envelope tighter. Did this mean?

His eyes were on her. She knew it and heat flooded her cheeks. But she couldn't look at him. Not yet. Not until her system adjusted and let her not say something stupid. She'd remember this moment for the rest of her life and what she didn't want to remember was that she'd blown it. It had to be perfect. Well, as perfect as the two of them could manage. Which was usually decidedly less than perfect.

Gabe let out a small breath. "You don't have to answer now. Maybe think about it."

Still not looking at him, she held her free hand out. "May I have that pen?"

He slapped the pen into her hand and she crossed out what he'd written.

"Oh, *ouch,*" he said.

"Sit tight, Gabe. I'm not done."

Below where he'd written "JOANNA POMEROY-TOWNSEND????," she jotted an alternative and handed the envelope back. "That's my final offer."

He read what she'd written and his reaction, the shocked gagging, set loose a monster giggle that made her eyes water. This was what life should be. Good, solid laughter that reminded her certain days could be extraordinary.

"Now this is a pisser," he said. "You want to drop Pomeroy? You'd be plain old Joanna Townsend?"

"Any day of the week. Any. *Day.* The sooner the better."

She crawled into his lap and straddled him. "I love you. I'm sorry I cause you stress, but it's over. I'll be happy being your wife and a lawyer who stays in her office."

He smacked her on the butt. "Love the wife part. I have my suspicions about you staying in your office. But, we'll see. Either way, I love you and I want to come home to you every night. So, Counselor, wanna get hitched?"

"I sure do, Mr. August. I sure do."

A NOTE TO READERS

Dear reader,

Thank you for reading the Justifiable Cause series box set. I hope you enjoyed it. If you did, please help others find it by sharing it with friends on social media and writing a review.

Sharing the book with your friends and leaving a review helps other readers decide to take the plunge into Jo and Gabe's world. Even a few words expressing what you enjoyed most about these stories is a huge help. Thank you!

Want to find out what's coming next?

Sign up for my newsletter at www.adriennegiordano.com.

Happy reading!

Adrienne

ABOUT THE AUTHOR

Adrienne Giordano is a *USA Today* bestselling author of over thirty-five romantic suspense and mystery novels. She is a Jersey girl at heart, but now lives in the Midwest with her ultimate supporter of a husband, sports-obsessed son and Elliot, a snuggle-happy rescue. Having grown up near the ocean, Adrienne enjoys paddleboarding, a nice float in a kayak and lounging on the beach with a good book.

For more information on Adrienne, including her Internet haunts, contest updates, and details on her upcoming novels, please visit her at:
www.AdrienneGiordano.com
adrienneg@adriennegiordano.com